JONATHAN GRIMWOOD

◆

THE LAST BANQUET

Complete and Unabridged

CHARNWOOD
Leicester

First published in Great Britain in 2013 by
Canongate Books Ltd
Edinburgh

First Charnwood Edition
published 2014
by arrangement with
Canongate Books Ltd
Edinburgh

A catalogue record for this book is available
from the British Library.

ISBN 978–1–4448–2021–8

Published by
F. A. Thorpe (Publishing)
Anstey, Leicestershire

Set by Words & Graphics Ltd.
Anstey, Leicestershire
Printed and bound in Great Britain by
T. J. International Ltd., Padstow, Cornwall

Jonathan Grimwood was born in Malta and christened in the upturned bell of a ship; he grew up in Britain, Southeast Asia and Norway in the 1960s and 1970s. Upon completing his studies at Kingston College, he worked in publishing and as a freelance writer for magazines and newspapers including the *Guardian*, the *Daily Telegraph* and the *Independent*. He is married to the journalist and novelist Sam Baker; they divide their time between Winchester and Paris.

You can discover more about the author at www.j-cg.co.uk

And you can follow him on Twitter @JonCG–novelist

THE LAST BANQUET

We meet Jean-Marie d'Aumout as a penniless orphan eating beetles by the side of a road. His fate is changed after he finds patronage and is sent to a military academy. Despite his lowly roots, and thanks to wit and courage in great measure, he grows up to become a diplomat and spy. Passion, political intrigue and international adventure abound in Jean-Marie's life, yet he is driven by one obsession: the pursuit of the perfect taste. Rising through the ranks of eighteenth-century French society, he feasts with lords, ladies, and eventually kings at the Palace of Versailles itself. But beyond the palace walls, revolution is in the air, and the country is clamouring with hunger of a different kind . . .

Sam, always . . .

'The afternoon knows what the morning never suspected . . .'

Prologue

The angels of death scratch at my door.

Walking through the corridors, with my hollow eyes staring back from every tarnished glass, I can no longer believe the mirrors lie. These are the last days of my life. Schoolmasters say to children start at the beginning. When writing stories people say begin where it begins. François-Marie Arouet, who wrote as Voltaire, began his *Essay on the Customs and the Spirit of the Nations* by tracing human development from its earliest days. But how does anyone know where anything really begins? Did this story begin the day I met Virginie, the day I arrived at the military academy to be greeted by Jerome and Charlot, that day, years before, I first met Emile, or did it begin with the dung heap, when I sat in the sun eating beetles? Looking back on the days of my life, I can't think of any time I was happier. So let me say it began there, as good a place as any.

Jean-Marie d'Aumout
1790

1723
Dung-heap Meals

My earliest memory is sitting with my back to a dung heap in the summer sun crunching happily on a stag beetle and wiping its juice from my chin and licking my lips and wondering how long it would take me to find another.

Beetles taste of what they eat. Everything edible tastes of what it eats or takes from the soil, and the stag beetles that fed on the dung in my father's courtyard were sweet from the dung, which was sweet from the roadside grass. I had fed the horse the last of the hay and knew it was in a ramshackle stall behind me so the clip clop echoing in the courtyard's arch had to come from another.

I could stand and bow as I'd been taught. But the sun was hot that summer and my mother and father were still asleep in their room with the shutters closed and I'd been ordered not to disturb them so I stayed where I was.

Luck brought me another stag beetle as the stranger cleared the arch and I popped it into my mouth before he could demand that I share. The stranger swore and the two men with him trotted forward on either side.

'He'll poison himself.' The stranger had a deep voice and a lined face and eyes shaded by the wide brim of a hat with a feather in it. He looked sterner than anyone I'd met. 'Stop him, vicomte . . . '

The man addressed slid from his horse and knelt in front of me. 'Spit it out,' he ordered, holding out his hand.

I shook my head.

Irritation flickered across his face, although he kept his voice kind and crouched a little lower until we were almost level. He had blue eyes and smelt of wine, garlic and cheese. Just smelling him made my mouth water.

'You'll poison yourself.'

I chewed quickly and swallowed, spitting the beetle's broken shell into my hand and dropping it beside the others. His eyes followed my movements and widened at the sight of a dozen little owl pellets that had to be mine.

'Your Highness . . . '

Something in his voice made the stern man dismount to crouch opposite me, although he crouched less low and winced at a pain in his leg. He too looked at the scrunched beetle shells and their eyes met. Together they glanced at the door leading to my parents' house.

'A week,' the man said. 'Two?'

'When was the letter written, Highness?'

The old man pulled folded paper from his pocket and skimmed its contents. 'A month ago,' he said, voice grim. He looked around and scowled at what he saw. To me it was home, the courtyard of a crumbling chateau, which I would later realise was a chateau in name only. A crumbling farmhouse then. On the slopes of a vine-clad hill that had been sold to a local

3

merchant to raise money for my brother's commission.

'Go check,' he said.

The vicomte scrambled to his feet.

It was now that the third man decided to dismount, and as he came close I realised he must be little more than a boy to them, though he looked a man to me. Whatever he was about to say died at a warning glance from the stern man. There was a family likeness between them. Father and son? Grandfather and grandson? Brothers if the gap hadn't been too great. 'Help the vicomte,' the older man ordered.

'Help him with what?'

'You will address me properly.' The voice was sharp.

'My apologies, Highness. With what should your servant help your aide de camp?'

'Philippe, you are my son . . . '

'I'm your bastard.' He shut the door into the house with a slam and silence fell, although it held a different quality, being the silence of people who were there, rather than the silence that comes with being alone. The sun was warm and the horse dung smelt sweet and a smaller beetle chose that moment to venture from a crack between the cobbles. My hand flicked out and was locked solid as the old man's hand closed on mine. He was staring at me intently, eyes dark and hooded.

'Mine,' I said.

He shook his head.

'We share?' I offered. I didn't believe he would. Grown-ups never shared but it was worth

4

trying and he seemed to consider it. At least his grip lessened and he looked thoughtful and then sad.

'It's not very big,' he said.

'I'll find you another.'

'You like eating beetles?'

'Black ones,' I said, pointing to the line of chewed carcasses that had dried to sharp crackle in the summer sun. 'Brown ones taste sour.'

'Let it go,' he ordered. His voice was so firm and certain of being obeyed I released the insect and watched it scurry away to hide beneath a broken cobble. It waited, perhaps feeling itself watched. After a while it ran for the safety of another dip in the cobbles, hesitated on the edge of stopping and kept going. We lost it in the shadows where the roof of the stables obscured the sun and put that corner of the courtyard into darkness.

A shutter was opened behind me. Without looking round I couldn't see if it was the vicomte or the sulking youth, or both. The old man looked up and words must have been mouthed because he nodded grimly, then forced a smile when the time came to face me again. He didn't say anything and the noise of crows filled where his words should be. Since I knew that grown-ups spoke and children listened I waited.

Crows kept quarrelling, a dog barked in the village, and behind me shutters clanged as the men inside opened every window they could find, and the old man and I squatted in the sun and waited patiently. A beetle shook itself free from the dung heap and my hand twitched to catch it but I didn't and the old man nodded approvingly.

'Are you hungry?'

I nodded.

'Come with me,' he ordered, climbing slowly to his feet.

Instead of mounting his horse, he gripped its bridle and led it under the arch with the other two horses following, as if they'd been trained to do so. We walked slowly, because my legs were short and his were bad and it obviously hurt him to walk. He was a big man, dressed in a long red coat decorated with strips of gold, his hose were black and his shoes had red buckles. I decided he'd once been bigger because he didn't quite fill the clothes he wore. There were food stains on one sleeve and his nails were dirty. I could see lice in the folds of his long wig. You can eat lice. I didn't know that then but you can. They are best fried and hidden by the taste of other ingredients.

As we walked under the arch and into the sun I discovered he'd brought an army with him. A dozen soldiers on horses stood silhouetted to one side. Directly in front of us were fifty more men, all with swords but lacking uniforms — unless frock coats and wide-brimmed hats with feathers counted. One kicked his horse forward and the old man raised a hand so abruptly his friend almost tripped his mount bringing it to a stop. A small man in a brown coat ran forward when summoned.

'Food,' the stern man ordered.

A wicker basket was bundled from the back of

a pack horse and a carpet — a real carpet — rolled across the dirt of the track leading to our house. They used the track because the banks on either side were too steep. I recognised bread and cold chicken but the rest was simply unknown to me. The man in the brown coat, who had to be a servant but a very grand one, bowed low as he presented the spread to the old man.

'Not for me, fool. For him.'

I was pushed forward and stumbled, falling to my knees in front of the food, with my fingers landing on a cheese that squished stickily. Without thinking, I licked my fingers and froze at the taste of a sourness so perfect the world stopped. A second later it restarted and I nibbled another fragment from my knuckle. The flesh of the cheese was white and the blue of the veining so deep it belonged to a jewel.

'Roquefort,' the old man said.

'Roffort . . . '

He smiled as I stumbled over the word and tore me a piece of bread before his servant could do it. He wiped the bread up my fingers to clean away the cheese and seemed unsurprised when I reached for the scrap. The bread had a lightness I'd never met and went perfectly with the cheese. A second piece of roffort followed the first and then a third, until the loaf was half its size and the cheese was gone and my stomach hurt. A hundred courtiers, soldiers and servants watched me eat. A hundred peasants watched them from the vineyard slopes, too far away to see what was happening, but transfixed by the largest group of men on horseback the area had seen in years.

'Highness . . . ' The man speaking was the one he'd called vicomte.

'What did you find?'

The vicomte glanced at me and the stern man nodded, his face resigned. 'Take the boy to clean his hands,' he told the brown-coated servant. 'And his face while you're at it.'

'Into the house, Majesty?'

'No,' the old man said sharply. 'Not into the house. There's a stream behind us. You can use that, and this . . . ' He held up a napkin.

The water was cold and fresh and I drank enough to take the richness from my throat and then let the grand servant clean my fingers in the stream and wash my face, rinsing his cloth out between washes. Tiny fish danced below us and one came into my hand and wriggled inside my fingers. It was still wriggling when I swallowed it.

The servant looked at me.

'Do you want one?

He shook his head and wiped my face one last time, brushing crust from the corner of my eyes and snot from beneath my nose. When I returned to where the others waited they were more solemn than ever. The one called vicomte knelt in front of me, despite the dirt, to ask what had happened to the things in the house. 'They were taken,' I said.

'By whom?'

'The villagers.'

'What did they say?' He looked serious. So serious, I understood he wanted me to understand he was being serious.

'That my father owed them money.'

'They told you not to go inside?'

I nodded in answer. They'd told me my parents were sleeping. Since my father had already told me I was not to go in because he and my mother would be sleeping this had been no surprise. That the villagers had gone in and returned carrying my parents' few possessions had been strange. But most things I asked about came down to 'That is how it is', and I imagined this was the same.

'Where did you sleep?'

'In the stable if it rained. In the yard if it was fine.'

He thought back and maybe it hadn't rained in his last few days but it had rained on at least two of mine and I'd been grateful for the shelter the stable offered. Its roof leaked, because every roof in the house leaked, but the horse slept in the corner that got most of the wet and I liked the company. Before the vicomte climbed to his feet, he said, 'He is le Régent. Call him Highness.' He was looking at the old man who stood supporting himself on the neck of his horse, watching us in silence while everyone else stayed back.

'And bow,' the vicomte said.

I bowed as ordered, the best bow I'd been taught and the old man smiled sadly and nodded his head a fraction in reply. 'Well?' he said.

'Stolen by peasants,' the vicomte answered.

'Do we know their names?'

The vicomte knelt again and asked me the same question — despite the fact I'd already heard it. So I told him who'd come to the house and the old man nodded the answers towards the brown-coated servant to say he should pay attention. The servant spoke to one of the soldiers who rode away with three others following after.

'Your name?' the sullen young man asked me.

'Philippe,' le Régent said.

'We should know his name.' The young man's voice was as sulky as his face. 'He could be anybody. You don't know who he is.'

The old man sighed. 'Tell me your name.'

'Jean-Marie,' I replied.

He waited and then smiled indulgently and I realised he was waiting for more. I knew my name and I knew most of my letters, I could count to twenty and sometimes to fifty without getting any of them wrong.

'Jean-Marie Charles d'Aumout, Highness.'

He looked at the vicomte at the last and the vicomte shrugged. I could see that the old man was pleased and that the vicomte was pleased with me. The boy called Philippe just looked furious but that was all he'd looked since I'd first seen him so I ignored it.

Le Régent said, 'Put him on the baggage cart.'

'We're taking him with us?' the vicomte asked.

'Until we reach Limoges. There must be an orphanage there.'

The vicomte leant forward and spoke too quietly for me to catch the words but the old man looked thoughtful and then nodded. 'You're right,' he said. 'He can go to St Luce. Tell the mayor to sell the manor and the horse. He can remit the money direct to the school. Make sure they know my interest in the child.'

Bowing low, the vicomte sent a soldier for the mayor.

The soldier and the mayor returned but — before they did — the other four soldiers who'd been sent into the village earlier came back with the first three of the men I'd named as taking things from the house. They were hanging from trees before the mayor even appeared at the bottom of the road. I tried not to look at them kick and when the vicomte realised I was watching he sent me to sit in a cart and stare in a different direction.

I couldn't see them with my back to the trees.

Their protests were loud enough for me to hear though; and their begging, when they realised protests were not enough. Finally they cursed the world and its unfairness and insisted my father owed them all money. This was not in doubt, apparently. It was the taking of what had not been declared theirs that was the crime. Besides, my father was noble and the law distinguished between those who were and those who were not.

The not, hanging from the trees, had better clothes than me. In one case the man kicking his heels had leather shoes instead of the wooden sabots peasants usually wore. But he was still a peasant, bound to his land and owing duties to his lord. The villagers could be taxed and beaten and thrown off their fields and tried with the most perfunctory of trials. Those things could not be done to me. Nor could I work, of course.

Unless it was my own land, and I had no land. I understood now that my parents were dead.

Tears would have been right, perhaps sobbing . . . But my father was a sullen and silent man who whipped me without thought, and my mother had been the shadow at his side, no more effective in protecting me than a real shadow.

Even now I would like to miss them more than I do.

All I could think about, as the cart trundled away from the manor that was soon to be sold, was the miraculous taste of the blue cheese I'd been allowed earlier. And the only thing I mourned was leaving my father's horse behind. It was old and lame and fly-ridden, with a moulting mane and a ragged tail, and was believed by everyone else to have a foul temper, but it had been my friend from the day I first toddled unsteadily through the open door of its stall and plonked myself in the straw at its feet.

'Don't look back,' the vicomte said.

From his tone I knew they were still hanging villagers. A line of kicking shapes throwing shadows on the dusty road. Shadows that stilled in order, like a slow rolling wave on the irrigation ditches when the water is released.

The vicomte was Louis, vicomte d'Anvers, aide to the stern-faced man, His Highness the duc d'Orléans, known to everyone as le Régent. Until February that year he'd been guardian to the young Louis XV. Although he looked impossibly old to me he was forty-nine, more than twenty years younger than I am now. He would die that December, in the year of our

12

Lord 1723, worn out by responsibility, childhood illness and the disappointment of having his power removed.

As for my parents. My father was a fool and my mother starved to death rather than steal apples from a neighbour's orchard and disgrace the name of the family into which she'd married so proudly. There are two ways to lose your nobility in this absurd country of ours . . . Well, two ways before self-elected committees began issuing edicts banning titles and taking away our lands.

Once these mattered but soon they will become so obscure as to be forgotten. *Déchéance* — failing in your feudal duties. And *dérogeance* — practising forbidden occupations, roughly, engaging in trade or working another's land rather than your own. My father had few duties, no skills to speak of and had sold what little land he inherited for enough coin to buy my brother a commission in the cavalry. Dying in his first battle, my brother wasted the sacrifice and was buried next to some mud-filled ditch in the Lowlands, and promptly forgotten. He was dead before I was alive.

1724
School

My next real memory is a year later. What happened between leaving my parents' house and joining St Luce was too predictable to make firm memories. The sun rose and the sun set and an old woman who lived in the school's gatehouse fed me twice a day in between, once in the early morning and once before dusk, and in return I fed her chickens and took care of myself during the day. The meals were poorly cooked and monotonous but filling and frequent enough to keep me fed and my body growing. Tossed corn brought the cockerel and chickens running. The cockerel was old and vicious and soon for the pot. The hens were safe so long as they kept laying and I lied occasionally, saying I'd tripped and dropped this one's egg or forgotten to put out the previous night's food, which was why that one had not laid. Maybe the old woman even believed me.

When eggs were plentiful I took the occasional one and let the richness of its yolk run down my chin before wiping the yellow away with my hand and licking my fingers. Winter yolks tasted sourer than summer ones. Autumn yolks were rich with burnt earth and sunshine. Spring yolks tasted different again. They tasted of spring. Everything caught and killed or plucked from the ground or picked in spring tastes of spring. You can't say that for the other seasons.

She called me her strange one, barely slapped me when she found me stealing food. What tastes the old woman's cooking didn't provide I found for myself. The crab apples growing up the side of the gatehouse were sour, the grubs that bored through them sourer still. The beetles in her yard were less sweet, the cheese in her shabby kitchen hard and waxy, without the imperial blue veins of roffort or its rottenly glorious smell. In my days at the St Luce gatehouse I tasted whatever I had not tasted before: cobwebs and earwigs (dusty, and spit), spiders (unripe apple), dung, the chickens' and my own (bitter, and surprisingly tasteless). I ate new laid sparrow's eggs and tadpoles from the brook. Their taste was less interesting than their texture. Both were slimy in different ways. The old woman helped look after the boys at St Luce and had the task of fielding me until I was old enough to go myself, which moment soon arrived.

There were men who liked small boys more than they should, she warned me. And boys could be cruel to boys in that way and others. I would have to stand up for myself. She could look out for me but I would have to be brave. There had been discussion about making me wait until I was seven. But almost seven was fine the headmaster said. I should call him sir. I should call everyone bigger than me sir, except the servants; they should call me sir. 'You understand?'

15

She had wiped my face and washed my clothes and forced me to eat a bowl of porridge. It was only when I saw the bundle with my other clothes, a slightly smarter jacket, a different pair of breeches, that I realised this was my last morning feeding chickens. Tonight they would have to wait until she could feed them herself.

'Courage,' she said. 'You'll be fine.'

Her face wobbled as she looked at me and she paused as if she might kiss or hug me goodbye. She spoke well and knew her letters, but was poor enough to need to work and the gatehouse was small for all it was clean. And the food . . . Perhaps she didn't care for food; the same dishes again and again, the same tastes. She looked at me and I looked at her and eventually I understood I was to walk to the school on my own.

Picking up my bundle, I headed down the drive and found it was further to the school than I'd thought. After a few minutes I turned to discover she was still standing in the gates at the top of the road, so I waved and she waved back and then I turned my face to the school and kept walking, with my bundle swinging at my side.

The wind was warm for early autumn and the track dry and the grass slightly yellowing. The cow parsley was bare, waiting to be made into whistles or blowpipes, both of which I'd discovered for myself. The chestnuts on both sides of the drive were rich with conkers and I took the largest I could see and polished its gleaming swirls before dropping it in my pocket. Another and another fat conker lay on the road in front of me and I took those as well, stuffing my pockets until they were bulging.

The boy who came towards me had his hand out. 'Give,' he demanded sharply.

Such was my greeting to a school where I knew no one; after a year in a gatehouse with a woman who was neither family, friend, servant nor mistress. I was to learn later that the drive was out of bounds and a dozen pupils had watched me approach, dressed in clothes that I didn't know represented their school uniform, and wondered where I'd come from and how severely I'd be punished for going beyond the courtyard. For now there was the outstretched hand.

'I'll hit you.'

Silence, while I looked at him.

He was my species but the only boys I'd seen were at a distance. I played by myself from necessity, and sat alone when I couldn't be bothered to play. The woman in the gatehouse hadn't suggested I find friends and I'd felt no need of them. The idea I might want to share my conkers with him was absurd.

'I warned you.' Watched by his friends, he made good his promise and I rocked back, hands to my already bleeding nose as someone started laughing.

'You want the conkers?'

'Uuu wan da conkers . . . ?' His voice mocked the pain in my nose, my split lip, the trouble I had speaking.

'Have the conkers.'

Closing my fingers round a handful, I threw

17

them as hard as I could straight into his face and then punched him hard while his eyes were still shut. He rocked back as I'd done and I punched again, harder, splitting my knuckles. The boy was some inches bigger and obviously older but he sat down hard on his bottom and cowered back to stop me hitting him again.

St Luce had rusting wrought-iron gates to the forecourt, with an arch through the main building that led to a courtyard beyond. 'You, boy, your name . . . ?' I turned to see an old man shambling from a door that had been shut seconds earlier. 'Well?'

'Jean-Marie.'

A boy laughed, a different boy from before, falling into silence when the old man glared at him. 'He's young. He doesn't know our ways. You will give him two weeks' grace. You understand me?'

'Yes, headmaster.'

'Your family name?' He said kindly.

'D'Aumout, sir . . . Jean-Marie Charles d'Aumout.'

He was asking so the others would learn it, I realised many years later. Dr Morel was the old headmaster and the new headmaster's father. In his seventies, and looking impossibly old to me then, he put an arm around my shoulders and steered me under the arch through the school and into a dark courtyard overlooked by rooms on all sides. A smaller arch led through to whatever was at the back of the building. 'You'd better come too,' he said over his shoulder to my attacker, who followed after us like an unwilling

18

shadow. 'Duras,' said the boy, sticking out his hand.

I stared at it.

'You have to shake.'

'You hit me.'

'You still have to. That's the rules.'

I took his offered hand and he nodded. 'Emile Duras,' he said. 'I'm in the second class.' The old man chose that moment to turn and smiled to see us shaking.

'Don't be late,' he told Emile. 'But first show him to class.'

'Which one, sir?'

'You can read?' the man asked me.

'Yes, sir.' The old woman had taught me the rest of my letters.

'What's fifty minus twenty?'

'Thirty, sir.'

The old man looked thoughtful, then decided. 'You can be in my class. I'm putting you in Emile's care. His punishment for what happened.'

'Sir . . . ' Emile protested.

'You expect me to believe he punched you first?'

'What you believe and what can be proved are different.'

Dr Morel sighed. 'Leave the law at home, Duras. Leave it to men like your father.' Taking the other boy's face in his hands he turned it sharply until they met each other's eyes. 'Now, the truth. Did you hit him?' The boy's face narrow and watchful, his curls dark and his nails clean. I was surprised by that. I hadn't met

19

anybody whose nails were clean. He seemed to be considering what it would cost him to admit this.

'Yes, sir,' he said.

So I first met Emile Duras, son of a lawyer and here because his father paid for him to come here to be educated. He went home at the weekends, which made him an outsider. His father was a rich lawyer and as St Luce was for the sons of destitute nobles, of whom there were enough to fill five classes of forty boys each, that also made him an outsider. But the biggest thing that set him apart, the thing that sent him out to punch me when other boys told him that was what he must do, was his name. Had he been de Duras, should such a family exist, his life would have been easier. The lack of the *particule*, the *de* in his name, set him apart from the others and from me, although I was too young to realise it.

My first day was simple. I trailed behind Emile and sat quietly at the desk I was given and answered the three questions the old headmaster asked me. Luckily I knew the answers to those, because there were others to which I did not. When Emile dipped his head for silent reading I did the same, looking over to see which page he read and fumbling to find my place. I read the page three times — and, though it made little sense, when asked to read a line I did in as clear a voice as I could manage. 'The glory of great men should always be measured by the means they have used to acquire it . . . '

Emile's sentence came from further down the list of quotations because he sat two desks away.

In the weeks to come we managed to sit side by side, when it became obvious our brief fight had made us friends. Emile's sentence read, 'Before we set our hearts too much upon anything, let us consider how happy those are who already possess it.'

Later I learnt the name Rochefoucauld, later still who he was and why his maxims were famous. His name reminded me of the cheese I'd eaten with le Régent and Emile brought me a sliver from home, wrapped in paper. It tasted as I remembered, of mould and horses' hooves clipping on brick and dung beetles and sun.

★   ★   ★

I learnt a lot from Emile in my first two weeks at St Luce, which boys and which masters to avoid and which could be trusted, and at the end of that I discovered what two weeks' grace meant and that Emile had truly become my friend. A boy — older and bigger, because all the boys were older and bigger, since I was the youngest and smallest in the school — walked up to me and tried to take my work book, having had his own stolen, the loss of which was punishable by beating. And instead of letting it happen, Emile stepped up beside me and together we saw off the would-be thief.

It was a friendship that was to last for years and only be broken by something bigger than friendship and fiercer than shared bonds. That was so far into the future we could barely imagine it from a world of small boys where days

21

stretched for ever and our memories hungrily swallowed every detail of the world around us.

'You can be good at sport, you can be good at learning, you can be good with your fists . . . ' Emile grinned ruefully and touched the yellowing fringes of the black eye I'd given him a few weeks earlier. Out of friendship I touched my lip, although the scab was mostly off and the swelling long gone. The written rules were on a board in the main hall. They were few and easy to understand. The unwritten rules more numerous and more complex. In the school as in the later world I was to find: but like the rules of the later world they could be simplified and reduced to those that really mattered. That was what Emile was doing, while standing with his legs apart and his hands behind his back as his father might do in court. 'You should punch, but you should also read to yourself.'

I looked at him.

'The masters will leave you alone.'

He seemed to be saying that Dr Pascal and the other masters should see me read books and the boys above should see me punch people. I checked, and that was exactly what he meant. I was six and he was nearly eight, older and worldly wise. I did my best to obey his suggestion. The result was the masters liked me, and my friends grew in number. Those I hit wanted to be friends so I didn't hit them again, and their friends wanted to be my friends so I didn't hit them to start with. Inside a year I stopped having to hit people and stopped worrying about being their friends. They were still friendly to me but got little in return. Emile was the exception.

We played together and he got permission from his father to bring me home for a weekend. I arrived in near rags and left wearing Emile's old clothes. More to the point, I left fed and with my pockets filled with slivers of five different cheeses. Emile's mother thought my passion for Roquefort funny and asked who'd given it to me.

'Monsieur le Régent.'

She looked at her husband, who looked at Emile, who shrugged slightly to say he didn't know if it was true but it was possible. And so I came to tell them about the day the duc d'Orléans rode into my father's courtyard and left a row of kicking villagers strung from the trees behind him. I left out eating beetles.

Emile told me later what she said. Sometimes life is kinder than one thinks. Sometimes it is even kind to those in desperate need of kindness. I adored her and she became the mother mine had never bothered to be. This amused Emile as his possessiveness of me extended to expecting his mother to like me also. An only child, in his home he was as spoilt and cosseted as a dauphin. Even the prickly Maitre Duras approved of my friendship with his son.

A small man with expensively tailored clothes and a jewelled ring on one finger, his coat was buttoned tight to the neck and his nails always clean. Occasionally I would find him staring from me to his son as if considering the difference. Emile was cleaner and still taller, although I was catching up. My appetite was bigger and I ate everything put in front of me, which endeared me to Madame Duras, a large woman fond of her gold bracelets, her supper parties and her garden. Maitre Duras acted for the school, and for baron de Bellvit, which was how Emile came to be at the school and why the school agreed when Maitre Duras suggested I might come to his for a few days over the holiday since I had nowhere else to go.

I was noble and instinctively polite and treated his son as an equal because no one had suggested I shouldn't. Later, other boys became my friends. Some of them in the first few terms suggested Emile was too common to be friends with people like us. And I looked at them and I looked at myself and I looked at Emile and wondered what the difference was. We wore the same uniform and went to the same school, we ate the same food and attended the same classes. The only difference was that Emile looked a little cleaner and had clothes that were a little neater and slept at home rather than in the dorms. To me that made him luckier than us not worse. All of us knew we were different from the peasantry.

That sullen indistinguishable mass who stared at us with flat eyes from the fields on the two occasions a year we were allowed to leave the school grounds: once to visit the fair at Mabonne and again to be fed by the baron de Bellvit, our local landowner and titular master, under its founding articles, of our school. The peasants dressed in rags and dirt and lived in hovels — it was hard beneath the mud and sweat and stink to tell the men from the women. And though we might see a wide-eyed boy only a little younger than we were, or a girl pretty enough to make us notice her, we knew what they would become. It had always been this way and we believed it always would. More to the point, they believed it and so it was.

1728
Hanging the Dog

To cook mice

Drown first. Clubbing produces sharp fragments of bone. Gut, skin and clean in water. Wrap three or four together in wet clay and bake in a bonfire. Alternatively, halve along length, fry with sliced onions and season with salt, pepper and thyme. This also works for sparrows. *Tastes like chicken.*

To cook sparrow

Gut, pluck, remove legs and clean carcase in water. Alternate layers of salt and cleaned sparrow in a jar. When needed, wash away salt and fry with a little olive oil. In a separate pan fry onions until clear and add diced tomatoes. Put sparrows on top of sauce and garnish dish with basil. *Tastes like chicken.*

To cook cat

Gut animal, skin, remove head and tail, cut off paws and lower limb at joint, wash body cavity thoroughly. Carcass looks just like rabbit and can be roasted in similar way. Spit, brush with oil, season with tarragon. Cook until juices run clear when meat pierced with a knife. *Tastes like chicken.*

To cook dog

Gut, skin and joint. The thighs are too fatty to make good eating, the flanks can be trimmed for steak, the rest can be stewed or fried at a pinch. Boiling the meat before roasting or frying removes fat and helps lessen the distinctive flavour. Sauce heavily or season with chillies. *Tastes like sour mutton.*

★   ★   ★

The sad truth is that, apart from dog, one animal tastes much like another, and those that don't taste like chicken mostly taste like beef, with the rest tasting like mutton. The secret of variety for meat is in the spicing. Vegetables, fruits, herbs have far wider variations in taste than the creatures that pick, browse or gnaw upon them. Even the way we describe the taste of meats other than the obvious ones is wrong. We say cat tastes like chicken when, had we been weaned on kitten stew, we'd say chicken tastes like cat.

'To cook mice' was my first recipe, written in careful lettering in a small notebook stolen from a master. I was ten and lied about the taste. It tasted more like chicken than beef because my palate was too inexperienced to make a better comparison. A cat and a dog changed my life. The cat came first, although the cat in this bit of the story is not that cat, simply a wild cat found trapped in a bush. But before this cat came a whipping. The old headmaster died the winter I was nine. The school was hushed into silence and slow movement. We knew in our common rooms and dorms that something was wrong because that afternoon's lessons were cancelled and the doctor was seen entering the gates in his cart and was hurried up the main stairs by the old headmaster's son himself.

The whole school attended his funeral.

The year I was ten no one died — and the year I turned eleven Dr Faure arrived. He taught Latin and theology and disliked me from the start. He disliked my face, my friendship with Emile, which he found suspicious, and he disliked that I was due to stay with Emile during the coming holiday when the terms of my attendance said I should remain at St Luce. He whipped me in his first week at school for being disgusting.

That is, he whipped me for eating a raw snail. Snails were common in the stews we were given and the masters ate snails boiled in butter and seasoned with garlic. This was different apparently. Because I took the snail from a pile of night soil collected from the school's latrines and I ate the snail raw. He announced he would transfer that rawness from the snail to my buttocks. After Friday prayers and the blessing, I was called forward, climbed the steps to the dais, and told to drop my breeches and grip the far edge of a small table — a position that left me stretched across the table with my behind exposed.

He used a switch of willow twigs, soaked overnight in a tub of brine that was carried in between two boys. The salt water makes the twigs subtle and acts as an astringent to stop the stripes going bad. The first blow made me jump so fiercely my knuckles cracked where I gripped the table. I was eleven. Everyone I knew in the world was watching in silence as I fought the pain that scalded up my body. Emile had told me to scream. He said people like Dr Faure liked you to scream. There would be fewer strokes and it would be over quicker if I screamed. Only my throat was too tight and the scream would not reach past my teeth.

The second blow was fiercer, the third so fierce that the wall of the assembly hall swam in and out of darkness. A whimper left my lips and I heard Dr Faure mutter in satisfaction. I kept silent for the fourth blow, helped by the darkness that washed over me the second it landed. The fifth had my mouth open in a silent scream and I would have howled my lungs out with the sixth had I not looked up and seen a girl staring at me through a crack in an almost closed door. Her dark hair was greasy, her eyes wide and shocked, her mouth slightly open. She was my age, perhaps a year older.

A girl, in a school of a hundred and fifty boys.

The sixth blow shocked me into a low moan and the headmaster stepped forward before Dr Faure could decide to launch another. When I looked up the girl was gone and the side door to the assembly room shut again. I was helped to my feet by the headmaster and put into the care of two of my classmates, who were told to take me to my classroom and report to his wife if I showed any sign of fever. Dr Faure glowered at the fuss and scowled at me so fiercely I grinned, which only made him angrier.

They clapped me into the classroom, the other boys. I was a hero, the boy who took six strokes of the birch and barely murmured. I had to drop my trews and stand there while classmate after classmate came to stare at the bleeding. It was the best, several agreed, beating the existing record for damage, which had been inflicted by ten strokes of the cane laid on with full force by the headmaster the summer before. The previous record holder spent a full minute with his face a hand's breadth from my rear while the class waited in silence for his verdict. Magnanimously, he agreed this was better.

A round of clapping saluted his sportsmanship.

'Are you an idiot?' Emile hissed, dragging me to one side when the clapping was done and the class had returned to flicking over the pages of the books they should have been reading or baiting each other. 'He'll just whip you again harder.'

Emile was usually good at knowing what others thought but he was wrong in this and I told him so. Dr Faure could not risk that I would hold out again. He'd failed to get a scream out of me and the headmaster had stopped him before he could inflict lasting damage. I'd made an enemy for life; neither Emile nor I doubted that. But Dr Faure could not risk another so very public humiliation in front of the boys. We should have guessed his response. Since he couldn't break me he would break Emile. It happened the following week. Some imagined infraction on Monday afternoon saw Emile stretched across a table in the assembly hall on Tuesday morning, Dr Faure with a sneer on his face and a birch gripped firmly in his hand. Emile did scream. He screamed so loud that some of the smaller boys covered their ears. The headmaster stepped forward when blood began to flow after the third stroke, not to stop the whipping but to indicate Dr Faure should lessen his vigour. It made no difference, Emile was sobbing by then.

No one clapped him into our classroom. No one suggested he drop his breeches so I could see if I'd lost my title, although his bruising was every bit as bad and his welts as bloodily raw as mine had been. They avoided him as if cowardice was catching. His bourgeois birth, the fact his grandmother was meant to be Jewish, his going home at weekends were rolled out as reasons for his weakness. He went to bed still crying and woke looking even more hollow-eyed than the day before. At lunchtime, unable to stand his silent tears or the insults of my companions, I went to find the headmaster's wife and insisted Emile had a fever.

'What are the symptoms?'

'He cries,' I said.

She sighed heavily, muttered something about that bloody man and told me to fetch Emile immediately. He should spend the night in the sanatorium and since I was his friend I could sleep there too. In the meantime I was to bring her Emile and then return to my lessons. I was d'Aumout, wasn't I? I agreed this was me and did what she said, collecting Emile under the scornful gaze of my classmates. 'I'll see you later,' I told him.

'Don't bother,' he said bitterly. 'I want to be alone anyway.'

'Don't you want revenge?' The plan had been forming since that morning. It was risky but what good plan wasn't? And it would give Emile back his confidence and even impress the rest of the class. Not waiting for his reply, I left him at the door of the sanatorium, a dark room overlooking a small courtyard in which Dr Faure kept his dog. Dr Faure's quarters were opposite so we would need to act quietly.

Back in the classroom I told them Emile needed volunteers for a plan he was going to put into action that night.

'What kind of plan?'

'He needs a judge, a scribe and a witness to swear that the trial was fair. Emile will act as the judge.'

'And you?' someone demanded.

'I'll be the executioner. Should one be necessary.'

'He's going to try Dr Faure?'

I shook my head. 'Even better. He's going to try his dog.'

32

Marcus, our class captain, grinned and I knew that if we brought this off Emile would be forgiven. Dr Faure's dog was a foul-tempered hound on which he doted. It spent its nights in the locked courtyard howling at the slightest noise and keeping the dormitories awake. The beast was walked religiously each day and was, everyone agreed, the only thing in the school with a fouler temperament than the man who walked it. The boys in my class began to draw up a list of crimes with which the dog should be charged.

*   *   *

By the time the shadows thickened to darkness everyone except Emile knew he'd sworn ferocious revenge on Dr Faure, and he greeted my news of this with wide eyes. His lips were bitten, his face puffy and his nose red from crying. So I told him to rinse himself in the cold water the headmaster's wife had sent up for us. When he just stood there, I put a china bowl on a tripod stand and poured the water myself, then gripped his head and pushed him under. He came up spluttering and flailing at me with useless fists.

'You do it for yourself then.'

He scowled furiously and splashed his face noisily, spilling water down the front of his uniform, since neither of us had changed for bed and nor would we until justice had been done. I explained what I wanted from him. He'd seen his father in action in a courtroom. He was to be that man. This was to be done seriously.

'I'm the judge?'

'Yes. You prosecute and Marcus defends. But the final decision is yours and you are the one who passes sentence.'

'But how can we get the dog to stay quiet? It will bark itself mad and Faure will come. He'll see us.' Another thought occurred to him. 'And how do we get into the courtyard? It's locked at night.'

'That's the point,' I said. The little courtyard belonged to the Faures' quarters and though a dozen windows looked into it there were only two doors: one into the main body of the school and one across the way into where the Faures lived. Dr Faure locked the first when he retired for the night and the second after he'd put his dog out. Only one man had the keys to those doors. Well, perhaps the headmaster had a spare set. But only one man had ready access. 'We don't get into the courtyard. The trial takes place on the roof overlooking Faure's door. As for keeping the brute quiet . . . '

I pulled a bag from under my coat, feeling its stickiness.

Emile looked in horror at the chunk of bloody meat I offered him. He stepped back and seemed to be reconsidering the whole idea.

'What's that?'

'Madame Faure's cat. I took a piece for . . . experimentation.' I didn't share the fact I'd fried that piece and still had slivers of cat and onion trapped in my back teeth. 'This is the rest of it. It should be enough. Although we'll need a quick trial. A decisive judgement.'

His eyes widened at my attempt to sound grown up and I almost smiled but caught myself in time. Serious. For this to work we had to be serious. Was he always so thin? I wondered. Had he always looked so weak? His eyes were watery, his lips bitten with anxiety. In my head he was bigger than me, this boy who punched me that first day and demanded my conkers. Now I realised I was looking down on him.

'You killed her cat?'

'It was fat and ugly.'

'This judgement . . . ' Emile sounded anxious.

'Execution. Death by hanging. To be carried out immediately.'

He mouthed the words, trying to make them his. Then it was time to meet the others in the lesser attic. Being caught out of bed would see us all whipped and I hurried Emile up the stairs, his steps slow and his face tight from his earlier beating. A broken harp loomed over us, leather cases rotted to spill their contents, a pair of ruined rapiers, their snapped blades rendering them exactly the right length for boys our age. Marcus grabbed one and tossed the other to a friend. Their clatter of enthusiastic battle was stilled by my outraged hiss.

'Leave the blades here,' Emile whispered. 'Take them on the way back.' Ordinarily Marcus would never take orders, but the fact Emile was judge in what came next was enough. Marcus put down the broken foil and his friend did the same.

At the far end of the attic was a door to the

roof. Most of us had come this way for bets or to cut lead from the flashings to be melted to make silver rivers or dropped into water to make strange shapes. That was the way we went, up one side of a gully where two roofs met and down the other side, to a parapet overlooking the courtyard where Dr Faure kept his dog. It was late summer and the air was rich with the stink of recently manured fields. The countryside was a dark sea around us. The peasantry were like their animals, early to rise and early to sleep, driven by the seasons and the length of the day.

'God's farted,' Marcus said. Someone sniggered and someone else muttered about blasphemy. I ignored them, already reaching into my bag.

'May I go ahead?' I asked Emile.

He stared at me, his hollow eyes half lit by moonshine the yellow of a cheap rush light. He was rocking slightly on his feet.

'You're the judge. May I go ahead to quieten the dog?'

'Go,' he said. So I opened my bag and pulled out a sliver of bleeding meat and lobbed it underarm along the edge of the parapet so it just cleared the top and splattered down onto the courtyard bricks. An eruption of barking greeted its landing, and I heard Marcus swear and Emile groan, and then the barking became snuffling. No lights showed in Dr Faure's house, no windows were thrown open. The snuffling became a whine for more.

'Here.' I gestured the others closer.

They huddled around me and I had to burrow

through them to reach where Emile stood on the edge. His face was white.

'Do this,' I whispered.

He raised his chin and his face changed as if his body were a house inhabited by different owners. He moved confidently through the small crowd and stared down at the foul-faced dog. 'Feed it again,' he ordered. The dog took its bloody mouthful and looked up to hear the charges. 'You are charged,' Emile said, 'with being owned by Dr Faure. You are charged with being a vile four-legged monster no better than your master. You are charged with being ugly, noisy and foul-tempered. How do you plead?' The animal whined for another sliver of meat and Emile nodded. 'The plaintiff pleads not guilty.'

I tossed the plaintiff another chunk of Madame Faure's cat and wondered if I had enough to last the trial. Emile must have wondered the same, because he turned to the defence and ordered him to keep his speech short and to the point. He then ordered the official witness to watch carefully. It was important that justice was seen to be done. This was an Emile none of us had seen before. Very different from the snivelling wretch who had sidled into our classroom that morning on a sea of his own tears.

'Begin,' Emile ordered.

'To sentence a dog for its owner's sins is no fairer than punishing a servant for obeying his master. The dog is not at fault. If it were my dog or your dog instead of Dr Faure's dog it would still be the same dog. Would you judge it then?'

A couple of the boys clapped softly and I agreed. It was a good speech — to the point and clear about the potential for injustice. I wondered how Emile would answer.

'The charges are in two parts. Both are serious. It is Dr Faure's dog, and it is an ugly brute no better than its master. Where those points overlap is where the seriousness of this offence lies. When two men gather together for the committal of crime this is conspiracy. In this case we have a conspiracy of ugliness. This court requires you to prove two things to establish innocence. That the dog is not ugly, and that it is not owned by Dr Faure . . . Jean-Marie, more meat.'

I threw it down as the lawyer for the defence began his hasty summary. He could not prove either point, but repeated that the dog was of previously good character and threw himself on the mercy of the court. It was a poor dog, a dog that knew no better, that had fallen in with bad company and was being judged for the sins of others.

Emile, however, was not swayed. 'There can be no mercy for crimes of this nature.' He looked to the boy acting as witness. 'You accept the trial is fair and carried out in accordance with the law. You hold witness to this fact?'

The boy nodded seriously.

'Then all that remains is for me to pass sentence.' Emile leant out over the parapet so he could see the dog clearly. Staring back, the dog wagged its tail and whined for treats. 'Pleading now will not help you. You have been found guilty of crimes so serious that there can only be one sentence . . . ' Emile let the pause stretch. 'And that sentence is death.' A couple of our classmates looked at each other and he raised his eyebrows as if wondering what they thought we were doing out here on a rotting roof.

'You may carry on,' he told me flatly.

I reached for a rope coiled under my jacket, its noose already prepared, and hesitated. 'The condemned deserves to finish his last meal . . . ' The remaining pieces of meat splattered onto the brick below and the dog wolfed them down, thrashing its tail with delight and licking its chops. I felt sick at the thought of what I was to do next and furious with myself for suggesting it. The last chunk of meat vanished down the dog's gullet with barely a chew of those fearsome teeth. And as the hound looked up and whined expectantly, my noose dropped over its head and I yanked furiously, desperation putting steel in my muscles. One handful of rope followed another. The dog rose rapidly until my grip slipped, it plummeted a few feet and came to an abrupt halt. The drop broke its neck. The whole thing was over in seconds.

'Help me,' I said desperately.

'Do what?' Marcus and the others looked puzzled.

'Drag the carcass up here. We can't simply leave it.' That obvious point had passed them by in the excitement. A huge dog dead in the courtyard would inevitably point suspicion at us. The animal had to vanish. That way, the servants would decide it was witchcraft and the headmaster would waste his time telling them not to be so stupid. Forming a line, my classmates began to pull on the rope while I kept the pendulum dog away from the wall. Our victim was almost at the parapet when I looked up and froze.

'What?' Emile demanded.

I grabbed the noose and wrestled the dead dog onto the parapet. 'Nothing,' I said hastily. 'Simply shadows.' A girl stared at me from a window opposite. White as a ghost against the darkness of an unlit room. Her hair was down and she wore a thin shift. I swear, even from across the court-yard, I could tell she was grinning.

'Sleep well,' I told Emile.

'You're going to . . . ?'

'Yes,' I said. 'I'm going to dispose of the body.'

I shook away offers of help from those who wanted a further part in the adventure. How well Emile would sleep in the week to come was down to him — and how brutally the lacerations on his lower back and buttocks hurt. But he would be allowed to try, and that was down to me. He could take to his bed tomorrow night and close his eyes without risk of a further beating from classmates who'd felt themselves shamed only hours earlier.

And me? I tunnelled happily though the darkness of midnight woods towards a shimmering ribbon of shallow river that edged the school grounds. One more dead dog for its cargo? Barely worth anyone's notice and miles down-stream by morning. Extracting my lock knife, I flicked out the blade and cut a strip from the beast's back, washed the meat in the river and wrapped it in dock leaves. I would grill it over an open fire, away from everyone's gaze come morning. In my head, as dry leaves crunched underfoot and an owl's sudden hoot lifted my soul into my mouth, I was already asking Dr Faure's wicked-eyed daughter if she wanted to share.

What the Chinese eat

Emile declared himself in love with the goose girl. A ragged child of twelve, if that, who dreamed and dawdled her way along the lanes with her stick and her brood, only hurrying them when she crossed school land. We caught her once where the road passed under the shadow of the oak trees, and demanded a kiss as the price for passing. But she gripped her staff like a Gaulish queen and her geese clustered around her, honking in agitation, and we let her pass unkissed for her bravery. Emile claimed he kissed her later. No one believed him, not even me and I was his best friend.

She was a princess in hiding, he said. Lots of goose girls were princesses in hiding or the bastard daughters of wicked dukes. Emile's flights of fancy were few and quickly over, but he turned this one into a long and twisting fairy tale that he told himself in corners, his head nodding in agreement to something he'd just said. The others allowed him his strangeness. He'd judged Dr Faure's dog and found it wanting. Emile was small and strange and common and far too brash in how he displayed his intelligence, but he was ours. We were the best, the bravest, the fiercest, the most proudly foolish year the school had seen.

And we were bound by a lie, all of us. The morning after Dr Faure's dog was tried, convicted and executed for the sins of its owner, the headmaster appeared in our classroom and asked if anyone had heard anything strange the night before. His gaze swept across our attentive faces so blandly I wondered if he suspected us but kept his suspicions to himself. Dr Faure stood behind him, face pale and mouth tight. He'd been having trouble meeting our eyes since classes began that morning.

We shook our heads, glanced enquiringly at each other, put on a very pantomime of innocence and ignorance. 'What might we have heard, sir?' Marcus took the lead and that was as it should be. After all, he was class captain.

'That,' the headmaster said, 'is a very good question. Dr Faure's dog has disappeared.' Maybe I imagined the headmaster's eyes settled on me. Although why would they not settle on Emile, since he was the last boy Dr Faure had beaten . . . ? 'It disappeared from a locked courtyard to which only I and your master have the key.'

'Witchcraft,' a boy muttered.

The headmaster scowled and thrust his hands in his coat pockets, leaning slightly forward as he told the boy not to be so ridiculous. It was bad enough the scullery maids thought such things in this day and age. Witchcraft was rare, and serious, a sin against God and punishable by death, but nothing like as common as servants seemed to think. He expected better from us. The boy he berated apologised, and I caught the boy's smile as the headmaster looked away.

'Did anyone hear anything?' I risked.

He stared at me long and hard. 'No,' he said finally. 'Dr Faure's daughter sleeps in a room overlooking the courtyard and she heard nothing. In fact, she slept the sleep of the angels . . . ' His mouth twitched at the words, which had to be hers. Theologians doubted that angels slept at all.

'Could it have escaped?' Marcus asked innocently.

The headmaster turned to Dr Faure as if inviting him to answer. When Dr Faure stayed silent the headmaster shook his head. 'Unlikely,' he said. 'The walls are three storeys high and the roof is steep. Unless, of course, it sprouted wings.'

'Like an angel,' Marcus said.

'Indeed. Should you discover anything I'm relying on you . . . '

'Of course, sir.' Marcus said. 'We'll organise a hunt this afternoon. I'll divide the class into teams. You can rely on us to search everywhere.'

'I'm sure I can.'

'It could have been worse,' Emile muttered. The entire class stilled and the headmaster turned to look at him. Dr Faure stared hardest, his face a stern mask as if his suspicions were confirmed. 'Obviously, a missing dog is sad. Its vanishing from a locked courtyard serious. But it could have been much worse. It could have been a member of Dr Faure's family. Say, his daughter.'

'Indeed,' the headmaster said slowly. And he said it in a very different way from the way he'd used the word earlier. The joke had gone out of the room and our classmates were shifting uneasily on their benches. The headmaster let himself out of the room and Dr Faure set us a page of Latin to translate and retired to his thoughts. A brooding presence hunched in a high-backed wooden chair at the front of the room. The meat was in my pocket, still wrapped in leaves, and I wondered whether to toss it into the privy and remove the night from my memory. But I had not tasted dog, and for all the beast had not deserved to die, that scowling brute in the chair at the front had deserved punishing more than we ever had. Emile translated the Latin quickly and cleanly, and since we shared a book, I simply copied his. I could have done it myself but it would have taken me twice as long, and my thoughts were on Dr Faure's daughter, my namesake, Jeanne-Marie.

★   ★   ★

Her grandfather is a cloth-cutter, her grandmother a Basque, those people who straddle the border between France and Spain and keep their own customs and speak their own language. 'My uncles and cousins make cheese. Well, their wives probably,' Jeanne-Marie mutters crossly. 'They do all the work.' We're jammed in a doorway, arms around each other and noses touching. 'You can kiss me,' she says. A minute later she sighs at my efforts and pushes me away. Perhaps she's already been kissed by someone better. Perhaps she's simply disappointed by the thing itself. She sucks her teeth.

'Now you can kiss me,' I say.

She grins, mood changing quick as the wind. Stepping closer she raises her lips to mine. I'm stood on the lintel; otherwise I'd have to raise mine to hers since she's half an inch taller. The kiss is soft, growing harder. Her mouth opens for a moment at the end. 'That,' she says, 'is how you do it.' I insist we do it again to make sure I understand. We kiss ourselves from spring into summer and through an entire winter beyond. We kiss ourselves into the following spring, and the only person who doesn't know is Jeanne-Marie's father. Perhaps her mother also. Although the woman looks at me with a mixture of amusement and worry.

A year to the day I first kiss her, Emile is five rooms away telling Dr Faure he hasn't seen me, but will be sure to tell me the headmaster requires my presence the moment he does. Emile says this with such politeness Jeanne-Marie's father doesn't know if he's being mocked. It is the same politeness with which Emile has asked, every day for a year, if there's any news of the missing dog. Dr Faure has come from asking Madame Faure if she knows where Jeanne-Marie is. Luckily he doesn't put her absence and my absence together and come up with my hand under his daughter's blouse, her ribs sharp as twigs and a slightness where her breasts are budding. 'The fat boy in your class has bigger tits than me. It's not fair. My mother has udders like a cow.'

I say it's hard to believe they're related.

46

'That's because we're not. I was found in a basket in the reeds. My mother, my supposed mother, found me when she went to the river to wash clothes.'

'That was Moses,' I tell her, grinning. 'And Pharaoh's wife went to the river to bathe not wash clothes. She had servants for that.'

'I'm serious,' she says. 'My real mother was a princess who loved unwisely . . . '

I grin at her words. So obviously overheard. 'Why didn't Madame Faure give you back? Surely that would have been sensible?'

Jeanne-Marie steps closer and rests her forehead against mine, her words a garlic-soaked whisper. 'She tried. But my mother's enemies gave her gold. Thousands of *livres* to keep me . . . ' She pauses, aware she's spun her story into a corner, and adds, 'It was stolen, almost immediately. By bandits.'

'Unlucky,' I say.

'Tragic.' She grins at me. The bell is being tolled laboriously by one of the junior boys for luncheon and our stolen time is at an end.

'My princess.'

She accepts my bow with a curtsy and skips away humming. Even Emile telling me the headmaster requires me isn't enough to destroy my secret happiness. I tell him that, like his goose girl, Jeanne-Marie is another noble orphan stolen from her rightful parents. 'Do you believe her?'

I look at him. 'Do you believe your goose girl?'

He grins. 'As much as you believe your beloved namesake.'

47

That's when I know I've done him wrong and he has kissed his goose girl.

'You should hurry,' Emile says, 'There are men with the headmaster. He calls one of them sir.' He watches me scurry away and goes to his lunch at the long table in the refectory, where we sit on benches and the older boys steal from the younger and our bowls are emptied as swiftly as if biblical locusts fly in one window and out the other, barely pausing to feed. Others will eat my lunch.

'So here you are.'

I bow and risk a glance at the headmaster's companions.

'These men are here to see you.' The headmaster notices their amusement at his words and amends them. 'These men are here. They have asked to see you. This is . . . ' He indicates a magnificently dressed comte whose name I miss because I'm looking at the man in the middle, who is staring at me intently. The man to his other side is a colonel, in uniform for all he's retired and head of a cadet academy.

'And this . . . ' The headmaster names the third man last. 'Is the vicomte d'Anvers.' It's obvious the vicomte is the man who matters, despite being younger than the colonel, and being outranked by the comte. The headmaster looks to him for approval.

'This is the boy?'

'Yes, my lord.'

'He looks well and stands straight . . . ' A buffet catches my shoulder and rocks me on my feet. 'Stands firm enough. Looks one in the eyes

48

when angry. Is he intelligent?'

'We have several cleverer. A fair number who are not. He manages Latin well enough. Can tolerate a little Greek. Knows his map of France, and his map of Europe. Mostly he's interested in botany.' How does the headmaster know this? Unless Dr Faure has told him, but why would the headmaster be asking about me? Nothing in his or the vicomte's face give me an answer to that.

'What do you want to be?' The colonel's voice growls like gravel under a cartwheel. 'Let's start with the obvious question.'

'No,' says the vicomte. 'If I might rephrase that? Boy — if you could be anything, what would you be? No job is forbidden. Simply tell the truth. That,' he adds, turning to the colonel, 'is how you judge a boy. By the measure of his dreams.'

'A cook,' I tell them.

Everyone except the vicomte scowls. 'You are noble,' the comte says. 'Try to remember that. Choose again.' His tone is so contemptuous the colonel comes to my defence.

'Come now. No doubt the meals here are sparse and repetitive. What would any sensible boy think of, if not food? It's all they fuss about at the academy.'

Vicomte d'Anvers snorts. 'At his age my interests were . . . ' He pauses, searching for the perfect phrase. 'Let me just say — it was not my stomach that hungered.'

The comte shoots him a reproachful glance.

'Tell me,' the vicomte says, obviously not

finished with the subject. 'Are my dear friends right? Is it hunger that makes you dream of having the run of a kitchen and the keys to the larder? Is this fantasy driven by a surfeit of winter vegetables, poor-quality bread, a simple lack of meat?'

I want to tell him food is plentiful enough, for all it is repetitive. And though recent bad harvests mean the peasants starve as often as their animals, vegetables and flour still find their way to our kitchens. As for meat . . . My recent understanding with the cooks, which saw any 'rabbits' I caught exchanged for the occasional *sou*, means meat has started to turn up in our stews. I doubt the cooks really believe I bring them rabbit, but a skinned, gutted and beheaded cat is indistinguishable in looks, taste and texture.

'Well?' demands the vicomte.

'I'm interested in the science of taste,' I say as seriously as I can.

'There,' he says triumphantly. 'The boy's a natural philosopher, who naturally wishes to go about his experiments in the laboratory of his choice. So,' he says to me. 'What is your favourite taste?'

Fresh sweat from the edge of Jeanne-Marie's hairline when I am kissing her neck. Although her tongue after she's eaten oranges comes close. In Jeanne-Marie, my search for the next taste and my hunger for the secrets of the other sex come together. I could not tell then if the search and the hunger would remain entwined or separate again. 'Roquefort,' I tell the vicomte. He smiles somewhat sadly.

'You don't remember me, do you?'

'No, my lord. Forgive me.'

'You were eating beetles, with your back to a dung heap and a smile on your face. It was summer and a horse was in the stall behind you.'

'You were with le Régent?'

'I was his aide.'

'The other man . . . ?' I remember the youth who scowled and growled and wanted as little to do with a dung-stinking, beetle-eating boy as possible.

'He died,' the vicome says flatly. 'An accident.'

'He didn't like me.'

'He liked very little. There were reasons, but none that need concern a boy of your age. All the same his death was regrettable.' Vicomte d'Anvers speaks to me seriously, as he might speak to a grown man. Although perhaps keeping his sentences short, his words simple and his wit under control.

'Am I going to have an accident?'

The vicomte lets a smile pull at the side of his mouth. 'Unlikely,' he says. 'A careful boy like you. We're dining here tonight. You should join us. No doubt the cooks will excel themselves.'

'You want him at the table?' The headmaster sounds horrified.

'A bad precedent, you think?' The vicomte pulls a handkerchief from his sleeve and flaps it vaguely. 'You're probably right. He can serve the wine. You know how to serve wine, don't you?'

I shake my head.

'Then I suggest you learn . . . '

51

I am sent from the room with instructions to wash and make myself as presentable as possible. I will be sent for when needed.

★ ★ ★

What I remember most about that night is the food. A pike was dressed in hot vinegar that turned its scales to the blue of a gun barrel. Its cucumber-and-black-pepper sauce had the texture of cream and smelt of spiced grass. The fish itself tasted of river weed and should have been soaked to remove its muddiness. I discovered its taste when I returned to the kitchens to fetch another bottle of Graves and helped myself to a sliver of pike from an abandoned plate. They ate rabbit next, three of them, stuffed with chestnut forcemeat and roasted. Since I hadn't delivered any of my rabbits to the kitchens that week I imagined this was the kind that hopped around fields rather than hunted on the school roofs or infested the ruined village beyond the stream. Pudding was a mess of cherries in brandy, mixed with broken honeycomb and meringue. The taste was sour and sweet and wet and dry and close to perfect. The pike had returned to the kitchens almost untouched, the rabbits had been mostly eaten but this simply vanished. I had to scrape the plates with my finger to taste it at all. Our visitors had eaten with forks, using the forks and scraps of bread to separate the fish and rabbit from their bones. I resolved to try the method for myself.

'The kings are much alike,' the colonel was

saying as I returned with brandy and glasses on a tray. I wondered which kings and listened harder, discovering that he meant ours, the young Louis XV, and the king of China. Although listening more carefully still, I wondered if he meant the Chinaman and Louis the Great, the man still called the Sun King. The colonel's voyage to China seemed to have occurred long before I was born.

'Vast empire, absolute ruler, troublesome family . . . '

The headmaster seemed worried by the last comment and glanced pointedly towards me. 'Listening, are you?' the colonel said.

'Yes, sir.'

'Wise man. You can learn a lot by listening. Any questions so far?'

'What do they eat, sir?'

Vicomte d'Anvers laughed.

Taking a glass, the colonel smiled. 'Can't tell you what their king eats. Never met him. Doubt any foreigner has. His subjects, however, eat dog, cat, snake, chicken's feet, eggs soused in horse urine and buried in the dirt to rot for a hundred days, sea cucumbers, insects, lizards, goat's embryos. It's hard to find something they won't eat . . . '

Hearing this I wondered if I should have been born Chinese.

'His subjects ascribe medicinal qualities to their food. This for calmness, that for strength.' Looking down the table to where Madame Faure sat prim-faced beside her husband, he smiled. Her primness was at odds with the ampleness of her overflowing and barely-covered bosom and the colonel had been glancing in that direction all night. 'For example,' he said, 'snake is believed to impart vigour in men. And cat is believed to impart agility. Together in the same dish called Dragon & Tiger they are believed to make a man both insatiable and subtle in his matrimonial duties . . . '

Madame Faure blushed and her husband scowled. The headmaster simply looked at me, decided I had no idea what the colonel was talking about and was thus too young to have my ears scandalised and joined his guests in their laughter. The evening broke up shortly after-wards, with Dr Faure's wife excusing herself first. I fell asleep half an hour later, wondering how hard it would be to catch a snake. And woke to the cockerel's crow, wondering if I should cook the snake by itself or with cat.

You're no better than Emile's goose girl, I told myself as I watched them ride away. No different from Jeanne-Marie, a schoolmaster's daughter, for all I loved the taste of her lips and the secrets she hid inside her blouse. You were not found in the reeds floating in a basket. No Pharaoh's wife plucked you from the waters. No princess pushed you into the current further upstream. Idle curiosity brought the vicomte here. You are Jean-Marie d'Aumout, scholar — child of nobles so destitute they starved to death.

But what if? said the voice in my head.
What if . . . ?

The Thorn Bush

Jeanne-Marie vanished the following week. There was little secret about it. She climbed onto a cart beside her mother, and the carter whipped his horse and they lurched forward as the shafts of the cart engaged with the leather harness straps. Gone, in an echo of hooves from the arch and a shuffle of gravel on the drive beyond. Dr Faure watched them go, his face impassive: then set us some Caesar to translate and five pages from Montaigne to précis in no more than three hundred words and no less than two hundred and fifty . . .

It was a long time since Dr Faure had flogged anyone. He clipped us round the ear, threw books at our heads, kicked chairs from under us as the temper took him, but no one had been forced to stretch across the table in full assembly and bear their buttocks to the willow twigs. For all that, the school ran as well as it ever did. The headmaster controlled the masters, the masters controlled the upper school, the upper school controlled the lower. It was, Emile told me, a very microcosm of the French state. He read in corners books he hid from masters and took from a locked cabinet in the library. He'd forced the lock, and for that he would surely be beaten, but the cabinet was in the darkest corner and everybody knew it was locked and the lock looked fine at a glance. Inside, the wood was splintered and the brass bent. The only damage outside was a dip where Emile's knife pushed so hard against the cabinet door that the edge bruised. I was there when he did it.

'Emile . . . '

He'd jumped at his name, not sure if he was furious or relieved to see me. 'What are you doing here?' he demanded. At which, I'd nodded at the knife in his hand and the half-forced lock and told him I could ask the same.

'Freeing knowledge.'

He scowled when I laughed. But how could I help it. He was as absurd as an Athenian demagogue, about whom Dr Faure had that morning been characteristically rude, since they were foreign, given to unnatural vices and favoured democracy. Being mostly thirteen, it was the unnatural vices that interested us.

The first plate we turned to in the first book showed a baby being extracted from between a woman's legs with a hook. We assumed the baby was dead. The second showed an arm being sawn off. Emile shut the book with a snap and slid it into its gap on the right-hand side of the top shelf. It had a fraying leather spine like every other book in the cabinet. We both memorised its position and knew we'd be back for another look later.

'How are you?' he asked.

'Well enough.'

Jeanne-Marie and I had been friends for more than a year. It was not just the kissing and my hands under her blouse I missed. I'd grown used to talking to her. She was the person I could say things to I couldn't say to anyone else. Emile still saw his goose girl. It was rumoured they'd been seen together in the woods flattening bluebells as she laughed and fought off his closer attentions. He never mentioned her to me. It was a kindness.

Most of my spare time I spent in the kitchens, the vicomte having suggested to the headmaster that I be given the run of them. After the head cook had recovered from his fury that anyone outside the kitchens should dare tell him what to do, he granted me one half of an insufferably hot and extremely small room next to the great oven. I still brought the man rabbits, although fewer than the previous year, and anything else I caught that he might use. He no longer paid me in greasy sou, having decided access to his kingdom was payment enough.

My recipe book grew week by week as that spring turned to summer and the harvest was brought in. Rats from the rubbish dump tasted sour. Rats fed on grain from the new harvest had a cleanness that required only frying in butter and a few leaves of shredded mint to make palatable. I gave some to Emile and told him it was chicken. He didn't doubt it, although to me it tasted more like owl. I killed a sleeping grass snake and stewed it with cat as the colonel said the Chinese did. The effects on my subtlety and vitality, if any, were minimal. The hiding place for my journal was obvious. It lived beside the first book we'd taken from the locked cabinet, its spine worn and shabby enough for the book to fit happily among its brothers.

It was while writing notes on a disappointing dormouse recipe that my life changed. The sauce had curdled, the clove spicing was entirely wrong, the taste was as sour as if I'd been chewing crab apples. I was wrestling with my foul humour when I looked out of the library window and saw a cart trundling down the drive towards the gates. The carter sat on a plank at the front, and behind him, on trunks, were Madame Faure and Jeanne-Marie, who looked a little more like her mother than when she'd left six months earlier. No one knew why they'd gone. A sick grandmother was the sensible suggestion. The most popular was that, having been bedded by the colonel, Madame Faure threw a hairbrush at her husband and left, taking her daughter with her. And here they were, almost inside the gates and headed for the arch into the main courtyard. I was hurtling down the back stairs, the grand stairs being forbidden to pupils, when I realised I could hardly burst into the courtyard and simply embrace Jeanne-Marie.

Dr Faure looked round as I stumbled to a halt in front of the cart.

'The cases,' I said. 'I thought you might need help carrying the cases.'

'Why not?' Dr Faure said. He signalled to a couple of other boys and between us we wrestled the luggage from the cart and onto the cobbles, having first stepped back to let Madame Faure and her daughter down. Jeanne-Marie passed me by without a glance. She was nowhere to be seen when we finally laboured the first of the cases into the smaller courtyard and up the outside stairs that led to her raised door. The school was old, and this bit the oldest; built in the days of rebellions and civil wars, when it was dangerous to have a door at ground level. We lugged another two cases up those stairs, listing in whispers what could be in them to make them so heavy, our hissed inventions growing wilder with each step. The lead-encased corpse of Madame Faure's lover was our last suggestion before we staggered through the door and found Jeanne-Marie waiting.

'I want to talk to you,' she said.

The others took one look at her scowling face and left with their half-completed goodbyes trailing after them. 'Jeanne-Marie . . . '

She stepped back as I stepped forward. 'You owe me a cat,' she said fiercely. 'I've thought about it and I don't mind the dog. But you owe me a cat.'

'You said it farted and its fur stank.'

'Don't be rude . . . ' She sounded almost grown up when she said that. Her face was rounder, her hips a little wider, her blouse had filled to reveal a definite curve. Impatiently, she pulled the coat she was wearing over it tighter. 'You understand? You owe me a cat.' She turned to go and my stomach tightened.

'Wait,' I begged.

She kept walking.

'What kind of cat?' I asked desperately.

Jeanne-Marie turned back and I could see that question hadn't occurred to her. Thought pulled at one side of her lip and she looked for a second as I remembered her. Searching inward, asking herself questions. When her eyes refocused she looked a little kinder, as if the answer itself made her smile. 'A kitten,' she said. 'I want a kitten.'

'I know exactly where to find one.'

She looked at me, considering. Was this a trick? How desperate was I to keep her talking? Later, I wondered if her harshness to me was a game. Or simply a way of saying don't think we can go back to where we were. Or maybe she really did miss having a cat and believed I should provide one having been responsible for the death of the other.

'Where?'

'Beyond the ruined village.'

'You know that's out of bounds.'

I nodded, and interest entered her eyes. She smiled for the first time since I saw her on the cart and let go the coat she'd gripped tightly around her. 'You go then,' she said. 'Bring me a kitten and we can be friends again.'

I shook my head. 'You must come too.'

'Why?' Jeanne-Marie asked.

'So you can make your choice.'

It was an answer she liked. 'When?' she demanded.

'Tonight . . . '

She shook her head. 'My mother's tired and my father will want to talk about my grandmother.' She saw my question and said, 'She died.'

'Your mother's mother?'

'My father's. He had his work so we went.'

'Was it hard?'

Her glare said it was.

'My parents died,' I told her. Hoping for forgiveness.

'I remember. You said they starved.' Jeanne-Marie considered that and decided it counted. 'Tomorrow night. Where do we meet?'

'By the bridge.'

★ ★ ★

The bridge is what the goose girl used to scurry for before we stopped trying to ambush her. The land our side of the bridge is school grounds and we could rightly demand a toll. After the bridge was common land belonging to the village. Well, so the village said. The local baron disagreed but was too lazy to go to court over scrub and marsh and thorn. Had it been forest he'd have asserted his rights years ago. Tonight's moon lights the bridge's weathered handrails and glitters on the shallow stream, revealing gravel at the bottom and a single stickleback hanging in the water like a miniature pike.

Jeanne-Marie is there before me. 'You're late.'

'How did you get out?'

'Through the back door from our quarters.'

That part of the school has doors at ground level so all she had to do was keep to the shadows as she headed for the gardens and across the inner field towards the bridge. 'I left through my dorm window,' I tell her. 'Walked the ledge around that side of the tower and climbed down the guttering.'

She agrees this is more difficult. 'Where are the kittens?'

I take her hand, and though she doesn't fold her fingers in mine, she doesn't pull away either, as I lead her across the bridge and along a bank that separates two water meadows that have returned to marsh. We walk in the shadows of willow trees along the way and cut across a patch of drier ground towards the ruined village. No one knows when it was ruined or why. Maybe plague passed this way. Maybe soldiers. Most of the walls are broken at hip height, and the highest only rises to my shoulder. There's a rotten door leaning drunkenly from a broken frame, and we slip into the ruins of a house and out through the back into a field beyond. I want to stop in the ruins, kiss Jeanne-Marie and feel the new ampleness inside her blouse but common sense stops me. The kittens are the key. Without the kittens we can't go back to where we were.

'Up here,' I say. 'We're almost there.'

She takes my word for it and doesn't complain when up there turns out to be another half mile of scrub and hedge. Silhouetted in the darkness, a dead oak separates its trunk into branches and spreads those branches into twigs. Like veins in the flesh of the sky. I marvel at my thought. The thought of any twelve-year-old who considers himself a thinker. But to me it feels original. 'In here,' I say, pointing at a bank of thorns. 'I heard them yesterday.'

Jeanne-Marie stops and stares at a woven mass of twisting tendrils, each one studded with nail-length thorns. 'How do we . . . ?'

'Under there.' The entrance is low and worn to

grit by the feet of animals forcing a trail through the bushes. I doubt anything larger than a badger has tried to come this way before. 'I'll go ahead.'

She nods doubtfully.

Thorns snag my shirt and I crouch lower, realising I'll have to crawl on my belly if I'm to reach the cat. It's a slow process that sees a thorn scrape my temple. Blood slithers on my cheek and drips like slow tears on the broken leaves in front of my face. I can hear Jeanne-Marie's sour muttering behind me and hope we find kittens. This seemed such a good idea when I suggested it, but with my face in the dirt and thorns tugging at my back and Jeanne-Marie's sudden ouches behind me I'm close to deciding it was really stupid. And then, somehow, I see moonlight ahead and crawl out into a tramped circle set in the middle of the thorns. A slab of fallen wall stops their growth. And though they reach in it's too large to let the thorns close over the top. Jeanne-Marie looks around her.

'Heavens,' she says. 'How did you find this?'

I didn't, I almost tell her. I simply heard the kittens mewling from outside. But she's looking round with a grin on her face and I can see why. We're protected from the world by a razor-sharp circle of thorns. This is a place where magic happens — and we're the contents of the magic basket. 'Hush,' I say, putting my finger to her lips.

We listen for the kittens and I hear squeaking, slightly back the way we've come. So I turn until I face the other way and crawl into the tunnel, stopping to listen again. They're to the side and sound loud enough to be within reach. I push my hand between branches and feel fur, the kitten tiny and noisy. I expect the mother to savage me but am allowed to remove a kitten without being attacked. There are five, six if you count a dead one. All thin and mewling and too weak to stand. My fingers reach again and I touch the mother's side, ribs thin as bare bones. Dead, I think . . . She stirs, however, and tries to snap but something stops her reaching me. It's dark inside the thorn tunnel, the moon slivers of yellow lighting brief lengths of brutal branch. I have the kittens; I have the key back into Jeanne-Marie's heart. All I have to do is take them.

Jeanne-Marie's voice calls me.

'Wait,' I whisper, reaching again. The cat's front leg is trapped between strands of thorn that have hooked their claws into her. She could be snagged in a snare given the mess they've made of her. She explodes into hisses as I touch the wound and tries to fight free. 'I'm trying to help,' I say. Thorns scratch my wrists as I push one strand away, freeing her leg. Breaking off the sticky spikes smooths the branch, and then I pull the other branch towards me, breaking its spikes in turn. Very slowly her leg comes free.

'Follow me,' I say to Jeanne-Marie, and tuck the kittens into my shirt and crawl down the dirt tunnel until I'm out in the moonlight and the thorn bank is behind me. Jeanne-Marie struggles to her feet a moment later, her face furious.

'Why did you . . . ?' She stops at the sight of the injured cat, her eyes widening as I pull the five kittens from inside my shirt.

'Take your pick.'

'What happened to her?'

'She trapped herself on thorns.'

'And so did you.' Jeanne-Marie wipes blood from my chin.

My face is a mess where I stretched for the twisting branches that trapped the cat; a long thorn dips under the skin of my wrist and reappears half an inch later. She watches intently as I pull it free and check for others. There's a stream a hundred yards behind us and I wash myself there, splashing water on my face and rinsing my hands until blood stops welling from a dozen different cuts. I wash the cat's back leg and she barely protests. All the flesh is gone from her sides and her hips are hollow, her teats sucked sore by starving kittens. As I lift her free, a single drop of milk spills onto my finger. It tastes of sadness and despair.

'Food,' I say. 'She needs feeding.'

Jeanne-Marie's eyes are alight with an expression I don't recognise. An inner light that makes her face glow and her expression soften. 'Give me the kittens.' She folds a mixed bundle of mewling fur into the front of her blouse, exposing the softness of her stomach, a softness missing the last time my hands passed that way. I put the cat over my shoulder and hold the creature in place with one hand. As is always the way, the return trip seems to pass more quickly than the trip out. The solid mass of the school rising in front of us.

'What does she need?'

'Eggs. Six raw eggs and chicken if you can find any.'

Jeanne-Marie leaves me with the cat and the kittens and returns within two minutes, clutching a chicken leg, and with the eggs folded into her blouse where the kittens had been. She drops to a crouch and watches while I break an egg and feed the cat, which licks overflowing white and yolk from the bottom half of the shell. A second egg vanishes as quickly. Water, I think. I should give her water. I fill two half shells with water from a butt against the school wall and she drinks those down while Jeanne-Marie peers closer.

'Which kitten do you want?'

Jeanne-Marie squints at the squealing mass of half-naked kittens and shakes her head. 'It wouldn't be fair. She should keep them all.'

I try hard not to sigh.

We leave the kittens under a bush at the far end of a garden where the boys are not allowed to go and rest the cat beside them, her injured leg splayed in front of her. I break the remaining eggs and shred the chicken and leave both within reach, lowering the branches we hope will keep the cat and her kittens hidden. 'You're brave,' Jeanne-Marie says, the glow still in her eyes. She steps closer and lifts her face for a kiss. Her mouth opens readily and our tongues touch in a tiny spark of electricity that has her shivering. Her breasts fall readily into my hands and she smiles as I grin. So beautiful. Sometime between the kissing and the touching my hand slips down and though she freezes for a second she lets me delve.

I take two new tastes away with me. Cat's milk and girl. Ones I'd never tried before.

The next day my life changes and for unexpected reasons. Vicomte d'Anvers and the colonel reappear, without the comte this time. I am sent for, examined and asked to explain the scratches on my face and hands. Unable to find a better answer I tell the truth. I leave out the where, the when and the who with. But the kernel of the event remains. For reasons that escape me, rescuing a trapped cat and her kittens from a thorn bush at the expense of my own skin appeals to the vicomte and helps convince the colonel that I'm right for what vicomte d'Anvers has in mind. I'm to be offered a place at the academy, studying artillery and explosives.

'Almost like cooking,' the vicomte says.

The colonel snorts but lets the comment stand unchallenged.

1730
Military Academy

The larger of the two cadets is Jerome, round-faced and pock-marked and as red-cheeked as a washerwoman who spends her days by the river. He introduces himself in a thick accent that his friend mocks, whereupon he clenches his fist and his friend raises his hands placatingly. There's an element of ritual about the exchange.

'He's Norman,' Jerome's friend says, as if talking about a dumb beast. 'He still has black mud on his boots.'

'Good mud,' Jerome says. 'Rich mud. Acres of the bloody stuff. Better than that sticky red shit Charlot owns . . . ' They insult each other some more and then their gaze slides to Emile behind me and they wait for me to introduce him.

'Emile Duras,' I say. 'He has brains.'

They look at each other and what they're thinking goes unsaid. He might have brains but his name lacks the particule that says he's noble.

'A friend of yours?' Jerome asks.

I nod. Emile is here because I am here. His father, or perhaps his mother, decided I was a good influence on their son, or perhaps a good connection, and so Emile has come with me. I have no idea how much money changed hands to make this happen. 'We were in the same class.'

'And will be again,' Charlot says lightly. 'You're in my house, my year.' He's still looking at Emile, who is the smallest and obviously weakest of the four of us. Charlot nods as if this is how it should be. 'Duras?' he says. 'From where?'

Emile names his town and Charlot considers his answer.

'Protestant?' he asks finally.

Emile hesitates a second too long. 'A good Catholic,' he says, 'like my father.'

'But your grandfather . . . ?'

As Emile admits the truth of it, I remember Marcus's whisper — Marcus, our form leader, now left behind — that Emile's grandfather was Protestant, true enough, but before this was Jewish. He converted so that he could change cities and convert again.

'I had a Protestant great-aunt,' Charlot says graciously. 'Strange woman . . . Of course, she was a duchess.'

'Of course,' Jerome says.

Our new friends go back to insulting each other.

The academy is recently built, in the baroque style and with stucco mostly unstained. Time will blend it into the hill it commands, but for the moment it looks down on Brienne le Chateau, with the River Aube in the distance, still starkly white and obvious as our destination since we first turned onto the road out of Troyes.

'Where's your luggage?' Charlot demands suddenly.

Emile points to a leather trunk with wide

straps and brass buckles. I see amusement flicker on Charlot's face, and maybe Emile sees it too, because he blushes slightly. The trunk is too new, too obviously bought for this occasion. I have no doubt that Charlot's case is old and battered, probably belonged to his grandfather, and has an earlier version of his arms embossed into the lid.

'And you?' he asks.

I turn a circle, displaying my pristine uniform, a long grey coat, lined red and faced at the cuffs in red with gilt buttons. 'This is my baggage.'

'A philosopher.' Charlot grins. 'Hear that, his body is his baggage.' He turns to Jerome. 'We have ourselves a philosopher.'

'Better than a saint, I suppose.'

'Can you fight?' Charlot asks.

I look at him and remember my first day at the previous school, my fight with Emile that ended with us both black-eyed and bloody-nosed. Maybe this is how it works. Every school you go to you have to start with a fight. 'Why?'

'The philosopher's question,' Charlot says.

'Can you?' Jerome asks.

'If necessary.'

Jerome smiles and nods. 'Good,' he says. 'Tonight our dormitory will be attacked by the class above. We have to defend ourselves well.'

'But not too well.' Charlot looks serious. 'We must lose but bravely.'

'How do you know we'll be attacked?' Emile asks.

'My father told me.' Charlot looks at us and decides he'd better introduce himself properly. 'I'm Charles, marquis de Saulx, my father is the

70

duke. This is Vicomte Jerome de Caussard, second son of the comte de Caussard. We'll be attacked because that's what happens. We'll lose bravely because that's common sense.'

'If we win they'll come back tomorrow night?'

'And bring the class above with them,' Jerome says.

A master is at the stone steps gesturing us inside. We have this afternoon and tonight to settle in. Lessons start tomorrow after breakfast, which is after chapel, which is at 7.30. Waking bell is 6.30, no one will be late for chapel, breakfast or lessons. We nod to say we understand and take his words seriously. The man grunts and then sees Emile's trunk.

'Mine,' Emile says.

'Carry it yourself. You don't have servants here.'

I wonder if he thinks we had servants at our last school and realise he knows almost nothing about Emile and me. It's a strange feeling. Our form room is through the main hall, left into a darkened corridor and right at a door that looks like half a dozen others before and after it. A handful of boys who arrived before us look up and Charlot makes introductions. All nod and I realise Charlot's amused approval is enough to ensure we belong. There are desks, tables, old chairs missing half their stuffing. A suit of armour rots quietly in one corner. Since it's far older than the school someone obviously brought it here. A deer's skull with a spread of impressive antlers looks down from one wall. A boar's skull, missing one tusk, sits on a desk I realise Charlot has claimed when he drops languidly into a wooden chair and leans back to examine the ceiling. 'Killed it myself,' he says, seeing my gaze.

'With the help of a dozen huntsman, his father's hounds and a musketeer on hand to shoot the beast in case little Charlot misplants his spear.'

Charlot blushes and then laughs. 'I was eleven,' he protests. 'My mother was anxious.'

'Your mother is always anxious.'

For a second I think Charlot is offended by Jerome's comment, but he shrugs at its fairness. 'Mothers usually are.' He turns to me. 'Let's ask our philosopher. Wouldn't you say that, in the general run of things, mothers are anxious?'

'In the general run of things, perhaps.'

'Yours is not?'

'Mine is dead,' I say. 'My father also.'

I could have added that the only mother I'd met — apart from Madame Faure, who didn't count — was Emile's, and she was stubborn, ambitious, built like a brick wall, and told her husband what to do, for all she was unfailingly kind to me. To say that would have been unfair to Emile, however.

'Your parents are dead?'

I nodded, and the room waited to see how far Charlot would push this. Already he was our leader; taller, blonder, unquestionably grander. But it was more than that. We were newly arrived at a strange school, mostly strangers to each other, and we would be required to fight to order in the dorms that night. But Charlot behaved as if he'd been here for ever. As if the coming fight were a minor inconvenience to be dealt with when it arose. His utter confidence calmed us. 'How?' he asked.

'The philosopher's question.'

Charlot's grin was approving. 'And when?' he said.

'I was five, maybe six . . . ' I was too ashamed to say they'd starved to death in the ruins of a house they'd mortgaged deep into debt. 'My brother died in the Lowlands. They'd bought him a commission in the cavalry. It was his first battle. They never recovered.'

'They died of grief?'

I shrugged. It was better than hunger.

Charlot looked at Jerome, who shrugged in his turn.

'And your home?' Charlot persisted.

'Ransacked,' I said. It was a grand word for a slow procession of shuffling *jacques* who wouldn't meet my gaze, if they bothered to look in my direction at all. They'd arrived like ants, in a line, carrying away whatever they could on their backs. The house, the stables and the outbuildings had been stripped bare by the time le Régent arrived. I had no idea why they didn't take the horse. Looking up, I realised I still had the room's attention whether I wanted it or not. 'By peasants. The duc d'Orléans hanged them.'

'Le Régent?'

'He found my mother and father dead.'

'And you?' Jerome asks. 'You were where?'

'Eating beetles.' Seeing his surprise, I say, 'I was hungry. I was five.'

73

They nod, the boys in that room. They nod and mutter comments from the corner of their mouths, and someone offers me a slice of cake, as if I might be hungry still. The talk turns to what they've brought from home — cakes and cheeses, fresh bread, dried dates, a sweetmeat made from egg white and candied fruit — and I realise this school, this college, has proper holidays and pupils who have real homes. Emile no longer seems so exotic.

'I didn't know we were allowed to bring food,' he whispers.

'You will next time.'

The fight that night is fierce and ritualised.

The bigger boys face off against each other, the smaller boys match themselves — those, like Emile, who don't really want to fight at all, find others who feel the same and pretend. We let them creep into our dorm an hour after lights out and then throw ourselves from our beds before the attack can properly begin. It is a night campaign and we fight in furious silence by the light of the moon through three long windows along one wall. A thickset boy punches me and flinches as I punch back. He hesitates and I punch again, seeing him clasp his hand to his mouth and look for an easier target. My stomach is a knot and my legs are shaking. I feel no excitement at the fight. I want to hide.

It is over in a handful of minutes.

Charlot stands, unbloodied. Jerome stands beside him with a swollen lip and a ferocious look on his face, his hands clenched into huge fists. He has the build of a cart horse. I stand slightly behind them, not ferocious and not unbloodied, but standing and ready. The rest crowd behind us and wait to see what happens next.

A boy with curls to his shoulders steps forward. 'You,' he says, looking at Charlot. 'What's your name?'

'De Saulx,' Charlot says. 'This is de Caussard, and this d'Aumout . . .'

The boy scowls as if wanting to match our names to our faces. 'This is Richelieu,' he says, naming the house to which we've been assigned. 'We win. We win at everything. You let us down and we'll be back.'

'And we'll be waiting,' Jerome says heavily.

'We won't let the house down,' Charlot says. The boy takes it that Charlot speaks for all of us and that's fine because he does. The older boys file out in silence and we hear them on the stairs. Common sense makes us wait to see if it's a feint and they plan to return to finish what they've started but that's it, the battle is done. None of the masters ask about our bruised lips and black eyes but I see the colonel at a distance in a corridor and he smiles.

Unlike my last school the masters change according to subject. They are severe, mostly military, and leave us alone if we do our work and give the right answers. I follow Charlot's example and read the books I'm told to read, work out what is likely to be asked and read enough to answer those questions only. My marks are good. My horsemanship, almost as bad as Emile's when we start, improves week by

75

week. I enjoy sword work — the clash of steel, the noise of our practise, the chatter of the sluice rooms and the lazy exhaustion that takes us afterwards. They work us hard. They work us hard at everything.

That Christmas I spend with Emile and his family. A quiet week filled with questions about the academy and our new friends. Madame Duras seems content with our answers and impressed with the casual way Emile talks about the marquis de Saulx and the vicomte de Caussard and a few of the others, as if they're the closest of friends. Just occasionally I feel him watching me as if worried I'll contradict and say they're my friends really, but he grows more confident as the week progresses, and why shouldn't he claim their friendship? We go around in a group of four and if occasionally I find Charlot regarding Emile as if examining an interesting specimen . . . Well, he uses that expression often, sometimes on me. I am the dung-hill philosopher, without family or home, and to the best of his belief content with that.

Charlot lives in a huge chateau, obviously. One of several belonging to his family. His mother is beautiful, his father is brave, his family are rich beyond belief. In someone less cavalier the idle boasting would grate. Somehow Charlot carries it off. He takes our homage and protects us lazily. If a Richelieu boy in our year is in trouble with an older boy, Charlot deals with it. He treats everyone as his equal: those younger than him, those older than him, even masters. It takes me two terms to realise he barely sees servants.

Another term to realise no one else in my year sees them either. Even Emile learns to look through them. I stop to talk to a red-haired laundry maid and she's so shocked she turns scarlet and rushes away. She's young, probably no older than me. The next time she sees me she turns on her heels and hurries back the way she came.

'Jean-Marie . . . ' Charlot and Jerome are in the corridor behind me. 'You can't make friends with loons,' Charlot scolds. It's the name we use for servants.

'He doesn't want to *make friends*,' Jerome says.

I blush. 'She's a person.'

Charlot rolls his eyes. Jerome smirks. The next time we see her, both of them are exaggeratedly polite and she retreats with tears in her eyes. 'She only likes philosophers,' Jerome says. But that's it. She refuses to come near me again.

Emile goes to stay with an aunt the next summer and I stay at school, somehow happier to be free of his family and have time for myself. I prepare my own food in the kitchens, which amuses the cooks until they realise I know what I'm doing. In between, to keep the colonel happy, I make mixtures that smoke, flash and explode. Filling a paper tube with three kinds of gunpowder I nearly lose my fingers when all three ignite at once before I'm ready. My next tube has cardboard spaces between the powders and a series of linked but separate fuses. The colonel comes to see what I am doing.

'Add colour,' he says.

To the flash, the smoke or the explosion? I wonder. In the end I add them to all three and produce something between a flare and a firework that flashes red, smokes a ruddy pink and then explodes in an impressive blast of vermillion. By the time Charlot, Jerome and Emile return from their holidays I have created tubes that will flare, smoke and explode in reds, greens and blues. The colonel is more convinced than ever that I have a fine future in one of the artillery regiments. 'Show-off,' Charlot says.

Jerome laughs. 'Ignore him,' he says, his Normandy accent thicker than ever from a summer spent at home. 'He's just jealous.'

'I was bored,' I say. As close to an apology as I can manage.

'Next summer you must come home with me,' Charlot says carelessly. 'You'll amuse my sisters.'

A year passes and summer comes round. Charlot has forgotten or never meant it. He spends the summer at Jerome's chateau. I spend it at the school. With the others gone, the red-haired laundry maid no longer hurries away at the sight of me and lets me inside her petticoats. The taste on my fingers is acrid, stronger. Roquefort to Jeanne-Marie's new Brie. I note both their tastes in my book, with the dates, and resolve to find a girl with fair hair to see if she tastes different again. The laundry maid disappears as summer ends and I discover she's newly married. By then the others are back, talking about the cold faces turned to them by the girls they love. Except for Charlot, who remains as languid as ever, slouched in his battered chair in the bigger study we've been given this year. He tells us nothing, I realise. His tales are of hunts and parties and could be pretty stories from a book.

His friendship with Jerome has grown watchful. Jerome's stomach has shrunk as his shoulders have strengthened. Our Norman bear looks dangerous now. Dangerous and amused and somehow stepped back from the bustle around him. The maids stare after him, looking away when they're noticed. Some of the boys too. He's the dark shadow to Charlot's lazy sunlight. On the afternoon of the first day back talk turns to our ambitions. Charlot tosses off some bon mot about maids deflowered and boars killed and Jerome rounds on him. 'That's it? The limit of your ambition?'

'And to be a good duke when the time comes.'

While I'm still marvelling that Charlot is prepared to admit that much, Jerome turns away peevishly. The rest of us shift uncomfortably.

'What do you want?' I ask Jerome.

'What does any man want? To make my mark. I should have been born when my grandfather was. A man could be great then.'

'Today is better,' Emile protests. 'We have science. We have thinkers. Superstition is vanishing. We are building better roads. New canals.'

'To carry what?' Jerome asks. 'Apples to places that have apples? Stones to places that have stone? Superstition will never vanish. It taints peasant blood like ditchwater.'

Emile blushes and turns away. I wonder how

many generations he's removed from that insult — his grandfather, the religious turncoat? I know how far I'm removed. One generation. Jerome would consider my mother a peasant. If he made an exception for her, he'd include her father without thinking about it. One of the villagers hanged by the duc d'Orléans for stealing was my mother's cousin.

My salvation where Jerome is concerned is that my father was *noblesse d'épée*, descended from knights. At least half our class are *noblesse de robe*, from newer families granted titles for civil work. Jerome lists what France needs: a strong king, which we have in Louis le bien-aimé, now twenty, and already tired of the ugly Polish woman they'd married him to and beginning to bed good French mistresses. A strong king, a strong treasury, a strong army. France must be the most feared state in Europe.

'It is,' Charlot says mildly.

'We must make her stronger.'

Boys around him are nodding and I wonder what it is like to have that degree of belief in anything, even as part of me is mocking his fervour and noticing Charlot's amusement. Emile turns, blurts out, 'We have a choice.'

'Between what?' Jerome demands.

Emile puts his hands behind his back, rises onto tiptoe and rocks back. It looks like something he's seen his father do. 'Between reason and ritual. Between what we can still discover and what we've been told to believe. Between the modern and the old.'

'And if I want both?' Jerome asks.

'You can't have them. They contradict each other.'

Charlot laughs and around him boys smile. 'Enough seriousness,' he says. 'Let's open our hampers.' He pats Emile on the shoulder as he passes, a move both comforting and dismissive, as if petting a dog. As always, knowing my strange obsession with taste, my friends let me try whatever they've brought from home. A wind-dried ham from Navarre that cuts so finely the slices look like soiled paper and melt on the tongue like snow. A waxy cheese devoid of taste from the Lowlands. Anchovies pickled in oil and dressed with capers. All of the boys bring bread. Two days old, three days, five — depending on how long they've had to travel. It must be what they miss most. The loaf Emile brings is pure white. Jerome's is solid as rock. He swears his cook doesn't knead the dough so much as punch it, pick it up and slam it on the table like a washerwoman beating clothes on rock. It can take an hour before she decides it's ready.

They watch me take their offerings. Occasionally I'll open my eyes after I've tasted something particularly fine and catch them looking at each other and smiling. I don't mind; at least I don't mind that much. Some of them, I suspect, barely taste what they eat.

'Try this, philosopher,' Charlot says. The pot he holds is small and sealed with clarified butter. He hands me a knife and tears off a chunk of oily bread and indicates I should dig through the butter to what lies beneath. The taste I know — goose liver. But this is rich beyond description. *Parfait de foie gras.* 'Now clear your palate with this.'

He hands me a second pot and a tiny spoon. This pot is sealed with cork and the darkness beneath has mould that he tells me to scrape away. The sourness of the puréed cherries cuts through the richness of foie gras. He laughs at my expression and I think no more about it until a year passes and summer comes round again and Charlot stops me in a corridor to say, 'You must see our cherry trees.' I look at him, remembering that earlier invitation.

'The colonel agrees,' Charlot says. 'My father has already talked to him.'

1734

The Injured Wolf

'My mother . . . '

'Will be distant but polite. Your father, whom I will see when I first arrive at Chateau de Saulx and again when we leave, will be too busy to bother with either of us in between. Your sister Marguerite, who I may not call Margot unless she invites me, is beautiful, distant, cold and older than me. I must not fall in love with her. Your middle sister Virginie may be friendly, she may be reserved, who knows. But Élise, your littlest sister, will crawl all over me and want piggybacks. Your mother thinks she is too old for piggybacks so I must refuse . . . '

Charlot laughs and slumps back into the leather seat of our carriage. 'You've been paying attention . . . '

'Of course I've been paying attention.'

The oddity is I think Charlot is more nervous of bringing me home than I am of visiting, though God knows I'm nervous enough. The colonel called me into his study before we left and told me the duc de Saulx would judge the academy on my behaviour. I was to bear that in mind. The duke has sent a carriage for us. A carriage, a coachman, outriders. The carriage is lined inside with red velvet, has red leather seats and the de Saulx arms on the door. Charlot thinks it is new. It is the most elegant vehicle I have ever seen and moves with surprising speed.

We stay at the best inns, eat what we like but drink surprisingly little. I think Charlot is worried that any misbehaviour will be reported to his father. Only once does my own behaviour worry him, when I disappear into a kitchen to ask what gave a stew its taste. Juniper, the cook tells me. I know the taste of juniper and think there's something else. In the end, after questioning, he produces a sliver of bark and lets me sniff it. From the Indies, he tells me, claiming not to know its name. Only later do I realise I don't know if it's East Indies or West. 'At home,' Charlot begins . . .

I know what he intends to say. 'I stay out of the kitchens?'

He nods, relieved I understand and we slouch back in our seats to watch the countryside flow past. This coach has springs so fine only the biggest ruts in the road throw us into each other or against the sides. Blossom is still out on the hedgerows, the wheat has turned from green to pale yellow in the fields, the sky is deep blue and strangely cloudless. The peasants work their fields like animals, silent and unchanging. Eyes glance towards us and glance away as our worlds slide by each other without touching. Their expressions are blank, their feelings unknowable. A young woman squats by a hedge curling out a turd without bothering to hide herself from our passing. Charlot laughs. He's right, she's young and comely for all she's filthy and craps with the unthinkingness of a cow.

'My lessons . . . '

'Are going well,' I agree. 'You ride the best, you fence the best, you can read maps and choose the right bit of high ground or defensive position faster than the rest of us.' When I see him flush I realise he thinks I'm mocking him.

Our days at the academy have traditional lessons in the morning and drill in the afternoon. We can march, we can ride, we can charge our pistols, prime our pans and change our own flints. I can oversee the loading of cannon, even load it myself. I understand elevation and arc. No longer being first years we are allowed to wear the cockade of our academy on our tricorne hats. We are progressing as well as can be expected according to our instructors. That is high praise indeed.

'I mean it,' I tell Charlot. 'Stop worrying.'

We travel the rest of that afternoon with Charlot wrapped in the silence of whatever troubles him. Whatever private storm he is suffering passes and by the time we reach the drive for Chateau de Saulx he is himself again. A long line of chestnuts both sides of the road usher us to a castle that takes my breath away. A cliff of towers and turrets and sharp roofs rises from the middle of a moat thick with lily pads. A wide stone bridge crosses the moat and enters a huge courtyard where a fountain splashes in the middle.

'Diana, the huntress,' Charlot says. She's magnificent. Tight and twisted and pert and dangerous. He grins. 'Thought you'd like her.'

We dine in silent splendour in a long room filled with mirrors and huge paintings of classically draped men and women being approved by cherubs and angels, and in one case by the Virgin Mary herself. They are, I realise, Charlot's ancestors. We have a footman each, behind our chairs and stood back against the panelling when not needed. They wear short white wigs and livery in the de Saulx colours, scarlets and greens. Charlot kicks me under the table when I peer at one too closely.

His father sits at one end. The duke wears a wig in the old style, falling to his shoulders. He does everything slowly, from saying grace before we eat to reaching for his glass, utterly secure in his certainty the world will wait at his pleasure. Charlot's mother sits at the other. Her hair is piled high and she wears a green silk dress and a shawl. Opposite Charlot sits his elder sister Marguerite, who looks as grown up as the duchess and a good deal more serene. She is strikingly beautiful. Far more so than her mother. As if it has taken the duke's blood to give Margot the quality that lets her turn heads, as indeed it has. Opposite me sits Virginie. She stares at her bowl of venison soup and scowls. Perhaps the bowl offends her, perhaps it's the soup, perhaps simply the company. Looking up to see me watching she looks sharply away and goes back to scowling at her bowl. Only Élise chatters. About our trip, about how much Charlot's grown, about a blue ribbon she wants for her hair. In the end, her mother scolds her into silence and Élise scowls at her bowl as well.

Margot and Charlot share an inner fire that Virginie seems to be missing. It might have missed Élise as well — although it is probably too early to say. In Margot the fire is contained. In Charlot it usually blazes but tonight it smoulders. The food is obviously fresh and undoubtedly beautifully cooked but I taste none of it as one course becomes another. And I bow my way from the room at the end of the meal still ravenous but with my stomach full to aching. 'I'm sorry,' Charlot says, when we're back in the linked rooms we've been given. One is Charlot's bedroom, the other a dressing room that has been emptied and filled for me with a huge bed, washing stand and looking glass.

'For what?

'You know what. For my family.'

'Do your sisters always curtsy when they see you?'

He considers this as if he's never asked himself the same question — and maybe he hasn't. 'On first meeting my father I bow to him, on meeting my mother I bow to her and kiss her hand. My sisters receive a bow but only after they have curtsied to me first. It will be better tomorrow. Tomorrow they will leave us alone. The first day is always like this.'

Leaving him to his sourness, I retire to my room and stare down at the bronze goddess with her bow. Her arrow points straight at my window and I smile. We have two months to waste before we must return. I am sure Charlot's temperament will improve.

Next day we rise early, rinse our faces in cold water and dress quickly. There is something Charlot wants to show me.

'There,' he says on reaching the ragged shore of a lake below the chateau. Tied to a post in the reeds is a punt, with a strange wooden vee at the front as if for a huge oar. Charlot pulls a key from his pocket with a flourish and leads me to a low hut I'd overlooked, sturdily built and roofed with turf. The hut is in darkness until Charlot finds a catch and the top half of the wall overlooking the lake falls forward with a crash. 'For the light,' he says. 'We'll put it back.'

An old chair, a decanter, chipped glasses, a boar spear and a hunting dirk, discarded powder flasks and a filthy leather hunting jacket hanging on a hook . . .

'There you go,' says Charlot, pointing to a long, dark and slightly rusting iron tube on the floor against the wall. It's a gun barrel, ridiculously long, with steel lugs either side that obviously drop into the wooden frame at the front of the punt.

My friend is grinning. 'Wait until you hear it. We'll wake the entire chateau.' This is a very different Charlot to the one who sat in scowling silence, in his best academy uniform, at the dinner table the night before. The punt is only really big enough for one of us but we pole it out into the middle of the reeds and squeeze down together.

'Now we wait,' he says.

As well as hiding us, the reeds stop us drifting. A breeze carries the smell of a distant marsh into our faces. The sun rises high enough to burn off the last of a low frieze of mist that obscures fir-covered hillsides beyond the marsh. Charlot sees our prey first, because he knows what he's looking for. A neat formation of dark specks in the sky. 'Here they come.' He blows on a coiled match until the end glows under its ash. 'You're the artillery man,' he says. 'You take the shot.'

The geese drop as they approach the lake but land way beyond the range of any gun, even one with a barrel like this. I look to Charlot and he nods towards the far horizon where other formations are showing.

'Where do they come from?'

'Another lake? Does it matter? The point is they come.'

An hour later I finally take my shot. Our match is down to single string and I know — from his shifts and sighs — that Charlot has grown impatient. There have been other possible shots before this, but the birds were too high or the distance too risky. Only when a dozen birds drop towards our lake heading for a patch of still-clear water, spook themselves at the sight of our punt and try to rise again, does the perfect shot occur.

The explosion is so fierce I fear the punt gun will shake itself free and sink us. The punt itself whooshes backwards and grounds on a mud bank, Charlot banging into me. He's laughing. 'How much powder did you use?'

'As much as I dared.'

'The gun's a hundred years old,' he says.

'Maybe use less next time?' He grips my shoulders and hugs me. 'Only you,' he says. 'Let's go and claim our prize.'

A dozen dead or injured geese float or flap in the water. We collect the dead ones easily enough, and break the necks of the living and toss them on top of the dead. Then we punt back to the hut, unfix the gun, replace the side of the shooting hut and struggle back to the chateau under the weight of half a dozen dead geese each. The duke himself comes to the main door to greet us and he's smiling.

'Impressive,' he says.

Charlot turns red with pleasure and is happy for the rest of the day.

So our pattern is set. We shoot geese on the lake and pigeon in the woods. We pull speckled trout from the river and eat them where they die, cooked in a pan over an impromptu fire of twigs, with butter and whatever wild herbs I can find. We are, for those two months of the summer at least, inseparable. Charlot's desires are simple. He wants to make a good duke. He would like his father to love him. He hopes for a wife who will be faithful and a friend. He would like to live a good life.

We swim naked in the mill pond, and cross the lake one night for a bet, dragging ourselves exhausted up the distant shore then turn round and swim back because neither of us dare back down. We wrestle half naked in the makeshift ring of a clearing in the woods and listen to each other's dreams, take bets on who can piss the highest, climb the tallest tree, shoot an arrow the furthest. Margot, whom I must still call Marguerite, treats her brother with outward politeness, as is his due as the next duke. But always mixed with quiet disdain. She is a grown-up and in her eyes we are still children.

Worse, we are noisy, irritating, ever-present children given to secret plots and laughter. I overhear her telling Virginie she fears I am not a good influence on her brother. Charlot tells me I was meant to overhear. Virginie simply does not see me. I might as well not be at Chateau de Saulx for all the notice she takes. When we meet on the terraces, taking our walks before supper, she nods politely to her brother and simply looks through me. Only Élise wants to be my friend. She curtsies clumsily every time she sees me and breaks into giggles.

'Ignore them all,' says Charlot, with the resignation of someone outnumbered three to one. We barely see his mother, although his father appears to approve of me. 'He can afford to,' Charlot says, and I ask him to explain. 'He's de Saulx, if he wants to like you he can. My mother is less certain you're a good influence . . . '

'Margot?'

Charlot sighs. 'Margot's a snob,' he says. 'She wants to marry a prince, live at Versailles, spend her days playing cards and listening to the harpsichord. She thinks I should bring back older boys, with grander titles.'

'With any title . . . '

'You're noble,' he says. 'That's enough.'

He's Charlot, marquis de Saulx and heir to the

duke, he is allowed to say that. He tells me about tomorrow's hunt, organised by his father as a final treat before we return to the academy. A wolf has been taking lambs from one of the fields that border the forest and we will beat the woods tomorrow and kill or capture the beast. We must sleep soon because it will be an early start.

★　★　★

I'm woken by a tap at my door. Charlot is already dressed in simple trews and a leather hunting coat, with a dirk at his hip and long pistol in his hand. He waits while I splash water onto my face, strip off my nightgown and change quickly into clothes he grew out of last year if not the one before. The first surprise of the day is that Élise is allowed to come on the understanding one of her sisters looks after her. Since Margot refuses to have anything to do with the hunt, Virginie has that duty. Her scowl greets us as we hurry out to find the others waiting. 'You're late,' she says.

'And a good morning to you, dear sister.'

She blushes, drops a brittle curtsy and turns away. I grin at Élise and she grins back, slipping away from Virginie to stand beside Charlot. 'You'll protect me from wolves, won't you?' she demands.

My friend grins, glances at his middle sister and says, 'I should help Papa. You'll both be quite safe with Jean-Marie. I'm sure he will protect you both grandly.'

Virginie's scowl at this is so black I'm on the

point of suggesting he and I swap places, when Charlot shoulders his musket, clicks his fingers for a dog that is apparently his in the holidays only, and hurries after the departing hunters, leaving us at the edge of the lawn.

'I'm going back inside,' Virginie says.

'You can't,' Élise protests. 'Mama says you have to look after me.'

'Monsieur d'Aumout can look after you.'

'That wouldn't be proper,' Élise says loudly. 'I'm not a child.' At eleven that is exactly what she is, and her face, usually so sweet, is so childishly stubborn I have to turn away to hide my smile. 'I will tell Mama,' Élise adds, her winning salvo in a battle that ends with Virginie sighing heavily and turning for the path to the forest without looking to see if she is being followed. 'Ignore her,' Élise says loudly.

'I don't need to,' I whisper back. 'She's doing the ignoring for me.'

Virginie's hearing is obviously good because her neck reddens. So begins a long day that sees us arrive, time and again, after the excitement is done. We see two dead females . . . Grey-coated and lean. A young male wolf the duke's huntsman says is no more than a year old. Charlot shoots a boar that the duke finishes with a second shot. We only learn this later, from the duke's servants who are loading the boar onto a litter to be dragged back to the chateau. The hunters have already moved on.

Virginie vanishes twice into the undergrowth, furious that I am there to see and red with embarrassment when she returns. She shouts at

Élise, who also vanishes, for not going far enough to be completely out of sight. Élise returns unhappy and we agree . . . Well, Virginie and Élise agree, and I agree with their agreement, that we've all had enough and it is time to go home. A shot comes from deep in the forest and we think nothing about it, until there is a second shot and someone shouts.

'They've got him,' Élise grins. 'Let's go see.'

'We're going home,' Virginie says.

'No,' Élise stamps. 'We're not. I want to see.'

She heads for the shouting and I look helplessly at Virginie, who scowls. 'I'll fetch her back,' I say.

'You do that. I'll wait here.'

I catch up with Élise where two paths cross. The oaks make a cathedral above us and I wish the day had been better, that I was with Charlot and the excitement, not trapped with the girls.

'Where's Virginie?' Élise demands.

'Waiting for us back there.'

'We haven't seen anything yet,' she protests. 'This is my first hunt and I haven't seen anything at all.' Her face floods with disappointment and for a moment I fear she's going to cry.

'I'm sorry,' I say.

'Not sure why you're sorry. She's not your sister.' Élise puts her hand over her mouth at her own rudeness and I have to smile. My smile makes her smile. We walk back in easy silence and then I hear Virginie's voice, low and urgent.

'Jean-Marie . . . ' She's never used my Christian names before.

'Wait here,' I tell Élise. Dry leaves crackle

94

underfoot as I abandon Élise and head to where Virginie should be. I have no idea what worries her but her voice sounds anxious enough to make me hurry. In the clearing stands Virginie, and directly in front of her the hugest wolf I've ever seen. Blood streams from a wound in its shoulder and its teeth are bared. Virginie is frozen. Half a dozen paces away from the beast at most. She is blocking the animal's escape.

'Move,' I tell her. 'Step out of its way.'

I'm not sure she even hears. Glancing down, I discover Élise has joined me. 'I was scared,' she mutters.

'Stay here,' I say. 'Don't move again.'

Without waiting to see if she obeys I walk into the clearing, my arms spread wide to catch the wolf's attention. Virginie is white with terror, her hands trembling, her feet locked into place by fear. Her eyes — brown and haunting — find mine, and her gaze is so beseeching that I swallow. I'm without musket or pistol. Without even a hunting dirk. All I have is the leather hunting coat I've borrowed. The one I'm sliding from my shoulders. The wolf turns at my movement, then turns back. Virginie still blocks its way. The creature glares at her, its hackles rise higher and its lips pull back to reveal fangs.

'Run,' Élise shouts.

'Don't,' I say. 'Step aside.' Virginie should give the wolf his path — but she backs away and the beast stalks after her. If she runs, and I realise with a hollow gut that she's on the edge of running, it will kill her.

I yell furiously and Virginie and the wolf look

at me together, Virginie in shock, the wolf already dropping its haunches for a spring as I lurch towards it, throwing Charlot's coat over its head and gripping tight as we roll in the dirt together. Élise screams, voices rise and branches break as people come running. I can hear Charlot shouting but my attention, my full attention, is on the beast trying to free itself.

'Stand away,' someone orders.

The duke, I think. Charlot is shouting my name, telling me to let go so the hunters can have a clean shot. I'm too terrified to let go, too terrified the wolf will free itself from the coat and rip out my throat. I can smell its stink and my own fear. My grip tightens without me telling it to and I hear a crack like a branch breaking, everyone hears the wolf's neck crack. The animal goes limp and hands begin lifting me away. The duke is pounding my shoulder. Charlot hugs me. Élise is sobbing as she tells the story of how the wolf was going to kill her sister. Some huge man, dressed in green with a beard big enough to house owls, is doing his best to comfort her. Hush falls for a second and I realise Virginie is in front of me. We look at each other and then she steps forward and puts her forehead against mine. 'Thank you,' she whispers.

Patronage

Marguerite came to thank me warmly, telling me to call her Margot and apologising for not taking me seriously. Charlot had had close friends before, usually local boys, but I was different, her family and especially her sister were indebted to me. My courage was astonishing in a boy so young.

I wanted to say Charlot and I were not young — we were sixteen, which was almost adult — but I understood that, to Margot, her brother would always be a child. So I told her the wolf was injured and already dying and I'd only done what Charlot or any of my other friends would do. She smiled at me then, kissed me briefly on the cheek and left a book of Latin poems on a table beside my high-backed chair.

She'd written my name, her name and the date inside.

I sat in the window of my chamber that looked down to the bronze huntress, and was dressed in a nightgown despite it being early evening. A blanket covered my gown for decency's sake. I'd been in bed when Margot knocked but swapped to the chair while she waited to come in. Her mother, the duchess, had already been and gone. Fussing so furiously that I finally understood that, for her, fussing was a form of affection. She might fret over Charlot's drinking, Virginie's lack of eating or Élise's manners, and I had seen her do all of those, but she would never have fussed over me before this.

Élise had been the first to visit me, pushing past a doctor to see what he was doing with my arm. The wolf's teeth had bitten through the coat and into my flesh without my realising it. The frenzy of battle was how the doctor described my brief tussle, while explaining how excitement and shock kept the pain at bay. I resisted pointing out that his prodding and pulling and bathing my arm in brandy hurt me far more than the wolf had managed. Only the fact Élise watched gave me the courage to bear the doctor's ministrations in silence.

Had I known the duke was in his study on the floor below exaggerating my bravery in a letter to the colonel, I might have complained more loudly. Margot was behind the letter. She'd told her father I'd said any boy at the academy would have done the same. A sentiment, the duke decided, which proved the calibre of the academy's pupils and the soundness of the colonel's teaching. The letter was to endear me to the colonel, as killing the wolf had endeared me to the duke.

Having made sure I would live — it was a bite to my arm, I'd told him, not to my throat — Charlot vanished. I discovered later he went to find his father's huntsman to give orders for the wolf to be beheaded, its pelt skinned, and its head boiled in a copper. The boiling was to be done immediately so I would have its skull to take back to school. Only Virginie didn't come. Dusk fell and the family went down to supper.

I was dozing when I heard a knock at my door. A young servant scurried in with a tray, put it down beside my bed, dipped a blushing curtsy and scurried out. She'd brought me fresh bread and cheese Élise knew I liked. A glass of wine beside it had been heavily mixed with water so maybe the doctor had given orders I shouldn't drink until my arm was better. The bread was yeasty and the cheese tart, and I was savouring both when there was a knock on the door between my room and Charlot's own. This was unlike him since he was given to bursting in without bothering to check if I was naked or pissing in a pot.

'Come in then.' The knock came again and, sighing, I slipped from the bed to see if the door had been locked. The bolt was drawn back on my side and since the key was on Charlot's side that couldn't be the problem. 'Such frigging delicacy,' I said, dragging his door open. 'How very unlike you . . .'

Virginie stood blinking at me.

My face reddened. 'I thought you were . . .'

'My brother? No, he's at supper, no doubt getting drunk with my father while my mother fusses and my elder sister politely mocks and my younger sister tries to sneak a glass for herself and sulks because she's not allowed to come up here to play nursemaid.'

'You didn't join them?'

'I'm excused. Mama thought I should rest after,' she smiled ruefully, 'the excitement. But I thought I should thank you. I wanted to thank you . . .'

99

I looked at her properly then. She was two years younger than me. Her upper lip seemed to pull naturally at one side as if in casual amusement at the stupidities around her. Charlot said it was the result of a childhood fall. Maybe that was true.

But in my heart she seemed to dance across my cares and dreams so lightly she barely risked breaking their shells.

'What?' she asked.

'You're beautiful.'

Her cheeks reddened and she scowled. 'Margot's beautiful and Élise is pretty. I'm neither of those. And don't you dare tell me I'll always be beautiful to you.'

'Any man who doesn't think you beautiful is an idiot.'

'Man?' she said slyly

It was my turn to blush and she grinned.

She flinched a little when I put my fingers to her cheek, then leant her face into my hand and closed her eyes. You kissed Jeanne-Marie readily enough, I told myself. There had been others too. A girl at a dance the previous winter. That scullery maid at the academy. 'Your hand is shaking,' she whispered.

'Shock. The doctor says it's shock.' Carefully I leant forward and kissed the corner of her lip. Her eyes flicked open, but she tipped her head so we could kiss again. The next was slow and soft and gentle, with only the corner of our lips touching. 'Virginie . . . ' I tasted her name and smiled as she raised her head, her eyes now shut and mouth slightly open.

'I haven't . . . ' She stopped. 'This before. I haven't . . . '

She wore a silk banyan over a white nightgown. Perhaps she'd gone to bed early. Perhaps she'd simply been told to rest. I had no idea what she was doing in Charlot's room before she knocked on my door. I only knew she was beautiful and her face was raised to mine. 'Again,' Virginie whispered.

I folded my fingers into her long thick hair and turned her head so our lips met properly, feeling her mouth open and tasting her breath. The kiss was deeper than the one before but no less languid. She was in a dream it seemed, a dream that remained unbroken as I kissed her neck. My hand dropped towards her breast, and I let my fingers caress the silk of her banyan, expecting her to pull away, or tell me off, or simply stop my fingers with her own. But she simply shivered and bit her lip as my fingers closed over her breast. We stood like that for a long second, her nipple hard beneath the silk.

'I should go,' she whispered.

'Not yet.' I pulled on the banyan's belt to loosen it, and slid the banyan from her shoulders, revealing white cotton with mother of pearl buttons beneath. When I reached for the first Virginie stepped back.

'Jean-Marie.'

My fingers shook as I reached again. 'Let me,' I begged.

She stayed silent as I undid the first four buttons of her gown and pulled it open enough to expose heavy breasts tipped with dark nipples

101

in paler circles. The scent of soap and orange water rose like heat between them. Without even thinking I put my mouth to her nipple and sucked. Virginie's hand came up to grip my hair and for a second she held me against her, then dragged my head away. Her eyes were wide and her mouth was open. 'You mustn't,' she said.

The neck of her gown held shut with her hands, she turned to go and shook me off fiercely when I put a hand to her shoulder. I asked the first thing that came to mind. 'Why were you in Charlot's room?' For a second I doubted she'd answer.

'To get to your room obviously. There are stairs between our chambers. We used to use them every day when we were . . . younger.'

There was such regret in her voice I suspected she'd been about to say *friends*.

'Don't tell Charlot,' she said. 'About this. About any of this. Don't even say I was here. He'll be jealous. Charlot's always jealous if I . . . ' She hesitated, a pretty hesitation but real, her cheeks reddened slightly. 'Want to be friends with his friends.'

'I thought you didn't like me.'

She turned away to button her nightgown, turning back as she adjusted the shoulders of her banyan and tightened its belt. 'I made the mistake of telling Charlot you seemed nicer than his usual friends. That was the first night. He's been teasing me ever since. It was easier to ignore you both.' Virginie picked up the book Margot brought and flipped it open, smiling at the inscription. 'Your name. Her name. The date.

For Margot that's enough. Her view of life is simple.'

'And yours is complex?

'More complex than hers certainly.'

I took the book from her fingers and put it back on the small table beside the chair. There was a bed behind us. Was I the only one to realise that? But the moment was gone if it had ever been there at all. The ghost of the moment perhaps.

★ ★ ★

I was dozing when Charlot came in. 'How are you feeling now?' he asked, sounding almost worried. 'Sorry supper took so long. Mama wanted to talk about the events of the day. She always does if something serious happens.' He stared round my room looking puzzled, as if a piece of furniture might have been moved or one of the pictures changed. In the end he simply shrugged and turned back for my answer.

'Well enough.'

'This might help . . . ' Lifting the flap of his coat, he produced a bottle and half a chicken. 'I had to beg dear Mama for the wine you did have, and even then she diluted it to ditchwater. This should help put you right.' He put the bottle on the table and took a bite from the chicken before passing it over. 'Eat up,' he said. 'Hungry work killing wolves.'

We grinned at each other.

'What do you think of Virginie?' he said. My face must have betrayed something because he scowled darkly. 'She's not that bad.'

'She's not bad at all,' I said hotly.

His scowl became a grin. 'You like her,' he said. 'I told her you did.'

'You don't mind?' I said, remembering Virginie's warning and wondering if this was some test. Charlot finding out where my loyalties really lay. But his face was open and his smile looked real enough.

'Of course not. You're my friend and she's my sister . . . That said,' Charlot produced two glasses from his coat pocket, the glass very slightly green, the stems thinner than a child's little finger, 'if you hurt her we'll have to fight and I'm the better swordsman so I'll probably kill you. Regretfully, of course.'

He filled both glasses, handed me one and raised the other.

'Your health. My health. Virginie's happiness.'

I felt he believed we'd settled something without my quite knowing what. Charlot's father, however, disagreed. When the duke called me to his study the next day it was to say two things. The first — that in saving the lives of his two younger daughters I had put him forever in my debt. He regarded me as a son and I would have his patronage for life, provided I did nothing to disgrace it. No small thing, even in 1734, when dukes no longer took their dukedoms to war or fought kings for territory. The second — Virginie was out of bounds. I was too young to know how women worked but her gratitude would make her believe she loved me. He trusted me not to take advantage of this.

104

Inventing Old Recipes

After a supper almost as formal and uncomfortable as the supper of our first evening at Chateau de Saulx, we set off next morning in the gilded carriage that had collected us from the academy at the beginning of our holiday. Virginie is not at the steps to see me off. My last memory is her sitting red-eyed and silent at supper. She ate little and asked to be excused early, the duke granting permission before the duchess could refuse.

Charlot is silent for the first fifty miles. Not fury or sulking, it takes me a while to realise he's embarrassed. 'My mother can be obstinate,' he says finally. 'I shall not stop asking you to come.'

'Has she told you to stop?' I ask, feeling sick.

My friend shakes his head crossly. We travel more miles in silence. 'What you should understand,' he says as our coach slows on the approach to an inn, 'is that my sister can be obstinate too.' We eat rabbit stew that I don't bother to tell him is probably cat, and drink a bottle of bad red wine I enjoy far more than the fine Bordeaux of our previous evening. Charlot takes the innkeeper's daughter upstairs and returns an hour later.

'How was she?'

'Flea-bitten.' He mimics a line of bites from shoulder to hip.

'But . . . ?' I say, seeing the grin on his face.

'Beautiful. And willing. And bubs so big they bounced when I rode her.' He's drunk enough not to notice the half a dozen men watching as he jiggles his hands up and down in front of his chest, among them the girl's father.

I suggest we go back to the carriage.

'So,' I say, helping him in, 'how much did you tip this beauty?' If the figure he tells me is true he could probably have bought the entire inn for that. He could certainly have bought her attentions for a year.

'You should have had a turn.'

I shake my head and take my place on the leather seat beside him. Above us, the coachman cracks his whip and our change of horses pulls away with a jangle of harness and clatter of wheels on brick.

'Why not?' Charlot asks.

Something in his voice gives me pause, and Virginie's warning about his jealousy comes into my mind, and I feel disloyal for putting the words of a girl I barely know over my faith in a friend. But what I want to say seems inappropriate. *Because all I would have seen is your sister's face* is not something you can say to a girl's older brother. When I look up from my thoughts, Charlot is watching.

'I love your sister.'

He sighs. 'Oh gods . . . I thought it might be something like that. She's pretty enough in a plain sort of way, there are certainly prettier. Margot for a start, although I don't suggest you fall in love with her. She collects hearts the way my father collects boars' heads. Break it to me gently. What is it you love about my sister?'

Her taste — orange water and soap, salt from sweat and a musk like the ghostly trace of a single sliver of truffle in an overflowing tureen. I can hardly say that either, so I simply repeat my original declaration.

'I just love her.'

'This is bad,' Charlot says. He sees my hurt and punches my arm lightly. 'Idiot, not like that. It's bad because Virginie will run you ragged if you let her. It's not enough simply to love her. Jerome says women are like horses, they need a bridle.'

'Charlot . . . '

He buries his face in his hands. 'Gods, now you're offended on her behalf.' It helps that he's drunk enough to be talkative and not so drunk that he's argumentative or wants a fight, and I've seen Charlot in both those states, often. 'Believe me,' he says. 'She's trouble. I'm not saying you shouldn't love her . . . '

'Can I ask you something?'

He looks at me owlishly, and I realise that at least half of the look is pretence. 'Ask away,' Charlot says. 'I can always refuse to answer.'

'Why don't you mind?' He waits for more and I fill the silence, wishing I had simple questions to which he could provide answers rather than have to lay it out in all its nakedness, but the question needs answering. 'We're friends, she's your sister, that's complicated, but that's not what I'm talking about. Virginie is a marquise, the daughter of a duke. Not just the daughter of a duke, the daughter of the duc de Saulx. I'm

107

nobody. Your mother minds. Your father probably minds. Why don't you mind?'

'You're my friend. You saved her life.'

He says it so simply that tears come to my eyes.

'And don't assume my father minds,' he adds. 'My mother is far more concerned with these things. My father can afford to be . . . '

'More generous?' Of course he can. Amaury de Saulx is rich beyond counting, one of the premier peers in France and has the ear of Louis XV. More to the point, he is said to have the ear of the young king's new mistress. In fact, he is the girl's godfather, guardian and first cousin combined. Still, it is interesting that Charlot would stress that it is his mother behind this. 'Madame la duchess sometimes changes her mind?'

'My father has been known to change it for her.' With that, my friend settles back into the corner of our carriage, shuts his eyes and retreats into gentle snoring, apparently exhausted by the unexpected seriousness of our talk, the wine he drank at luncheon and the success of his tussle with the flea-bitten girl.

We arrive at the academy later that evening and find ourselves clapped into the courtyard. The colonel has read the duke's letter aloud to that morning's assembly. Had it been taken badly by the boys his reading of the letter would have been an act of savage cruelty and my remaining days would have been blighted. As it is, everyone basks in our glory and we are heroes.

I'd been wondering about cooking the wolf's heart when Virginie came knocking at my door. And cook it I do, with the colonel's amused permission, removing it from the salt in which it has been packed for our journey. The recipe is my own and perhaps, with hindsight, over-complicated.

Pickled wolf's heart

Half a tablespoon each of yellow mustard seed, black mustard seed, coriander seed, peppercorns, cloves, celery seed. A quarter tablespoon of dill and fennel seed, mace and shredded bay leaf. Crush all together firmly. Rinse the heart in water, cut six diagonal slits and fill each with a clove of garlic. Mix cider vinegar with water, two parts to three, add a sliced onion and the spices, well crushed in a mortar. Simmer until the meat is soft, remove from the pan and slice finely, then return to the water and simmer slices briefly. Let stand for a day. Serve cold with bread and pickled cabbage. *Tastes like dog.*

The boys in my study treat eating the heart as a ritual. A warrior's ritual from the darker days when magic ruled France. Charlot lights a white candle and sets it in the middle of a table he moves from the wall to the middle of the room. Jerome — altogether more practical — produces a jug of dark beer.

'You first,' Emile says, pointing to the pickled heart. I take a sliver, chew it and think instantly

109

of the night we hanged Dr Faure's dog. The garlic is complex, the cider vinegar sweetly sour, the mustard seeds hot and the clove smoky. But under it all is dog. The taste is unmistakable.

'Bravo,' Charlot says.

He is the only other boy to eat it on its own. Everyone else, including Jerome, eats their slivers on bread, or mixed with sour cabbage, or on bread with sour cabbage. Emile eats his on bread with sour cabbage, liberally coated with mustard and washed down with beer. The point is he eats it. We become the boys who dined on wolf's heart. The colonel smiles at us. The instructors nod as they pass. We are Richelieu. Our reputation grows.

Charlot is for the cavalry and believes war an art and that art is in his blood. Hadn't one of his ancestors been a marshal of France? 'A successful one,' he reminds Jerome, whose own family provided a general who lost half of the Lowlands. Emile will be one of life's quartermasters if he goes into the army at all. Famous for the neatness of his camps and the efficiency of his supply lines. I tell Charlot war isn't an art any more than cookery is — at least not only an art. It is a science as well. I learn triangulation, theoretical mathematics, cartography, siege warfare, the strength and weaknesses of star forts, even how to manufacture gunpowder. Charlot can flaunt his art. I intend to win my battles with science. Charlot thinks it hilarious.

We study, we practise, all of us. In the end all the colonel's teaching comes down to a few words . . . Fight to the end, die well, make those

110

around you do the same. We know — how can we not — that anything is forgiven those who sin elegantly, while gaucheness sours even the noblest deed. So we fence with our wits and our blades, using both alike on friends and enemies. Afterwards we laugh and joke and scold, and worry we should have done better. The academy has no need to police us, we do that for ourselves. And looking back, I can see how even our rebellions are foreseen and required. Only Emile flounders. My friends whisper about blood outing. I wonder now if he was simply more intelligent than the rest of us.

Charlot and I go drinking in taverns where the tables serve to keep enemies apart as much as the wine and noise bring friends together. In the Hog, an inn so squalid even the owner won't eat there, Charlot meets a series of local girls who take his silver in food and wine and little gifts in return for letting him finger the underside of their petticoats, always promising him more next time. I sit in a corner — that after enough nights, on certain days of the week becomes my corner — and try to guess that night's meat. The rabbit is undoubtedly cat, the beef is probably horse, the mutton is too greasy to be anything but mutton, although so tough the sheep obviously died of old age.

All of it is cooked terribly with hastily fried onions and sour gravy. Students eat there, lost in their philosophy and rhetoric. Mostly the Hog is used by thieves and bankrupts, moneylenders and poets, highwaymen and cut-throats too, if one believes the rumours. Prosperous townsmen and the God-fearing avoid it for the place of pox and sedition it is. Charlot, of course, adores it.

'Somewhere else,' I beg him.

'What's wrong with the Hog?'

'The noise, the stink, the people, the whores . . . '

He grins at me. 'Good girls all,' he says. 'Don't believe nasty rumours.'

I sigh. 'The food is terrible.' He asks if I'm serious and I watch his face fall when I nod.

'But who can I go with?'

'Jerome, Emile, Armand, Marcel . . . ' I name the first four classmates who come to mind.

'Jerome's too serious. Emile would wet himself. The others are idiots. Besides, we're brothers in arms . . . '

We continue to go.

1736
The Hunt

Winter came and Charlot asked if he could take me home for Christmas but his mother refused. Well, she wrote that she felt it was inappropriate. Spring came and Charlot asked if he could take me home for Easter. This was also refused. As was summer.

It was, he told me later, with a heavy heart that he wrote at the beginning of the following summer to ask if I could join him at Chateau de Saulx. An answer came two weeks later, written in the duke's hand. Charlot could bring home three friends, the duke assumed one of them would be me. This last was written in haste and with a slightly different ink at the end of the letter, below the swirl where the duke signed himself Papa.

Jerome was Charlot's first choice to join us. Emile his second. Poor Emile looked stunned at the invitation, then embarrassed himself with the fulsomeness of his thanks, and then retired to a corner of our study to write home. Who knew what his letter actually said? But the gist of it, that he'd been invited to stay at Chateau de Saulx by the future duke, was enough for his father to send a purse of gold so Emile could dress appropriately and pay his way in such company. Charlot laughed, telling Emile that we'd travel in our uniforms and dress, for the most part, like gardeners and huntsmen, since we'd be spending our time hunting and fishing. But that if Emile wanted to have a smart coat made then his own mother would undoubtedly approve.

We set off a week after the letter arrived, the four of us crammed into the coach that had carried Charlot and me two summers earlier. The leather was slightly worn, the gilt a little tarnished, the coat of arms on the door less bright than I remembered. It was still enough, however, to turn heads on the road. We stopped twice. Once just before Dijon, and again on the Dijon-Lyon road. At the second inn, Charlot looked out for his innkeeper's daughter. She had a baby in her arms and another in her belly. I have no idea if she recognised him, but after one glance Charlot shot me a look that said say nothing about her to the others. The service in the inn was surly and the atmosphere bitter. On the road peasants spat as we passed. Last winter had been hard, plague sweeping the south. Spring had been no better and the rains endless. Those who lived close to the land already knew this year's harvest would be terrible. Poaching was on the rise and, as always happens, punishments became more severe. Where first-time offenders might have been whipped, they were sent to the arsenal at Marseilles to serve in the galleys. Where repeat offenders might once have been sent to the galleys, now they were hanged. Not always after due process.

'A mistake,' Emile said.

114

'A necessity,' Jerome replied. They squabbled for a few miles as to whether a man who didn't own forests should have his opinion taken over a man who did. Somehow, Emile won all the debating points and still lost the argument. His sulk lasted until we turned into the approach to Chateau de Saulx and then disappeared at the fairy-tale sight of the chateau's towers and turrets and moat.

'We have three chateaux,' Charlot said. 'Five if you count the little ones.' The rest of us hushed him into silence and we were all grinning as we tumbled out of the coach and found the duke and his family drawn up to greet us. We bowed to the duke, all of us, including Charlot, and kissed the duchess's hands. We bowed to the girls, who curtsied in their turn. Then Élise broke ranks and hugged Charlot so hard round the middle that he gasped, unless he was pretending. She did the same to me.

'You've grown,' I said. The kind of idiot thing an eighteen-year-old boy says to a thirteen-year-old girl he hasn't seen for two years. She grinned.

'You haven't.'

I tousled her hair, which produced an outraged shriek and a complaint that it had taken Mama's maid hours to arrange it and she wasn't going to have it done again, even if we were having a proper supper in the dining room. Charlot laughed, and nudged me towards Virginie, but his sister was already following Margot and her mother back into the house.

This time we were given rooms in a tower.

There was a drawing room we could share with three chambers off it, set on the floor above Charlot's own quarters, which, I knew, were a floor above Virginie's. Our luggage was waiting for us and a fire was laid but not lit in the grate. Looking from a window I saw mist and flooding across distant fields. Burgundy was a country of grapes and wheat, orchards and cows. None would do well in this weather and the savage winter and poor spring would make things worse. ' . . . Isn't she?' Jerome asked.

I turned to find my friends looking at me. 'Who?' I said. 'And what?'

Jerome sighed. He came to stand beside me and, for a second, as he looked where I'd been looking, he was serious. 'We have flooding at home,' he said quietly. 'My father writes that the crops are bad. The potato harvest has failed and the apples have already started to rot. We're lucky to have the sea. If nothing else we can eat shellfish.'

'Isn't she?' Emile echoed.

'Who? What?' I demanded, more crossly than I intended.

Emile looked at Jerome who became the Norman bear again, his shrug huge and exaggerated, his gut large from winter. He would thin down again. He was always that way. Eating in winter and bored with food in the summer. 'We were saying Virginie is attractive,' he explained. 'The way Charlot talks about her you'd think she was ugly.'

'They're rivals.' I said it without thinking.

'For what?' Emile asked, sounding interested.

116

'For everything. Margot's too grown up to bother him and Elise too little. Only Virginie is close to him in age. Well, she's two years younger.'

Jerome considered this and admitted it was possible. 'I'm going to kiss her,' he announced. 'See what happens.'

'She'll slap you.'

'Tried it, have we?' He grinned, and grinned some more when my face reddened and I swore she'd never slapped me. 'Well,' he said, 'my turn now.'

'Mine, actually,' Emile said.

'A wager,' Jerome said. 'The first to steal a kiss.'

'Without Charlot knowing,' Emile added. 'The first to kiss, and touch.'

It was as well he couldn't see my face. My feelings for Virginie were unchanged, and her turning away in the courtyard had put a darkness in me that the mist and flooding and Emile's stupid bet did nothing to lift. 'Are you in?' Emile asked.

Jerome said, 'What's the prize?'

'The honour of the kiss,' Emile replied, then smirked. 'And the thrill of the touch, of course. We mustn't forget that.'

Jerome was smiling. 'And you?' he said.

I shook my head, excused myself and went to unpack my case. What little it contained had been bought with money Charlot's father had sent the colonel so my life at the academy could be more comfortable. My uniform was cut from decent cloth, I had my own leather hunting coat and a decent sword in place of school issue. I unfolded the coat, hung it on a hook and put the book of poems Margot had given me on a table beside the bed. Then I washed my face, checked my nails were clean and went downstairs without waiting for the others.

Weeks passed and we emptied a copse of wood pigeon, killed an elderly boar under a cathedral oak in the forest beyond the river, and took as many trout from the streams as we could manage. We failed to find a stag big enough for our pride to allow us to kill it. And by the time we returned to that part of the forest a few weeks later even the smaller bucks were gone. 'Poachers,' Jerome muttered.

Emile scowled until he realised he was being teased.

Our first month became a second, and half of that went before we began to talk about returning to the academy and how we should spend the last few weeks. Virginie remained unkissed by any of us. Whether by intention or design, Margot, Virginie and Élise had spent much of their summer with an aunt in the Loire. Charlot simply shrugged when I asked him about this, saying the ways of his mother were beyond the wit of man. They returned eventually, however, and Charlot invited them hunting.

The day came and Margot declined, having already said she thought it unlikely. Élise was not allowed to go, retiring to her chamber to sulk furiously. That left Virginie, who came down the steps of the chateau with her chin up, looking

118

uncomfortable and red-eyed, obviously aware she was out-numbered four to one by boys, even if one of them was her brother. I discovered later she'd had a furious argument with her mother immediately before. An argument so serious her father intervened, requiring Virginie to apologise to her mother for rudeness, while decreeing she could join us after all.

We'd been warned to be careful. We'd been advised that the temper of the jacques was sour. We'd been told they'd burnt a manor in the next province. We'd been exhorted and instructed so comprehensively that half the pleasure was leeched from the day before we even left Chateau de Saulx. We carried boar spears like lances, rising to the trot and then beginning to canter as we tried and mostly failed to stick cabbages as we passed cottages and fields. And found our humour again in the lunacy of our play.

Charlot, being Charlot, took us beyond the second wood, the first wood being as far as we'd been told we could go. There was a boar apparently. And if not a boar then a five-point stag. His thrust was we'd find something in the old forest better than anything we could find in the woods. Charlot led us down the track, while Emile and Jerome reluctantly rode side by side when the path was wide enough. Reluctantly, because that left me to ride beside Virginie, who stared straight ahead.

'I'm sorry,' I said.

'For what?' Her face was unreadable.

'That you had to come with us. That we're

here.' I gestured at the canopy of oaks above us, the mulch and loam beneath our hooves, which should have been drier at this time of year, even this far into the forest.

'This is the most beautiful thing I've seen in weeks.' Her face hardened. 'It's the only beautiful thing I've seen in weeks. Have you met my aunt? No, of course you haven't met my aunt . . . ' Up ahead, I could see Jerome and Emile trying to hear what made Virginie so unexpectedly impassioned. They could catch her tone but not her words. 'I've spent my summer being introduced to one fool after another . . . '

'Why?' I asked.

She sighed. 'Why do you think? My aunt is helping my mother choose me a husband. He has to be rich. He has to be grand. He should have a position at court, or the expectation of one . . . What?' she said, seeing my expression. 'Did you think it would be different?'

As the path narrowed I let Virginie edge forward and fell back to take the rear, which was as well as I had no answers to her question. All I could do was try to look at the cathedral oaks with her eyes and see them as beautiful. And they were in their way, huge branches like beams above our head, trunks rising like pillars, the greatest trees buttressed by lesser oaks that tumbled against them. We'd begun to pass charcoal clearings within a few minutes of entering the forest. Wide circles of hacked-back undergrowth with smouldering earth-covered mounds where the charcoal baked. Naked children watched us pass, filthy as animals. Their faces black with soot, their hair matted and grown together in the way hair is if it's never washed. We saw hard-eyed *charbonniére* women with wooden shovels in their hands. Occasionally they worked topless so the brats bound to their chests could feed. The youngest children sat naked in the doorways of earth huts, slightly older ones scavenged the undergrowth collecting twigs, their shifts and filthy shirts too short to cover their buttocks.

'Gods,' I heard Virginie mutter. She dropped back to bring her horse closer to mine. Emile looked nervous, Jerome blind to the ragged misery around him. Charlot . . . ? Who knew what he thought. He rode ahead humming some song to himself. After the charcoal clearings we reached a wide river and a ford where the depth of the water and speed of the flow made me fear for our horses. I was beginning to wonder how much further Charlot intended to take us when he splashed through the ford, pulled up on the far side and turned back, grinning. 'We're here,' he said, his first words since leaving Chateau de Saulx.

1736
Charlot Injured

Sliding from his horse, Charlot drops his reins to the dirt. Anyone else's mount would bolt at the spookiness of the river's edge or wander off and need recapturing. His horse stands patiently while he walks back to help his sister dismount. We're right in the heart of the forest, an hour's ride along wooded tracks from the nearest village. The trees overhanging the river are hundreds of years old but they feel older.

'We'll tie our horses here,' Charlot says.

'And carry the damn buck ourselves if we catch one?' Jerome demands.

'All right, we'll take one horse. Emile's . . . It's the least spirited. Mine would dislike the smell of blood and so might the others. You happy to lead it?'

Emile nods, sullen-faced. He rides less well than Charlot and Jerome, who both rode from their earliest years, although only slightly less well than me. Charlot has simply given me the better horse. No insult; at least no intended insult. Virginie's mare might do but Charlot doesn't want to risk her refusing.

Virginie steps closer to me and I crook my arm. She hesitates for a second, then takes it. She's trembling. 'What is it?' I ask.

'This place. Can't you feel it?'

All I can feel is her hand resting on my arm. We have a rifled musket, two boar spears, a couple of pistols . . . And a hunting dirk each. We also have lunch in a pannier slung behind Virginie's saddle. Charlot says we should leave this. He takes the musket and Jerome and I take boar spears, with Jerome also taking a pistol, leaving a pistol for Emile. Virginie smiles sourly as we divide the weapons among us.

'Would you like the pistol? I can give Emile my spear . . . '

'Jean-Marie . . . ' Charlot is laughing. 'Don't you dare arm my sister. My mother would never forgive you.' At which Virginie mutters that her mother is unlikely to forgive me anyway. And I suffer five minutes of sideways glances from Jerome and Emile, even though I'm not part of their stupid bet.

'This way,' Charlot says.

We push through the undergrowth, making our own path or widening those used by deer. Charlot first. Emile always bringing up the rear. We pass a ruined charbonniére hut, the charcoal mound dead and the circle deserted. Thorns have taken back the edge and bracken shows in the hut's doorway. A fire pit is filled with the cold bones of a wild pig. 'Poachers.' This time Jerome isn't teasing, simply stating the truth. We pick up the fresh spoor of a deer a few minutes later. Its tracks lead further into the forest and we follow them.

'I can hear something,' Emile whispers.

Charlot stops his humming and we all listen. The sound of breaking branches comes from behind thorns to our right. 'Wild boar,' Jerome says. Swiftly, Charlot draws back the hammer on his musket, Jerome lowers his boar spear and Virginie drops her hand from my arm, leaving me free to lower my own spear.

'You stay with Emile,' Charlot tells his sister.

She looks mutinous and Emile opens his mouth to protest, then looks at me, shoots Virginie a sideways glance and decides he doesn't mind that idea after all. Charlot, Jerome and I push our way through a cascade of thorns towards the noise and find ourselves in a clearing. A dozen charbonnières look round, and then one of them rips his knife across the throat of a struggling deer. The animal's death frees those holding it down to stand and face us. An old man behind them carries an ancient musket that he lowers and fires. No thought or hesitation.

The ball hits Charlot, who drops his own musket and tumbles to his knees, his hand clasping his shoulder. Jerome dives for the musket, raises it and pulls the trigger. The flint slams down and the gun misfires. The old man laughs and I throw my boar spear. It is to be the first and only time I kill anyone. Something I have no possible way of knowing then. Jerome raises his own spear as another man reaches for the old man's musket and powder horn. We advance on the charbonnières, who retreat. All I have now is my hunting dirk, but it's the spear in Jerome's hand and the death of their leader that stills them. Faces blank as millponds watch us.

Reaching the old man, I rip my spear free. It's a fearsome weapon. A long blade ending at a crossbar to stop a wounded boar forcing its way up the hilt as it tries to reach its killer. Jerome stabs the man who reached for the musket. It's a fast, vicious and unexpected blow. One that would impress our instructors at the academy. He's already withdrawing the blade when the man begins to fall. Another man dives for the musket and rolls away as Jerome stabs a second time.

'This is the duke's son,' he says. 'Harm him again and the duke will slaughter the lot of you, and your families.' He has greater faith in words than me. And greater faith his words will be taken the way he wants them to be taken. He thinks he's given them a reason to fear us. I suspect he's given them a reason to kill us all.

'Fall back,' I say. Seeing Jerome's scowl, I add, 'We have Virginie to protect.'

'We should lead them away from her,' Jerome growls.

I'm about to agree when Charlot shakes his head. 'And leave her for Emile to protect? No, I need a surgeon and we must get her home.' Jerome dips for Charlot, and since he stands to Charlot's right, and holds his spear in his own right hand, this is easy enough. I change my spear to my left and steady Charlot's other side.

When Charlot says we can't leave the muskets, I point out, briefly, that I cannot carry two muskets and a boar spear and protect anyone usefully.

'Cover me,' Jerome orders. He lets go of Charlot, stabs his boar spear hilt-first into the dirt, grabs the older musket, puts his heel to the barrel and strains. Wood splinters and the barrel comes free. It's an impressive show of strength.

Two young charbonnières kneel by the one Jerome stabbed in the throat, who must be dying by now. Their uncle, perhaps their father. The others watch Jerome with flat eyes as he smashes the second musket. 'Follow us,' he snarls at them, 'and we'll kill you all.' Reclaiming his spear, he twists it in his hand and pretends to launch it at the nearest, who stumbles back as the others scatter. 'Now we fall back,' he says. Virginie comes running the moment we're clear. 'You must take your brother back to the chateau,' Jerome tells her.

'That nag won't carry both of us,' Charlot says.

'Emile should go,' I say. 'You know the way?'

He nods, white-faced.

'Then ride back and raise the alarm. Tell the duke to have his huntsmen meet us. And he should call out the militia . . . '

Emile looks at me.

'This is a *jacquerie* — or will be. You think this ends here?'

'I want to stay,' he insists.

'You can help us best by going.'

He scowls and I think will refuse; pride or fear of being alone in this forest. But Virginie touches his arm and looks pleading, and that decides it. Emile mounts the horse and trots away without a glance. All I can do is hope he keeps his head down. Most of the branches on our way here were low.

★ ★ ★

126

We knew we'd hit disaster when we found our mounts gone. Sabots had churned the loam so badly that the clearing where we'd left our horses could have been freshly dug. 'Bastards,' Jerome said.

'Downriver,' Charlot muttered. 'We must follow the bank.'

'Why?' Jerome demanded.

Virginie folded her fingers into mine and gripped so hard her knuckles turned white. She took my hand without asking, without saying anything, for all I knew without knowing she'd done it. 'Charlot's right,' I said. 'We need to find a boat. It's too far to walk back through the forest and we'd have to pass those encampments.'

'You think it's a full jacquerie?' Virginie whispered.

I shrugged. 'The last harvest was bad, the next will be worse. The taxes are high. Their children are starving. What have they got to lose?'

Jerome obviously disliked my choice of words but he put his arm round Charlot to support him, then hesitated. 'Can you ride on my back? It'll be faster.'

Charlot lifted bloodied fingers away from his shoulder and considered the wound. 'Bind this first,' he said, 'then carry me.'

Having eased off Charlot's jacket, we tore the arm from his shirt and used it to pad his wound. Then we put him back into the jacket, buttoned it tight to keep the padding in place and Jerome knelt so he could climb aboard. We did all of this in less time than it takes me to write. Charlot bore the pain in silence. 'Will we make it?' Virginie asked.

'Jerome will help Charlot and I'll keep you safe.'

'You shouldn't make promises you can't keep.'

'Who says I can't keep it?'

She laughed and Charlot glanced back. Something passed between them because Virginie blushed and put her head down and walked in silence for several minutes, keeping her thoughts to herself. A mile ahead, we found three small boats on a sand spit where the river turned. Trees overwhelmed the far bank but our side was clear and the boats there for the taking. I cut two free and drove my spear through the other's bottom to ruin it. Virginie and I dragged the first boat to the water.

'Get him in,' I told Jerome, who lowered Charlot to the ground, picked him up as if he was a child and did as I said. 'Now go.'

Jerome looked at Virginie and hesitated.

'Please,' she said. 'Get him to safety.' It was enough. Jerome nodded and all together we pushed Charlot towards fast water and Jerome clambered in as the flow caught the boat and whisked it away. 'Hurry,' Virginie said.

Shouts came from the trees as we reached our boat and began hurrying it down the sand. Virginie scrambled in with a flash of bare leg and I pushed her into the stream and dragged myself after, the boat rocking violently. The flow caught us and hurtled us after our friends as charbonnières reached the sand spit, screaming in anger. We'd left the boar spears and they hurled both after us.

The spears fell short and were lost.

The river narrowed and the banks rose, matted with wild scrub, dog rose and Corsican mint, and dotted with an occasional pine that peered at us from above. We came out on the far side of the ridge and chased Charlot's boat towards a stone bridge that carried the road through the forest across the river. Charbonnières lined its side, pointing and shouting. I saw Jerome raise his pistol and watched those nearest shrink back. He and Charlot passed under the bridge and I saw Jerome jerk forward as a stone caught the side of his head.

'Tip the boat,' Virginie said.

She was right. We flipped the boat, cold water closing over us, and I grabbed her and held fast, holding to the bench inside the boat with my other hand. When we surfaced it was under our upturned hull. Stones clattered on the wood above our heads as we approached the bridge and again after we passed under. A musket was fired and another, the first ball missing and the second smashing a plank as it bounced away. The river widened and the current slowed and through the split the musket ball made we could see ragged men lining the bank. Some had ancient muskets, others spears, most carried wood-axes or farm implements. There were dozens of them, then hundreds, for all we knew thousands. Misery on the move. They shuffled and stared at each other blank-eyed as if trying to find a purpose. When we saw a church in flames we knew they'd found one.

The Upturned Boat

Our shell bobbed and swirled and once bumped into the body of a gamekeeper floating face-down in the river — and we bobbed and swirled and bumped along beneath it, sometimes bruising our legs on rocks in the shallows and sometimes hanging on to stop ourselves sinking beneath its surface with exhaustion, but always hidden from watching eyes. Virginie had not then learnt to swim, and the shallowest bits of the river always seemed to have banks dotted with peasants. The gap between water level and inside keel was small but it was all the safety we had.

'I'm cold,' Virginie muttered. 'My hands . . . '

'Mine too.' I was terrified my muscles would cramp and I'd lose my grip and Virginie and the boat would be swept away. 'We should land.'

'Soon,' she agreed. 'We should land soon.'

Trees ran down to the river on both banks and we were back in the forest, which followed the river in a curve along one side of the duke's domains. He had more lands than a man could ride in a day and Virginie, although certain her father owned the trees we passed through, had no real idea where we were. What worried me, although I was careful not to say so, was not where we were, but how long we'd have to stay hidden. Alone, I might have risked trying to reach the chateau. Virginie's presence made that idea impossible.

Charlot's sister was torn between terror her brother had drowned, been killed or died from his wound, and certainty that he was Charlot, so of course he and Jerome would reach safety. They would reach safety and raise a rescue party. And if they didn't — not because they were dead, but because they were hiding — then Emile would undoubtedly get through. I could sense she was less convinced by that idea but she repeated it as if it were obviously true.

'Over there,' she said.

The very beginnings of a gravel bank showed where the river bent around the edge of a slight hill. It was as good a place to put ashore as any and better than most of the sites we'd seen. I put my feet down, felt nothing and pushed myself under, my heels digging deep enough into the riverbed's gravel to bring the boat to a brief stop. Pushing towards the shore I found my feet could reach the bottom. Even then the current was strong enough to throw us into the bank a hundred yards further along.

'Too fierce,' I said, after we'd tried to push our shell upstream.

'We should let it go . . . ' Virginie was right. Dragging it up would tell the charbonnières this was where we landed. That is, if they were looking for us still.

'Ready?' We came out from under our boat and the flow carried it away as we trudged back to the gravel bank. It shifted noisily underfoot and I looked round. A hundred peasants could be watching without us knowing. But no one shouted or shot at us as we scrabbled ashore and reached the safety of the undergrowth at the river's edge.

'Now what?' Virginie asked.

I took her face in my hand, my fingers so cold they could barely sense the flesh of her cheek, and kissed the corner of her mouth. Only once and gently. 'I've missed you,' I said. 'All summer and the two years before. I missed you.'

Huge eyes considered me, brown as cut agate and twice as bright. Then she nodded and looked around her, my words held somewhere for later. 'We should find safety,' she said softly. I agreed with her; I simply wasn't sure what safety was in the middle of a jacquerie. A stone house if we could find one? A church? Although we'd seen one of those on fire. A cave in the hills, if there were hills nearby?

'This is safe,' I told her. 'The trees will hide us.'

'And when night comes?' The day was barely afternoon but night would come as it always did.

'We sleep in the trees.'

'Separate trees?'

'If you want. Although we'd be safer together.'

Again that nod, as if she were saving the words. Maybe she was, because she looked around her as she'd looked around her before and finally nodded. 'We stay here,' she said. 'And we sleep like animals in the trees.'

Unbuckling my belt, I put down the hunting dirk I'd been issued that morning. Then I unbuttoned my jacket, which was so heavy with water I would have discarded it had I been able to while clinging to the upturned boat. After that

I struggled out of my wet shirt. I'd long since kicked off my boots in the river, as they'd filled with water, but I kept my breeches, although I undid the knees and dragged off my stockings. It was only as I stood in the clearing in the afternoon sun in my wet breeches that I realised Virginie was staring at me. 'I'm frozen,' I said.

Pushing a stick through the arms of my shirt I hung it from a jutting branch and began looking for a stick thick enough to support my jacket, which had been heavy enough when it was simply dry leather. Finding one, I hung the garment from a thicker branch and draped the stockings next to it. 'Where did you learn to do that?' Virginie demanded.

'At the academy.'

'Why would they teach you something so strange?'

'So we can dry our clothes in situations like this.' I meant we the students, me, Jerome, Emile, her brother . . .

But she simply said, 'Turn away.' And a few moments later, her voice resigned, she said, 'I need your help.' She still wore her sodden dress and still shivered from the cold despite standing in the sun. 'My fingers.'

Her fingers were those of the dead, blue and shrunken where water had leached oil from her skin and bleached her nails. She could barely hold still as I examined them. 'Let me do it,' I said. My fingers trembled both from cold and nervousness as I struggled with the first of her buttons. Where I had huge buttons, her dress had dozens of tiny ones, arranged in twos, which fed through cotton loops that seemed to have shrunk. It took me minutes to undo the bodice of her wet dress and she dragged herself out of it rather than face the embarrassment of having me undo more. Her chemise was also sodden but she was naked beneath. It clung to her hips as she turned away from me.

I hung her dress in direct sunlight and told her I would find food.

'What?' she said. 'Where?'

When I returned it was with three small trout, a handful of mushrooms and, unexpectedly glorious, a summer truffle with pale flesh and the most elegant scent. I used the hunting dirk to gut and fillet the trout, slicing carefully along each fragile spine. I stripped skin from the first fillet, broke off a piece of flesh and offered it to Virginie. She shook her head so I ate it and offered her the second piece. She swallowed the raw fish so quickly she could barely have tasted. 'Slowly,' I said. 'Eat it slowly.'

'I can't,' she said, looking sick. 'I can't eat it at all.'

We found a beech tree just beyond the clearing twisted with age and split by lightning. In the top of the cavity inside was dry wood so rotten it crumbled in my fingers. I had my flint and steel, because what boy didn't travel with such in those days. Putting the rotted wood on a flat stone out of the wind, I cracked the flints together. The kindling caught and I blew it ablaze, adding a handful of rotted wood ripped from the tree's innards.

'I suppose they taught you that at the academy too?' Virginie demanded. She was smiling as she said it. Finding the driest twigs I could, to keep smoke to the minimum, I left her holding a stick-skewered trout over the first flames and returned to the river. By the time I came back with a larger trout that I'd tickled from the water, she'd eaten the first and was looking at the second hungrily.

'Have it,' I said. 'I'll catch others.'

She took a bite and grinned at me; the relief of eating, the warmth of the sun, the fact we were now on dry land putting light in her eyes.

'No,' I said, before she could ask. 'I taught myself how to fish.'

I could have caught her rabbit or wildcat or water rat but I knew trout would make her happiest so that was what I offered. I would love to write that we stripped and I took her in the clearing in the sight of the sun and the trees, or that we kissed and pleasured each other as we discovered secrets hidden to us before this, or even that we lay naked in each other's arms and kissed. But the truth is we kissed once, right after we landed, the slightest kiss for all the touch of her lips skewered through me like the lightning that blasted that beech tree. And though we held each other through the night we were dressed by then, and we huddled together for warmth, and when she slept I held her so she wouldn't fall.

Who knows what another day alone in the forest and a night in the trees might have brought us. But the next morning, before I could even catch us breakfast, a large boat filled with soldiers sailed down the river, with the duke himself in the prow shouting for us to show ourselves if we were within hearing. Emile had delivered our plea for help. Charlot and Jerome had put ashore further downstream than us at the first sight of soldiers. Charlot had a cracked shoulder and Jerome a split head but both would be fine. Since Emile had saved us, I was unsure why the duke spoke his name with such distaste. I was to discover the reason soon enough.

On our trip back to Chateau de Saulx we passed gibbets filled with slowly twisting charbonnières and peasant cottages burning and carts full of blank-eyed prisoners, as silent and solid as the animals with whom they shared the land. The fire in their eyes was gone, extinguished by the sight of the soldiers around them and the ropes that fixed their hands behind their backs. Cows lay dead in the fields. Crops had been trampled. In a town square on the way home a half-naked woman was being whipped, her rags ripped from her shoulders and her breasts bare to the jeering crowd. She was gagged, probably against the risk of sedition, since her cries wouldn't have worried the soldiers. A small child at her feet sobbed loud enough for both of them.

Virginie saw none of this. She sat next to me in her father's carriage, her face buried in my neck and her fingers twisted so hard into mine that her knuckles were white. She would not let go of my hand or move further from me despite her father's silent gaze. As we entered the courtyard at the chateau she ground her face into my neck and wrapped her arms tight around me as if she would never let go. But she did without being asked and was the first from the carriage, greeting her mother with a kiss.

'That's the second time he's saved me.'

The due de Saulx looked at me. 'We must talk.'

★ ★ ★

They took Virginie in one direction and the duke walked me in another towards a knot garden he'd planted when he first married. He told me about the planning and the planting of the garden as we walked. So far as I could tell his story existed only to fill the silence until we reached the middle of the garden and a circular pond filled with gold fish.

'D'Aumout,' he said, and it was unlike him to use my name so formally. 'Did you take a bet with your friends as to who could be the first to kiss my daughter? Who could do more than simply kiss her?'

'No.' I said with such fury that he blinked.

'I require your word on this.'

'You have my word on this. I did not take part in any such wager. Nor would I ever take part in any such wager.'

'You love her, don't you?'

'Since the first moment I saw her.'

The due de Saulx sighed. 'And from the moment you saved her from that wolf she's loved you . . .'

'Before, perhaps.'

He looked at me strangely and I blushed. 'Charlot teased her about liking me that first summer I was here. Before the wolf.'

'My son told you this?'

'Your daughter.' I didn't offer when she'd said it or that she'd been in my room at the time, with the rest of his family at supper. He thought I meant in the day and night just passed and I let him think it. The duke nodded thoughtfully and looked beyond me to a man I recognised. It was the doctor who'd treated me for the wolf bite.

'Wait here,' the duke said.

The two men spoke quietly and briefly and then both bowed and the doctor retired while the duke returned to where I waited. 'My daughter has been examined,' he said. 'Her mother insisted and I'm not sure Virginie will ever forgive her, or me for agreeing. The doctor says she is intact. That she is untouched. So I ask you honestly, have you been . . . ' He chose his words carefully. 'Close to my daughter?'

'We kissed,' I said. 'Once, when we climbed from the river. It was a small kiss.' I touched the corner of my lip. 'Here.'

The duke smiled at me. 'Oh, to be so young again.'

'May I ask . . . About that wager?'

'Something Emile said to Jerome when he thought he was alone and not overheard. To the effect they had no chance of winning now. Virginie does not know how they dishonoured her. A boy like Emile, I would expect no less. But

I am ashamed for Jerome. Although he redeemed himself saving my son.'

And Emile brought you warning of our trouble. I kept that thought to myself, still cross with Emile for the original bet, and lacking the courage to defend him.

The King's Mistress

Our engagement began with an argument. Of course, I didn't know it was an engagement then. After supper, the duke and duchess and Margot having left the room, Virginie walked up to me and slapped my face, hard. 'How dare you,' she said, her face white. Her eyes were on the edge of crying and her temper looked barely under control. Jerome stopped what he'd been saying, Emile stared at us, and Charlot smiled.

'She does that,' he said.

Virginie shot her brother a look that would have turned another man to stone. Being Charlot, he simply pointed to his heavily-bandaged shoulder and said, 'You wouldn't slap an injured man, would you?' Virginie stalked from the room.

'What was that about?' I asked.

Charlot looked at Jerome, who blushed, and his gaze dismissed Emile, who pretended not to notice. 'I wouldn't know.' He stared at me. 'Well, go after her then. Unless you're a complete fool.'

I caught up with Virginie in a corridor. 'What have I done?'

She swirled round and raised her hand, wrenching free when I grabbed her wrist before she could slap me again. 'You know exactly what you've done.' She turned from me and hurried though a door at the end of the corridor and out onto the terrace, leaving me to follow like a stubborn shadow, across the terrace and down stone steps to a lawn. We ended up in the knot garden where I'd talked to her father earlier. 'Go away,' she ordered.

'Not until you tell me what I'm meant to have done.'

She glared at me, eyes huge in the darkness. 'How could you?'

'Virginie. Tell me.'

'How could you have wagered with those . . . ?'

'I didn't,' I said fiercely. 'I didn't. I wouldn't. I told your father.'

'My mother said . . . Why didn't Charlot stop it?'

'He didn't know.'

'So there was a wager!'

'Jerome and Emile wagered on which could steal the first kiss.'

'And you?' she said.

'What could I have told you?' But that wasn't the question she was asking. She planted her feet solidly on the gravel of the knot garden and faced me full-on.

'Swear,' she said. 'Swear you weren't part of this.'

'I wasn't part of it. I would never have taken that bet.'

'Why not?' She demanded.

'Because I love you.' The truth fitted the moment, and I had a sense my life was about to change here among severely cut shrubs under a cloudy night sky. 'Because I've loved you since that summer.'

'You barely noticed me. All you did was gaze at Margot.'

'Because I didn't dare to look at you.'

'A sweet lie,' Virginie said, but she was smiling.

'A sweeter truth.'

Sometime later, when our kisses become so deep we stopped caring if people wondered where we were, I dropped my hand to the front of her dress and closed my fingers around the slight mound between her legs. Virginie's eyes widened and she bit her lip. A minute later she lifted her dress out of the way so I could touch her again, this time with her hand holding mine in place. Her other hand covered her mouth until her whimpers died away. 'So much for untouched,' she giggled.

*   *   *

The duke had moved swiftly to put down the riots, mobilising the local regiments and ordering courts to sit day and night to try those captured mid-riot or later arrested. The sentences were harsher than normal, far harsher than for an equivalent crime tried in the same courts a year before. Examples were made. Youths were whipped through the streets, young women pilloried for days in the town squares, with all the risks that brought them. The ringleaders were hanged, the lieutenants sent as slaves to the galleys at Marseilles, or to work out their lives chained together at the arsenal there.

The duke's personal vengeance was brutal. The charbonniére accused of leading the riots

142

was tried for treason and convicted — even though the man swore on his soul he was innocent. He was whipped through the streets, then lashed to a wooden frame in the local town square and the long bones of his body broken with an iron bar by the sergeant of the watch. After that he was hanged, dragged from the cobbles by a rope around his neck since he was no longer able to stand. Only the duke among us watched. He reported the crowd had been respectful but sullen. Which is what he would expect.

'Necessary,' was all he said to me on his return. Jerome and Emile had been sent back to the academy. Charlot and I would not be joining them. Charlot was to take up his duties at Chateau de Saulx. As for me, I was waiting to be introduced to Louise, the king's mistress, who was Margot's age but even more beautiful. Virginie was furious about this. A fierce sulk from her produced pleading from me, which became a sulk on my part the moment she began relenting. We made up shortly before Louise arrived, in what was becoming our traditional way. 'You look flushed,' was all Charlot said.

'It's hot, I'm nervous.'

'That's my sister,' he reminded me. 'It's as well I like you.'

We stood in the courtyard awaiting Louise. She arrived in a royal carriage, bearing congratulations from the king on the duke's handling of the uprising. She refreshed herself and then disappeared into the duke's study. An hour or so later she entered the drawing room,

143

smiled at all of us and turned to me.

'Will you walk?' She asked this in a gentle fashion, as if she really expected me to say I was busy or had better things to do. She was beautiful, this king's mistress. Looking, to me, little older than Virginie, and I was still an age when a few years either way really counted as a difference. I bowed and offered my arm, and she smiled as she might at a clever child. 'This way, I think.'

She led us down to the little lake and we walked its edge, ducking under willows and watching coots steady in the water as little battleships. We stopped to marvel at an ancient trout, large to us and monstrous to the insects that kept it fed. 'What are you thinking?' Her question made me stutter.

'I'm wondering if a large trout would taste better than a small one.'

'Worse,' she said with certainty. 'Old things always taste worse.'

I could think of exceptions but didn't contradict her.

'You keep looking at me,' she said a hundred paces later. 'Why?'

'You're younger than I expected.'

She stopped, turned in a slow circle beneath a willow tree, her smile suddenly coquettish. Her cream dress was rich with brocade, its neck cut low enough to show the slope of her breasts. She smelt of rose water and musk. 'You like what you see?'

'How could anyone not like?'

'Unfortunately ... Some men are more

144

exacting than you.' She sounded sad and her face fell a little. 'You think I'm beautiful?'

I blushed, but nodded all the same.

'Is Virginie more beautiful?'

I nodded again and she laughed, taking my hand and squeezing it. We walked on while she told me what her cousin, the duke, wanted of her. That was when I first realised he intended to let me marry Virginie. He was not simply humouring his daughter while he found other ways to deal with her infatuation. 'Do you know the marquis d'Aumout?'

'No, my lady.'

'So polite. We are friends. You may call me cousin . . . D'Aumout is old,' she said. 'Only bastards for children and none he likes. You are family.' She glanced at me, looking doubtful. 'Distant family. The duke is sure of it. I am to ask the king on my uncle's behalf for permission for the marquis to adopt you.'

'Why would he do that?'

She stopped, put her hands on my shoulders. 'Do you really know so little of the world? He is poor, the duke is rich. Why would he not? You will become comte d'Aumout, and marquis in time. The marquis lives in Paris. But there is a castle in the south, probably hideous. But it will become yours.'

'I will be suitable for Virginie?'

'You are suitable already,' she said seriously. 'In the duke's eyes you are already suitable. This makes you suitable in the eyes of everyone else.'

'The duchess?'

Hélène nodded. 'In her eyes too. Now go tell

that girl of yours to stop scowling at me.' I turned and saw Virginie watching us from the terrace. When I turned back Hélène was already walking away.

'You held hands,' Virginie said furiously. 'She held your shoulders. She turned circles in front of you to show herself off. You talked and you talked. What did you talk about?'

'She asked if she was more beautiful than you.'

Virginie went very still. Until I told her I'd said no. At which she relented, hugging me fiercely when I said I believed her father would let us marry within the year.

1738
Marriage

As though amazed that cooks this far south knew how to prepare something that complicated, Charlot examined the pigeon pasty, peeling strips of parchment-like pastry from its case and selecting the largest chunks of meat.

'You have a prize bull. Those apple trees are skilfully pruned. Your servants wear shoes. There are carp in the moat . . . ' I thought him surprised to find the south so civilised, until I realised he was mocking me to hide the fact that he was surprised. At school he'd regarded southerners as little better washed or mannered than Moors.

The sun was blade sharp, the sky the blue of the royal banner. 'It is a good day for France,' Charlot said. 'Chateau d'Aumout has a new lord to make it strong. And the new lord will have a new wife to keep him strong.' Like most of the things Charlot said it lingered somewhere between brilliance and idiocy. It was hard to know if he meant it or was simply playing with words. 'I hate goodbyes,' he added.

'Charlot, I'm marrying your sister.'

'Exactly.' He gripped my shoulders hard. 'Goodbye to childhood. Goodbye to the old world. Goodbye to freedom.'

It is the spring of 1738, Virginie is eighteen and I am almost twenty-one. Charlot is my best friend and my best man. Behind me is the lonely tower of the village church next to a pine twisted into arthritic fingers. Under our feet the earth is red, virulent as powdered paint. For a second I see my new estate through Charlot's eyes; ruined and ragged and far from Burgundy's richness, or France's heart, which lies at Versailles. Down here we hear not the beat of the king's ambition but the slow clop of mules on empty roads and the caw of crows rising like black rags from stony fields. Charlot laughs when I tell him this.

'There's room for dreamers in this kingdom of ours.'

Keep his sister happy and I'll have his family's friendship for life. It means something, their friendship. They have the ear of the king. More to the point, the duke has the ear of his mistress. That's why we are there, at the head of the drive watching for the carriage that will bring Virginie to the altar.

Of our wedding itself I remember little. Prayers and hymns and vows. Virginie in a simple white dress looking closer to angel than human. There is a feast afterwards, obviously enough. And then we retire to our bed and leave the others to sly jokes and laughter. As I say, of the wedding I remember little. Of the morning after I remember everything. I wake and she is smiling, her lips almost on mine and her breath on my face. She pulls back, covering her mouth and freezes as my hand reaches out to find her shoulder. Her fingers close over mine after a second, tightening slightly, and then she slips from beneath the covers and I see the white of her gown cutting through the warm light of the early dawn as she heads for the closet, closing the door behind her.

She pisses after several seconds' hesitation.

A full bladder's worth from a healthy girl who's drunk more wine than was wise the night before, for all her old nurse kept mixing it with water. We have a pot under the bed, as most couples do, but I realise from the blush on her cheeks when she returns that she's been too embarrassed to use it. I wonder if I'd be embarrassed to stand there and piss in front of her so soon and am grateful I'd woken in the pre-dawn and used the pot then.

Sliding into bed beside me, she jerks back a little as my fingers reach between her legs and touch moisture. Her urine tastes much as mine, flavoured with food from the night before and scented with herbs used in its cooking. At least the drop I taste does. Her eyes are wide and uncertain as she watches me.

'You're beautiful,' I tell her.

She smiles instinctively, shaking her head to brush aside the compliment. Margot is beautiful, as shinily perfect as a Limoges figurine, her composure uncracked and unchipped as the finest glaze. Élise might be beautiful if she grows into the body nature intended to give her. But my lovely Virginie . . . ? Her hair is brown, with slight waves, thick enough to be a mane. But her

149

body remains the one Élise is already growing out of. Her breasts are full and her stomach soft, her hips slightly wide and her buttocks broad. I have still to see her naked and the night's sleep has only delayed the moment for all we look at each other with clearer eyes. 'How are you feeling?'

'Better than I should.'

'Drink some water,' I suggest. 'That usually helps with a bad head.' The water is in a carafe on her side of the bed and as I lean across her I can feel her breasts against my chest and then against my thighs. She is blushing deeper than ever when I offer her the glass. 'Sip it,' I say, and she does. Small sips, looking to me for approval.

Our bed is huge, curled at both ends and inlaid with black woods from the Indies and pale woods from Malacca, its legs thick and squat. The whole thing a mix of the old solid simplicities and the new elegance. Much like Virginie's father, the man who gave it to us, along with two dozen of the finest sheets, and a Gobelin tapestry to hang on our bedroom wall. He is the man whose approval she's wanted before now. Now that man is me, and watching her sip carefully from the glass I know I want her approval in return.

She lets me take the glass from her hands and put it carefully on the sideboard and she smiles a little nervously when I rest her back on the pillow and kiss her deeply.

'My breath,' she says.

'Is sweet . . . ' We kiss again and I feel her lips soften and her nipples harden as my hand

150

reaches up to hold her breasts through the gown. I want to strip her and taste her, see her naked and put my fingers and tongue into every part of her. But she is trembling and her kisses are becoming unhappy and distracted. So I let go the breast I am gripping and roll myself above her, taking my weight on my hands.

'I love you.' I mean it without reservation. She has brought me titles and lands, her father's patronage and the approval of his friends. I am Jerome's equal, Charlot's dearest companion, Margot's dear brother, Élise's imaginary knight . . . But most of all she has brought me herself. And it was this I wanted more than anything. Her self to go with my self, so the two of us can make a better person together.

She smiles. 'I love you too . . . '

Pulling her nightdress to her hips, I stare for a second at the thick dark tangle between her legs and the glint of her sex, remembering something Charlot said years back about using spit to make entry easier. Talking not about his sister then, of course, but about some servant girl he claimed to have taken. Virginie's eyes widen as I spit onto my fingers and smear it where I've previously sought the taste of piss.

I spit again, discreetly. Tasting her on my fingers as I coat them with my own spit and put it between her legs, letting my fingertips reach deeper until she opens her knees wide without being asked and I put myself against her.

'Gently,' she says. 'Margot said I should say gently.'

Dipping forward, I try to push in. She is tight

and nervous and it takes another mouthful of spit on my fingers and her promise that she is all right, not really afraid, before I put my hardness against her again. This time she pushes up as I push down and gasps as a little of me enters. We hang like that, me suspended above her and both of us suspended in time, and then she grins.

'More,' she says. So I pull away and, feeling her relax, drop my hips until she squeaks and I am mostly in. We kiss with only our groins and lips touching and clean morning air between the rest of us. It is a sweet kiss, as perfect as it's possible to imagine. Then she shifts a little, so that I slide slightly out of her, and pushes up until we are joined, hilt to quim, my body resting along the length of hers and her body utterly still beneath me.

When I looked at her she is crying.

'What's wrong?'

Virginie turns her head in embarrassment, only to giggle when I kiss below her ear. Liking her giggle, I kiss her ear again and her arms come up to hold me tight and she stays like that as I plough her slowly, finding it easier with every stroke. At last, sooner than I would like, but as long as any other man could have managed with a new bride, I feel my body spasm.

'Well,' she says, when I am done.

Her grin is wider than ever. Later, she will tell me Margot had said the first time was usually painful and men usually brutal, which said more about Margot's husband, the Prince de Ligney, than it did about nature itself. Her mother had told her to bear it well and then ask, tactfully, with words of love, to be excused further such duties until she'd had time to recompose herself. Her mother suggested three days should be sufficient.

Virginie tells me all this as she crouches on top of me several hours later, her legs drawn up and her chin resting on her hands, which rest on her knees. Her full weight is on my hips and I am buried deep inside. Before this I have lain two or three times between her thighs, with my mouth to the tangle of hair, my hands holding her thrashing hips in place as she bit her own wrist to muffle the cries of her excitement. The bouts ended with my mouth so bruised and bottom lip so swollen from where she ground against me I could have been punched.

'Take off your gown.'

She scowls and stops rocking.

'I want to see your body. It's beautiful.'

Virginie shakes her head fiercely. 'It's not,' she insists. 'It's ugly.'

'No, believe me. You're beautiful.'

Her face takes a petulant look that turns from playful to real as the thought behind it takes hold. 'I suppose you've seen lots of girls naked?'

I shake my head.

'You shouldn't lie.' She is glaring at me.

'A handful,' I say. 'None as beautiful as you.'

'Charlot said . . .'

'Your brother has seen several handfuls and would still need to count on all the toes of both his feet. I don't care what he told you. A handful is the most I'll admit to. And I'll only admit to them if you believe none were as beautiful as you.'

'He said you loved me.'

'Of course I love you. Why would I marry you otherwise?'

Her lips twist in sadness rather than joy. 'Because my father is the duc de Saulx? Because you have lands that were his lands? Because Monsieur Duras says . . . '

'What does Emile say?'

What Jerome and her brother say can be embarrassing, mischievous even and possibly both. I'm coming to realise, however, that what Emile says can be dangerous to my happiness, to my safety and to the health of my marriage if Virginie ever decides to believe I was part of that bet. 'That you married me for what you could gain.'

'The man's an idiot and blind. I married you because I love you.'

'You swear it?' she says fiercely.

'On my life and soul, on everything I believe in. On my happiness.'

She bends forward and kisses me slowly on the lips, opening her mouth to take my bruised lip between her teeth and pull back a little. And then my fingers are in her hair and I kiss her hard until she breaks away and sits upright, still half supported on her knees and half supported on my hips and begins to rock in earnest. She doesn't remove her nightgown and won't the whole of the first month we lie together. As I watch her raise her face to the ceiling and stare intently at something inside her eyelids, I know

I've never been happier and suspect I'll never be this happy again. She comes the second before I do, the wave that sweeps her inside pulling a fountain from me that fills her so full it oozes from between her thighs for the next half hour as we lie in each other's arms and find our breath and kiss, not with passion, which is entirely spent, but with a fondness that silences us both.

Jean-Pierre is conceived that day.

Virginie is sure of it. Not the first time, when I lay between her thighs, but the second when she knelt above me in private communion with the spirit inside her. 'I love you.' She repeats it endlessly, as if she doesn't realise she's said it already a few seconds earlier. 'I love you.' And I nod and am grateful.

Our first son was born nine months later and we adored him, because he was ours, because we had made him in the coolness of the evening after a day in each other's arms. Virginie's body was that of a woman, at least I thought so then. Now I look back and see a girl. Although, even then, I knew the face smiling down at me had little more than a child's experience such was its innocence. We called the boy Jean-Pierre and counted ourselves blessed.

1742
The Barbary Goat

Emile is the next to marry, a porcelain-faced, blue-eyed bourgeois with blonde ringlets and a father so rich he owns two chateaux in the Loire, a long strip of the Lot valley and a vineyard outside Bordeaux large enough to count its vintages in thousands of bottles. The marriage takes place at Église Saint-Séverin in Paris, across the river from the Louvre and just north of the Sorbonne. Whichever way you enter Paris you hit squalor. Rue Saint Jacques is ankle deep in shit, the church cold and Emile's bride so brittle she could be spun sugar.

Église Saint-Séverin is the southern archdeaconry of the diocese of Paris, and its marble choir a gift from the duchesses of Montpensier. Emile told me both of these facts without saying why he thought they mattered. We stand before the altar, Emile and I, shivering in the cold while his spun sugar bride takes her place beside him and I step back.

Charlot and Jerome are in the front row of the pews. Emile's mother insisted, giving up her place and that of her husband, probably without consulting him. I'm surprised to see Charlot, and Emile's face tightened when I made my excuses for Virginie. It's the second year of our marriage and she's miscarried our second child.

156

But Jean-Pierre thrives and she's stayed with him at Chateau d'Aumout.

'How is my sister?' Charlot mutters. He should be concentrating on the marriage being solemnised. Jerome is concentrating, although I suspect it's on the young bride in front of us. The dress is pinched tight at the waist and cascades in pleats across her buttocks. It's also cut square and low at the front but that's not where Jerome's interest lies.

'Well enough, considering.'

'But too ill to travel?'

'She's weak, a little tearful. We were lucky . . . ' I wonder if I can say that. She lost the child early, months before she was close to full term. If it had been a month or two before that we might never have known she was pregnant. 'Well, perhaps not lucky.'

'Ahh . . . ' Charlot looks to where Emile stands beside Thérèse and nods. He understands that his sister's decision not to travel turns on more than simple tiredness. She has not forgiven Emile the bet and she would hate Emile's new bride, I'm certain of it.

'White,' Charlot mutters.

I can hear the disgust in his voice. Virginie married in a dress of green silk, patterned with roses, with a train that fell from her shoulders. Thérèse's dress is white and lacks a train. If it had a train I imagine Jerome's interest would be less. 'Behave,' I tell Jerome, who glowers at me. That burning Normandy gaze girls find so affecting. 'I mean it.'

'A man can dream . . . '

'Dream on that instead.'

He follows my gaze to where one of the bride's cousins sits across the aisle, and she blushes and looks quickly away as he smiles. They spend the rest of the service throwing glances when each thinks the other isn't looking. At the meal that evening their chairs are empty and neither can be found. Four months later Jerome marries his slight, dark-haired girl at a service in Mont Saint Michel. Eugenie's waist is already thickening and Jerome is convinced she will have a boy. He tells me her pregnancy is a secret. He also tells Charlot, who tells me and then sulks when he discovers I have the secret before him. Emile knows already through his wife, Eugenie's brother having married one of Thérèse's cousins. Eugenie's family are old, Jerome is at pains to tell me, noblesse d'épée rather than noblesse de robe. And he dotes on her. Charlot and I doubt it will be enough to keep his eyes and hands and cock from roving, especially when Eugenie's stomach begins to swell, but she looks at him with real fondness and we decide she's probably the forgiving kind.

The abbey at Mont Saint Michel is on a rocky outcrop reached at low tide by a causeway. Stone walls run round the base of the island making it a fortress. Indeed, it once withstood an English siege and was both rich and famous in its time. Now it is near dilapidated and a handful of monks hover at the back of the cathedral like unhappy ghosts. Jerome's family have been patrons of the abbey for centuries, and with the death of Jerome's father that spring he inherited the title his elder brother would have had, had he not been killed in the siege of Prague the previous winter. Jerome is now comte de Caussard, and Mont Saint Michel's best hope of money to rebuild the abbey roof and pay for candles to burn in front of its altar. A choir has been borrowed from Rennes cathedral and shipped to the island, along with the local bishop to perform the service. We meet, attend the service, eat our feast and sleep on the island. 'Tradition,' Jerome says.

'One so old,' Charlot mutters, 'that no one can remember it.'

Jerome scowls, and is swept away by Eugenie who rushes across to find out what is wrong. It is those awkward minutes before a feast when the lower tables are settling themselves and those at high table wait to go in. 'We're teasing him,' I say. Whereupon she looks so appalled that Jerome grins, uniting himself with us in complicity, and lets Eugenie drag him to the far side of the room to talk to the abbot. The only difficult moment comes when Virginie and Emile meet, her nod so cold he blushes.

'Why me?' he demands of me later.

'You set the bet.'

'And you all took it.'

'Not me. And not Charlot, obviously.'

Emile looks mutinous until I stare at him and he glances away, realises Virginie is watching and his mouth tightens still further. 'Jerome took it.'

'Jerome's Jerome,' I say.

* * *

It was a stupid thing to say. I should have still been angry with Jerome, had been angry with Jerome, brutally angry at the time, with the fury of a young man who thinks no one should touch, or even think of touching, or have ever touched, the woman he loves except him. But Jerome was Jerome. Even then at his own wedding his eyes noted the women around him. Not hungrily but contentedly, like a lion in the grasslands lazily confirming it lives in a world where there will always be another meal.

I followed Emile across the room to where he'd gone to sulk. 'Make your apologies,' I said. 'That's all it will take. Say you were younger. You were stupid. You wish to say sorry and hope she can let bygones be bygones. We all make mistakes . . . ' Instead of understanding, he shook my hand from his arm.

'Have you suggested Jerome does the same?'

'He didn't set the wager.'

Emile's face grew cold. 'No. He simply took it. Apparently, that's entirely different. Obviously, it's a difference you can't expect people like me to understand.'

This time when he walked away I let him go and watched him join Thérèse, who stood in a window overlooking the darkening sea, her dress a little richer and a little more showy than any other. Marriage had made Emile rich. In time the death of his father-in-law would make him richer still.

'You were right to let him go . . . ' Charlot pushed a glass into my hand and grinned at my expression as I took a sip. 'Apple brandy,' he

160

said. 'Finer than the best cognac.' His voice mimicked Jerome's exactly. 'To go with the magnificent feast.'

The last hundred and fifty years might never have happened given the food Jerome served his guests. Perhaps in Normandy it didn't. Louis XIV would have been appalled. But Henri IV would have recognised the meal instantly. I was surprised Jerome let us have forks and didn't make us eat with our knives off rounds of gravy-soaked bread. What the food lacked in subtlety it make up for in quantity. A whole ox, roasted over a fire pit, was dragged in, still on its spit, on a cart made for that purpose. Whole boars and whole deer, endless pike roasted in long clay pots and herons on wooden platters. It was a feast in the old style and as tasteless and poorly cooked as anything I'd eaten since leaving the academy.

'Your face,' Charlot said.

'Don't encourage him,' Virginie hissed.

'The bread is good,' I said.

She looked at me. 'That's all you have to say? *The bread is good?*'

'Freshly baked, good yeast, not too much salt. With a slight sense of oil in the aftertaste, like an echo from a low note.'

Virginie sighed and Charlot grinned. 'You deserve each other.'

We watched him slip away towards a door into the courtyard. It was possible he was visiting the latrines or else simply wanted air. 'His turn next,' I said.

'His turn?'

'I'm married, Emile's married, now Jerome. Charlot's turn surely?'

'After my father dies . . . ' Her look was considering, on the edge of comment. We had been married two years, nearly three. We were happy in bed and in each other's company, and happy enough together not to grudge the other solitude if it was wanted. I suspected that Virginie was pregnant again, but she had still to say, and after the miscarriage of our last child I would wait rather than ask. 'Charlot is hard to know.'

'I know him better than anyone,' I said, hurt.

'Better than me?'

'Well, better than anyone but you.'

'And I know him not at all.' Virginie shrugged. 'I doubt sometimes that he knows himself. My brother will not make a good husband. And he will make his match only after my father has died. It is their final battle. The first of my father's desires for him he has been able to refuse.'

'Your father has someone in mind?'

Amusement crossed her face. 'Of course he has someone in mind. He probably had someone in mind before Charlot was born. My brother's revenge is his refusal to marry while my father is still alive.'

'Revenge for what?'

She shrugged away my question as if it were irrelevant, unless she simply thought the answer was obvious, and told me what I'd already guessed. She was three months pregnant and hoped we could return to Chateau d'Aumout more slowly than we'd travelled on our way here, as the travelling made her sick and she feared for the child. We made love slowly that night, with her sitting above me and moving gently, as her doctor had suggested for the previous pregnancy after she'd crossly dismissed his idea that I take a mistress and leave off troubling her until after the birth. It made no difference. We lost the baby at five months, as we had lost the one before. We lost the one after that in the sixth month and I began to wonder if Jean-Pierre was to be our only child. The doctor insisted Virginie's body needed a rest and this time we both listened. In the privacy of my study the doctor opened his leather bag and pulled out a scrap of leather, resting it on the desk in front of me.

'This is among the finest made.'

Reaching for his offering I unrolled it and looked at the ribband around the lower edge and the crude stitching at the top. Maybe my face revealed my thoughts, as it often did, which had been a frequent nuisance at school and remained one still.

'I can assure you it is of the best quality.'

I thanked him for his kindness, assured him my comptroller would pay his fees promptly and showed him to the door. He bowed. The man could find his way out. He had been here often enough. That evening, as supper was finishing, I told Virginie I would be going to Paris for a week and asked if could I fetch her anything while I was there. It was as if I'd said I was leaving her forever. She abandoned her chair, pushing past a footman who only just stepped back in time, and fled the room, her feet hard on the stairs. Her sobs as I made my way along the corridor to our room were as loud as I'd ever heard.

'Virginie, open the door.'

'I won't. You can't make me.'

I considered putting my shoulder to the door and decided the wood was too thick and the hinges too heavy for that to do anything but bruise my muscles and my pride. It would be absurd to send for a man with a hammer and I felt ashamed for even thinking of it. 'Virginie,' I said. 'Please. Let me in.'

There was a heavy silence and I was listening for her refusal when the key turned in the lock and she opened the door a fraction. 'I hate you.'

'At least tell me why.'

'You know why.'

'You want to come to Paris too?'

'And help find you a whore? Marseilles must be full of them. Why do you have to go to Paris? Or have Jerome or my brother shared their dirty little secrets? Have they told you where to find the best brothels and gaming dens?'

'This is absurd . . . '

'Don't you dare call me absurd.'

She beat her fists against my shoulders but let me pull her close and suffered me to hold her after a slight struggle. Her mouth was open and her face twisted to an ugly mask as she sobbed into my coat. Like all her dark moods the storm was fierce but brief. The face she raised to me was tear-streaked but calm.

'If you must,' she said.

'If I must what?'

It was, she told me later, my apparently wilful stupidity that convinced her I had no idea what this argument was about. Except that by the time she raised her face for me to kiss her gently on the lips, I did. It seemed Dr Albert had told Virginie we should have no pregnancies, but her previous reaction to his suggestion that a mistress might lighten her load had dissuaded him from telling her how we could achieve this, while sharing a bed and remaining man and wife. She'd assumed I'd agreed to take my comfort elsewhere.

'And what was *I* meant to do?'

Pushing her back on the bed, I lifted her petticoats and put her hand between her thighs, folding one of her fingers inside her. 'I believe this works.'

Virginie swiped at me with her free hand and then pulled me close to kiss. She closed her eyes so she couldn't see me watch, kept her finger where it was and finally bit hard on my shoulder to muffle her cries. When she was done and her breath returned she opened her eyes and swiped at me again for grinning. Then allowed me to take her finger and suck it clean. She tasted salt as tears and I could tell everything she'd eaten in the previous two days.

'And you?' she asked.

I rolled her onto her front and rode the crease of her buttocks, wiping her clean and curling up behind her when I was finished, my arm folded so my elbow rested on her hip and I could cup one beautiful breast.

'I love you,' she said. 'I always will.'

I left for Marseilles the next morning, having agreed with Virginie that Marseilles would be as good for what I wanted as Paris, being a port and near Italy, a place Virginie believed libidinous and licentious; both qualities likely to encourage trade in what I sought. I kept from her that what I wanted was not the thing, but a man who knew how to make the thing. I travelled quietly, inasmuch as a man who travels in a coach and four with his arms gilded on the side and his coachmen in livery can travel quietly. The mayor heard of my arrival within the afternoon and offered me the use of his house. I had to explain my presence in his city was a matter of delicacy and I'd be grateful for his discretion. He bowed himself out of my chamber, which was the largest on the upper floor of the hotel I'd chosen, and left still offering me any assistance I might need. If he left also with the idea my visit to his city was officially unofficial then that was his choice.

The city stank so richly I spent my first morning simply losing myself in tiny back streets as I hunted down the source of the smells. Strange fruit were piled high on barrows in a market peopled almost exclusively by Moors and other sorts of North African. I bought two or three of each fruit, asking for and noting down the name and making notes of the taste, texture and consistency. Wild-looking goats hung in a window, throats cut and bodies gutted, but unskinned and still with heads and hooves. I

166

asked where they came from, meaning the country, since I didn't recognise them as French, and my question was misunderstood. I left with the name of a market in the port area. The first recognisably French man I asked for directions told me a gentleman like me didn't want to go to a place like that. So, smiling, I made my other request and he offered to guide me to a brothel he knew where the girls were clean and willing and the price reasonable. Having thanked him, I asked again and he said he knew three men who made *redingotes Anglaise* and I told him to take me to the best.

We parted ten minutes later outside a workshop that stank of sulphur and rotting meat and he took his coin and my thanks. I wondered if he was one of the mayor's men sent to keep an eye on me and decided it didn't matter. Inside a small Italian scowled, noted the quality of my clothes and found a smile instead. Light streamed through a glassless window from a squalid courtyard behind and a brazier in the yard billowed yellow smoke while a boy thrust one hand into the smoke and kept his head turned away. Seeing my gaze, the Italian told me I'd come to the right place, he made the best *baudruches* in the world.

'I need you to teach me how . . . '

His gaze was unreadable as I looked round his grimy workshop. I'd gutted enough animals to identify the entrails in a bucket as sheep. The yellow smoke was sulphur, its stink unmistakable. A second bucket full of milky liquid rested on a bench, with short lengths of small entrail floating on its surface, and a long knife honed thin from sharpening showed I'd interrupted him in the middle of scraping a section of entrail clean. There is little enough space between cooking and chemistry, and this obviously combined both.

'You wish to manufacture and sell condoms?'

'I want to know how they are made, how long they last, what is the best quality that can be produced.' Pulling out my notebook, I reached into my pocket for my tiny silver inkwell, flipped open the lid and fitted a nib to the shaft of a pen, putting them all on the cleanest section of bench I could find. My actions convinced him I was serious.

'My secrets are expensive.'

'More expensive than other men like you?' The price was unimportant, within reason, but there are certain rituals to be observed when dealing with someone like this.

'There are no other men like me,' he said flatly. 'I am the best.'

'Which is why I am here and not with them.'

He smiled, flattered. And named a price for his knowledge that was probably double what he expected but still less than Virginie would spend on a single dress. We settled on a little less but still enough for him to believe he'd driven a hard bargain. As we worked — and he taught me as a master teaches an apprentice, by showing me how and then making me try for myself — he lectured me on the value and uncertain history of condoms. They were named for an English earl who gave some to his king, in an effort to stop him having so many bastards; they were named for a French Colonel Cundum; they were old as history itself; they were relatively new. It seemed their history was whatever the customer wanted it to be. 'Take the lamb's intestine and wash it in water for several hours ... ' He scowled as my mouth opened for a question and then he shrugged. I was paying him.

'Does it have to be lamb?'

'Lamb is traditional.' He considered the point. 'But I can see no reason why you should not use another animal if the idea of lamb offends you.'

I nodded for him to go on.

'After washing, mash it gently in a weak solution of lye.' He tapped the bucket of milky liquid. 'And then turn it inside out and mash it again. After that, scrape away the sticky membrane very, very carefully, and then we do this.' He took the scrap of entrail from me and led me outside, where he used wooden tongs to hold my offering and threw a small handful of sulphur onto a hot plate, pushing the tongs into the smoke. 'Now wash it in soap and water, blow it up to check for holes and tie it off at six or seven inches. You have a *baudruche*.' The man looked at my offering, and rolled his eyes. 'One so bad I doubt I could even give it away but a *baudruche* all the same.'

'And how do I make it better?'

'You practise.'

'No, how do I make it better than the ones you sell? How do I make it cleaner, thinner, more supple? How do I make it *better*?' He sighed. Another gold coin later I left with the knowledge of which bit of entrail was best to use, and a secret method for preparing this bit supposedly known only to the condom-maker to the Ottoman sultan and the man teaching me. I also left with the address of a glass-maker who would and, apparently, frequently did make dildos for the finest families. The glass-maker was where I headed early next morning, and it was only after explaining exactly what I wanted, which was a life-size dildo, no larger and no smaller, correctly shaped and mounted upright on a wooden base like a small statue, that I found the market the Moors had mentioned, in the shadow of a shipyard.

'That,' I said. 'What kind of goat is it?'

The old man I addressed looked for help to a boy who hurried over to act as his grandfather's translator, or great-uncle's, or whatever the relationship was. They were undoubtedly family, sharing cheekbones and mouths in the way Charlot and Virginie shared deep-set and ridiculously beautiful eyes. 'It's a sheep that looks like a goat.'

The animal's horns were large and swept out and backwards, its throat, chest and front legs covered with long yellowy-brown hair. Its tail hung to its heels. It looked like a goat to me. 'Smell it,' the boy said at a whisper from the old man.

The old man was right. The animal lacked a goat's distinctive stench and, now I looked closely, it lacked the beard as well. Other than that, it was so goat-like as to be indistinguishable. Nearby stood two bleating kids and their mother. 'What do you call them?' I wrote *Arudi* in my notebook and agreed a price for their delivery to my hotel, payment on delivery.

I was in my room, eating a bouillabaisse that needed more saffron but was otherwise passable, when there was a knock at my door. 'My lord, sir, I'm so sorry but there's a boy . . . '

I had the innkeeper tell the boy to wait until I'd finished eating, and later went down to pay the child and instruct my coachman to bind the arudi's front and back legs and stow them on the roof of my coach for our departure. 'Hurry home,' I told the boy, then stopped him from doing so with another question and rewarded his answer with a sou. The beasts bred easily and were best fried swiftly with garlic or cooked slowly in a fruit stew.

To cook arudi

Prepare a marinade by mixing torn rosemary, chopped mint, chilli and garlic with a cup of good olive oil and the juice of two lemons, two limes and a blood orange. Add salt and crushed pepper, pour over two pounds of meat cut from the legs of a young arudi, chopped into thumb-sized chunks, and mix well. Cover with a muslin cloth against flies and leave overnight in a cool larder.

Next day blister the skin of two red and two green peppers over flame and remove skin as cleanly as possible. Put peppers to one side to cool. Repeat with a large aubergine, cut into slices and squeeze between two plates with a small weight on top to remove sourness (drain away any liquid). Now sear meat by frying in marinade mix to seal, adding extra olive oil if necessary, then add peppers and aubergine, and fry fast. Can be eaten with rice or pain de campagne. *Tastes like mutton.*

To make the perfect redingotes Anglaise

Take the caecum[1] from two smallish animals — arudi are ideal — and soak for a day in fresh water, changing the water twice. Turn both inside out and mash gently in a weak solution of lye for a further two days. Scrape carefully to remove the mucous membranes, leaving the stronger outer coats. Expose to vapour from burning brimstone, then wash carefully with soap and water. Turn the

---

[1] There is a naturally-occurring pouch in intestines where the big and small intestines meet, called the caecum, which is ideally shaped for the human male member. Unlike condoms made from lengths of intestine, those fashioned from caecum do not require tying, sewing or sealing at the top. This makes them more comfortable. All condoms can be soaked in milk or water before use but the best redingotes Anglaise-maker in Marseilles recommends dressing caecum condoms only with first-pressing olive oil. *Wash well after use and hang out to dry.*

second length of moist gut back to its original configuration — with the scraped surface on the inside — and put aside. Smooth the first length onto an oiled glass dildo and draw the second length over the first. The two insides will seal together. Burnish the condom with a glass weight to polish its surface and thin the membrane. Dress with oil and slap the condom repeatedly against a table to break down the fibres and make it supple. Sew a red ribband around the lower edge for tying in place.

1748
Charlot Marries

The burial of Amaury, duc de Saulx, was the last of the great state funerals. There were others later that were as grand and equally impressive, but his had a solemnity that was missing from those that came later, as if we secretly knew the world was changing. Amaury de Saulx had been born in an earlier century, had grown up under the Sun King and been that king's godson and favourite. The men who turned out to mourn were as old as their houses. Marshals and generals, premier dukes and peers so ancient they had to be helped from their carriages and walked with sticks on both sides, shaking off offers of help as rude attempts to hurry them.

The old *légitimés de France*, Louis XIV's legitimised bastards, were dead but their sons represented them. The service was at Chateau de Saulx and the king himself attended. Fresh in our minds was the previous year's battle of Fontenoy in the Netherlands, where the king took to the field, along with his sixteen-year-old son, and with the help of his marshal, Maurice de Saxe, smashed the armies of the Dutch, the English, the Austrians and the Hanoverians. Charlot's cavalry attack on the English and Hanoverian infantry helped win that battle. He was twenty-nine then, thirty now. His face as he buried his father was unreadable. As we left, he gripped my hand firmly, hesitated and hugged me. He kissed his sister carefully on both cheeks and promised to write.

Virginie cried in silence for the first hour of our journey home, the first tears she had shed since receiving news of her father's death. I had no idea if she cried for her father, at the formality of her brother's farewell or from the emotion of the week now gone, which had seen her return to the room she'd slept in as a girl.

'He always liked you better.'

'Virginie . . . '

'It's true. You know it's true. I'm surprised he let me marry you. Sometimes I wonder if we're really brother and sister.'

'Of course you're brother and sister. It would be hard to find two people more alike. It's not just in your eyes and cheekbones. It's in how you behave, how you look at the world.' Virginie glared at me so fiercely she could have been sixteen again. 'He couldn't have stopped me anyway,' I said, attempting to make peace.

'Of course he could. My mother hated the idea. My father was uncertain. Charlot spoke up for you. He persuaded Margot to speak up for you in her turn. Do you think my father would have agreed if Charlot had protested?'

'I thought they disliked each other?' I'd never put that thought into words, and writing it now from this distance I'm ashamed at my poor grasp of how families worked. All I can say in my defence is that I'd never really had one, until I met Charlot and Virginie . . . I was her husband, the father of her child. But she was — and always would be — Amaury de Saulx's daughter. That she loved me, would take off her dress and spread her thighs for me remained a shock. Even back then, almost ten years after we married.

Virginie sighed. Her face grew thoughtful as she hunted for the right words and she wiped away the last of her tears with her knuckles without even noticing.

'He grew up in harder times.'

That was all she ever said about her father, all she ever said about Charlot's relationship with the man, which I now understood somehow mirrored her own. I had been the exception. His kindness to me allowed by the lack of blood tie. He was truly from another time.

Charlot married two years later, in the summer of 1748, a girl almost exactly half his age, seventeen to his thirty-two. Lisette had dark eyes and a round face, tightly curled black hair that fell to her shoulders, and a tight, almost muscled figure, with high breasts and hips like a boy. She looked more Breton than Norman. I wasn't even sure I'd known Jerome had a younger sister, certainly not one born when we were at the academy. Charlot was infatuated, suddenly kind and unexpectedly nervous. Virginie found comfort in this. As if her brother, who had always been a little too brave, a little too strong, and in her eyes a little too careless with the affections of those drawn to him, suddenly redeemed himself by showing the same vulnerability that the rest of us tried so hard to hide.

He married her in a private ceremony in the

176

chapel at Saulx, the same chapel that had been filled with princes and nobles for the burial of his father two years earlier. Jerome sat in the front pew, beside my wife and my young son, who was doing his best to appear grown up among his father's friends. I stood at the altar beside Charlot as Lisette approached, as I'd stood beside Emile, the difference being Charlot was invited to Emile's wedding, and had gone out of a sense of duty, but Emile was not invited to his. I'd received a letter beforehand from Emile asking me to intercede, and had to write back that I had mentioned the matter but he knew what Charlot was like and I was loath to make promises I couldn't keep. Emile didn't write again for three years. It would have been worse had he known Virginie was the one who banned him from her brother's wedding — and it had been her, not Charlot, I'd been unable to sway.

These were good years for Charlot, Jerome and me. We were in our prime, married, with children or with children on the way. Lisette fell pregnant almost immediately, and I stood godfather to Amaury, Charlot's first boy, as did Jerome. We were bound by our time at the academy, and by the fact our names were rarely mentioned separately. Charlot's father arranged my entry into his world, but my friendship with Charlot and Jerome consolidated it. At the academy they'd raised their eyebrows, muttered asides, called me *philosopher* and forgiven my strangeness because it amused them. But as the years went by my oddities became eccentricities, my eccentricities became virtues.

Society approved my marriage to Charlot's sister. We were politely formal in public, as manners required, but we were known to be affectionate in private. I kept no mistresses and she took no lovers. That made us unusual for people like us in those days. Instead we shared a bed and kept to ourselves as much as politeness and society allowed. Later, I wondered if Virginie had wanted more from me or from her life. If she did, it never showed. She was the perfect wife, the perfect mother, the perfect chatelaine.

Using a portion of the money she inherited on the death of her father, I had the kitchens at Chateau d'Aumout rebuilt in the latest style. A new bread oven was installed, and the old spit, driven by geese on a treadmill, ripped out and replaced with one of my own invention. My spit was wound by hand and powered by a steel spring that could have driven a town clock. A ratchet kept the meats turning at a steady pace. Gearing was used to adjust the speed. An artist from Paris came down at the king's command to make engravings of my design.

I had an ironworker make me huge pans with bases three times the normal thickness. They took far longer to heat up but retained their heat and could be set aside and continue to cook their ingredients until it was time to return them to the flame. I had a salamander made, longer than a spade, with a heavy metal circle at one end that could be pushed into the coals and left until needed to caramelise sugar or brown the skin of a goose or crisp the crackling on a boar. I began to work on my theory that the taste of food

178

should be treated not like the taste of wine but like music. There were rising notes, falling notes, harmonics. The perfect meal took all of these into account.

Tell me what you eat, and I will tell you who you are . . . A throwaway line in a letter of mine to Jerome, after he'd been boasting of his beef and root vegetables and other Normandy food, became a bon mot bandied about at Versailles and claimed by a dozen others. My simple comment that the years just gone had stretched our palates, and the discovery of cane sugar, and its different preparations, of alcoholic liquors, of white and red wines, vanilla, coffee and tea had given us flavours hitherto unknown, became a staple of commonplace books. Chefs in Paris dedicated their recipes to me, then chefs in Rome, and London, with which we were briefly at peace, and where all the best cooks are French anyway. Rousseau wrote to me. D'Alembert gave my theories an entry in the first edition of his *Encyclopédie*.

I was proudest of my championing of the potato, a vegetable from the Americas that produced more food per acre than wheat. It was filling, nutritious and wholesome, and would, I was certain, if grown in sufficient quantity, save France in times of famine for all my peasants knew it as winter food for their cattle. Unfortunately, the similarity of its root shape to deadly nightshade convinced many it was poisonous. I had even seen my kitchen maids wash their hands after handling it. It didn't help that the French Parliament had forbidden its cultivation on the grounds that potatoes caused leprosy, an absurdity I exposed by eating potatoes at every meal for a week and challenging the Faculty of Medicine in Paris to examine me and say I was ill.

In the winter of 1753 Virginie fell pregnant and I realised I would need to make a new redingotes Anglaise. Although we were worried, she carried her baby to term and we named our daughter Hélène after Virginie's favourite aunt. Jean-Pierre was fourteen when we discovered his mother was pregnant and fifteen when we sent him to stay with his uncle Charlot in the week that Hélène was born. He travelled alone from Chateau d'Aumout to Chateau de Saulx, except for a coachman. I have no doubt his trip was as interesting as mine would have been at his age. He'd been offered a place at the academy in Brienne two years before this, but had chosen to remain at home and Virginie was happy with that decision. He liked his summer with Charlot so much that he returned the following year. And the year after that, with Charlot promising to introduce him at Versailles. It was here that tragedy happened and we were in the gardens at Chateau d'Aumout when we received news of it carried by a royal messenger. Jean-Pierre had been thrown from his horse while hunting with Charlot and the dauphin. He broke his neck in the fall and died immediately.

I can remember the moment of the letter's arrival, the beads of sweat on the royal messenger's face as he was shown to the knot garden Virginie and I had planted to mimic the one at Chateau de Saulx. I remember the deepness of his bow before he handed me the letter, and my voice faltering as I read Charlot's words aloud to my wife and we reached the import of their meaning. I can remember Virginie's sob, and the rustle of silk as she fell to the ground. I cannot remember what I thought at all. I suspect I thought nothing beyond the need to help Virginie. As for what I *felt* . . . I never cried for Jean-Pierre. But in the weeks that followed his death I walked the walks he and I used to walk when he was small; around the little lake, and through the knot garden as far as the monkey puzzle tree and back again. I walked them until my heels cracked and my ankles bled and the bones in my feet hurt as fiercely as if someone had broken them with hammers.

1757
The Lover

Virginie took Jean-Pierre's death badly as mothers do. She withdrew from family life and our three-year-old daughter clung to me like a shadow, until I appointed a young woman from Limoges as Hélène's nanny. Fierce and wilful, Hélène took after her grandfather in temper and her mother in looks. Perhaps I should have let her cling. It was only later I realised the child needed me to make up for her mother's absence.

The years of Jean-Pierre's life had been good for us but bad for France. Louis XV, once loved, became hated. When Emile and I finally met, in Paris at supper with his family, Madame Duras told me in all seriousness that her local police were abducting the children of the poor so the king could bathe in their blood to heal his diseases. Since this was treason, I took Emile aside and told him he should guard what his wife said since not everyone was his friend. He looked at me a little strangely, and replied she said nothing everyone else in Paris was not already thinking. The execution of Damiens the following year, in the spring of 1757, made matters worse. The man had tried to murder Louis — of course he had to be executed. But four hours of public torture with molten lead poured into his wounds? While fools like Emile's father-in-law paid seven hundred livres for a balcony on the Place de Grève so he could hold a party and watch a screaming halfwit die in agony ... We disgusted Europe with our degeneracy. We disgusted ourselves.

The years of Jean-Pierre's life had passed, as they do as we get older, ever faster for me. Although not so fast as they do now, where each New Year's Day seems followed almost immediately by another with nothing but a few letters written and a few books read in between. I can remember weeks that lasted longer as a child than this last year. The day I sat with my back to the dung heap and watched the duc d'Orléans ride under the arch into my father's courtyard felt longer than the whole of this last year of my life. Some days I feel I would like to find God, but we keep missing each other in the gaps in our lives. Well, my life, his eternity. The fact I don't really believe in him probably doesn't encourage him to approach. Virginie believed, properly and without question. I envied her that in the months following our son's death, in between feeling irritated at how little she questioned what she'd been told. We took communion together each Sunday in the local church rather than invite the priest to come to our private chapel, and Virginie mouthed private prayers while I made the public responses and tried not to think ungodly thoughts about a local farmer's daughter or the young wife of a wine merchant. My thoughts might stray but my hands did not and I thought she knew this. Evidently, she did not.

Virginie took a lover the year after Jean-Pierre died.

Whether they were lovers in the physical sense I have no idea. Père Laurant was a young priest in the next village and she was five years his senior. She took her pain to him and somehow over the months that followed he did what I could not, lifted the grief from her shoulders and put the smile back on her face and eventually back into her eyes.

The benefice was mine and I could have dismissed him had I wanted. But he was liked by all for his freshness and lack of guile. His sermons were short, his penances lenient. It was whispered he'd read Voltaire and believed God had a use even for such a man. If they were lovers, and there were many who whispered that was true, and in the dark of the night my fears saw her naked above him, smiling down with those same dark eyes, I could have had him defrocked by the bishop, although if one were to defrock every village priest who slept with unhappy wives and lonely widows half the vicarages in France would fall to ruin.

Charlot solved the problem eventually.

He arrived unexpectedly one afternoon in the autumn of '57, in the coach that had been so grand and new the year it collected us from the academy. Now it looked tarnished and outdated. He greeted me kindly and folded his sister in his arms and took her for a walk around the little lake until they reached a bench beneath a willow where they stopped to talk until the sun set behind the trees and the sky changed colour and the world shifted a little on its axis and for a while seemed to settle back into place.

Virginie came to my bed that night.

With the windows open and the sound of peacocks scratching on the gravel and a dog howling in the village, I heard a creak as the door between our rooms opened and the curtains of my room billowed as the night breeze was allowed free rein. A glimmer of white was framed in a square of darkness. 'May I come in?' it said.

'Of course . . .'

Her hair was unbound and her feet without slippers, she lacked the lace shawl she usually wore around her shoulders. The night takes away the years. A woman by candlelight is younger than a woman in the light of an oil lamp, a woman in darkness younger still. I have no doubt the same is true for women when they look at men. Virginie seemed to me as young and as beautiful as in the first weeks we shared a bed. She hesitated, when she was halfway across the room, and I shifted on the mattress and pulled back the covers and she slid in beside me. That night neither of us really slept. Although for different reasons this time. We held each other, stiffly at first and then more naturally as we relaxed into the shape of each other's body, and the tightness in her shoulders softened and she smiled when I kissed her hair.

We made love next morning, because she found that easier than doing so late at night. We never talked about why — though I knew. Virginie could dislike her body enough to feel uncomfortable around it when it was full. In the morning when the food had settled and her bowels and bladder emptied she could afford to be kinder to herself. We're animals made complicated by the belief we're something more.

She made me go slowly the first time, grinned when I took her hard and finally crawled on top of me, as she'd done in the early days, and rode herself to relief, collapsing in a sprawl on my chest and biting my shoulder when I slapped her buttocks. She put aside her sadness that morning, as if it were a burden she'd been waiting for the year just gone to put down. Without saying . . . At least without saying clearly, we knew we'd agreed to resume our life as a couple and try for another son. Jean-Pierre could not be replaced but we would try to replace him anyway.

Charlot left at the end of the week and took Père Laurant with him to a new post at the Sorbonne. It was a big promotion for a village priest, albeit a young and intelligent one who should probably not have been a village priest in the first place. He went with the new duke's patronage, and Virginie's tears, as she watched her family's old coach trundle away. A few years later Père Laurant wrote a treatise explaining away the contradiction between God's kindness and the world's cruelty, and dedicated it to Charlot and an unnamed muse. By then Laurant was born. I let Virginie have the name since I knew, from the time between the coach's departure and the baby's birth, that the child was mine. Besides, she had an uncle called Laurant and said the child was named for him. I pretended to believe her.

1758
Responsibilities

Laurant's birth gave me a son and lost me a wife. The woman I'd loved and briefly lost to another and got back, mostly through her brother's good graces as much as any virtues I might have, vanished again and remained gone. My second son was born in the summer of 1758, two years after the death of the brother he'd never meet, and a little over twenty years after Virginie and I married. It was a bad birth and lasted longer than she or any other woman could endure. Her screams were so fierce I abandoned the chateau and walked in the woods praying to a God I barely believed in to let her live if he had to make a choice between mother and child. The labour left her ripped, and pain clouded how she looked at the child. She'd part-fed her other children but could barely stand to have Laurant in the room and gave him over to the servants within days. I kept waiting for the Virginie I knew to reappear. She had to be in there somewhere. But her eyes remained dull and her gaze fixed on her feet and I'd find her frozen on a chair blank-eyed but crying. 'I'm fine,' she'd say.

Pretty much all she ever said.

She repeated it to me, to the doctor, to her brother who came to see the new heir to the marquisate his father had worked so hard to have transferred. In desperation I sent to Paris, to the Sorbonne, for Père Laurant, the man for whom I believed the child was named. He came at once, trundling through the night over rough roads through bandit-infested forests to arrive dust-covered and exhausted. I showed him into her room and took another turn around the gardens. I no longer cared what anyone thought.

Père Laurant sought me out several hours later.

He looked drained and exhausted and older than in my memory. Paris had been unkind to him and his skin was blotched from poisons in the water. The year away had taken the hair from the crown of his head and thickened his waist and broadened his shoulders so they stretched the cloth of his cleric's gown. His was a face pretty in youth and coarsening with age. Round faces do that.

'Well?' I spoke as I would to my village priest and he bridled, swallowing his pride in the next second. The man had been alone in the room of my wife for the last several hours and my heir was possibly named for him, I felt entitled to be short.

'Marquis . . . '

The silence stretched between us and I used the beating seconds to pour us both a glass of wine, putting it silently on the table in front of him. The servants were banished, gone from the room and gone from the corridor outside the door. This was a conversation I was determined to have in private. Although there was little conversation to be had. Père Laurant expressed his regrets at how he found my wife, muttered a platitude about God's healing kindness and asked what the doctor had said. Since the doctor's answer was much the same as his, give her time and trust in God, I thanked him for coming so far, offered him the use of a chamber and told him to stay for as many days as he liked. He left that afternoon looking as dusty and exhausted as the horses that brought him.

Maybe I was wrong to translate 'give her time' as limiting my visits to her bed. All the same, our lives became separate and the door between our chambers remained closed far more often than not. Some weeks it was locked, others unlocked; I never discovered the logic behind her choice. That she was reading gave me faint hope. Anything was better than sitting at the window staring out at the lake.

I knew that in any city I could find brothels, there were enough of them. Not that I needed to go that far. A dozen innkeepers between my estate and the nearest town would have turned over their daughters, wives or sisters for coin. The first place I stopped was a staging post, offering cheap rooms and cheaper food to farmers and shopkeepers and sour-faced bourgeoisie who looked appalled by the crowds and the noise. The dining room was full, the public bar overflowing with drunken locals. Couples staggered into the afternoon, laughing, their arms around each other. I looked at the dozen youths and girls scurrying to serve customers and wondered how many were conceived against the wall at the back of that very inn.

I rode on and stopped just beyond the next town, dust on my boots and in my throat. The innkeeper's daughter had black hair falling in filthy curls around her shoulders, a soiled white blouse boiled so thin it billowed every time her breasts shifted. The landlord saw my gaze and came across, his eyes dark with calculation and greed. No price was mentioned and I had no idea if he'd sold her before. He simply told me what a good girl she was, how hard she worked, how devoted to her mother, who watched from the kitchen door. I nodded to say I understood and took my place in a private room upstairs and waited for the girl to serve me.

'My lord.' She curtsied clumsily and looked to see if I was impressed.

I smiled and some of the tension left her face.

'Should I get you food, sir?'

Or shall I simply pull up my dress? I understood the words she left unspoken and told her to fetch me bread and cheese. The bread as fresh as she could find and the cheese as old. She checked to see she'd understood what I'd said and scuttled from the room, her shoulder and hip pushing against me as she went. When I looked after her she was blushing. She stopped at the top of the stairs and took a deep breath before descending.

'Sir, my mother has this.' She unwrapped warm bread that stank of yeast and took the imprint of my thumb in its cooling crust. 'And this is the cheese.' Beneath an upturned bowl lay an eighth of Camembert so rancid it could walk off the plate, next to a fat sliver of goat's cheese white with bloom. She looked at both doubtfully. 'You said old . . . '

'So I did.' I covered the Camembert with the bowl before it could sour the room. 'You can take that back . . . ' Like duck's egg soaked in horse urine and buried for a hundred days in the Chinese style, some tastes do not need repeating. I'd already tried Camembert ripened beyond the point of deliquescence and felt no need to try again. She trotted away with her tray, the rotting cheese and upturned bowl and hurried back a moment later, face warm from climbing the stairs. 'Sit,' I told her.

She did and watched me trim away mould until I was left with a sliver of goat's cheese the colour of tallow and the texture of hard wax. Cutting a slice, I laid it across a strip of bread crust and offered it to her. She chewed two or three times, swallowing hastily. When I offered her another bit, she shook her head, looking anxious that she might have offended me and said, 'I've eaten,' by way of explanation.

I ate the rest myself while she watched. The taste was divine. As I ate I tried to guess her age — and realised it was impossible. Thirteen? Fourteen? Younger than Jean-Pierre when he died. Perhaps Virginie's age when we first met. Too young for a man like me, even one in search of withered dreams.

I left the girl with a gold livre and a handful of greasy sou. If she had sense, she'd give the gold to her father and keep the smaller coins for herself. I also left her untouched — at least by me — and rode home, torn between shame at the instinct that took me there and delight at the taste of the cheese. I knew I needed to find another outlet for my needs.

I took a mistress, the wife of a doctor who'd treated Laurant when he was sick. My neighbours discovered soon enough and treated her as one would expect, with a mixture of envy and disdain. Her husband being my physician provided enough respectability for my coming and going to her house to pass almost without comment. I have no idea if Virginie knew or cared. Or even if the doctor did. Our affair began in summer and ended in the autumn as the leaves were turning. She cried.

In desperation, I turned to food. My recipes becoming ornate, my tastes more complex. At school my attempt to recreate the Dragon & Tiger dish the colonel had told me about was basic and disappointing. So I refined it, and revised it, and experimented, and though I finally came up with a heavily seasoned stew that was passable, I realised that cat and snake were best eaten separately and I preferred snake to cat anyway. In a month I cleared the chateau grounds of adders, and arrived at two recipes that amused me. The bouillabaisse involved treating snake like fish, the fried dish involved treating it like chicken.

Three-snake bouillabaisse

Take two each of adder, grass snake and slow worm and gut, skin, cut into sections and let soak in salted water while you fry in a pan three diced onions, six unbroken bulbs of garlic and six ripe tomatoes, skinned over flame and seeded, in a cup of good olive oil. Add the snake, cover with boiling water and add cayenne, salt, fennel and saffron to the liquid, plus parsley, thyme, rosemary, black peppercorns and tarragon all bound in a small muslin parcel, simmering the ingredients together until the oil, water and tastes have mixed. Separate the snake from the broth and serve with thickly sliced potatoes on the same dish. Pour the broth individually over thick slices of pain de campagne rubbed with raw garlic. A rouille of oil, egg yolk and garlic maybe floated on top. *Tastes like fish*.

Fried snake

This is far simpler. Gut, skin and cut into finger-length sections a snake and let soak in salted water while you beat together three egg yolks, a tablespoon of olive oil and a little sour milk. Whisk the egg whites until stiff and fold into the mixture. Prepare a bowl of crumbs from stale bread, mixed with coarse black pepper. Dip the snake pieces into the egg mixture, dredge through the pepper crumbs and fry immediately in an inch of good oil. Eat while hot. *Tastes like chicken*. (The above recipe can be used for frogs' legs. Use only the upper section of the rear legs and season with lemon juice. Alternate pieces of snake and frog dredged

193

in the pepper mix and cooked on a skillet make for an interesting exercise. The similarities of texture, taste and afternote are closer than the differences.)

I served these two dishes to my guests and was complimented on both. But the truth is taste no longer excited me in the same way. I had eaten everything France had to offer. One pig, one mouse, one owl tastes much like another. Ravens taste little different from crows. Eels from the Seine might taste subtly different from those from the Garonne but they are still eels, even if sauced with a mixture of lovage, dill, celery seed, fried mint and rue, and garnished with pine nuts and honey, as served to the Emperor Tiberius and recorded in *De Re Conquinaria* by the Roman epicure Apicius.

At a loss, I began improvements on the estate and in the lands beyond, doing things I could have done long before. The marsh was drained in a single season. Huge ditches were cut to take the waters, until long straight lines sliced a landscape that had always been chaotic before. The marsh plants died, of course. The small animals that had lived at the ragged water's edge died out or moved away. The ducks had nowhere to land that winter and the hunting was bad. Villagers went hungry, refused to eat the cartloads of potatoes I provided and openly cursed me. Their newborn no longer died from marsh fever but now their mothers had no food to feed them or themselves. I tried to undo the worst of the hunger, even knowing that the really destitute were never dangerous, that it was those on the edge of destitution who could be led against those they held responsible. Even knowing this, I released grain from my own granaries at prices so low the local merchants complained. The peasants, of course, said I overcharged.

I rebuilt roads, planted windbreaks, began building a school for the children of merchants and prosperous farmers. Voltaire himself wrote to me saying he approved of my work and my diligence. He'd heard I was a scientist. I wrote back denying it. The most I could claim was that I kept a book of the things I'd eaten, how they tasted and how that taste made me feel. If wine from vines grown on flinty slopes tastes different from wine from the valleys surely meat should be the same? I'd had my cattle herd split into four, I told him. Split into four and nurtured on uplands and lowlands, rich ground and poor. And having had four cows slaughtered I ate beef from each and discovered I could tell without being told which had been raised where.

Voltaire wrote back a long letter on the nature of taste and begged me to write to him again with news of my experiments. My reputation in the neighbourhood rose. Père Laurant wrote from Paris that he was master of a college now, to ask about the health of my wife and to say he'd heard I corresponded with Voltaire.

Dear Père Laurant
Virginie continues to favour a quiet life and solitude. But I can truthfully say that your

195

visit helped her find an element of peace
that had been missing from her life since the
birth of our son, and for this I am glad . . .

Not grateful, simply glad. That was the truth of
it.

She saw him and her mind settled enough for
her to stop weeping in corners over the damp
pages of a poetry book or be found sobbing at
the harpsichord as she played endlessly some
country tune she must have overheard in the
village. Seeing him again let her fall out of love.
The thin boy who'd arrived in the village in an
oversized cassock was gone. A thickset academic
with hair already beginning to recede and a
myopic gaze had taken his place. Seeing one
destroyed her memory of the other. I asked if she
wanted to invite him again and Virginie shook off
my suggestion as if I'd had the ill manners to
mention an embarrassing cousin.

1758
Hope

Hope came for me from the strangest of quarters. On a day I'd expected to spend only a few minutes at most approving a replacement wetnurse for my new son. Her name was Manon and the look she gave me was amused. I felt she understood how absurd a world it was where she was required to rent out her teats for another child's use so the mother should not have the inconvenience of feeding the child herself. Although maybe it was finding herself talking to the marquis because the marquise was too busy staring out of a window to notice the negotiations taking place in front of her that twisted the village girl's mouth into a rueful grimace.

The first thing I noticed about Manon were her freckles. The second, that her breasts were so full with milk they strained against a shift that was drab brown and recently washed. Her face was also recently washed and I had no doubt her straw-coloured hair had been rinsed through. She had the look of someone wearing her best in hope of making a good impression. All the same, that knowing smile undermined her politeness. It was amused and a little sharp. If it had been a herb it would have been hyssop. If a wine, a local white from the flinty soil above the quarry. She caught my gaze and looked away, wondering if she was in trouble. The curtsy she dropped spread her hem across the dusty floor.

Virginie frowned vaguely. A book lay open but unread on her lap. Her hair was scraggly at the temples where she kept worrying it with her fingers. She looked as she'd looked for months, sullen as a cloudy sky that threatens to tip over into rain. Like everyone else in the chateau I waited and waited and waited for the storm that never came.

'Come with me,' I told Manon. 'And bring my son . . .'

She lifted Laurant from the floor at my command and tucked him casually against her hip. Virginie watched us go like a child watching leaves blow across the grass. With vague interest but little understanding of what made a leaf move.

'She's ill,' I said before we reached the end of the corridor. 'You must understand the marquise is ill and make sure Laurant behaves quietly around her.'

The girl nodded meekly. As we reached the bottom of the stairs and headed for the front door Manon opened her mouth, only risking a question when we stood outside. 'It was a bad birth, my lord? If I might ask . . .'

I thought back to the white-faced midwife, and the hovering priest who'd arrived to stand outside the door long before my man found me fishing the lower stream. I'd entered Virginie's bedroom to a child as bruised as if the midwife had dragged it from my wife's splayed legs and kicked it into a corner.

'Forgive my question,' Manon said. 'It was insolent to ask.'

'She almost died,' I said fiercely. 'He almost died too.'

Manon looked at the baby banging its head against her side. 'He's hungry.'

'He's never anything else.'

She turned without asking off the gravel into the mouth of the maze. The puzzle garden had been planted when Jean-Pierre was born and had grown, been cut, grown and been cut until the yew bushes were thick and their edges sharp. I knew the way by heart, having designed the puzzle, but I let Manon head towards a dead end, where a small bench waited for those who wanted to rest before finding their way back to try again. Laurant was grinding his face below her breast by then and mouthing at the cloth until dabs of saliva darkened it.

Nodding at the bench, I said, 'Feed him.'

Manon sat without protest, matter-of-factly unbuttoning her shift. All I could see was the suddenly silent child and a squash of pink flesh behind. I stood and watched as my son guzzled. After a few minutes his hunger sated and he fell from the nipple, waking himself in the act of lolling. She tapped her finger to his mouth and he followed it until he found her breast again. Her nipple was the colour of raspberries from Laurent's feeding and he drained that breast dry in the next minute before lolling back as drunk as I've ever been on wine. Manon hoisted him onto her shoulder and began to jiggle him until he burped. All the while keeping her arm across her chest to keep her breast hidden.

'You're done?'

'He'll take more. But he'll do for now if you want me finished?'

Looking at my milk-drunk son in her arms and the sweet curve of breast behind, I shook my head. She was young, fresh-faced and so full of life her skin glowed and her flesh was as firm as a perfect peach. 'Feed him again.'

I came to sit beside her and made no pretence of looking away when she lowered him from her shoulder and shifted her dress to free the other side. Laurent fed less hungrily and dozed in the gaps between guzzling. His head lolling back to expose her nipple. The sun shone warmly on the three of us and chaffinches sang in the trees beyond the hedge. A robin dropped to the dirt at our feet to search for worms or crumbs, hopping in ever-wider circles until disappointment took him away. Finally, Laurant was done.

'Here,' I said.

She handed me my son and I held him as she had, jiggling him until he burped in my ear. Her dress was still undone but she was reaching for the buttons when I leant forward to stop her. Very slowly I opened one side to reveal where my son had been feeding. Her nipple was raspberry, the circle around it lilac. Milk oozed as I watched and collected in a bead that rolled to the underside of the raspberry. Her face stiffened when I wiped the bead free before it could drop and carried it to my lips. A second drop collected and I took that too. 'Chestnuts. You've eaten

200

chestnuts and fruit.'

'I took a plum from the orchard. But only from the ground.'

'Next time take one from the trees. And the chestnuts?'

'For lunch,' she said. 'My mother made soup.'

I shut her dress to the neck. 'You want this job?'

She nodded fiercely.

'And your own child?'

'My mother will look after.'

'Who will feed him?'

'Her, my lord. My ma will feed her. She has a baby that age of her own and, as she says, two tits for two mouths.' She blushed at her mother's crudeness and I waved her blush aside. So it was settled. Manon came to the chateau to take care of Laurant and the nursery. I explained what I wanted. I wanted him happy and well fed, on her milk and pureed vegetables from the walled garden. I wanted all responsibility for his care lifted from my wife. Manon would deal direct with me. She was to start today. She was to start now. Manon curtsied before taking Laurant back. And having told her to find my housekeeper and explain the arrangements, I sent for a stable boy and told him to find Manon's mother in the village and tell her what had been agreed.

1762
Master of the Menagerie

In the three or four years that followed, my love for Virginie was worn to tattered cobwebs by her tears and my own anger at being unable to change how she felt or comprehend the source of her sorrow. We had Hélène, now eight and the image of her mother, we had an heir, the building work on the chateau was finished and the grounds had never looked more beautiful. An Italian fountain cascaded cooling water in the middle of the terrace, peacocks roamed the grounds fanning their tails in grand display and puffing themselves up with pride. The king himself came with his retinue and emptied our larders of food and our forests of prey, and rode his hunt through the middle of the harvest, scattering silver to compensate the peasants.

I was asked if Virginie was seriously ill.

My answer, that I did not know but that I was worried, was greeted as a display of tact and kindness unusual in marriages of our kind. By the time Louis rode away I'd had three offers of friendship, and mentions of beautiful daughters, from members of his court. His majesty left with a smile on his face and his stomach full, although not as full as he left the stomach of a peasant girl who bore his bastard nine months later. And he left me a knight grand cross of the Order of St

Louis, with the promise that a place on the Privy Council was mine when one next came available, should I want it.

Virginie listened to all this with a tired smile and retired to her room to play sad melodies on her harpsichord, having first suggested I might want to take myself and Laurant to Paris to consolidate the impression I'd made on His Majesty, and I might like to take Manon too. My reply, that obviously I'd take her if I was taking Laurant, produced a sadder smile and a softly closed door.

We left a week later and slept at the duc de Saulx's chateau on the way. Charlot asked carefully after his sister, dandled his nephew on his knee and let his gaze slide over Manon without really noticing her. He could probably have told me she was female and from a peasant family, given the broadness of her face. I doubt he could have managed more without looking again. Later that night we shared a cognac on the terrace, looking down over a lake he was having widened and deepened so his son's sailing boat would not keep running aground and stranding the boy.

'How is she really?'

The cognac was old and almost auburn, with odours of quince and fig, perhaps a little jasmine and liquorice. 'Your own?'

He nodded, his face serious to show he still awaited my answer. I let him wait while I swirled the straw-coloured liquid round the glass to release its scent and then sipped, letting the complexity roll over my tongue. Maybe Charlot knew how hard I struggled to find the words; he certainly knew how much I'd loved his sister, and perhaps still did, because he let me have my tasting and my silence. In the end I told him the truth because he was my friend.

'She keeps to her room. She reads a little, writes a little, plays harpsichord, pieces by Rameau and Couperin, and walks occasionally in the garden.'

'Anything else, marquis?'

'She cries.'

Charlot came to stand beside me and rested his arm heavily around my shoulder. He had always been the biggest, at school and after. Age and good living had thickened his waist and filled his frame so the velvet of his frock coat stretched across his back and was cut in a curve at the hips to flatter his thighs. He'd be too heavy for the hunter he owned when I first knew him. Probably too heavy for the horse I rode now. We looked at the lake with its ugly mud scars and silvery water and let the silence lengthen. 'You are . . . ' he hesitated. 'Still man and wife?'

This was a conversation it would be hard to have with any brother-in-law but harder still because he was one of my oldest friends. I nodded, and then made myself put the situation into words. 'I go to her bed occasionally. She has stopped coming to mine and I do not send for her. Even in bed, even during that, we are polite strangers.' There were tears in my eyes and I knew Charlot had noticed because he shifted uncomfortably. He disliked strong emotions; his whole family disliked strong emotions. Before

today, before noticing Charlot's uncomfortable-
ness, I would have said I disliked them myself.

'You know I loved her . . . '

'Loved?'

'I would love her again if I could find her. But
she's not in there. I've been left with a husk,
beautiful and elegant, dutiful if required, but
wanting only to be left alone to her books and
her harpsichord and her walks and her tears. She
sits in her room playing Couperin to the mouse
that comes out from the wainscot and makes up
her audience in exchange for crumbs.'

'Is there anybody else for you?'

I shook my head.

'You must have mistresses? Willing wives
among the local gentry? Favourites among the
servants? That young woman you arrived with?'

So he had noticed Manon after all. 'She looks
after Laurant, no more.'

'Take a mistress, Jean-Marie. It's not normal
for a man to do without, you'll fall ill. Now, why
are you going to Versailles?'

He listened to my tale of the king's visit and
Virginie's suggestion that I follow up the promise
of royal favour. 'Do you want a post at the
palace?'

I could think of nothing worse. Charlot's
father, the previous duke, was of the generation
Louis XIV made live there, back in the days
when nobles were still rich and powerful and
influential enough to plot. The Sun King
bankrupted his own nobility with the fees and
attendance he demanded and the retinues he
required his court to keep. I knew the figures.

Almost 2,500 rooms, as many windows, a hundred staircases, more mirrors than had ever been gathered together in one place. He gave them a honeypot, his courtiers, the grandest there had ever been.

'So, why are you going?' Charlot asked.

'Virginie . . . '

'Is my sister. But that doesn't mean I don't know her faults. A worse man might have beaten her. A man worse still might have had her removed to a hospital or found a convent willing to take responsibility.' He looked at my face and knew I'd thought of the second and third if not the first. 'I'll write you a letter for de Caussard, although you'll hardly need it. Still you and me together . . . ' He stopped. 'You know Jerome has control of the appointments now? That he's comptroller of the household.'

'Jerome?'

'He's a marquis now, like you. De Caussard de Sallis. He made a wise marriage to a family with good connections.'

Also like me, I thought. Though Charlot was too polite to say.

'He would do whatever you ask anyway. But he owes me a debt and it won't do any harm to remind him.' Charlot's eyes hardened. 'He bets heavily and he bets often. Avoid saying yes if he suggests a hand of cards.'

I nodded, and left Chateau de Saulx early next morning, riding my horse while the carriage conveying Laurant and Manon trundled along behind me. We arrived at Versailles three days later, having stayed one night at a hotel, another with the mayor of a small city and finally with some distant cousin of Virginie's. The hotel was by far the most comfortable and least irritating.

Versailles was built to stun and impress and overawe, and I felt the effects of all of those by the time I stopped at the edge of the road on a gently sloping hill and heard the carriage draw up behind me.

'Bring Laurant here.' Climbing from the coach, Manon lifted the boy down, walking with him hand in hand until they reached the point where I had dismounted. 'The king lives there,' I told my son. 'With his courtiers and servants. It's the biggest palace in Europe. Quite possibly the biggest in the world.'

His eyes were wide as he stared at the huge baroque-fronted palace, with its almost circular courtyard in front, dotted with the dark specks of carriages. A long walk with wide paths either side of an immense strip of grass led to a huge fountain on a vast and crowded terrace, and where the terrace ended an ornamental lake began. We looked down on the nearest edge of lake and I realised the distance was greater from the fountain to the lake than from my chateau to the village. Hearing the cry of a wild animal and remembering the menageries I realised what it was I saw.

A human zoo built by a king to keep his courtiers captive.

It was not even a prison. Those in prison know that's where they are. That must be true. Animals born to a zoo know no other life; for them captivity is all the life there is and all there has ever been. Looking down at that edifice I knew I could never live there no matter what honour was offered. There was, however, something I wanted to see.

We rode into the courtyard an hour later, having been met by dragoons and escorted to a barrier across the road that lifted only after my identity had been established. A single dragoon rode with me to the next stopping post where I waited until word came that I should be allowed through. Even then there was another barrier. It was captivity so perfect that mechanisms were needed to keep people out. Finally, with a dragoon officer at my side, and his sergeant riding behind Manon's carriage, we reached the courtyard in front of the wide façade and I knew we were but flyspecks to anyone looking down from the hill.

The door under a heavy arch opened and Jerome strode through, his gut bigger than ever and his grin wide enough to make the dragoon officer stare. Jerome grabbed me before I could fully dismount, folding me into a bear hug and pounding my back until I was forced to push away. 'This is your son?' Jerome demanded.

I nodded.

A moment later Laurant was airborne, thrown up and then caught and thrown up again. When Jerome put him down again the boy was quivering with excitement and trapped between laughter and tears.

'He looks just like you.'

'More like his mother.'

Jerome shook his head. 'No,' he said, 'that

expression. He looks like you.' The dragoon officer was glancing between us and I could see him wondering if we'd been treated with enough respect and if his men had been sufficiently polite. I thanked him for his help and he withdrew gratefully, saluting before he went.

'You're important,' I said.

My old school friend grinned widely and shrugged. 'I keep the keys to the honey larder and only I may unscrew the pots. In the best interests of His Majesty, of course. France needs the money and these appointments help fill his purse.' He saw my face and his mouth opened, although he stifled his laugh. Stepping closer, he said, 'You knew all the appointments were paid for? That it costs to have a position in this place?'

I shook my head. 'I thought the king gave them.'

'He does,' Jerome said simply. 'But you give something first.'

'To the king?'

'To His Majesty, of course. To his secretary. To the master of the household. To me . . . There are others possibly, depending on the position. What did you have in mind?'

'Nothing,' I said. 'I came because Virginie suggested it.'

His face stilled and I knew he'd heard rumours of her illness or her madness or her unhappiness, who knew what her affliction had become by the time it reached the court. 'Let me show you some of the palace. What would you like to see?'

'Lions,' Laurant said loudly. 'I want to see the lions.'

Manon dropped to a crouch beside him and spoke softly. When she stood, Laurant was biting his lip and looking serious. Turning to Jerome, he bowed. 'If it is allowed and you don't mind I would like to see the lions.' He said the words so carefully I knew that Manon had put them into his mouth.

Jerome bowed in his turn.

A pair of women turned to look at the comptroller of the palace bowing to a small boy while trying to stifle a grin and one of them smiled, caught my eye and did so again, only this time it was a very different smile. She drifted across, as a ship might drift in the wind if it slipped its moorings, and waited for Jerome to introduce her.

I bowed, she curtsied.

'The lions,' Jerome said firmly. 'We're off to see the lions.'

If the palace was a zoo for people the menagerie at Versailles was a walled city for animals; entered through a huge arch and laid out in the baroque style with roads radiating from a two-storey central pavilion. Houses for animals had brick on three sides, and bars on the side facing the central pavilion. There were woodland areas for wolves, and an enclosure for ostriches where the ground had been scratched bare. Many of the enclosures within the walled city were filled with exotic birds, their wings clipped to stop them flying away.

'Don't say it . . . '

'What?' I looked at Jerome, who was regarding a field of tired-looking flamingos with something approaching sadness. His answer was halted by the sight of a uniformed keeper who bustled towards us and bowed low when he recognised Jerome.

'My lord, I had no idea you were visiting.'

'We're here to see the lions. Well,' Jerome ruffled Laurant's hair, something my son usually hated, but the boy just grinned, 'he is.'

'Of course, of course.'

We were led through a crowd of courtiers watching an elephant being bathed and all bowed low to Jerome, and again to me, because being with Jerome obviously meant I mattered. I noticed this dance of politeness and deceit more these days. The bowing, the curtsies, the words used to turn aside questions and hide lies. When I said this without thinking to Jerome, as I would have said it without thinking at school, he stopped to look at me.

'My country mouse,' he said. 'You should avoid the cats of the city.'

I flushed, because in part it was true. Life at Chateau d'Aumout had softened me and removed my ability to cope with crowds. The press around me, the number of people, the stink in the air . . . Jerome barely noticed but I did.

'You think this is bad,' Jerome said, when I complained of the smell. 'Inside the palace is worse. The air here smells like a spring meadow compared to the stink in any of the corridors. Men piss against walls, women squat in cupboards rather than go outside into the rain.

And the dogs, all those endless little dogs, they shit everywhere.' He saw my horror and smiled. 'Later,' he said. 'You can see for yourself.'

Laurant loved the lions, as I knew he would.

His Majesty had five of them, the biggest collection of any king in Europe. The male lay in lazy splendour while his wives circled slowly and occasionally snarled and bared their teeth at each other. There were no cubs, though the uniformed keeper said he was still hopeful. After the lions, Laurant was taken to see a rhinoceros and an anteater. The latest of the lions was a present from the Bey of Algiers, the rhinoceros the gift of some African king. The wolves came from Russia, but were the children of the children of the children of those originally sent.

'And here we have the tigers,' the uniformed keeper said.

I knew from the way he said it that there was a problem. Jerome, of course, barely noticed. He had always had an ability to ignore anything unpleasant unless it was put directly under his nose. An enviable talent for someone living here. Peering through the bars, Laurant wrinkled his own nose and looked uncertain. 'What's wrong?' he asked.

A huge tigress lay in one corner licking her front leg, which was raw almost to the bone. A cub, perhaps older than a cub, circled the straw in front of her, occasionally bumping into a water bowl left in the middle of the floor.

'She's dying,' the keeper said.

Laurant's lip trembled.

'You shouldn't have shown him this.' Jerome's

212

voice was sharp. 'There are happier sights, animals he'd be glad to see.'

'My lord.' The keeper bowed his apology, then hesitated. 'My lord, what should I do about . . . ?' He indicated the sick animal.

'Let it die.'

'It may take months, my lord. And the dauphin's son . . . '

'What has His Highness to do with this?'

'He cannot bear to see the tigress suffer, my lord. Because of this he has stopped visiting the menagerie . . . ' The dauphin's son was a shy boy of seven or eight, given to tears and only important because his eldest brother had fallen from his rocking horse the previous year, taken a fever and died. Although in his early thirties, the dauphin had consumption. Suddenly Louis-Auguste was next in line after his sick father. Before this he had been virtually ignored.

Jerome looked worried.

'And the cub?' I demanded. 'What's wrong with her?'

'Blind, my lord. Almost entirely. She came to us in her mother's belly and it was a rough trip for both by all accounts.' The mother was a gift from an Indian prince we had been bribing or threatening. The man was now dead, overthrown by his nephew with help from the English. His offering remained, as unhappy, flyblown and worthless as his memory.

'Do what you need to,' Jerome ordered.

Everyone except Laurant knew a death sentence had just been passed for both animals. I thought of the sullen beast caught in the musket

213

fire of soldiers afraid to come too close, of a pistol held to the cub's head. I'll be honest, it was not entirely for my son's sake I spoke out. I wondered about the taste of tiger meat and knew both carcasses would be wasted.

'No,' I said. 'Send the beast to me . . . No, I'll take both with me.' The plan formed as I thought about it. Turning to Jerome, I said, 'Tell his young Highness the tiger and her cub have gone to live happily in the country — where the air will make her better. I will write to him of her happiness in her old age.'

'Jean-Marie . . . '

'I have the space, the gardens are walled . . . We can find her somewhere to live out her days. The cub will do well enough and being blind will limit her range.'

'You're serious about this?'

I nodded. Laurant was grinning, at the thought of having a tiger at home, most probably. And Manon, whom I'd almost forgotten was there, was watching me with a slightly strange expression. I raised my eyebrows, inviting her to speak. The woman hesitated, glanced at Jerome and said, 'Do you mean to make it travel in the coach with us?'

Jerome roared with laughter, but I knew that was not what had been in her mind, and resolved to find out what had been later. Laurant was tugging my hand.

'In the coach,' he begged. 'In the coach.'

'There's not room,' Jerome said diplomatically. 'She would need a carriage of her own . . . We'll lend you one.' He turned to the uniformed keeper and said, 'There must be a cage on wheels or somesuch we could use?'

The man hurried off to find it.

'Show the comte the lions again.' Understanding that Jerome meant Laurant, Manon glanced to me for approval and then hurried off, leaving me with my old school friend, who began smiling. 'You never cease to impress me.'

I wondered what he found impressive but he was still busy smiling. A moment later, he clapped me on the back so hard I stumbled forward and had to grab the bars. The tiger snarled and her cub looked round but that was it.

Felis tigris said their plaque.

'Which one's felis?' Jerome laughed to show it was a joke and he remembered enough Latin to know this was their species. But I liked the conceit and decided that should be their names: the mother would be Felis and the cub Tigris.

'Lord Master of the Menagerie . . . I can't believe I didn't think of it for myself. You have no idea how hard it is to keep coming up with new positions.' He looked thoughtful. 'Perhaps a Lord Master of the Gardens. A Lord Master of the King's Maze. I'll need to think, there must be others. This war with the English is ruining us. How much will you give?'

I looked at him.

'For the position of Lord Master of the Menagerie? Don't worry, there will be no official duties and you don't even have to live here if you don't want, since the king hasn't demanded it . . .'

215

'Jerome, I can give you nothing.'

He scowled in a way I remembered from school. A sudden black cloud that could lead to a fight or blow over. This one blew over as he considered my position. The chateau was mine, given me, as he probably knew, through the good graces of the old duc de Saulx, Virginie's father. The monies from the rents kept me in hunters, books and small objets d'art. They even allowed me to save enough for a porcelain dinner service, which had been my aim for the last five years. This was not the kind of sum that would interest the comptroller of the king's household, and even if it was, I wanted the china more. But I wanted the tiger also, and that must have shown in my eyes because Jerome sighed and chewed at a nail. 'Say the position came with an income of seven and a half thousand livres . . . Let's be generous and make it ten thousand. Say you were to remit this income to my office for ten years . . .'

'You pay me but I don't take the money?'

Jerome nodded happily. 'That would work and it would set a price for similar new positions at court, which is always useful.' He thrust out his hand and I took it, feeling his fingers fold around mine as we shook on this strange agreement. As always he had the strength of a bear.

I stayed one night at Versailles, in a guest room provided on Jerome's orders. My chamber was grand but dusty, foul-smelling from a flowerbed below my window used by many as a latrine. I saw a procession of buttocks that evening, female and male, quickly bared and wiped and put away. I have no idea where Manon and Laurant slept but it was not in the same corridor. In my time at Versailles I ate a breakfast of brioche and cream, an afternoon picnic of chicken breast in aspic, ending the day with pork loin in puff pastry served with clove-spiced apple purée. The brioche melted on the tongue, the chicken was perfectly carved and obviously fresh — and the pork and pastry confection was so hideously overcooked I had the first taste again to make sure. All the food from the kitchens seemed to have an underlying sourness. I wondered if I imagined this, so perfectly did it mirror how I felt about the palace. I was about to ask Jerome what he thought of the pork he was cramming into his mouth and swallowing, without chewing or tasting, when I realised he could tell me nothing useful. In an hour he wouldn't even remember whether it was pork or lamb.

The next morning, quite unexpectedly — to me at least — I was introduced to the dauphin's son as the man who would be giving the sick tiger a happy home. The small boy peered at me nervously, glanced at his grandmother, glanced back and risked a smile. The queen, a round-faced Polish woman, was so surprised she also smiled. Courtiers and servants alike bowed me out of the palace.

To celebrate my new post as Lord Master of the Menagerie I ordered a 200-piece set of Chinese porcelain from the English East India Company, paying their agent half in advance. It was to bear the d'Aumout coat of arms on the rim and a lion, tiger, elephant, rhinoceros or giraffe on the main part of the plate. They were to be painted by local artists from engravings I included with my order.

The porcelain took many months to arrive. Felis and her cub arrived rather sooner. They were with us within the week. Virginie was appalled and Hélène scared but Laurant loved them both. He called Felis *old cat* and Tigris *new cat* and petted the second and helped me dress the sores of the first. I was proud of him.

1763

Virginie

The porcelain dining set with the d'Aumout arms arrived over a year after I ordered it. It had been carried, I was told, by Chinese barge and river boat and on the backs of peasants across wild mountains before being loaded into more river boats and barges to be carried to the coast and loaded onto an English merchantman. It was thus delivered to Bristol from where a French lugger arranged by Emile carried it to Bordeaux from where I went to collect it myself, taking Laurant to see the boats and Manon to look after him while I was busy. Three pieces out of two hundred broke on a journey that took my plates halfway round the world.

I paid the captain for transporting my cargo from England, and stopped at my bank to remit the other half of the original costs to the East India Company's agent in London. Then I had the strange Chinese boxes loaded onto my own carts — well-packed in straw — and sent them back to Chateau d'Aumout with outriders to keep them safe. I kept three plates and three cups from the crate I'd opened last, and we ate our supper from these in the upper room of a hotel I'd taken for myself that morning, having arrived early and told the owner to accept no further guests and dismiss those he already had.

My fear was that the mayor of Bordeaux or governor of the province might hear of my presence and offer me lodgings at their mansions. I had no desire to stay with them nor with the bishop nor any of the local dignitaries. The owner of the hotel glanced doubtfully at my gilded coach with its brightly painted coat of arms when I said I expected my arrival to pass unnoticed, but shut his courtyard gates and warned his servants not to gossip.

His wife took Laurant for the day, I went to oversee the unloading of my porcelain and Manon went to the market at my suggestion, returning with fresh Brie, new-made bread and a fist-sized lump of unsalted butter tied in the muslin in which it had been lifted from the churn. That night we ate at an oak table in my room, Manon, Laurant and me. The table rocked slightly when I leant on it until Manon stuffed the butter muslin under the shortest leg, watched by a dim reflection of herself in a dusty and flyspecked glass.

'Sleep now,' I told Laurant.

He looked up from his bread and his head drooped with tiredness before his mouth could open to protest. Smiling, Manon scooped him up and carried him to a side room. I could hear her chatter and the silence as my son knelt by his bed to say his prayers. She returned, still smiling, and sat when I indicated.

'I should sleep soon, my lord. If you're finished with me.'

Her figure had filled a little in the years she'd been with us, her skin had improved and her hair was almost always clean. Breadcrumbs dusted the front of her dress and she blushed when I leant forward to brush them away. Something put the taste of milk into my mouth and I felt my groin stir as memory matched the taste to that afternoon in the maze when I employed her. She said nothing when I reached for the buttons of her dress. Perhaps she always knew it would come to this. It occurred to me that maybe the easy companionship I found in her company was false and intended to bring me here. Then again, maybe it was real, because without it I'd have coaxed her into my bed long before. Everyone at Chateau d'Aumout assumed I already had.

My wife certainly did.

'My lord . . . ?'

'Jean-Marie. You can call me Jean-Marie when we're alone.'

She smiled and her eyes went bright. Amused, I thought, remembering her wry expression the day I employed her as Laurant's wetnurse. I realised it was more than that. Manon was touched by my words, and I was touched by that fact. We're animals, I know we're animals. As caged by our lives as those in the royal zoo. But the look in Manon's eyes made me wonder, just for that moment, if we weren't also something more.

'Please, my lord . . . '

She shook her head but by then I'd begun unbuttoning her blouse and didn't stop until it was open to the waist and her breasts exposed. Gently, I opened her knees, but only so I could kneel between them and put my mouth to her breast and suck. In my mouth her nipple turned from strawberry to deep raspberry but the taste I wanted was missing. I had sweat and what had to be soap from washing her dress or herself. Reaching behind me, I found the Brie and broke off a fragment, sucking her nipple through it. She tasted almost as she had the day I took the drop of milk on my finger.

Manon smiled when she realised what I was doing.

You know the peasant saying? If you can't imagine how neighbouring vineyards can produce such different wines put one finger in your woman's quim and another up her arse, then taste both and stop asking stupid questions . . . My fingers found both vineyards. At the front, she tasted salt as anchovy and as delicious. At the rear, bitter like chocolate and smelling strangely of tobacco. My tongue explored each and she shivered at one and giggled with embarrassment at the other. 'My lord, please . . . '

'Call me Jean-Marie.'

Perhaps I was unfair, with her face-down on the table, her skirt drawn up at the back, to expect her to call me that so soon. 'You like me?' she asked.

I stilled, wondering at her question. I'd always liked her. But there was more to her query than that. I could have had her years before. I could have had any one of my servants. I knew men who would have taken all of them without thinking. 'Since I first saw you,' I said. Manon had her own bed in Laurant's room but I scooped her up in my arms and took her to

222

mine. The heavy oak frame supporting the horsehair mattress had probably seen its share of couplings, although few as hungry as ours. Before we began, I ripped away her skirt and, having stood her naked in the middle of my bedroom floor, examined her by the light of a candle. So young, so perfect. At last I put the candle down and slid two of her fingers inside her, tasting them afterwards. The second time I took her fingers, she slipped free and took two of my fingers in turn, slipping those inside her and locking her thighs. What I remember at this distance is the taste of her nipples, the richness between her legs and the bready sweetness of her breath as I slammed into her and heard her gasp.

'My lord, if I get pregnant . . . '

'I'll acknowledge the child.'

I rode her hard, ploughing deep and savouring the feeling of myself inside her. The heat was incredible, the sense of flesh dizzying. After a few moments, Manon's legs hooked over mine and she ground herself against me, her grinding ever more urgent. She spent fiercely, bucking beneath me with her nails in my back to hold me still while she wrung the last from her moment.

Taking her arms, I put them flat above her and held Manon down as I took my turn, coming with a fierceness beyond anything I could remember even when young. She let me sprawl on her a while, then shifted as if to say I should move as she wanted to sleep, which she did with her back to me, her buttocks against my thighs, and a warning that I should be careful where I jabbed that thing of mine. At dawn, I remembered to ask about the daughter who'd gone to live with her mother the day she came to the chateau to look after Laurant.

'She died that first winter,' Manon said.

Her one remaining link with her old life had succumbed to fever and been buried in the village churchyard. I felt ashamed I didn't know that, and hadn't thought before to ask. She heard out my muttered apology and her reply was sharp. Why would I know? Why would she expect me to ask? She dozed for an hour in my arms, her body soft under my hands and her rebuke sharp in my mind.

I didn't know it then but Manon changed me that night.

Whether she changed me into something better rather than something simply different is hard to say. I would tell you if I knew how to judge the change. I was too drunk on the sweetness of her body and what I saw as the rightness of her rebuke to do more than concentrate on the mechanism of re-making myself in the years that followed. As if an architect decided to replace one bridge with another without first asking if the bridge had ever been needed . . . All I knew was that I liked her honesty. I liked the way Manon looked me in the face and spoke her mind. All the careful courtesies with which I approached Virginie were missing. It was as if that night with Manon had removed a veil and let me see another person for the first time. There was a fierceness to this gaze. An animal rawness to life that some might prefer to keep hidden.

On my return I had silt dug from the stagnant river that gave rise to the poisoned air that infected Manon's daughter. I had the roads widened from the chateau to the village and from the village to the town beyond. I gave the town the right to hold its own markets every second Friday, I issued licences for more mills and reduced *banals*, the duties peasants paid to have their flour ground by my miller and their bread baked in one of the communal bakeries. I also opened the forest to scavenging for wood and mushroom. I reserved the right to the boar and the deer, and when they took those anyway I let it pass, unless the act was contemptuously open and thrown in my face. There were riots in Normandy that summer, which spread south to Bordeaux. They never reached Chateau d'Aumout.

Things at home were less happy.

Virginie disliked my tiger cub and had tried to ban Laurant from playing with the animal. He ignored her. She cried when a cart arrived from Versailles with half a dozen sad flamingos, which can be found in this part of France anyway but had obviously hated life at court. Within a month they lost their ghost-white hue, began to regain their pink and no longer looked like moth-eaten relics dragged down from an attic. Four lived, and I ate the others, cooking their tongues in the Roman style, using a recipe from Apicius. The fat, which was rich as goose fat, I drained into a bowl, let set and kept for special occasions.

Virginie made clear she had no interest in roads or river flows, in improvements to our estate, the animals that now arrived every few weeks or so, or my recipes. After I began telling her how I planned to adapt the Apicius recipe, she turned on me. 'What you fail to understand is I have no interest in *any* of your hobbies.'

I cooked the dish all the same.

To cook flamingo tongue

First a note — the tongue is fat and runs along a deep central groove in the bird's heavy lower bill. This plumpness is what makes it attractive to cooks. Take one tongue per guest and scrub well with a mixture of equal parts salt, water and white wine vinegar. Soak the clean tongues in fresh water overnight and then boil in new water for at least an hour. Let cool and carefully strip away the outer skin. Slice each tongue diagonally into finger-width sections and braise in freshly made butter over a high heat. Serve with an already-prepared leek and date sauce that has been flavoured with coriander, mint, cumin, crushed black pepper and good wine vinegar. (Adjust quantities based on the number of tongues, but allow at least eight dates per tongue and replace leek with onion if preferred.) As an alternative, fry one red onion per guest in a shallow pan with cumin, ginger, saffron, a little crushed dried chilli and crushed black pepper, until onion is clear. Add cubes of tongue and braise well, along with three diced tomatoes

226

per tongue, and one large wine glass of water. Now add twelve dried dates and eight dried apricots per guest and cook very slowly for at least an hour. Serve à l'Indien (over rice). *Tastes like chicken.*

After this meal my wife withdrew into herself until she was a ghost of the woman she'd been, and that woman was already a ghost of the girl I'd first met. Becoming more worried than ever, I wrote to Charlot, who wrote to his sister, who wrote a polite and distant reply that read as if addressed to a passing acquaintance. Charlot quoted extracts in his return letter.

Life continues as it always has, she wrote. *When not scribbling his recipes, Jean-Marie works incessantly for the good of others, Laurant continues to grow* ... The only time Virginie seemed animated was when she mentioned Hélène, who had grown pretty and remained as clever and industrious as she'd always been. She hoped Hélène had a happy life and Charlot and I read her own unhappiness in that line. What was to follow came as no surprise to Charlot and that was a huge help to me. He turned aside the gossip and kept rumour at bay. The fact he came to see me, stayed with me and left reluctantly, swearing his friendship, helped protect my good name.

On a Sunday afternoon, after her usual attendance at mass in the morning and a light lunch alone in her room, Virginie took a book of poems to a bench by the lake where Tigris was not allowed. She disliked Tigris and resented my having made such a fuss of burying Felis, the cub's mother, the previous week. I had my reasons, of course. The cooks were used to my peculiarities and thought little of my retiring to the smallest of the kitchens to work on a sauce. Obviously, it was not the sauce that interested me but what it covered. Tiger meat turned out to be sour and stringy. Well, meat from this one did. But it tasted well enough fried with onions and seasoned with black pepper and turmeric. I chose the spices for the colour of her coat, obviously.

Maybe Virginie did read poems for a while. I'm not sure when she took Laurant from the nursery but it was Manon who told me she'd sent him up for an afternoon's rest and he was missing. Maybe I knew. The bench by the little lake was certainly the first place I went looking. I went alone, having told Manon to search the house without alarming the servants. There would be time enough for that later if necessary. I saw the splash of white in the water before I was halfway along the path. I ran, what man wouldn't, recognising his wife's dress rippling like weed on the surface of a lake? Of Laurant there was no sign.

'Here, Papa,' he called when I shouted his name.

By the time I reached him he'd scrambled to his feet, but he'd been sat on the far side of a beech tree peeling the nuts that littered the ground around him, discarding the husk of the nut he'd chosen before finding another. 'You're meant to be resting.'

'Mama said . . . ' he protested, lip quivering.

Scooping him up and keeping his head turned away from the lake I carried him back through the formal gardens and up the stone steps to the chateau. Manon stood near the top, one hand on a balustrade, her other against the base of one of the urns that broke up the balustrade. She must have seen what was in my eyes because she took him without being told and carried him inside. I could hear her chatting as they disappeared through a salon door towards the hall and the main stairs up to the nursery.

Virginie hung face-down in the water, her arms limply at her sides, her back bobbing with the waves that the wind made and her hands and feet slightly below the surface, one shoe missing. I found it on the lake's edge, which was where I dragged her, surprised at how heavy the water in her dress made her. I was trying hard to avoid the unthinkable but then found myself thinking it anyway. I was lucky to find Laurant still alive. Perhaps she'd taken pity; perhaps she simply wanted him close so she could say goodbye. He'd told me as I carried him that she'd said he should wait behind the tree.

She'd known what she was doing.

The little lake at the end of the formal gardens was reserved for family, a place where we could go to be out of the gaze of those who kept the chateau functioning. It had once been one of Virginie's favourite spots . . . The sun was hot and the afternoon young and the idea came to me as I struggled to lift her. Virginie believed, and if the Church knew she'd taken her own life they would refuse to bury her in hallowed ground. For her sake, for Laurant and Hélène . . .

Removing my shoes and stockings, I slipped into the water and unbuttoned her dress. My fingers shook and the buttons were slippery but in the end it was done. Her chemise was easier to remove. Her body was unchanged by motherhood. Her hips no thinner or thicker than the first time I saw her. She bobbed in the tiny waves, her legs trapped by the shallows, her hips and back and shoulders free-floating. She'd come to the lake with her hair undressed and it spread across the water as if she slept on a pillow. I felt the tears well up and wondered how much of this was my fault. There would be time for that later. For now, I needed to hurry.

Leaving Virginie where she floated, I took her dress and wrung it out as carefully as I could, removing most of the water. I was afraid the stitches at the hems would burst with my twisting but they held and when I shook the dress out to remove the creases it was already halfway dry. I spread the dress on a bush in direct sunlight, as I had done once before many years ago on a river's edge. Having wrung out her chemise in the same way, I hung that beside her dress and went to wash the mud from her shoes. Our last hour alone was spent with me sat on the bench where my wife should be sitting, while her clothes dried in the sun and she floated in the water, as much in the shade as I could manage. The lake did more than hide her from idle gaze; it cooled her body and kept it from spoiling. I rolled her over once, knowing how blood could pool in resting meat, and wondered at my coldness. I should be weeping or on my knees and yet my initial tears were already drying and my main concern was how fast the dress would dry.

It was late afternoon before her dress and undergarments and shoes were ready and I could pull Virginie from the lake and rest her in the shade of the bush on which her clothes had been drying. I drove what water I could from her lungs by pressing on her back, and then dressed her clumsily, pulling the chemise over her head and buttoning the dress. Her shoes were clean enough for my servants not to notice one had been in the water and the other lost in mud at the edge of the lake. I wrung out her hair and dried it with the inside of my jacket, combing it with my fingers as I'd done when we were young. Finally, I sat her on the bench and took the upturned book of poems and rested them on her lap, folding one arm across the book. The sadness took me then. This was the Virginie I knew, sat with her book on a bench in the gardens. Tears rolled down my face and I knelt beside her, drying my tears in her lap.

That was how Manon and Laurant, Charlot and his family found me.

The duke had come from Saulx, drawn apparently by the flatness of Virginie's reply to his letter and the sadness of my last to him. Lisette was with him, and their son. The boys had Tigris with them on a lead. She was getting too big to be led but her blindness made her

231

more docile than nature intended. They were grinning. At least they were until Charlot froze and ordered them back to the house. Manon took one look at me in tears beside Virginie and said she'd take them. After a glance from Charlot, his wife said she would return to the chateau too.

'When?' he asked, once we were alone.

'Just now. I thought she was sleeping.'

He looked down at his sister, eyes closed in the shade, her hand draped across a book split at the spine and worn at the edges from use, and smiled sadly. We both knew what Charlot was thinking, that she looked happier now than at any time in the last five years. Losing Jean-Pierre began her sadness, having Laurant made it worse. Only I knew it had taken the lake to end it.

'I'll stay with you until the funeral.'

He took my hand as if to shake it and kept it gripped. The years had given his face a gravitas his youth had never hinted at. Somehow he'd turned from the wild one, dangerous and beautiful, to a solid member of the nobility, a counterweight to the dissolute fops who'd encouraged the king so disastrously in our recent and ruinous wars. His friendship could make or break a man's life and prospects, and looking into his eyes I knew I had his friendship for life. Whatever doubts he might have had about my marriage to Virginie, and I had no idea if he had had doubts, they were gone. He gripped my hand one last time and let it drop.

'Do you want me to stay with her while you send for servants?'

I shook my head. 'You go,' I told him. 'I'd like a few last minutes alone.'

Charlot looked at me with pity and turned away, his back heavy and his head bowed with grief as he left the garden Virginie and I had made for ourselves when we were young enough not to know how young we were, and life was happier. I knelt beside her, and breaking the private habits of a lifetime, because I only paid public dues to religion, I closed my eyes and prayed. When I opened them again it was to stare across the lake into the bushes beyond. There was a flash of white as a small girl stepped back into the shadows. Hélène. How long she'd been watching, I had no idea.

1763
Funeral

I've been told that François Couperin cannot really be considered the heir of Jean-Philippe Rameau, but since they were both French, both famous and both composed for the harpsichord people talk of them as if they're interchangeable. Virginie certainly spoke of them as if they were brothers, Rameau the elder and a little more serious, Couperin younger and known to be flighty, although Couperin died the year I first met her brother and Rameau was dead before she was born.

I hired musicians from Bordeaux who claimed to have played at Versailles and charged accordingly. The afternoon of Virginie's funeral they alternated between her favourite two composers and the women smiled at me through tears and the men took me aside and said seriously it was touching how deeply I'd cared for her.

Only Charlot muttered that he'd always hated that tinkling rubbish but if his sister had liked it he supposed I was allowed. Emile came across to say he remembered Virginie playing the piece the musicians were playing. No doubt he was right.

What matters is intelligence and ability, not bloodline.

That should have been a harmless enough

statement from a man like Emile Duras. His grandfather and father had been lawyers, he was a lawyer . . . If I'd been feeling difficult I'd have said he'd already established his bloodline — a bloodline of the law. In time he could hope to become noblesse de robe. If not him, then his son certainly.

Instead I just nodded. We were at Virginie's funeral and I was making my round of those remaining at the chateau. Many had come to the church, the law stating that weddings and funerals must be open to all; fewer came to the feast afterwards, but still enough to make a sizeable crowd. It was inevitable Emile would be invited. He was my oldest friend and had known Virginie when she was young. If our lives had drifted apart it was because they no longer ran on parallel lines.

Emile was someone now. A representative of the local assembly, as well as a successful lawyer. I knew he had ambitions to represent the third estate at the assembly in Bordeaux. He wore expensive shoes with pompadour heels in cork and leather that added a good three inches to his height. His coat and waistcoat were dark blue with fine black embroidery on the edges, deep cuffs, and pocket flaps. His waistcoat reached his thigh. A fob chain vanished inside a pocket. Seeing my glance he pulled out a small pocket watch. 'Thomas Mudge, London,' he told me. 'It has a detached lever escapement. It's the newest thing. No one in Paris is doing this yet.'

'Monsieur L'Ingénieur.'

He flushed slightly at my gentle mockery but I

could see he was pleased. I mentioned a problem with a weir on one of my rivers and he listened carefully and made two useful suggestions: that I rebuild the weir in brick, and that I consider straightening and widening that bit of river and linking it to the Canal du Midi. The frequency of barges would increase and the extra revenue collected in taxes could pay for the river-widening and weir. I thanked him for his good advice. He'd married again after the death of his first wife and now had a son to go with his daughters.

Before Emile and I talked I'd been watching his son. A handsome young boy of eleven or twelve — already close to his father in height and probably destined to be taller. Looking at Emile's wife I could see where Georges Duras got his height, his figure and his blue eyes.

The boy was dancing attendance on Hélène like one born to be a courtier. And though my nine-year-old daughter pretended not to notice I could see that she was flattered. Smiles had been rare since her mother died. Manon had tried talking to her and got nowhere. Charlot's wife, whom Hélène adored, did little better. But here she was, talking to Emile's son as if they'd known each other forever.

'Let them be,' Charlot said, materialising at my side.

I smiled, took his advice, felt grateful my daughter was prepared to talk to anyone, and wished the day would be over. Only when the last of the mourners had gone would I have my own chance to talk to Hélène, who'd been avoiding me, and to Manon, who was doing the same. A week had past since Virginie died and most of that had been taken up by administration and formalities. Jerome had already warned me the second week was worse. He based this on losing his oldest sister but said he imagined losing one's wife would be much the same. He came, of course. Jerome was one of us. An original.

'I hear you've reduced the banals again . . . '

Charlot meant the duties peasants paid to have their flour ground by my miller and their bread baked in one of the communal bakeries. 'The last harvest was bad,' I told him. 'The one before little better.'

He sighed and patted me on my shoulder. 'Peasants will always tell you the last harvest was bad, this year's will be terrible and next year's probably worse.'

'I should talk again to Emile.'

Charlot smiled. 'Ever the diplomat,' he said, before returning to his wife and leaving me wondering what was diplomatic about what I'd just said. He smiled at me across the room to say he was with me, that all of my friends were with me, as Emile turned and smiled to see me coming. His was a tighter smile. We'd seen almost nothing of each other since Laurant was born and little enough before that. He had his law offices in Paris and Limoges. I'd been told his company acted for wine shippers in their disputes with vineyard owners and had handled more than one complicated inheritance case. He was known to be clever, none of us had ever doubted that, but in the intervening years he'd developed a reputation for ruthlessness as well. He left his enemies not only poor but broken.

All the same, Emile smiled. And glancing to where my daughter and his son talked — their heads close and their voices low — said the words that shaped the last third of my life. 'What matters is intelligence and ability, not bloodline. Don't you agree?'

Charlot's father would have regarded that as blasphemy, but I was not Charlot's father or even Charlot. So I nodded and thanked him for coming, in such a way as to avoid implying that I'd thought he might not. We gripped hands and he told me how sorry he was, how he knew what it was like to lose a wife, how impossible he found it to consider life without her replacement. Of course, he understood things had been complicated . . . Of course he did, everyone in the room did. People danced around the subject of Virginie's illness with varying degrees of delicacy and Emile showed more finesse than most. I turned the conversation to more general matters and somehow we ended up talking about religion, a subject on which Emile was indiscreet. 'I'm not sure the people can cope without the idea of God,' I told him. 'Without spiritual heights to which they can aspire, like young men looking at a rock face and daring each other to climb. If we abandon our belief in God we become God and take his powers.'

Emile laughed. 'Don't tell me you've started to believe?'

I stared at him. 'I've always believed.'

'In God the father, God the son and God the holy ghost?'

'Of course not. But in something. We all have to believe in something.'

'If we don't . . . ?' He let his question hang.

'We start believing only in ourselves.'

'Belief in God is the cause of war, superstition, irrationality . . . And has been the cause of those since time began.' What Emile spoke was treason, and if not treason, then certainly blasphemy, but I'd heard it from him so often it barely registered. He was hunched forward, knuckles white around his wine glass from where his fists were clenched, like a boy trying to make an impression on the classroom. As he'd been when I first met him, a lawyer's son sent to live among the children of impoverished nobles.

'Without God the wars will get even worse.'

'We'll see,' he said. And there our conversation ended. I told him there were things I needed to do and he nodded at my convenient lie. We clasped hands one last time and I crossed the room to talk to Père Laurant, who had made the trip from Paris. Each year seemed to age him faster than the one before and listening to him it was easy to understand why. He'd gone to the Sorbonne foreseeing a life of study and found himself in a world of politics, backbiting and intrigue made all the worse for being regarded as irrelevant by everyone else. Apparently his recent promotion was a poisoned chalice and a dozen atheists and heathens were waiting for him to fail. He added that he was drunk, apologised for his indiscretion and agreed with my suggestion that I have a servant show him to his chamber so he could rest. This was my last unwanted conversation of the day. After that, I bade my guests goodbye, Emile and his son among them, and went to repair the damage with my lover and my daughter.

1768
Mission to Corsica

Five years separated my bidding goodbye to the last of those unwanted guests and a letter arriving from the king. Five years in which I tried to re-make my heart and settled instead for a comfortable routine. Virginie's death made me rich; that is, I'd always been rich if you regarded her money as mine, but now it was truly mine and I no longer felt guilty about spending it. So I had the kitchens rebuilt, installed a huge ice house, extended the herb garden and had a second lake dug to house aquatic mammals sent from Versailles. I even had a wall thrown right around a small wood to give Tigris somewhere safe to wander.

Manon took the place of my official mistress without being asked, and because I'd done my public grieving when Virginie was still alive, few understood how hard her death hit me. Only once did the grief fight free; on a night when I walked down to the lake to get clear sight of the constellations. Walking back beneath the stars I started to sob, fierce tears mixing with ferocious anger. At what, I didn't know. At Virginie leaving me perhaps. I felt a sense of abandonment and guilt. Only next morning did I wonder if perhaps I'd been the one to abandon her. Either way, we forsook each other before death gave us no choice.

I married Manon eighteen months after Virginie died, in a quiet ceremony in my own chapel. It was a morganatic marriage, as I was noble and she was not. She took the title vicomtesse with the king's permission, although most called her marquise from politeness. I doubt my servants understood the difference anyway. Charlot came to visit us twice, Jerome once. I met Emile in Bordeaux and we ate at his hotel, an indifferent meal to accompany indifferent conversation. I wondered later if he found the few hours we spent together as difficult as I did. Manon took over the running of the chateau and responsibility for Hélène. There was a familiarity in the way she talked to me that troubled some of our neighbours. Our conversation lacked the formality found in their marriages, our affections and occasional irritations, best kept behind closed doors, bled into open conversation. So be it. We were shaped by how we'd begun.

I started to think of my life as clay. That day by the dung heap, my life was entirely malleable, soft to the touch and easy to shape. Slowly it dried and grew stiff, until I began to accept the shape it had because change was hard. One day in early summer, Manon found me in a potter's shop, stripped to my shirt, which was splashed with clay water like earthy blood, the wheel spinning erratically as I treadled. A lump of drying clay twisted and twitched beneath my fingers. '*Jean-Marie.*' She realised there were people around us, the potter's family, his neighbours, a ragged apprentice younger than my son, and her tone softened. 'What are you doing?' From the way the apprentice hid behind Manon's skirts, I wondered if he was the one sent to tell her where she might find me.

'Wondering if my life is really like clay.'

She looked at the misshapen mess under my fingers and the potter hastened to assure her that working the wheel was hard and mine was a very good first effort, many did far worse in their first attempts and not everyone had the skill. I thanked him for his time, which embarrassed him, and washed my hands under a squeaking pump outside. The sun was hot enough to turn the remaining splashes of clay on my wrists to earthy scabs. They tasted of metals and salt, like raw liver or fresh blood.

Père Laurant, who now styled himself Maître Laurant, wrote from the Sorbonne to say he heard I worked simply like a man of the people, stripped to the waist, and my love for the natural over the artificial was an inspiration. I don't bother to reply. That didn't stop him writing a pamphlet proclaiming the best of the French aristocracy as instinctively noble and quoting me as a suitably Rousseauian example. Jean-Jacques' *Du Contract Social ou Principes de Droit Politique* had been published a few years before, and, like others, Père Laurant was busy trying to dress what already existed in new clothes to show we already had the framework for creating the best of all possible worlds.

His pamphlet and my foolery with the potter's wheel were behind the royal letter, although I only discovered that later. By the time it arrived, the estate was running smoothly, the animals had settled, even the proudest of my neighbours had begun to think of Manon as the chatelaine of Chateau d'Aumout, as long as they didn't think too deeply. There was no reason for me to worry about leaving her, not that I was presented with a choice. But still I wondered at the words. *The king requires your presence.* That evening Manon asked me what was wrong and took the letter, and my silence as permission to read.

'You must go.'

'Of course I must. I just wish I knew what he wanted.' I was fifty, married for the second time, with a son to take my place and a daughter soon ready to be wed. I had my kitchens, my recipes and my mountain of notes. I was a good subject of Louis XV, quiet and unambitious and untroublesome. What could the king possibly want with me?

★   ★   ★

Manon and I make love that night and I doze in her arms, my wrist still trapped by her thighs, her fingers stroking my neck. 'It might do you good,' she says.

I drag myself out of sleep enough to be querulous and feel her smile, her hand stilling for a moment as she waits for me to answer. The peacocks are noisy outside despite the darkness of the night and I can hear sabots crunch on gravel. A kitchen maid returning from a tavern or a groom sneaking into the village. In a quiet part

244

of my mind, where Charlot is still thin and Jerome fierce, Virginie beautiful and I'm young, I envy them.

'I like it here.'

'No,' she says. 'You're comfortable here, there's a difference. Cross your heart and tell me honestly that you're happy.'

'I'm happy enough.'

Manon sighs. 'What is it? Is it us?'

I assure her that it isn't. And in the aftermath of that, because Manon's good at letting silences lengthen and I always feel the need to fill them, I admit that nothing seems to matter as much as it once did. My waist has thickened in the years since Virginie died, the stubble beneath my wig has thinned and grey shows in the fur of my chest and groin. I tell Manon that I know I've acquired the habits middle age brings; that I eat more and taste less, I walk the same path through the gardens after lunch, lost in my thoughts and no longer see the trees and water around me. Sometimes Laurant trots at my side, very occasionally Hélène will deign to walk with me, but Tigris always comes. Her head nudging up under my hand if I ever forget she is there.

'All the more reason to go.'

'What about Tigris . . . ?'

'You should think of your children first,' Manon says. She prods my ribs with her elbow less gently than she could. 'You should think of me.'

'You would hate court,' I tell her. 'And Hélène is exactly the wrong age. As for Laurant, I'm taking him with me.' Manon has other ideas. In the end I agree to leave Laurant to keep Tigris company. In return, Manon will protect Hélène, and I will hurry home as soon as I'm allowed. I'm required to make two promises: that I will spend as much time saying goodbye to my children as I do to my big cat, and that I will spend as long saying goodbye to my daughter as I do to my son. Rolling off Manon, which is where I've been while negotiating this, I kiss her cheek and feel her arms close around me.

'Come back happier,' she whispers in my ear. I tell her I will and believe it. Visiting Versailles always makes me grateful I don't have to live there.

★ ★ ★

'You are the marquis d'Aumout?' The boy who asks is about Hélène's age — although a boy and a girl at fourteen are very different beasts. He has the hesitancy some boys get at that age, his voice is a scratchy embarrassment. We have not met for six years but the retinue behind him proclaims his rank.

'Yes, Your Highness.'

The dauphin smiles. 'The marquis de Caussard said you were coming. How is . . . ?' He sees me smile in turn. 'The old cat is well?'

'The old one died, Highness. She was old and sick. But the young one is as proud as a princess.' Behind him courtiers stiffen. 'And as beautiful,' I add hastily.

The dauphin laughs. 'I wish I could see her.'

'I will have her portrait painted for you.'

246

My promise earns me a warm smile and a slight nod that I answer with a bow, and then the prince and his entourage move on, some smiling, others casting dark glances as if the dauphin's kindness to me offends them. A few seconds later the rose garden is empty and I can hear their voices and laughter from a fountain beyond a hedge. If anything, Versailles feels a little more crowded and looks a little more tawdry than I remember. The laughter has a sycophantic edge. Unless I am simply more jaded.

'That was well done.'

The words come from behind me, and turning I see Jerome leaning on the arm of a blonde-haired girl who looks, at first glance, little older than Hélène. When I glance again I realise she might just be in her twenties. She shares startling blue eyes and a slightly pink complexion with a young man standing behind her. Her neckline is a little too low and the velvet of his frock coat slightly faded. She drops me a curtsy so perfect she must have grown up at court. The young man's bow is equally polished.

'You can go,' Jerome tells them and they walk from the rose garden together. The girl touches the boy on his wrist to stop him looking back.

'How was your journey?' Jerome asks me.

'Long, uncomfortable, boring.'

He laughs, as if at a joke, and asks what I know of Corsica, laughing again when I tell him the national dish is *brocciu*, a ricotta-like cheese made from goat's milk. And the island is famous for the quality of its ham, which is made from pigs fed in winter on sweet chestnuts and grazed in summer on the *maquis*, the wild herbs of the Corsican uplands.

'You've read Diderot's encyclopedia.'

'I wrote that entry.'

He glances around him. 'You understand the encyclopedia is banned?'

'I understand the king has his own set, as did la pompadour. No doubt you have copies of your own.'

'That is beside the point.' I'd always thought he'd grow to resemble the bear we'd joked he was in our youth but Jerome looks more like a bullfrog, all puffed chest and round belly and fat cheeks. It is three years since I've seen Charlot and I wonder how he's aged and whether I've aged this badly as well.

'You're looking fine,' Jerome says.

'And you,' I lie in my turn.

'We'll play a hand later?'

I remember Charlot's warning from years before and shake my head. 'I'm useless at cards,' I say. 'I always have been. You know that.' Jerome's patronage comes at a price in this place, you play cards and his winnings are a tax. But I want nothing from him, and he wants something from me. I don't see why he should have my money as well.

'Still the country mouse.'

'Says the palace cat . . . '

He laughs, and nods towards a path. I follow him towards a maze and guards step back from the entrance to let us pass. They accept Jerome's order that no one but His Majesty or the dauphin should be allowed inside. 'Now we can talk freely,' he says, leading me deeper, until he reaches a bench and slaps himself down and lifts his wig to wipe his skull.

'This has to do with His Majesty?'

Jerome looks at me, obviously puzzled.

'I had a message that His Majesty required my presence.'

'That's a form of words,' he says with a sigh. 'I sent for you.'

'Why?'

'Because I've bought Corsica.'

Jerome's story is long and complex, or maybe it's short and simple and I'm simply too removed from politics to grasp it easily. He tells me Corsica has been a self-proclaimed republic for the last thirteen years, ruled by president Pasquale Paoli. This I know. I admire Paoli. Jerome doesn't. As far as Jerome is concerned, Paoli is the only man in the world rash enough to let women vote in local elections. Worse than this, Paoli has established a constitution based on Voltaire. The real owner of Corsica is Genoa, only that Italian city is too weak to take it back from the rebels.

'So Genoa sold its claim to you?'

'Its *rights*,' Jerome said. 'But yes, basically that's it.'

'What has any of this to do with me?'

'I want you to negotiate the island's surrender.'

'Jerome.'

'I'm serious. The king wants this . . . ' He caught my glance and shrugged, his shoulders heavy inside his brocade frock coat. 'Well, I want this and the king agrees. He will raise Manon to the nobility, confirm her title as marquise, recognise as noble any children you might have ... ' Something must have shown in my face because he nodded. 'Ahh,' he said. 'I wondered. Charlot said he thought you were simply being careful.'

'We can't have ... '

'*You* can,' Jerome said.

'And Manon once did. But between us, nothing.'

He clapped me heavily on the shoulder. 'You have an heir. That's enough.'

'How am I to do this?'

'You agree then?'

'Do I have an option?'

Jerome shook his head. 'But I expected you to put up more of a fight.'

The Fall

I remember that I want to see the menagerie. Of course I do, but before we part that night, and I'm left in a squalid room that stinks so fiercely from a nearby latrine that no amount of gilded cherubs or paintings of pink-nippled shepherd-esses can make good the smell, Jerome tells me he's arranged for me to ride in the royal forest instead. This is a privilege apparently, one reserved for those in favour with the king. Two friends of his will accompany me. He knows they are looking forward to my company.

'You're sure I can't supply you with servants?'

My room has a commode, a basin for washing, a jug already full of tepid water. My cases have been brought up from the coach. 'No,' I say, shaking my head and wishing only for some peace. 'I can manage for myself.'

'As you will.'

Morning comes and with it a knock at my door. Jerome has sent me a serving maid whether I want one or not. She changes the water, empties my commode, draws back the curtains having asked permission. She leaves when I tell her she can go. A second knock an hour later produces a liveried messenger with a note from Jerome saying he's waiting, and Armand and Héloïse with him, if I'd like to join them. Since I'm already wearing breeches and my riding coat I have the messenger show me to the stables, a set of low buildings I would never have found for myself.

'Sleepyhead,' Jerome says.

There's something forced about his greeting but I smile anyway and nod to his companions, the young man and fair-haired girl I saw briefly the day before. The boy bows and she curtsies and grooms bring out our horses, already saddled and brushed to the shine of newly fallen chestnuts. Jerome's animal is huge, and still it dips dangerously under his bulk as he clambers onto his saddle. The young man mounts easily and I realise the girl is waiting for me to help her. She smiles her thanks and Jerome laughs.

'Héloïse de Plessis,' he says. 'And Armand de Plessis. There's no need for me to give your name. Everyone knows the marquis d'Aumout.'

We set off with a single servant on his own animal, leading a second animal loaded with wicker panniers. Jerome and I lead, the other two ride behind us and the servant and the pack horse go last. Courtiers bow or nod stiffly to Jerome as he passes. He barely notices. The royal forest is a wood filled with neat little bridges over bubbling streams. A grotto squints from between mossy rocks. A spring rises high on a grassy slope where no spring could rise and trickles over gleaming gravel into a little pool below. Butterflies fill the air around us.

'It gets better further on,' Jerome growls. He kicks his mount and we keep riding until we reach a clearing in the middle of a patch of what could almost be a real forest, but for its neatly cleared paths and lack of charcoal burners. 'We'll breakfast here,' he says. A blanket is spread over the leaf mould, the first of the wicker baskets is opened and the servant produces fresh bread, newly made butter and jam. A bottle of Champagne follows and elegant little glasses. The wine is cold and the glasses sparkling clean.

'Your health,' Jerome says.

I return his toast, accept the toasts of his two companions and turn my attention to the bread and jam. They are as perfect as bread and jam can be. A surprise after the unpleasantness of my room, and my memories of the food at Versailles having an unidentifiable but definite sourness. When Jerome is certain I've eaten my fill — only the first few mouthfuls were really satisfying — our servant packs the basket and we mount again and ride deeper into forest. An hour later we stop to look at a waterfall. And then again to look at a pond with a fat carp that circles sadly until Héloïse tosses it scraps of bread and water bulges as it surfaces to take her bounty. An hour later still, we stop at a blasted oak so picturesquely stark that I look for chisel marks or proof it's been artificially scorched on the side that is burnt. The next stop is for lunch amid the mossy ruins of a little chapel. Jerome's servant unpacks the other hamper to produce more bread, Roquefort wrapped in linen and another bottle of Champagne. As always the Roquefort is sublime. Even after so many years the first mouthful, like the first sip of Champagne, sends a shiver down my neck.

When we remount, I expect Jerome to head for the next pretty sight in what I suspect is a well-trodden path through the beautiful forest. Instead he tells me he needs to talk privately with Armand and asks if I'd mind Héloïse leading me home? By which he means Versailles presumably. I shrug, before realising that's impolite and she's done nothing to deserve my irritation. I say I'd be happy to ride back beside her. Jerome tells me the servant will find his own way. He adds that we'll meet again that evening for supper, spurs his horse and leaves without another word. Armand gives Héloïse a single glance and trots after him.

Our journey back is uneventful for the first hour. We've gone deeper into the forest than I realise and we ride slowly, grateful for the shade the trees give us from the sun overhead. I'm almost dozing in the saddle when Héloïse gives a little cry and wrenches at her reins, dragging her horse's head to one side. Her animal shies and Héloïse is already slipping when its rear hoof comes down wretchedly and it whinnies in pain, bolting in the same moment towards a low-hanging branch. Héloïse shouts in real fear and twists awkwardly in the saddle as she tries to dismount. But a side saddle is no easier to dismount than mount and I've kicked my horse after hers before I realise it. I join her at the moment she falls, her foot still in her stirrup.

Sometimes the body acts ahead of the mind, which makes me believe the brain is not the body's sole coachman. I fling myself from my saddle without any thought for the conse-quences, and there will be many and they will stretch beyond trying to save a young girl from being hurt. Landing beside her horse's head, I grab its bridle, but this only infuriates the beast, which begins to rear, so I grab its skull instead, clinging tight with my body covering its eyes. The animal shies and shakes its neck and beneath its skin I can feel every one of a dozen muscles thick as a ship's rope. A slighter man would have been thrown and a less desperate one have had the sense to let go. Neither happens. In the end my weight brings her mount to a halt and blindness stills it.

Héloïse is sobbing, her feet still hooked in the stirrup as she sprawls in the dirt, a scar half a dozen paces long showing where she's been dragged through leaf mould. Her skirt has flopped across her face and she's struggling to move it. I'd help but the fallen skirt has revealed her raised leg, naked thighs and a patch of palest fur between.

'Please,' she begs.

Letting go of her horse's head, I stroke its neck briefly and mutter quick endearments until I'm certain it's stilled, and then, having patted its neck one final time, I reach for Héloïse's ankle and she whimpers. I end up unbuckling her stirrup leather since this is easier than trying to extract her bruised ankle. Obviously enough, that takes time, in which I glance occasionally, and despite myself, at the prize between her thighs. In the final moment, as the strap is about to come free from the saddle, I give in to temptation and slide my middle finger lightly along her cleft, taking its taste and smell. The slightest tang of urea, a trace of evaporating salts. It is exquisite.

'There,' I say, lowering her leg to the ground. With my help she stands unsteadily and smooths her skirt. She seems on the edge of saying something, but keeps silent. Her face is scarlet, from being head-down as much as embarrassment I hope. She doesn't protest when I kneel to remove her shoe. The bones in her foot are whole, the skin on one side broken, bruising already blooms on the other. We need cold water and the sooner the better. I walk her to a stream and she sits at the edge and whimpers slightly as it stings her broken skin. After a while she thanks me.

'What happened?'

She has trouble meeting my eyes, poor child. 'An adder,' she says. 'I saw . . . I thought I saw an adder on the path in front of me.' The afternoon is hot, the hour dappled with sunlight, and adders like sleeping in the open. It seems entirely possible.

'Can you ride?'

She looks at her saddle doubtfully. In the end she rides back sitting in front of me, her legs swung to one side and my arms around her to reach my reins. She's awkward, almost embarrassed at my touch and thanks me constantly. She is furious with herself. Quite obviously furious beyond what the accident demands and my comment that it could happen to anyone brings her to tears. Her eyes are still red when we ride back into the stables and a groom comes running, followed a few minutes later by Jerome and Armand, who appear from a door in a wing of the palace.

'Her horse bolted,' I say shortly. 'You might want to have a doctor look at her ankle, although it seems well enough to me. Don't scold her. She's upset enough as it is.' I hand responsibility for her care to Jerome whether he wants it or not, and turn towards the gates to the stable.

'Where are you going?' he asks.

'To play with the other animals.'

At least they, the ones in cages, knew they were trapped and probably suspected their lives were unnatural. I walk away and he lets me go.

Supper with Candles

To cook foie gras en croute

Make a pastry from a pound of flour, a third of a pound of good butter, a tablespoon of mildly salted water and one egg, and put aside in a cool place until needed. Vein a whole goose liver — foie gras — until all the veins are gone and only the flesh remains. The bigger and finer the liver, the easier this will be. Soak a Périgord truffle in good cognac. Now finely dice two slices of smoked wild boar and a small quantity of lard and shred the truffle, mixing the three together well. Wrap your foie gras in the forcemeat and hold in place with a sheet of fatty caul taken from a pig's stomach. (The birth kind works but this is better.) Using only as much pastry as is necessary wrap your parcel, seal the edges carefully with milk and smooth these away before brushing the whole with beaten egg. Cook in a medium oven for an hour and serve immediately. *Tastes sublime*.

★   ★   ★

Jerome and I ate that night in a private room near the Abundance Salon, which we passed through on our way to supper. The tables in the salon were crowded with plates of marzipan fruit, silver jugs of coffee and trays offering wines and liqueurs. The floor was as crowded with nobles as the buffet was with food, and the smell of stale coffee mixed with that of sweet chartreuse, the musk of urine and a miasmic stink of shit.

'Behave,' said Jerome, and I realised I'd named the scents aloud.

Small dogs cocked their legs to piss on people's shoes. A goat on a leather lead was as barbered as the fop who owned it. Cold eyes watched me pass and weighed my value. A tiny woman with a lined face and hair to her knees smiled knowingly, her hair filled with roses and peacock feathers. 'Madame de Laborde,' Jerome whispered. 'La Pompadour's cousin.'

There were a dozen lesser courts within Versailles, places where dukes and princes kept open table for their followers and friends, where politics could be discussed and alliances made. Jerome had quarters on the second floor overlooking the Royal Court. I asked about the apartment Charlot had and barely used, and my friend's mouth set. When at Versailles, Charlot had rooms on the third floor of the Old Wing, overlooking the Ministers' Court. From the sourness with which I was told this I imagined his were bigger or their location better. To smooth things over I asked about Lisette, and was told flatly she'd produced yet another son for the de Saulx family line. Jerome had daughters. That too was a touchy subject.

Inside the dining room Armand and Héloïse

were already waiting; her head slumped onto his shoulder, his arm around her shoulders to lightly touch the side of her breast. When Virginie and I were first together we sat like that for hours, half touching, grateful for the contact. Neither of us knowing Jean-Pierre was already in her belly.

'Husband and wife?' I muttered.

'Brother and sister. Well, half-brother and -sister.' Jerome didn't bother to lower his voice and I understood they were his creatures. 'She gets her looks from her mother. He gets his concupiscence from his father.'

I looked at Jerome.

'It is my knowledge of this that makes them pliable.'

The objects of our discussion smiled in Jerome's direction and turned to me as one to nod politely. Then all life left their faces and they sat back as if breath had gone from their lungs or the room was empty again and we had simply disappeared.

'Why are they here?'

'Armand is your secretary. Héloïse your housekeeper.'

'Jerome. Why are they here?'

'Half my reports say Paoli likes pretty women. The other half say he likes pretty boys. There are those who say he likes both. Sometimes at once . . . Don't look so shocked. It is my job to know these things.' Other words from a younger Jerome entered my head, brave boasts about keeping France strong and making her great. Now we sat in a room where the very roundels of the Sun King on the door mocked our childish idealism. His grandson was despised by his subjects. His palace stank like a sewer. Every war he fought lost us lands or cost us gold we didn't have. I should have stayed at home and pretended I'd never received Jerome's letter.

'Cheer up,' Jerome said. 'I'm going to feed you.'

The young man rang a glass bell and a door opened to admit liveried servants, who put porcelain plates on a marble-topped table and followed them with silver knives and forks and crystal glasses and jugs of wine. Finally, a huge silver-gilt platter was brought in on which sat four pastry-wrapped parcels. My dining companions watched carefully as I took mine, sliced it open and scooped a warm morsel from inside. I could taste fat, and discovered a texture close to bone marrow, which dissolved to liquid with the heat of my tongue.

'Well?' Jerome demanded.

'A whole foie gras, wrapped in a forcemeat of veal and lard, baked in butter pastry but first wrapped round with . . . ' The texture was parchment but the aftertaste was not. He had me and I wondered who Jerome had found capable of cooking like this.

'Wrapped in calf's caul,' he said, naming the membrane ripped from the face of new-born cattle. He smiled at my surprise and took one for himself, making a pretence of savouring the first mouthful. By the third mouthful he'd forgotten what he was eating and finished long before Armand or Héloïse.

'Now, to business,' Jerome said, when I had finished. 'You are being sent to Corsica because Signore Paoli respects you. He has read of your passion for hard work, your draining of marshes, your efforts to improve crops. He knows that you read widely, that you make scientific discoveries, that Voltaire answers your letters. You are kindred spirits. You will offer him hereditary nobility, a pension from the French state and the title of marquis di Bonafacio.'

'And if he refuses?'

'You offer him the title of duc de Bastia.'

Héloïse smiled and I knew she understood my question was not how high I could bid but what happened if Signore Paoli did not intend to be bought. Without being asked she poured me a glass of white wine and pushed it forward, revealing the valley between her youthful breasts. She blushed prettily when she saw me look.

'And if he refuses that?'

'You can offer him prince of Corsica.'

'I see. And his followers? His ministers?'

'Lesser titles. As many as you need without making us look ridiculous. They may keep their language and even teach it in schools. They may conduct local business in *lingua corsa*.' He nodded at his glass and Armand filled it. 'Their peasants can barely speak Italian, never mind French. At least Paoli is almost one of us. That will help.' Emptying his glass in a single gulp, Jerome said. 'Now, Armand and I have business. Héloïse can tell you the rest. Ask her about *brocciu di Donna*. That should interest you.'

'You shouldn't dislike him so,' said Héloïse,

once the door had closed behind Jerome and her half-brother. Leaving the sofa she'd shared with her brother, she poured herself a glass of wine and finished it in two gulps, poured herself another and refilled mine. Then sat herself in a chair directly opposite. That was when I realised she hadn't been drinking.

'Jerome is one of my oldest friends.'

'It shows.' She smiled sadly and looked around her, the subject apparently having changed. 'You hate this place, don't you?'

'I prefer my own chateau.'

Héloïse snorted. 'Your contempt for Versailles is obvious. You should have seen the marquis de Caussard's face when you said that about the *other animals* . . . '

It was odd to hear Jerome referred to by his full title, and I wondered if Héloïse suggesting I disliked Jerome was her way of saying she did. I certainly doubted Jerome's motives for so obviously bringing us together for the second time that day.

'Versailles is rotting,' she said. 'One day it will simply fall down.'

'It's rotten already. If it was going to fall it would have done so.'

'You'd pull it down?' She looked sly.

'I'd burn it. That's the only way to get rid of this stench.'

She glanced at the admixture of lavish and rancid around us, the crumbling drapes and dog-pissed rugs, the perfectly-breasted marble nymphs flanking the fireplace with their mottled drape of staining. 'You wouldn't save anything?'

263

'My animals. They didn't choose to be in prison.'

'Yet they say you keep wild animals yourself.'

'In better conditions than this.'

'Comfortable captivity is still captivity. Don't you agree?' The hem of her dress lifted slightly and for a moment I thought I'd imagined it, but she edged the hem higher and higher still, opening her knees until I could see a little darkness between. 'Marquis, you haven't answered.'

'Most would die if returned to the wild.'

'You think we've been rendered unfit for freedom too?'

'I've considered it.'

Of course I had, she told me. Everybody who wasn't a fool had. As she said this, I wondered if she realised I meant freeing my animals. I'd certainly considered releasing the animals kept at Chateau d'Aumout, but I was worried they'd simply be killed by my peasants or the authorities. And if I sent them back to their original countries, they'd be killed by animals who'd never been captive. Besides, I liked them around me. They reminded me we were once wild too. So yes, she was probably right, we had been rendered unfit. All of us.

'Marquis . . . If you'd like to put that candle on the floor.'

I placed the silver candle stick where she indicated, and she widened her knees and then spread them again until they would go no wider. Light from the candle revealed her sex, which glistened with a secret grin. To refill her glass I had to step over the candle and stand between

264

her legs, which closed to touch mine.

'They say you've tasted everything. Have you tasted pain?'

'Mine or another's?'

Her smile was bewitching. 'Either one counts.' Looking into her eyes, I wondered if she was serious and what Jerome had got me into. I'd thought his proclivities simple. Women, plenty of them. But there was nothing simple about Héloïse.

'Well?' she asked.

I shook my head.

'A pity. You should.' Dipping for the candlestick, Héloïse lifted it with steady fingers and tipped it sideways so wax trickled down her inner thigh. I was out of my chair before the wax was solid, only to be stopped by a smile so mocking I sat back, embarrassed. 'The great d'Aumout. The man who will eat anything scared by a little wax.' She tipped more into the palm of her hand and made a fist, droplets falling between her fingers like tears.

'Why?' I demanded.

'Why do you hunt for new tastes?'

'Because I want to taste them.'

'But what makes you want to taste them?'

When I told her that discovering new tastes helped convince me I was still alive, she smiled and said she'd known we were alike from the moment I'd stopped her horse bolting. That was the moment she'd stopped treating my seduction as a chore ordered by Jerome and turned it into something she'd do for herself. If not for the horse, she'd have fucked me by now and we'd be

265

done. She admitted this casually, smiling as she said it. I did my best not to be shocked. Manon, to whom I could talk, was far more open about these things than Virginie had ever been but she'd still never said anything like this.

'You could have been killed.'

'But I wasn't.' Putting the candlestick on a table, Héloïse asked, 'Do you like what you see?' The slyness of her smile said she already knew the answer. Of course I did. She was young and her skin was clear and her flesh firm. How could I not? Taking my silence for assent, she explained the rules of the game. I was to drip exactly twelve drops of hot wax on her body. Anywhere I liked. The choice was mine. If my choices were good I could have her any way I wanted. If they were poor we were done.

The hem of her dress dropped as she stood, turning away. 'You'll have to do the buttons.' There were a dozen of them running from her shoulders to her buttocks and I undid every one, my fingers no longer shaking by the time I reached the last. Only then did I lift the dress from her shoulders and let it fall into a puddle around her feet. She untied the ribbons on her petticoat herself, stepping out of both. Her figure was full and her curves soft, her skin the white of milk and her nipples strawberry, the hair between her thighs crinkly as saffron. A bandage circled her injured ankle. I glanced at the door, knowing I should use it.

'You want this,' she said.

She was right. I did. Héloïse let me stretch her face-down along a brocade chaise longue. The chaise curled up at one end, so that was where I put her legs, bending them at the knee. Her head I let hang over the foot of the chaise, feeling her smile as I used a rotting curtain tie to lash her wrists to the legs. I slid a second curtain tie under her waist and tied it like an over-tight belt, stepping back to consider the result.

'I knew it,' she said.

'Knew what?'

'That you would understand this.'

I almost protested that I understood little of what was going on in this room but it would have been a lie. I recognised hunger when I saw it. And could feel it grow in me to match the salt hunger that rose from her body. Taking the candle, I lifted away her hair and let it fall forward, dripping the first drop of wax onto her neck. She flinched. I made her wait ten seconds between each offering of molten wax, placing one on the underside of her foot, another on her shoulder, choosing carefully. By the time the last drop splashed between her perfect buttocks her body was rigid and she came with a cry.

The first sound since we began.

I left Héloïse where she was and, untying my breeches, knelt in front of her. Having come deep inside her throat, I cut her hand free and crouched by the foot of the chaise so we could kiss. She tasted of wine, foie gras, butter pastry and me. In some strange way she seemed happier than before. The fierce intensity she'd brought to the start of this meeting was no longer there. The rest of our coupling was ordinary. She knelt up, she lay flat, she rode me like a jockey. I had her piss into a pot, letting the last of it dribble into my hand so I could taste what she'd eaten previously. She took me into her mouth again — from choice this time — and tried to guess what I'd drunk. I pleasured her arse with a plum and her quim with the narrow end of a pear, eating both when we were finished. I licked honey from her navel and brandy from nipples, making her raise her hips high so I could fill her lower lips with Champagne. The bubbles tickled and her giggles spilt most of it before I could dip my head to drink.

Donatien de Sade, a young man and almost neighbour, knowing nothing of my encounter with Héloïse, sent me a note in response to a pamphlet I wrote after returning from Corsica. I'd said good food was civilised Man's primary pleasure. He replied that sex was as important as eating or drinking and I should allow that appetite to be satisfied with as little false modesty as any other. Mind you, he also wrote that sex without pain was like bread without yeast. By then I'd lost contact with Héloïse or I'd have introduced them. I suspect she would have liked him, and he would have been impressed by her lack of false modesty.

Later, much later, when the noise beyond the door had stilled to silence and even the servants who'd come to clear the Abundance Salon seemed to be in bed, I asked Héloïse about brocciu di Donna. She told me it was a cheese. A hidden one. I knew what brocciu was. But the di Donna version was unknown to me and 'hidden cheese' was not a term I'd met. When I asked what it was made from, she smiled and turned my head towards her breast and pushed one nipple against my lips until my mouth opened to suckle.

'There,' she said. 'You have your answer.'

The candles had burnt out and dawn was a smear against dirty glass on the other side of a curtained window. I only knew I gazed into eyes of the purest blue because I'd learnt their exact colour hours earlier as I hung above her. Peering into the shadows where her eyes should be I wondered if she meant what I thought she meant, and suspected from her grin that she did. I'd tasted almost everything a noble in France could procure. At least, until that moment, I'd thought I had. Sex with Héloïse was not meant to tie me to the mission. She was simply the hors d'oeuvre. I knew she was here on Jerome's orders to compromise me, should he need me compromised, but he had no need. I sucked her breast so hard it filled my mouth.

'Really?' I asked when I was done.

'Made from the finest milk, taken from girls fed on mountain food. No mixing of the milk unless the girls are twins. Each cheese is the size of my fist, wrapped in muslin and kept in spring water to keep it cool. It must be eaten quickly.'

'When do we leave?'

She laughed, but kindly.

Leaving Versailles

I remember the journey well, even at this distance. Maybe the sharpness of what had passed the night before gave the day a sweetness it didn't deserve but I have it perfectly, one of a handful so clear in my memory that I recall every moment.

As we leave the gilded cage through gates decorated with the boyish face of a long-dead king, I feel my headache lift and my lungs fill with fresher air. Within five miles my nose is no longer clogged with palace stink, within fifty its foulness is a memory. As Armand de Plessis picks at his nails and sulks, his half-sister gazes from the carriage window. In place of last night's troubled figure sits a smiling young woman, her hands in her lap and her knees together. For all I know her back is raw with burns but she sits neatly and shows no sign of discomfort. The most she says, as we trundle noisily over a stone bridge above a dried-out riverbed, is 'I'm glad to leave.' After inhaling deeply, she breathes out and I think I see the last of some strange sadness leave her eyes.

'Have you been to Corsica before?' she asks.

I shake my head.

'You'll love it,' she promises.

'You've been?'

'I'm Corsican. Well, my mother was.' Héloïse catches my glance towards her half-brother. 'His

270

mother too,' she says. 'Our father was French.'

'Where is he now?'

She looks at her brother. 'Dead.'

'Jerome is family?'

'He became so.' I get a sense of something unsaid. As if to confirm this, Armand pointedly sits back and closes his eyes. After a while his pretence of sleeping is replaced by tiny snores and Héloïse's smiles. 'Thank you.'

'For what?'

'Understanding.'

The moment for either of us to say more passes, and eventually she closes her eyes in turn, her head lolling to one side before falling forward onto her chest, until the obvious discomfort of that position makes me rest her head back against red velvet. She smiles. Even though I know she is asleep, Héloïse smiles.

Our coach, the one taking us south to Toulon, takes us through forests, wheat fields, vineyards and finally olive groves unchanged in a hundred years. The hedgerows are ragged, the roads rutted and old oaks stand abandoned by the lightning that killed them. And in the shadow of the hedgerows, and on the roads, and at the foot of those blasted oaks, the same sullen faces I'd seen thirty-five years earlier.

Men piss at walls and women squat, barely bothering to hide their buttocks. Armand, who has woken, scowls, shuts his eyes and loses himself in daydreams. Héloïse buries her nose in Rousseau's *Julie*, reading aloud the most touching of Jean-Jacques' lines, so far as I can tell entirely without mockery. Only I notice the animal-like shuffle on the road, and hours pass before I realise the difference between now and thirty-five years before. Where once the peasants' gaze slid across our coach, almost unseeing, our worlds not colliding, now they meet my stare and there is fury as well as desperation in their eyes.

We stay at inns in Auxerre, Beaune, Lyons and Valence, changing horses four or five times a day as conditions demand. Our coach bears state arms and our coachman wears the palace livery. Armand and Héloïse share rooms, as is allowed of a brother and sister. I sleep alone, even in those places where I am offered company. We are given the best chambers, served first and offered the fastest horses.

Mostly Armand dozes and I use the time to learn about Héloïse. She lives in an apartment in Paris and attends Versailles one week a month to fulfil her duties as a lady-in-waiting to one of the princesses. Her brother attends one of the lesser princes, and the half-brother and -sister arrange their lives so their duties at Versailles coincide and they can live the rest of the month together at their Parisian apartment. That is what everyone does, apparently. The old rules requiring courtiers to remain in residence are gone. The only exceptions are those who wait on the king directly, and the royal governess.

Héloïse tells me Armand's mother had been Paoli's cousin, and that she's been chosen to accompany me because her few words of *lingua corsa* will help smooth the way. I ask what she knows of the man I am to meet and it is little enough. Pasquale Paoli comes from a family of lawyers and his father was a nationalist before him. His republic controls the rocky centre of the island and we, that is, the French, control the coast. But there are six hundred miles of shoreline and two hundred or more coves and beaches. Héloïse shrugs prettily and I understand. Jerome is sensible to want a peaceful solution. If half of what Héloïse tells me about mountain strongholds, centuries-long vendettas and smuggling is true, pacifying the place would be a nightmare.

'Signore Paoli knows we're coming?'

'Oh, yes. The marquis de Caussard has informed him. The signore is expecting us.' Héloïse sits back, opens her Rousseau and within a mile the carriage has returned her to sleep, dozing as prettily as her brother. We make Toulon in good time, wait another day for our ship and a fortunate tide, and are met on the jetty at Calvi in the north of Corsica by a Gascon colonel who seems doubtful about the wisdom of our visit. A bottle of wine later I know why. Colonel Montaubon has been on the island for ten years, first at the invitation of the Genoese and then commanding local French mercenaries. The man I am going to visit is the man he's spent the last decade trying to kill. He has his doubts Paoli will receive me.

'We have a safe conduct,' says Armand, who takes a scroll from a leather case and passes it to Héloïse, who unrolls it and passes it to me. I give it to the colonel, who peers at the signature and a red wax seal showing the head of a Moor cut off at the neck.

'Well,' the colonel says. 'It looks real enough. You'll just have to hope you don't fall into the hands of Paoli's enemies.'

'He has enemies?'

'This is Corsica. Everyone has enemies.'

Picking up my bottle, Colonel Montaubon peers with pantomime disappointment into its emptiness and puts it back. I take the hint and order another. The girl who delivers it brings olives and bread at the same time. The olives are stale, the bread hard and the new bottle no better than the one before it. In fact, it is so sour it would have drawn complaints from a barracks full of soldiers. I wonder why the colonel has brought us here and must be looking around me a little too obviously.

'One of ours,' he says. 'The innkeeper is French.'

'You can trust him not to tell tales?'

'I can trust him not to try to poison me.' Colonel Montaubon sighs. 'You know little enough about this part of the world, don't you?' He speaks with the studied ennui of a long-term visitor who proclaims he hates where he finds himself while secretly knowing he loves it too much to leave. It is the tone Jerome uses to tell me how much he hates life at court, only to look appalled when I suggest he resign.

'It's all stabbings, ambushes and abductions,' the colonel says. 'The merchants are thieves, their peasants are worse than ours. Pasquale Paoli's parliament is proof of what happens when

274

you let lawyers loose. I'll give you soldiers for your protection.'

'We go alone,' I say. 'That is the agreement.'

Colonel Montaubon looks briefly querulous, opens his mouth to object and decides to fill it with wine instead. So I thank him for his advice, nod to Héloïse and Armand to say we should go, and leave the colonel what remains of my bottle. Eyes watch us leave. I can feel them as we move through a dusty square towards a dry fountain, with Armand leading the way. 'There,' Armand says.

Three donkeys and a ragged boy wait by the fountain, beyond which a handful of old men stand one side of a line scratched in the sand and throw heavy wooden balls in looping arcs to drop onto a smaller ball several feet away. The old men barely glance up as Armand hails the boy. 'Spies,' Héloïse mutters.

'I expected a coach . . . '

'Later,' she promises. 'A donkey is better for reaching the citadel.' She means the huge fortress perched on a rocky outcrop and overlooking the harbour.

'That's where we're going?'

She smiles and shakes her head. 'That's where we're pretending to go. You only have to travel by donkey for a mile at most. Then we'll change to a cart. It's all worked out.'

'By whom?'

'The signore.'

I take her word for it. There is little else I can do. As he'd said his goodbyes, Jerome had told me that Armand and Héloïse know where I should go and when. My job is simply to impress Pasquale Paoli with my sincerity when we arrive. I am a marquis, a friend of the great and beloved by the dauphin, yet I dress plainly and talk quietly of simple things. I'd started to tell Jerome that there was nothing simple about taste, but he moved on to how impressed Signore Paoli would be to meet me.

★ ★ ★

Very occasionally the boy leading the donkeys would drop back to swipe one of the animals across its rear but mostly his turning towards them was enough to have them pick up their hooves. The sun was hot overhead and the air rich with the scent of herbs: thyme, marjoram, mint, juniper and honeysuckle. Even my own kitchen garden lacked this wild and casual abundance. At the back of the citadel we kept climbing rather than enter the heavy arch that led to the headquarters of the French forces in this area.

'Soon,' Héloïse promised. Sweat beaded her forehead and dark patches showed under her arms. Since there was no one to see, I removed my wig and held it like a dead thing as I let the donkey carry me into an olive grove and over a small bridge to where a horse and cart stood. It would have blocked the traffic had there been any for it to block. Around us was red earth, rocks like weathered bone, sharp-leaved plants and coarse grasses. I wondered how far French authority really ran.

Fifteen minutes later I found out. As our cart turned a corner, it hit a rock and the carter swore, dropped his reins and lifted his hands in one fluid movement. His cart came to a trundling halt, one wheel dangerously askew. Three masked men stood in our path with drawn pistols while two others with muskets were silhouetted on a slope above. At a barked command, the carter clambered from his seat and prostrated himself in the red dirt, face-down and with his hands stretched in front of him. The man in charge spoke again.

I thought Armand would answer but it was Héloïse, her words fierce and her accent strange. If she was speaking *lingua corsa* she knew more than the few words she'd mentioned. She nodded at Armand, nodded at me and finally said something I understood. Pasquale Paoli. The man looked at me, looked at Héloïse and Armand and waved his gun to indicate they too should clamber down. When Héloïse shook her head, he raised the pistol and his hand tightened on the trigger.

'Wait,' begged Armand. He practically dragged his half-sister from the cart while the man stood there laughing. After which, he examined me slowly, asked a few questions of the two now kneeling on the road and began a heated conversation with his companions. They were obviously arguing about something and, after a particularly fierce glare, I began to suspect it was whether or not to shoot me. There comes, in such moments, a sweeping fatalism. Well, it comes to me in those moments when the world waits on the edge of change. I can remember red flowers like tiny blood splatters standing out against a grey rock. Every boulder in the wild fields around us was topped by a rough pyramid of stones, an offering to the god of high places or maybe a memorial to something.

I recognised the same stillness and calmness I felt when I realised Virginie was dead. If I could have fought them I might have done, having my training and a certain skill with a sword; but the three on the road had pistols and the two on the hill above had muskets and I was unarmed. That had been part of the conditions. I was to come unarmed. Without even my sword. Glancing up, I found one of those on the road examining me. 'Your name,' he demanded in French, his accent as thick as a Marseilles innkeeper.

I bowed. That was the first thing we were taught at school. When you need to make an impression, always bow. 'Jean-Marie, marquis d'Aumout. Here to meet Signore Pasquale Paoli, president of the Corsican republic.'

The man spat. He translated my words for his companions and they muttered among themselves. Héloïse was watching me and there was a message in her eyes; unfortunately I had no idea how to read it. She had her hands clasped behind her head as she knelt in the road and the position exposed sodden circles beneath her arms and pulled her breasts high. She was swaying in the heat. Armand had his eyes shut and the movement of his lips told me he was praying. Only our carter seemed untroubled, for all his awkward position and his face in the dirt he lay as silent and still as a man asleep. Looking at him, I wondered if he really was asleep and envied him if he was. The wine from the harbour inn had been heavy as well as sour and there was nothing I'd have liked more.

'Come here,' the man demanded.

'You come here.'

He raised his pistol and I looked into its muzzle. From this distance the ball would pass without trouble through my head. Such a death would be instant or as near as made no difference. I took a mouthful of hot Corsican air and savoured its scent. If I were to die it might as well be with the scent of wild herbs in my nostrils. The crickets were loud, the cicadas a constant background hiss like tiny steam engines. A kite called high overhead. *Falco milvus* Linnaeus had named the Corsican variety in his *Systema Naturae*.

'*Jean-Marie* . . . ' Héloïse was staring at me.

'What?'

Her throat rippled. 'He'll kill you if you don't.'

I was going to shrug but her eyes were so blue and when I looked back the black circle of the muzzle somehow looked bigger. I could remonstrate, demand the man find his manners and remind him he dealt with a French noble sent by the king. That's what Charlot would have done. But I had a headache and Héloïse's expression told me she feared the outcome of this. So I climbed down from the cart and walked to where he waited.

'A Frenchman?'

I bowed politely.

'Come to talk to Pasquale Paoli?'

I nodded, and the man muttered to his companions. The last thing I remembered was that he spat, before saying '*Traitor.*' And then the barrel of his pistol slashed towards my skull, bringing darkness.

Arrest

I wake to the rocking of a cart, the stink of dog shit on somebody's heel and my face hard against the cart's rough floor. My hands are bound behind my back and my head is trapped inside a sack that smells of wind-dried ham. Men are talking somewhere above me. *Lingua corsa* mixed with mainland Italian and borrowed words of French. My head hurts from the pistol blow and the after-effects of wine. My best hope is that I've been abducted in return for ransom. I try to remember if Corsica has that tradition too. Its neighbour Sardinia certainly does. I imagine I'll be murdered.

When my cart stops suddenly I draw breath and look for my courage. A man growls a question from several yards away. The man sitting above answers in a tone brutal enough to say this is no friendly conversation. The cart rocks forward, the first man shouts and the cart halts again, my head slamming into wood from the abruptness of the stop. There is shouting and then a shot. Above me someone jerks, gurgles and slips down as someone else fires. To the ham smell of the sack, and the stink of shit from the dead man's heel, is added the acrid tang of gunpowder smoke that thickens as other pistols discharge. In the end, only ringing silence remains. And then the cart rocks as someone clambers onto it. That person grunts as they drag a body off me and a scrabble of stones say they've tossed it over the edge of some slope. Two other bodies from within the cart follow, after which the cart begins to trundle through the heat of the Corsican afternoon, the only noise being the creak of its wheels. When it stops occasionally, as if its driver is deciding this way or that, a wild symphony of crickets reaches me on a wind that smells of herbs. We stop an indeterminate time later. Maybe an hour, maybe no more than ten minutes. Time runs differently when you have a sack over your head. Well, so it seems to me.

The next thing I hear is Armand's voice, then hands drag me upright onto a seat, remove the sack and I find myself staring into the soft face of a light-haired stranger with startlingly blue eyes. His mouth is full and his nose broad and his hands small, with long narrow fingers and perfectly clean nails. I see all of this in a second, perhaps because an hour earlier I'd been expecting to meet death and this man has taken his place.

'Monsieur le marquis d'Aumout?'

I bow as best I can, realise my forehead is sticky and find blood. It tastes fresh and I understand the cart's earlier abrupt halt opened a cut that was already there.

'We'll have that dressed,' he tells me. He peers more closely. 'Perhaps stitched. I'm Pasquale Paoli. My cousins tell me you have an offer from the king? They wanted to tell me themselves but I thought it would be best to hear it from you.' Héloïse and Armand look at me impassively from a yard or so away. There is a family likeness between the three. 'Second cousins,' Paoli says, seeing my gaze.

'They are your spies?'

'Friends,' he says. 'Family. Their father was French, true enough. A dreadful man. Luckily for me they take after their mothers. This was their chance to come home.' He says this easily, in an entirely friendly tone, and I wonder if they were always Paoli's spies or if he is simply lucky. Some men are.

'What went wrong?' I ask.

He understands my question. 'A faction not friendly to me heard of your arrival on our island and decided to interfere. They intended to discover what I might have to discuss with France. I must admit,' he smiles slightly, 'I'm at a loss to know what you think you could say to me that might change my mind.'

'About what?'

'Remaining independent.'

'That is what you are?'

He looks at me and his gaze hardens. Then the fierceness goes out of his eyes and he makes himself smile and keeps his voice light when he answers, 'You know, as well as I do, that Corsica has been independent for many years.'

'Genoa didn't agree.'

'The Genoese could barely hold a quarter of our coast. That's why they sold their supposed rights in my country to you. Now, I must send my friends away . . . ' He hugs Armand and Héloïse and they head in different directions, going downhill on red-earth paths, with armed men in front and behind. 'My soldiers found them by the road. My enemies didn't dare kill them. I suppose I should be grateful.'

'Your soldiers?'

He stops for a second, looks at me. 'I'm president,' he says. 'As such I'm commander-in-chief of the Corsican forces. I have generals but they report to me.' He shrugs. 'This is how it should be in a democracy.'

'I've heard your women vote.'

'In local elections. In time I can see no reason why they should not vote in the national elections or stand for the general assembly. We have a tradition of strong women here. When men die in vendettas the women take over.'

'And run the farms?'

'And the bakeries and breweries, and the fishing fleets and olive presses. And continue the vendettas.' Paoli sighs. 'I need to find a way to stop those. What would you think of civil courts, arbitration before a panel of equals and binding rulings?'

'It sounds like something Voltaire might suggest.'

'We write to each other. I don't wish to boast but I suspect François-Marie takes ideas from me in his turn.'

As we talk, he leads me along a terrace of olive trees towards drystone steps to a terrace above. We climb through the summer heat, Signore Paoli apparently unaffected by the sun beating down on our heads. After the sixth or seventh terrace, I stop to wipe my skull and he suggests I discard my frock coat and offers to carry it if I find it too heavy and the slope too steep. Pride demands I carry my own coat and I try to steady my breathing. When we stop, it's on a road along a ridge, and I look down over purple gorse towards Calvi, and the sea is a blue spread beyond. The view is beautiful and brutal, unlike even the wildest stretches of southern France. It is a country worth loving. On the ridge road a carriage waits. Not a cart but an open-top carriage with leaf springs and leather seats so hot they burn my legs through my hose. Signore Paoli sits more slowly, being a man used to life in this heat. I am impressed by him and I suspect he means to impress me. For my part, I say little and listen often, trying to judge who he is and how he will greet my offer. Jerome told me little enough about the man and what he did say was partial. In Paoli's face I see no sign of the sybarite Jerome said I would meet. He could be a minor noble, a successful lawyer, a rich merchant who'd turned his thoughts to good works; except a fierce intelligence far back in his blue eyes suggests something more.

The house to which he brings me is not the ruin I expect. It is low and long and sunk into the side of a hill, its red stucco faded to blend invisibly into the pink dirt behind. The gates, which are sturdy, are drawn back by two dark-skinned boys with coal-black hair and pistols in their belts. A groom rushes from inside a stable block to see to our horses and Signore Paoli helps him unfix the harness.

'Here we can talk,' he says.

I can understand why. There are men with

guns in every direction. Shepherds with muskets across their backs in the fields. A boy leading goats along a track has a pistol hanging from a lanyard around his neck. Two hunters carry a belt full of rabbits, one has his musket slung, the other has his muzzle forward. I doubt the colonel from Calvi could get his men within five miles of this place without running into an ambush.

'Come inside,' Signore Paoli says, 'you must be thirsty.'

I fear he is about to offer me wine but he produces a glass jug filled with cold fresh water obviously drawn from a deep well and joins me in finishing first one tumbler and then another. Only then does he take me into his study, sit himself in a heavy chair on one side of a simple desk and indicate I should take the chair on the other.

'So,' he says. 'Tell me about this offer.'

I begin, as Jerome had suggested, by telling him how much we respect Corsica. How being part of a great kingdom like France would be entirely different from being the colony of a poor and near-destitute Italian city state. That the island would be granted the status of a province, with all the rights and privileges that brought. Corsicans would have the right to an assembly, the right to their own courts. Corsica itself would be the equal of Normandy or Burgundy, both great countries that became part of the France.

'And to sweeten this . . . ' His voice was light. 'What does Paris have in mind for me?'

'Armand and Héloïse really didn't tell you?'

286

Pasquale Paoli shakes his head. 'I wanted to hear this from you myself. I already understand you're a friend of the duc de Saulx and the marquis de Caussard, and that when you speak it is with their voice, and when they speak it is with the voice of the king of France. The only thing I don't understand is why you came. I mean . . . I understand why they sent you. I'm simply not sure why you agreed to be sent.'

I tell him I came for brocciu di Donna.

He looks puzzled, and when I explain he looks a little cross, as if he thinks less of me now than when we first met. 'And you believe this exists? You believe we make cheese from the milk of our women and keep it hidden in caves to eat in secret?' He sees my face and sighs. 'Héloïse tells me you're a good man. That your life reflects your writings. She says you saved her life one day in the woods when her horse bolted. For that I can forgive you this ridiculousness. Tell me what they told you to tell me. Make their offer.'

'I am to offer you the title of marquis di Bonafacio. If you do not accept that I am to offer you duc de Bastia. If you refuse that I am to offer you prince of Corsica, with all the rights of a prince of France who is not of the royal blood.'

'And my men? I'm sure you have something for them.'

'Such titles as you think fit. A handful of comtes, more vicomtes, as many barons as you need. I doubt the king will be fussy about those.'

'Why would I accept this offer?'

'Because the alternative is war. The king will send soldiers and this time you will be fighting

France. You will find it very different from fighting Genoa.'

'Perhaps,' he said. He pours himself a glass of wine and then pours one for me as an afterthought. I can see from his face that his thoughts are turned inward. 'Do you expect me to accept?'

A silence stretches between us, broken only by footsteps on wooden boards overhead and a fiddling of crickets so loud it reaches through shuttered windows. There are two answers to that and they depend upon to whom he addresses the question.

'Who are you asking?' I say. 'Me? Or the French envoy?'

'Do you expect me to distinguish?'

'Of course.'

'Then you mistake me. I am Pasquale Paoli and I am the president of Corsica, the two are indistinguishable. There is no difference in the views of one and the views of the other. However, for you . . . What does the French envoy think?'

'He expects you to accept. Your acceptance is the only way to avoid war. The rewards of becoming part of France are great, and the rewards offered to you personally, and through you to your followers, will make you the equal of the great nobles of France.'

'And this other you?'

'You will refuse,' I say simply. 'You have no interest in titles or desire for your country to be ruled by Louis and have your children learn French.' He stares at me for a long while and asks a question that haunts me still.

'What would you die for?'

I give him the obvious answers. 'My family, my children, my wife . . . ' I add *My king* as an afterthought, not knowing if it is really true. But those are not the answers he wants. He means what *idea* would I die for. And I realise I do not know. Standing, I bow to show I accept his decision and tell him I will return to Calvi. With luck I will be in time to board the vessel that brought me.

'I'm afraid not,' he says.

'She's left already?'

Signore Paoli shrugs. 'I have no idea. But I cannot let you return so swiftly. We have preparations to make at this end. The longer you are here, the longer we have to make them. In a week they will wonder where you are. In a month they will send someone to find out and that person will fail. In two months, France will begin to worry and questions will be asked through intermediaries that will be answered, although the answers will leave them uncertain. In four months . . . In four months we will be ready.'

'You gave me safe passage.'

'True,' he says. 'But I said nothing about returning you.'

1769
Freedom

Since I am alive to write this you already know I didn't die in Corsica, although there were days and weeks, and finally months, when that seemed the likely outcome. First came a period of silence. I was held in cottages and fed well, moved every week or so, sometimes in the night and sometimes by day. This continued until Paoli himself appeared in the autumn to tell me his army had won a great victory over the marquis de Chauvelin. At the end of a ten-hour battle a thousand Frenchmen were wounded, six hundred were dead and another six hundred had surrendered, along with enough cannon, mortars and muskets to arm an entire new army. Corsica was free and would remain so.

Pasquale Paoli was almost right. Faced with the scale of the defeat, our good king Louis XV suggested the island was not worth such losses. But such was the damage to the duc de Choiseul's reputation as foreign minister that he begged the king to send more troops. Charlot objected and Jerome proclaimed himself appalled by the proposed cost, but the king let himself be swayed and de Choiseul got his way. At the end of winter a French army landed in Corsica, this time led by Noël, comte de Vaux.

The cottages in which I was held became

smaller, and I was moved more often, sometimes daily, sometimes not for two or three days at a time. Once I thought they'd forgotten me and the shepherd boy left to push stale bread under my door grew so frightened he unlocked it to ask if he could sleep inside. They would have beaten him, the men who turned up a week later, but I told them the boy had explained to me that if I tried to overpower him or run away the grown-ups would cut off my bollocks and hang me from an olive tree with my own entrails.

That night the boy brought me cheese in thanks. It was hard and stale and bloomed with mould but it was the first I'd eaten in three months and tasted so wonderful I almost cried. That winter was fierce. Winds howled though gaps in the walls, rain fell, food became scarce and my captors sullen and silent. They grew friendlier as the weather grew warmer and shared rabbit stew and small birds roasted over open fires. The kind didn't matter: we ate larks and thrushes, pipits, warblers and shrikes. And then they grew sullen again, and cast black glances, and I realised they had returned to discussing my fate. These were young men, sometimes very young, and I understood they were what Paoli could spare. The rest of his forces were engaged in running battles with my countrymen.

Towards the start of May I was taken to join a ragged column of soldiers. Maybe they were retreating. Maybe advancing. From their expressions as they squatted, crouched and sat in the dirt of a village square it was hard to tell. My guard that day had one good eye, his other as coddled as a half-cooked egg. He made me walk on his right where he could see me, called me 'old man' and said he'd break my legs if I tried to escape. 'Today you walk,' he said. 'You walk and you don't stop.'

'How far?'

'You will find out.'

I asked the question again of a rough-voiced soldier who joined us a mile or so later and to whom Milk Eye deferred. He said, 'We need to reach Ponte Novu. Twenty-five miles, perhaps more.'

'Where do we break the journey?'

He looked at me and saw my age rather than my Frenchness. He saw a person rather than my name or position in life, assuming he knew either. I understood that for me to know that meant I saw him in the same way. His voice was sympathetic as he said, 'No stops.' The casual kindness of his tone undid me and I had to hide tears.

We walked, I could not believe the distances we walked, as Paoli's peasant army sang songs around me. Some songs buoyed me on my way; others seemed so endless, I began to believe my exhaustion came not from walking but from the monotony of tunes that refused to end. I staggered, I swore openly, but I kept walking. There were women among the men and at least one of the sergeants was female. Filthy-faced and hard-eyed, she barked for her troop to keep moving and threatened a flogging for any who stopped. At about the nineteen-mile point my sides ached as if from the most vicious kidney punch. I saw one soldier stop to bend at the waist, and another stretch her leg muscles, but knew that if I did the same I'd never start again. A mile later, with the setting sun on my back and the column ahead, around and behind me I became determined to make it to the end.

My hair was to my shoulders and my beard long enough and tangled enough to need occasional combing with my fingers. My clothes were rags. So ragged that one of my captors had brought me a rancidly rotten coat the previous winter and I'd worn it gladly. I was unwashed and unkempt, hungry and thirsty and my eyes were raw from dust and that day's brightness. In short, I was enough like those around me to attract no attention. When a boy in front of me stumbled and almost dropped his musket, I took it from him. Milk Eye stepped forward, only for the rough-voiced man to pull him back. What damage could an unloaded musket do in a crowd that size? I gave it back to the boy when we reached the end, nodding curtly when he thanked me in *corsu* rather than speak and give myself away. The rough-voiced man brought me a cup of raw wine as reward. It was a year since I'd drunk anything but water and I grinned as its taste blossomed on my tongue.

'What will you do here?' I asked him.

'Die, most probably. You're free to join us.'

'It's not my war.'

Unreadable eyes examined me. 'It's everybody's war,' he said.

He stayed at Ponte Novu and my guard took

me through. At a church, in the next village that the milk-eyed young man led me through, I begged leave to say a prayer and he let me go up worn stone steps and into the gloom alone. It was not God I wanted but a moment to myself. And since God probably recognised this, if he existed at all, he left me alone too. All the same, habit made me use the water in his bowl by the door to cross myself, then kneel briefly before his altar. The windows around were high and narrow, one being broken near the top to let in a ray of light so sharp it pierced the floor.

Hunger, I told myself. *That's why everything looks strange.*

Away to one side, a marble bier supported a glass coffin. Inside it was a girl, perhaps a woman, her flesh as white as new ivory, her eyes closed and her hands crossed demurely over breasts that swelled sweetly beneath yellowing lace. I had no doubt she was wax, and was equally sure the village priest claimed she really was whichever local saint she was supposed to be. Her hair was blonde, her face serene, her toes delicate where they peeped beneath fading embroidery. She reminded me of someone so much that every time I turned to go I found myself turning back for another gaze — until the thought of Virginie finally slipped into my head and I stopped, appalled. Was this how I'd seen her? Perfect, unchanging, incorruptible? A wax girl? No wonder she'd been unhappy.

The question followed me into the brightness of the afternoon where the heat and dust drove it from my head before I could force myself to answer. That night Milk Eye left me in a narrow cave in the high central mountains, with a brick wall across its entrance and a low door and a window with bars and crooked shutters. Next day I woke to find him gone. No one brought me food that morning or night. The door was locked and the hinges strong. The shutters had been nailed from the outside. It was sheer luck this had been done hastily and using only two nails.

No one came the next morning or the one after. My diet in those first few days was mostly spiders. Spiders, beetles and water found on the cave floor. I felt that if I died here my life would have come full circle. The following morning I stopped being a fool and began hunting the bats that entered the cave at dawn through a high natural chimney to sleep out the day. There were thousands of them. Well, perhaps hundreds, hanging upside down from the rocky ceiling overhead. I took to throwing stones and enough dropped stunned or already dead for me to feed myself. I ate them raw, since I lacked kindling, flint or any wood to burn. Now, looking back, I wonder why I didn't simply wrestle apart a shutter and try to burn that. Holding the bats by their wings to give me something to grip, I would tear out their flesh with my teeth. Sometimes they were alive and other times dead. I ate several a day for maybe a week and though I never caught enough to assuage my hunger, they kept me alive.

At the end of that week I knew beyond doubt a battle was being fought because I could hear musket fire and the sound of cannon. It came and went on the wind for several hours, although I probably only imagined I could smell gunpowder. Another day passed and then I saw French troops on the road below. I shouted and they ignored me. So I shouted again. When this failed I screamed insults and that was enough to have a couple break off from the column and scramble through the scrub towards me. They came angrily and would have beaten me with their muskets had they not been stopped by the locked door.

'Break it down then,' I told them.

They stared at me, the pair of them. Young and sunburnt and stinking of sweat, garlic and cheap wine. They wanted to know who was giving them orders but something in my tone made them hesitate. 'You're French?' one asked.

'I am the marquis d'Aumout. Please call your commanding officer.'

They looked at me doubtfully, then looked at each other with the slightly helpless air of men who realise they'd have been better off staying where they were, and one of them stumbled his way downhill while the other attacked the door with a large rock. Since the door opened inwards he had better luck than I'd had pulling from inside. I was out, and crouched in the sunlight, when a grizzled lieutenant appeared. Up from a sergeant, I thought, remembering some of our trainers from the academy.

'You are the marquis d'Aumout?'

I bowed slightly and he remembered his manners and bowed in return. 'We were told you were dead,' he said. 'Everyone believes you dead.'

'There were times I believed that myself.'

He asked if I could walk and I said probably, but not swiftly. So he shouted for a man to find me a mule and three solders ended up carrying the ammunition the mule had been carrying and the mule ended up carrying me. 'There was a battle,' I said, before clambering onto the creature's back. 'A day or so ago.'

'Ponte Novu,' the lieutenant replied. 'It was a bloodbath. One of their generals refused to fight. Their Hessian mercenaries turned against them in the middle of the battle. Half their army cut and ran. The war is over. We're hunting their so-called general and his gang. We'll find them, don't you worry.' The lieutenant slapped my mule and we set off in a long ragged line up to the ridge of a hill and down the other side towards a small town nestled in a valley. The air smelt sweet and the crickets sang and I drank water from one soldier's canteen and ate another's bread. It was good, if surprising, to be alive.

★   ★   ★

The lieutenant passed me to a major who delivered me himself to the house in Corte commandeered by the comte de Vaux. Having established it really was me, the comte gave me his own quarters, found me decent clothes and had his own servant shave my head and remove my beard. He also lent me a wig and had

297

servants bring me endless jugs of hot water until I felt clean enough to join him. For a week I was tended by a doctor and fed food only fit for an invalid. De Vaux told me again that everyone had presumed me dead. My murder had been mourned and my reputation enhanced accordingly. He was glad it had proved untrue.

I thanked him for his sentiments and asked whom I should talk to about catching the next ship. I would go to Paris if summoned, and I would see Jerome, and Charlot, and anyone else who felt the need to see me, but first I insisted on going home. Manon and my children would be waiting. Tigris too. Tears came into my eyes at the thought of them. De Vaux made the arrangements, told me he'd sent messages ahead announcing my return, and asked, as a favour, if I could visit the gaol in Calvi where Corsican prisoners were being held. Pasquale Paoli had not been found, nor had most of his senior staff. It was thought they were hiding among common soldiers being held until the war was over. Seeing my surprise, he added that the war was over, in any real sense of the word, but a few of the Corsicans had yet to realise that and cleaning up might take another few months.

He fed me well on the last evening, and then I took myself up to bed, stopping only in a corridor to stare at myself in a flyspecked looking glass. My face was gaunt, my cheeks sunken. My shoulders had shrunk and my gut was as flat as a boy's. I'd not looked this thin since leaving the academy. There was far more grey than I remembered in my stubble. The next morning I climbed into a coach and was driven with only two changes of horse to Calvi where I presented a letter from the comte de Vaux to a major who saluted me respectfully and walked me to the prison. The cells were crowded and stank of misery. There were French soldiers with bayonets on their muskets to keep the prisoners back if they mobbed me.

I walked through three huge halls filled with Corsicans; some were wounded and others swaying with tiredness but all gazed at me with blank hatred. In the third hall I noticed a flash of blue eyes and glanced in that direction.

'Someone you recognise, my lord?'

Paoli had grown his hair and a beard and wore the tattered uniform of a private. He had a crutch under one arm and was supported by another man, having been shot in the leg. The man who supported him was Armand de Plessis. Without thinking, I looked round for Héloïse but realised quickly it was a room full of men.

'No,' I said. 'Similar but not the same.'

The major nodded regretfully.

'What will happen to them?'

He looked at his prisoners with distaste. 'We'll release them shortly. Take their names and the parole of any who are officers. Although most of those got away.' Pulling out a fob watch, he consulted it and told me my ship, the *Leopard*, would be leaving within three hours and I was welcome to dine with him or else join my vessel. Pleading tiredness I made my excuses and he had a cart take me to the harbour.

In the last few minutes before we sailed a boy

appeared on the jetty and begged to speak to me. A doubtful captain fetched me from my cabin with promises that he would have the urchin beaten if he was wasting my time.

'You are the Frenchman?'

I tried to smile at him, though desperate for my cot. 'I am Jean-Marie, marquis d'Aumout.'

He nodded, as if that was what he'd asked, and pushed a small parcel towards me. He held it out when I didn't take it and kept holding it out until I did. Then he turned and ran, losing himself in the evening crowd.

'Is everything all right, my lord?'

I assured the captain that it was, and took myself to my cabin with my heart hammering against my ribs and sticky liquid oozing onto my fingers. The muslin was filthy, tied by the corners into a knot that my hands scrabbled to undo. Inside was a cleaner cloth and inside that a fist-sized lump of cheese. Scraping my nail down one side I carried a fragment to my mouth. It was creamy with a slight taste of thyme and the faintest trace of lemon. I remembered Héloïse telling me the girls who gave milk were fed on the finest foods. I allowed myself a slightly larger piece and then wrapped the cheese again in its inner cloth and dropped it into a jug of water to keep it cool.

Corsica gave me back my curiosity and hardened my soul — not the way stale bread hardens in air, but the way steel hardens when put through fire and plunged into water. Long after I'd forgotten the exact shape of Pasquale Paoli's features I could summon fierce hunger and the scent of wild herbs on hot summer winds simply by thinking about those days. And Corsica taught me something else, something unexpected about myself. I was not as comfortable and complacent as I'd thought. In the cottages and ruins and caves of my captivity I'd clung to life with a ferocity that would have done Tigris proud.

It was Signore Paoli in that prison. I know it. But he had, in his way, treated me fairly and I had come through my experiences alive. More than that, I'd rediscovered my appetite and my hunger and my passion for food. That he sent me brocciu di Donna seemed fitting. It was the first truly original thing I'd eaten in ten years. More than this, much more than this, it tasted new. Only later did I realise he'd let me taste new ideas as well.

Brocciu di Donna

Take two pints of whey made from an equal mixture of ewe and breast milk and heat until hand-hot in a ceramic pot over a steady heat. (I've never produced satisfactory results, certainly nothing that equals the brocciu de Donna from Corsica using breast milk alone.) Add three teaspoons of salt and two-thirds of a pint of fresh breast milk and two-thirds of a pint of fresh ewe's milk. Heat to just below the simmering point without allowing the milk to catch on the side of the pan. Allow the mixture to cool to room temperature. Lift the cheese from the whey and drain though muslin. The result should be ivory coloured. *Tastes creamy, rich, almost silky.*

Simple brocciu di Donna

Heat a mixture of two pints of breast milk and two pints of ewe's milk to just below simmering, add a wine glass of good Champagne vinegar (or half that of fresh lemon juice) and allow the mixture to return to room temperature. Strain the mixture through muslin to drain away the whey and mix salt into the remaining curds. Eat within one day. *Tastes creamy and rich, but less elegant in its finish than the above.*

1770

The Return

I returned home to a fierce hug from my son, who at twelve was on the edge of believing himself too grown-up for such things. My fifteen-year-old daughter simply curtsied. Hélène now looked enough like her mother for me to bow back. As for my cat, Tigris barely deigned to acknowledge my return for two days and then refused to leave my side for a month, sleeping across my bedroom door when Manon refused to let her camp at the bottom of our bed.

I'll get to Manon in a moment — but first let me deal with the letters that awaited me. Jerome's announced he was forgoing the last four years of the ten-year period in which I was not to receive my salary as Master of the Menagerie. The treasury had been instructed to remit me twenty thousand gold livres, being the money for this year and the last, when I had been so abominably held captive by . . .

I didn't bother reading the rest. Charlot's letter was strangely formal. He stressed his friendship and our ties. He thanked God for my safety. So much went unsaid I wondered what troubled him. The king's letter, which was probably written by Jerome, thanked me for my efforts on behalf of France and promised me a position at court for my son. If I would rather,

Laurant could have a commission in the army instead.

Voltaire wrote too. I liked his letter best.

He gave thanks for my survival, talked of the trials that put steel in men's souls and ended by paying tribute to the rightness of the cause of those who had captured me. He understood I had met Pasquale Paoli in person. He asked me to write by return giving my impressions of the man, his followers and his politics. He'd heard Paoli had given women in Corsica the vote, that Corsican women not only fought beside their men but acted as NCOs and even commanded brigades. He wanted to know if I had seen any of this. 'It seems the Corsicans' principal weapon was their courage. This was so great that in that final battle near the River Golo they made a rampart of their dead in order to have the time to reload. Bravery can be found everywhere. But courage like that is found only among free people.' Reading Voltaire's words, I remembered those of the old Corsican on the march to the bridge. *It's everybody's war.* For the first time in my life I wondered if we were on the right side.

As I'd hoped, Manon came to my room the night I returned. She was my wife, the marquise, she'd looked after my children and run Chateau d'Aumout while I was away as ably as any Corsican woman widowed by a vendetta. Charlot's letter had stressed how well she'd done. Manon knocked once, pushed open my door and picked a fight.

'Why didn't you write? You should have written.'

304

'Manon, I was a prisoner.'

'From the day you left this chateau until this morning? Someone held you prisoner for all of that? They tied your hands and denied you paper?'

'I was captured almost on landing.'

'You should have written before that. From Versailles. And you should have written the moment you were released. What was it? Ten days ago? More than ten days?' She stood in her white nightgown in the doorway between my room, which had always been our room, and my dressing room, which now seemed to be her bedroom. Her fingers were folded into fists and hard against her hips like a furious child. Sighing, I climbed from my bed and went to hold her. She pushed me away. 'You should have written.'

There was something forced about her anger. 'What's wrong?' I asked.

'Everything. I thought you were dead.'

'Manon. What happened?'

There was anger in her eyes, that was real enough. Perhaps not as much as she pretended and about something other than my lack of letters. She was right, though. I should have written before setting off from Versailles, and at the point I landed in Calvi, and when the comte de Vaux was sending news of my safety to the court. But this was about more than my neglect in not writing, I was certain of that. And I understood Manon well enough to know much of her anger was turned in on herself. I'd known her for eleven years, we'd been lovers for eight and it was five years since I'd married her.

'Manon. Tell me.'

Something in my irritation gave her the courage to answer. Raising her chin, she said, 'Charlot came.' That she called him Charlot, when once she would have said le duc de Saulx or simply le duc should have warned me.

'Charlot came?

'A month ago. He came in person to say the comte de Vaux's campaign against Pasquale Paoli was coming to a head. He knew I still hoped you were alive but he thought it unlikely. He was sorry to be the one to tell me that, but he owed you the debt of treating me honestly. I said . . . ' Manon hesitated. 'What if he was wrong?'

'And Charlot replied?'

'If you were not already dead the Corsicans would kill you to stop you being retaken . . . There were tears in his eyes when he said that.' Manon looked at me, and I understood she was momentarily cross with me, when before she'd been close to pretending. 'You have no idea how he values you. He told me I had his protection. He would find a good husband for Hélène. He would treat Laurant as his own son. He would take over responsibility for running Chateau d'Aumout until Laurant came of age.'

'Manon, what happened?'

'I was lonely.'

She looked away. Her words when they came were a whisper. 'You'd been gone for over a year. And I was lonely.' She gave the tiniest shrug, without looking up from the floor. 'He said you were dead. And I believed him. And now . . . '

'I'm not.'

Tears spilled from her eyes and ran down her cheeks until they reached her jaw and splashed onto her nightdress, turning the cotton translucent. She let me take her shoulders and suffered me to lift her head and dry her eyes with my fingers.

I said, 'You know I love you.'

'How would I know? When have you ever said it?'

Remembering the number of times I'd said it to Virginie long after it stopped being true, as if hoping the saying could make things better, I wondered what had happened to me. I was a man waking to find myself ashamed of what he'd done in his dreams.

Manon hiccupped. 'Wait there,' she told me.

So I waited in my own bedroom, on the first night of my return, until she came back a few minutes later with an embroidered silk banyan I didn't recognise thrown over her nightgown and, hidden beneath it, the silver-tipped crop I'd given her when she began to learn to ride. It was the first year of our marriage. I'd been so proud of myself for thinking of the present.

'Three strokes,' Manon said.

'Why three?'

Sliding the over gown from her shoulders, Manon folded it neatly across a chair. She didn't look at me as she said, 'Work it out.' By then she'd turned her back on me and was bent over the end of our bed with her nightdress round her hips. I didn't know if she meant they'd gone to bed three times, or had gone to bed once and that was the number of times they coupled, nor could I bear to ask. The more I thought about it the sicker I felt.

'Jean-Marie. Do it. This is cruel.'

She was still waiting, bent over the bed I'd intended us to share, her bare buttocks sharper than I remembered, her sex a shadow below. If I whipped her things would be different forever, and if I did not . . . How could I guarantee things would not be different anyway? Tossing the crop onto the bed, I slapped her arse so hard she rocked forward, then steadied herself as I slapped again and again, my slaps explosively loud in the silence. Later, with Manon in my arms, my seed spilling from between her thighs, and her hand cupped lazily over me, she asked why I hadn't used the crop and I lied, saying that if I'd started I would never have stopped.

She kissed my ear and told me I was a good man, a better one than I knew, and I was flattered and wanted to believe her. Before dawn, hesitantly, she told me something I made her say twice, to ensure I'd understood it. Charlot had said — drunk and in the darkness probably, because this is not the kind of thing one says sober, clothed or in daylight — that he wondered how his life would have turned out if Jerome had been with Virginie in the boat that capsized. If I'd been the one to take him downriver that day in the forest when we were almost still children. From this I understood Manon now knew about that day.

Yes, Charlot was very drunk when he said this,

she admitted. Drunk enough to tell her he'd always loved me better than his sister ever could, and her love had cost him ours although he'd done his best not to mind.

'Manon . . .'

'That was what he said.'

'He meant the love of friends.'

She kissed my ear. 'Of course he did.'

1771
The Proposal

'Are you happy?' I asked Manon at the end of the month. Smiling, she nodded. 'Of course.'

'Because if you're not . . . '

Her mouth twitched in amusement. That look I knew so well. *If I'm not, what . . . ?* her eyes asked. *Which bit of what happened can you change?*

'Were you happier when . . . ?'

'Of course not,' she said crossly.

'Good,' I said. 'I'm glad.' Mostly to be spared asking the full question. Were you happier when I was captive? Were you happier with Charlot? Where you happier when you were simply my mistress, before Virginie died? My fear was not of framing the questions but of hearing her answers.

'I'm happy.' Manon leant her head into my shoulder. 'Happier than I've ever been. You should believe it.' I knew little enough of her life while I was in Corsica, and even less of her life before we were together, and nothing about Manon invited questions. I knew she'd lost a husband, and later a daughter — and since her daughter was recently born when she first came to the chateau, she'd lost her husband no more than a year before. Had she loved him, feared him, married him out of convenience? I knew no

310

way of asking and, more than this, knew the memories on which she drew for an answer would be tinged by being seen through the lens of what had happened since.

She came unasked to my bed every night in the month of my return; and took me in her mouth and let me taste myself on her lips and mix that taste with the taste of her other lips until salt and saliva mixed with olives, anchovies, pears, garlic, fresh bread, a black-pepper-and-butter sauce. What we'd eaten made our humours what they were. She laughed when I said that and accused me of wanting to be an alchemist, not understanding why I was offended. I had a hard time explaining I didn't want to change what was into something else. I wanted to record what was so it could be tabled.

I showed her my newest chart where I'd grouped foods into sweet, sour, bitter, salty and savoury the way chemists had begun to group the elements into gases and metals, not-metals and earths. I talked of how eggs coagulated, sugar caramelised, how one taste added to another synthesised a third that could be sweet and sour or savoury and salt. How these could be used to change people's humour. A woman could be brought to bed, a man made to fight, quarrels forced or mended simply by selecting the right foods.

Give me Jerome and Pasquale Paoli, and with the right cook and the recipes I'd prepared I could have brought both to a treaty faster than any periwigged and be-stockinged diplomat. Laughing, Manon reminded me that I habitually wore both wig and silk stockings and suffered me to slap her behind for the insolence. We made love after that and fell asleep in our own rumpled stickiness like bears in some cave.

Laurant adored Manon. Why wouldn't he? She'd fed him at her breast and brought him up as if he were her own. Better than if he were her own, to be truthful. And though Hélène was trickier she trusted Manon more than she trusted me, and somehow that brought them together. That year's seasons blended into each other the way they do as one begins to grow older. And, as they did, the grounds of Chateau d'Aumout filled again with animals too old or too ill to live at Versailles. Some survived and others died, to be fed to those who lived. We acquired pelicans for the lake and a stunted hippopotamus that spent its hours skulking in the shallows, eating grass and leaves rather than the fish I'd imagined. The lion died and tasted stringy as old saddle. I began to think there must be a better way to preserve meat than wind-drying or salting . . . Tigris retook her place as my most constant companion, walking at my side as I made my way round the gardens, my hand resting on her shoulder. She turned from a cub to a young tigress and then to a queen.

Hélène did the same but I was slow to notice.

★ ★ ★

It was the end of 1770, perhaps the start of 1771, around seven years after Virginie's funeral, that Georges Duras arrived on my steps and begged leave to speak to me alone. His coat was well cut but sensible, his breeches flattering without being vulgar, his hair combed back, arranged in curls around his shoulders and dusted with powder in the modern style. He rode a hunter as good as any in my stables and carried a silver-topped whip. His bow was almost courtly and he hovered nervously on the stone steps as he waited for permission to come in.

'We can talk in my study.'

The boy followed me up the stairs and along the landing, his hat in his hand and his steps confident. If he let himself look at the portraits lining the walls and the huge Chinese vase on the half landing he kept his gaze to a skim. I'll admit I was impressed with his blend of confidence and vulnerability, which is always endearing to women and respected by men who recognise it from their younger selves. The only sour moment came when Tigris raised herself from the study floor and Georges stepped back and raised his whip.

'Lower it,' I said sharply.

'My lord . . . '

'She won't harm you if you don't show fear.'

I had no idea if that was true but Georges was persuaded to lower his whip and stand still while she sniffed at his boots and then his breeches and his crotch. She looked at me with blind eyes, wrinkled her nose to say if you insist, and returned to the exact spot she'd been curled on when I'd opened the door. 'Well done,' I said.

He smiled nervously and took the chair I suggested.

Out of kindness I took the chair between the tiger and where he sat, so that what he wanted to say wouldn't be hindered by nervousness — at least no more so than that of any young man sitting silently in the study of a girl's father awaiting permission to begin what he wants to say. I recognised the situation for all I'd had the luck to avoid it.

'Let me get you something . . . '

'My lord . . . '

Our words collided and he reddened, upset to be denied his chance to make the speech he'd no doubt prepared, and rehearsed a dozen times on his ride from town.

'Georges, how old are you?'

'Nineteen, my lord.'

'So soon. One loses track of time.'

He smiled uncertainly. I wondered if he wanted to say only some people had the luxury of losing track of time . . . Except that I believe it's true for all of us. Taking a decanter from the side I poured him a dry and fortified wine and then one for myself, uncovering a dish of salted almonds and spooning some into two smaller dishes. I put a glass and one of the dishes on an occasional table beside him and settled myself with my own dish and glass, which I sipped from slowly. He took that as permission to sip his own.

'What do you think?'

'It's dry, my lord. Also well fortified.'

I waited. He swirled the liquid round his glass

314

in a way that said he knew a little of what he was doing and sipped again, sucking air through the wine in his mouth. He identified it as Spanish and aged in oak.

'Well done,' I said.

He blushed and waited to check that I wasn't about to speak again. The boy had no wish to have his second go at a speech interrupted as well. I was tempted to let him have his head but raised my hand before he could start.

'You have a speech prepared?'

He looked confused. 'Yes,' he admitted finally.

'Forget it,' I said. 'Tell me simply.'

'Hélène and I love each other. I would be honoured beyond belief if you would give me permission to court her, under proper supervision, of course.'

I wasn't sure I intended him to speak quite that simply. 'You've met only once.'

'Three times, my lord.' He spread his hands apologetically. 'The second time two years ago at the Sieur d'Alembert's party. The third, last month at the wine fair.'

'Three meetings are enough to produce love?'

'We write. After the death of . . . ' he hesitated, navigating what he wanted to say. 'After the funeral of your wife . . . Your first wife. I wrote to offer Hélène my condolences. She replied very sweetly and sadly. I wrote again and she replied to that. We have been writing ever since.' He shrugged, as if to say this was how love was born. In this he was right. It is shared sadnesses as much as the shared joys that bind men and women together. I tried to think back to the days

315

after the funeral and imagine my nine-year-old daughter, because that's what she'd been, reading a letter from a twelve-year-old boy she barely knew and sitting down to reply carefully in that beautiful neat writing that was one of the things her mother had left her. I imagined her writing, receiving a reply, writing again, and receiving another reply.

'How many letters?'

'Hundreds, my lord. Maybe more.'

All those shared memories. This was going to be more complicated than I'd suspected. Was already more complicated.

'She's young,' I said, holding up my hand to still his protest. At seventeen she regarded herself as a woman, obviously. And if he regarded her as a woman, and had done more than simply think that fact, I wasn't sure I wanted to know; for all fathers are meant to demand answers to these kinds of questions. 'Let me think on it.'

'My lord . . . ' He stood and bowed.

Maybe I should have rejected him flat out. Perhaps that would have been the fairest response. He certainly read more into my decision to think on it than I intended. Picking up his glass, he gulped his wine, left his almonds and made his farewells with a gaucheness that undid much of the impression he'd made on his arrival. A better-born young man would have known to re-sit himself, finish his wine and make conversation until I let him know he was dismissed.

When Tigris's hackles rose as he turned in the door, I wondered what she saw with those blind

316

eyes of hers that I missed. Her muscles were tense, her lips drawn back to show a little of her teeth. Georges was too full of the moment to notice.

'My lord, I won't disappoint you.'

'Disappoint me?'

'I have always admired this family. Have always dreamed . . . ' He stopped, glanced round the room and his gaze locked on a little silhouette of Laurant framed in an oval glass. 'I'm an only child,' he said. 'The son of an only son.'

'Laurant would be your brother?'

He nodded. 'Exactly. Laurant will be the young brother I never had.'

His voice was triumphant enough to trouble me. As if he were an officer who'd brought off a daring but risky manoeuvre. Maybe I only imagined this to justify the doubts I felt rising. 'Say nothing of this to Hélène.'

'My lord, she knows I'm visiting. She'll be waiting for news of your answer.'

'She knows?'

Georges looked surprised. 'My lord, she suggested I ask. My father thinks I should wait another year and I agree. It's Hélène who insists she's ready to marry. I wanted to wait until our new office in Bordeaux was established and I was full partner with my father in the affairs of the firm . . . I have a house,' he added hurriedly, although I'd cast no doubt on his ability to provide for my daughter. I imagined he knew she'd inherited property from her mother. If he could not provide for her before marriage, he

317

would certainly be able to provide for her lavishly once he had access to this.

'As I said, I will think on it.'

Recognising his cue to leave, Georges bowed himself from the room. After a second, Tigris stood lazily, arched her back to stretch her spine, then dropped her haunches to the carpet and raised her shoulders to stretch it in the other direction before ambling towards the door and nosing at it until it pushed open. The servants were used to her for all they gave her wide berth and some of the more nervous ones simply hid when they saw her. She followed Georges out of the house. I know this because from my window I saw her appear on the steps just as the young man swung himself onto his hunter.

The horse reared at the big cat's appearance and threw its rider.

Georges picked himself up, red-faced and furious, and turned on Tigris, raising his whip . . . Common sense saved his life. I forgot to mention that the year before I left for Corsica, she killed a gardener who entered the chateau and made it as far as the stairs between my study and my chamber on the third floor. He had no reason to be there and when I pointed that out, the other servants accepted he was there to steal and my tiger was not at fault. The point was Tigris would have killed Georges if he had struck her and, even in his fury, the boy had sense enough to realise this.

Turning he lashed his horse, which rose onto its hind legs and screamed as he lashed it again. One of my grooms came running to still the animal and Tigris turned as if her work was done. It was. I knew I'd been right in what I saw behind Georges' eyes. One day he would treat my daughter like that if they were to marry. She was fierce and beautiful and strong-willed, and he was weak. There are men who treat their wives and mistresses that way as a matter of course. I know men who say women should be beaten on the first night to let them know what will happen if they displease. That a single truly savage beating right at the beginning negates the need for later beatings unless that's what you want to do. I have never whipped a woman in anger or as punishment. Neither my wives, my mistresses nor my daughter. I have never seen the need. I would not let another man do to Hélène what had been done to that horse.

At a window in a tower opposite mine, two women were watching, one taller and older and less richly dressed than the other. I only knew this because I knew them, not because my eyes could see clearly at that distance. One of them was my wife, the other my daughter. Though they were unconnected by blood I could not help feeling they had somehow conspired to keep me in the dark over this.

'Naughty,' I said, when the door pushed open.

Tigris simply looked at me and slumped back into her favourite spot on the carpet, closing her milky eyes and beginning to purr. She sat there with the noise of gears grinding coming from the back of her throat while I pulled a sheet of good paper from a drawer, found a new steel nib for my quill, flicked open my ink and began to write.

My dear Emile

Your son Georges came to see me today to declare his love for my daughter and ask for my permission to let him court her. Hélène is still very young and has had a difficult childhood. You know that I hold you — and by extension your son — in admiration. So it is with great regret . . .

1771
Elopement

The recriminations heaped on my head were worse than the worst storm of the coming winter. Hélène was door-bangingly angry, loudly furious and driven from one rudeness to another in a litany of my failings as a father, the hideous tedium of our chateau and the unfairness of life, until all I wanted to do was what I feared Georges would do if I let them marry, and take a whip to her. Even Manon did not hide her disappointment in me. She sighed and looked at me sadly and pretended to believe Hélène when she retired to her chambers claiming a headache that kept her away from family meals for five days. I wanted to send for her but my wife dissuaded me.

Manon came to my room at the end of that week in her nightgown, with her Chinese banyan over it tied tightly at the waist. Her feet were hidden inside red Moroccan slippers with little curled up toes. Her hair tucked under a cap. I understood she was here to talk, no more. 'Why?' she said simply.

'He whipped his horse.' When Manon said nothing, I added, 'You saw it. You and Hélène were at the window. I know you saw it.'

'The beast threw him.'

'It shied at the sight of Tigris.'

'And who released the tiger?'

'Tigris released herself. The point is he thrashed his horse because he couldn't whip my tiger. If he had, we wouldn't have this problem.'

'Jean-Marie . . .'

I apologised, only half meaning it. I hated it when we quarrelled and always ended up saying sorry first, though she claimed I never said sorry and it was always she who had to make the first move. Her way of giving me back some pride, I imagine. Patting the bed, I waited for her to sit beside me, which she did, stiffly, until I moved away slightly to show I understood why she was there and she relaxed a little. So much of human negotiation is unspoken and depends on gestures we learn early to read.

'You need to talk to Hélène.'

My face must have shown reluctance because she repeated it more firmly. 'What do you think your daughter is doing in her chambers?'

'Slamming doors and sulking.'

'Crying,' Manon said, but had the grace to admit that banging doors and sulking, plucking at the little Spanish guitar Charlot had given her years before, and reading sad poems also played its part. 'You need to make your peace.'

'How can I possibly . . . ?'

'Tell her what you told me. Give her your reasons. Explain.'

'She's a child.'

Manon looked at me fiercely. 'How old do you think I was when I married? How old when I had my child? How old when I came here to feed Laurant?'

'You told me you were nineteen.'

'I lied,' Manon said simply. 'I needed the job and lied. I was fourteen when I married, only just fifteen when I had my child, sixteen when you bared my breasts in the maze the day you employed me, twenty when you finally took me to your bed. At Hélène's age I had been wed, bedded and given birth.' She looked around her. 'This world of yours keeps children young.'

No, I thought. *Yours makes them age too fast.*

When had it become my world? Except it always had been. I knew when Manon felt the difference between us. A sudden tightening of her face at a generalisation about peasants, a silence after the louder of our neighbours had visited, her admission she found Jerome blind and arrogant and so removed from any world she knew he could have been a different species. Seen through her eyes Jerome did indeed look different. The loose mouth, the puffy bags under his eyes, his habit of scratching his groin without care for who was around, the fact he never seemed to treat Manon seriously. He'd visited a handful of times since we'd married and he'd been polite enough. Jerome was never rude unintentionally and he knew better than to be rude to my wife, whatever he thought of our marriage. It was the fact he acted as if Manon were a child who needed everything said twice and clearly.

'Go,' she insisted. 'Talk to your daughter. Leave Tigris here.'

I knocked at Hélène's door, and announced myself when she asked petulantly who wanted to disturb her now. My answer shocked her into undoing the bolt. Her room was decorated in maroons and purples. I assumed Manon was behind the changes. The last time I'd visited it had been pink and my daughter still slept in a child's bed. Hélène waited, and since I was her father and it was my job to speak, I did. I asked if she'd seen Georges whip his horse repeatedly across its face and said any man who could do that to his hunter would do the same to his wife. I cared for her, whether she believed it or not. In fact, I loved her for herself and because she reminded me of her mother. Whom I had loved very dearly. The words were hard to say and surprised me as much as her.

She reminded me the horse had thrown Georges, insisting he could have been killed and had acted from shock when he whipped the animal. Anyway, Georges would never mistreat a woman, he was too charming and clever and handsome and ambitious. I resisted pointing out he was handsome for a small town and should he reach the peak of his ambition he'd still be more lowly placed than any of our neighbours' sons, who were no less handsome and had temperaments that were substantially less ugly. Was my belief that he was cruel my only objection? she asked me. When I said yes, she asked if that was true.

Of course, I told her. She knew I was a democrat, that I had corresponded with Voltaire, that I did what I could for my peasants. I welcomed the arrival of the professions. I saw no reason why the cleverest of the middle classes should not be allowed to rise. My daughter's eyes softened at this and she hugged me.

By morning she was gone. A horse missing from my stables and her day clothes vanished. Everything else remained where she'd left it, including her jewellery. On the table by her bed was a letter:

Dearest Papa

Georges is not the man you think him to be. He is charming and clever and has always been unfailingly kind to me. I know you will grow to love him as I do when you know him better. All he wants is to be a part of this family, as I will become a part of his. Forgive me for this.

Your loving daughter Hélène.

I sent messengers to the mayors of every town within a hundred miles telling them to have the local watch look for my daughter. I wrote to the bishops stressing she lacked my permission to marry and since she was noble needed the king's approval to wed; I expected them to make sure their priests knew that. I wrote to Paris to tell the authorities what had happened. I wrote to Charlot, since the girl was his niece, knowing he would begin his own investigations. Then I had my hunter saddled and went to see Emile. Our meeting was short and uncomfortable. I said I felt his son's temperament was wrong for my daughter, that I could not approve their marriage, and this elopement destroyed any chance I might change my mind. If he chose to believe it snobbery or an insistence on my rights, that was his choice and his right.

Customs officers stopped her in Bordeaux about to board a ship for Portugal. Emile's company had recently opened an office in Lisbon and I wondered how much he knew of what his son intended. When she returned, however, Hélène insisted that running away had been her idea and that Georges had been shocked when she had arrived on his doorstep in the early dawn declaring her love and suggesting they elope. I learnt all this from Manon, since Hélène retreated into furious silence every time she saw me. It was Manon who had the task of examining her, since I refused to involve the local doctor. This took place in Manon's room while I waited outside with the door slightly open.

She told my daughter to lie on the bed and there was a rustle of skirts and a long silence broken by Hélène's sobs as Manon did what I'd asked her to do. The silence lengthened and the sobs loudened and I heard a whisper of reassurance, and then the sound of Manon washing her hands in a bowl. She came to the door with her fingers still wet. 'Intact,' she said. I looked at her and she scowled. 'Do you doubt me?'

'Of course not.'

'Probably wise in the circumstances.'

She shut the door in my face and that was the last I saw or heard of either of them that day. I took the knowledge that my daughter was still a virgin despite having spent three nights in

Georges' company up to the study, where Tigris raised her head, examined me with milky eyes and lowered it again. Even she seemed disappointed in me. I tried to write my notes on a meal I'd eaten but the words wouldn't come and I couldn't pin the tastes to the page. After a wasted hour of blotting my letters and crossing out words I took myself down to the lake where Virginie had died and sat myself on the bench where I'd once sat her body when it was dressed and dry.

What had Hélène seen that day? We think we know what they see when our children look at us but what do they really see? Sitting on that bench, and remembering what it was like to be seventeen, and how much I had loved Virginie when she was that age, I wondered how badly I had got it wrong. Whether I should have simply let my daughter marry Emile's son, whether there was still time to change my mind. Night fell and made the decision for me. I returned to the chateau to find a letter waiting for me from Charlot, a second letter from him having already been given to my daughter. Hélène's letter was an invitation to Chateau de Saulx, where, he said, she could recover from her recent upsets and learn to enjoy herself again. My letter promised to keep her safe. I wondered if I was wrong to be offended and read in that promise an implication he would succeed where I had failed.

Corsica had given me a deeper taste for my own company than the one I'd already possessed before going, and a fiercer eye with which to watch the world around me. I saw us as Pasquale Paoli would have seen us and found myself disliking what I saw. When a letter came from Versailles the following year — signed by the king but first dictated to some clerk by Jerome, I imagine — offering my son a position at court, I called Tigris and took Laurant and my big cat for a long walk, and told my son I would not stand in his way. Maybe he heard the reluctance in my voice because he asked what I would have him do instead.

'There was talk of a commission,' I said. 'When I returned from Corsica there was talk of offering you a commission when you were old enough.'

It was clear from his nod that Laurant considered himself old enough now. He already stood a hand taller, and looked enough like his mother to discomfort me. Staring across the little lake, where he'd sailed boats as a child, he admitted he'd considered the navy. So it was settled. I wrote saying my son had a fierce desire to serve His Majesty at sea. I could have added *Where the air is likely to be fresher*, but restrained myself.

The boy left a month later; I've barely seen him since.

After that my life shrinks. The birds wake at dawn, thrushes and larks, robins and sparrows; they wake with the day and settle themselves come dusk. And so do the animals and the animals' owners, my peasants who live like animals themselves. Candles are expensive and finding food is as much as many of them can manage. My life falls into a similar pattern. I wake early, sleep early, tie myself to the rhythm of the land. Servants retire and are not replaced. Manon asks if we are become poor and I say no, I am simply glad of the peace. She should hire as many servants as she needs. We take on another girl to scrub floors and two boys to help in the stables. A footman or two. If she hires others I don't notice.

Emile dies in the summer of 1774, the year Louis XVI is crowned, and I am not invited to his funeral, although I am his oldest friend for all we parted badly. Charlot is invited and refuses. I have no idea if Jerome receives an invitation too. He has stopped writing to me so I must assume rumours of Hélène's near-disgrace have reached him. Unless he is offended by Laurant's rejection of a place at court.

Charlot, of course, regards himself as above scandal. He keeps Hélène with him, introducing her to the sons of his friends and followers. By the time Georges finishes burying his father, my daughter is married. Her husband is a diplomat, half-French and half-Austrian, a baron through his father, due to inherit a chateau and the title of comte when his mother dies, since she is her family's sole remaining heir. Charlot petitions the king for the boy to be allowed to adopt the title early, and this is given. My daughter becomes a comtesse and pregnant in the same month. She lives in London where her husband represents French interests in this war between our two countries, and writes infrequently. When she does, it is always about her children and in the most literal of terms. Her son has learnt to ride, he has learnt to write, he is learning Latin and English. Her daughter is having dancing lessons. She sends me silhouettes of both, black and anonymous, cut-out profiles of children I've never seen and maybe never will, since she moved to London two months before giving birth and has not returned home or visited France since.

1777
Ben Franklin Visits

Two years, possibly three after Hélène moves to London, an American diplomat arrives at my chateau and introduces himself as an old friend of Hélène's husband, the son-in-law I've met only once. He describes the count as an intelligent enough boy — and smiles the smile of old men amused by the presumption of those younger. Benjamin Franklin looks less heroic than his engravings, older and more portly, but I recognise him instantly.

We've met once already — in Paris, the year before I went to Corsica — at the Hôtel de Saulx, Charlot's house in the city. Then he wore a powdered wig, curled heavily at the sides, small spectacles, a white linen shirt with frilled cuffs, a stock tied neatly around his neck, and a powder-blue frock coat with heavily turned-back cuffs held in place with braid-edged lapels and gilt buttons. He could have been a successful financier or a provincial governor. Instead he was an agent for the American colonies, based in London and briefly visiting Paris. This afternoon he wears a brown coat without braid, the simplest of shirts and a fur hat with a tail falling down the back. I know him for one of the new congressional commissioners to the French court.

'Mr Franklin . . . '

'Monsieur le marquis.'

We bow to each other and his eyes flick beyond me and I turn to see Tigris padding towards us, her paws huge on the gravel that fills the circle in front of the chateau where the coaches turn. 'So it's true,' he says. 'You keep wild animals.'

'She was born in a cage.'

He looks at the chateau, looks back at a coach drawing up behind his then drops his hand to Tigris's head and tugs her ears. I'm impressed.

'Weren't we all?' he says. 'Weren't we all?'

Digging his hand into a crude leather satchel that looks as if stitched by wild Indians, he pulls out a rock-like object. 'I thought you might like this.' Mr Franklin has brought me an elephant molar the size of a large grapefruit and heavy as lead. *From the Americas*, he tells me. I look at him and he smiles at my expression and I know he's been waiting to savour this moment. He tells me the elephant's tooth is one of several found near his house in Philadelphia. Proof that there were elephants in America before the Flood.

'Unless something else killed them,' I say.

He glances around him, but his coachman is looking at one of my maids, and everyone else is looking at the young black woman climbing from the second carriage. She is young and full-figured, dressed in the latest Paris style. 'What but the Flood?' he begins, half-distracted by his own companion.

I shrug my shoulders. 'Who knows what killed

the elephants in the Americas? But it's an interesting question, don't you agree? Perhaps all animals once existed everywhere. Perhaps Noah's ark was less successful than God hoped . . . '

He smiles at me. 'Let me introduce Celeste to you. She knows a lot of Creole recipes. You'll find her interesting.'

'Monsieur le marquis.' The black girl curtsies deeply enough for me to see her cleavage and looks up from under long lashes, but her eyes flicker and I know the presence of Tigris at my side is unnerving her. Ben Franklin mutters something and she nods doubtfully.

'Take a turn in the garden with me,' I say.

'Later,' says a voice behind me. Manon smiles to soften her words. 'They've been travelling all day. No doubt they want to wash, freshen themselves. You can show Tigris off later.' She smiles at the girl, and says to her, 'Once the tiger knows you're friends with my husband she'll be friends with you too. Tigris can't see, but her sense of smell is excellent and somehow she always knows what's going on. I'm afraid we have quite a lot of animals. You'll find flamingos and an old hippo in the lake, a giraffe in the lower paddock. Just look for the stripped vegetation. We have a gazelle as well, too old to jump its fences. And parrots in most of the trees. If you're unlucky my husband will give you parrot stew for supper.'

'I like parrot stew,' Celeste says.

Manon's mouth quirks and she nods. 'Then you'll get on famously. Come inside. I'll have the servants find you a room.' Celeste glances at Mr Franklin, who nods, and she follows my wife up the stairs and disappears into the cool of the hall, leaving me with my visitor.

'Your mistress?' I ask.

'Not mine,' he says. Something in the way he says it suggests there's a story wrapped up inside his denial, and a twinkle in his eye says we might get to it later. But there is, it seems to me, a calculation behind the twinkle. Just as there is a calculation in the way his clothes have changed in the years since we last met. If I had not seen him in his powder-blue frock coat in Charlot's Parisian drawing room, smiling at the men and softly, carefully, talking his way inside the petticoats of a baroness known for her virtue, I would believe today's brown coat and simple shirt, fur hat and sturdy shoes indicated a man who came straight from the wild American frontier to plead with France for help fighting his colony's English masters. Mr Franklin asks what I'm thinking and I tell him.

He smiles, and flutters a liver-spotted hand towards my faded frock coat and old-fashioned wig. 'We wear what we have to wear to play the parts that we need to play. A man like you understands this.'

I'm flattered at his 'man like me', as I'm meant to be, and ask about Celeste, who is at a window with Manon looking down across the gardens. I see the black girl's gaze sweep across us and then stop on Tigris. She says something to Manon, who laughs.

'Your wife was not noble,' Mr Franklin says.

334

'You heard?' This is only half a question.

'Yes,' he says. 'How long is it now?'

Since we married? 'Thirteen years. Long enough to know we're happy.'

He considers this, and tickles Tigris's ears while he does, drawing a rumbling purr from deep in her throat. A sound that fills his face with sudden and real happiness. I decide in that second that I like the man for all that I don't really trust him or know why he has brought his coach south simply to reacquaint himself with me after all these years. My fame, which is slight, is for recipes, strange farming methods and an obsession with food. Court politics have long since ceased to have any interest. Those I leave to Jerome and Charlot. And the kind Emile once practised? They bore me. Emile's friends don't want to open the cage and return the animals to the wild, they simply want to change who owns the zoo.

'No falls from grace?'

'One each and both regretted.'

'So it's possible,' he says, and it takes me a moment to work out what he means, and another to frame my reply, which is that it is perfectly possible for a man to be content with only one woman if it's the right woman.

'And he's the right man,' Mr Franklin says.

I'm not sure if he means the right man for the woman or the kind of man who can be content with only one woman at a time. He tells me — and I am uncertain if he's tying this to my fall from grace or not — that he writes on occasion to Pasquale Paoli, who mentioned that in the last days of the Corsican republic my life was saved by the pleas of a young girl I'd saved from death some years earlier.

Swallowing my shock, I tell him that at best I saved Héloïse from a broken leg, and he nods as if I've just confirmed something he's suspected for a long time. 'Call me Ben,' he adds, before walking with me to see my gazelle, who looks at us with tired eyes and is so old she has trouble keeping her massive sweep of horns steady.

'She'll die soon,' I say.

'And then?'

'I'll eat her, probably slow roasted given her age. Maybe boiled and then slow roasted if the meat looks really tough when I come to prepare her.'

'You should talk to Celeste. She has eaten snake and alligator, puma and possum. She tells me she knows recipes that mix snake with chicken.'

'And I've mixed snake with cat. It's an old Chinese recipe,' I add, seeing his expression, and we walk on, taking a long turn around the paddock with the giraffe, and then back along the edge of the lake where the pygmy hippo floats as quietly as a log, his nostrils only just above the water and his eyes watching us pass. I'm proud of the hippo. It was almost dead when it arrived, and though I was tempted to let it die, my job as Lord Master of the Menagerie was to keep it alive for as long as nature would let it live. So maybe I was proud of myself for not giving in to temptation. Although it's easier not to give in to temptation when one's kitchen has a ready supply to hand of the exotic and near-dead.

Unbuttoning the flap on his breeches, Ben Franklin pisses against a tree without feeling the need to retire into the undergrowth or turn away. I'm not sure if it's affectation or he really doesn't consider it a matter of shame. The man interests me. He's probably used to that. As we walk back to the chateau he tells me more about Celeste. She can quote Voltaire, and talks of the tedium of Versailles with all the boredom of a French marquise. So far as Ben can tell there is no difference between her and any other woman he has befriended, apart from the colour of her skin and the darkness of her eyes. He's begun to wonder if our natures are a product of how we're treated rather than to whom we're born . . .

He tells me openly that his father was a soap-maker and the son of a blacksmith, his grandmother on his mother's side an indentured servant little better than a slave. That he grew up poor and knows the value of thrift, and that the years he wore silks did nothing to change his early life. Nor would he want it changed since the values and virtues it instilled outweigh any hardship. He looks at me to see how I take this. So I tell him my parents starved to death when I was small and I grew up in a school for the poor; that my title and the castle behind us I owe to having killed a wolf and travelled downriver under an upturned boat. Had those boyish adventures not happened I would, at best, probably now be dead on some forgotten battlefield. Had le Régent not found me I would never have gone to St Luce. For reasons that escape me, rescuing a trapped cat and her kittens from a thorn bush at the expense of my own skin appealed to a vicomte and helped convince a colonel that I was right for what the vicomte had in mind. Our lives are built almost entirely on a foundation of events colliding.

Ben smiles, and announces that that bon mot alone makes his trip worthwhile. He hopes we will have many more conversations in the week he would like to be allowed to stay, but adds that we should probably make our way back to the chateau to see how the marquise and Celeste are doing. He says one other thing, as we return, that gives me the frisson that comes from meeting for the first time an idea one has not had the intelligence to think for oneself. He touches briefly on the political uses of taste; not just in fashion or furniture but in wine and food. About how taste defines and separates the sexes and the classes and the cultures and the races. I had been lucky to fall so in love with Roquefort, and to do so immediately. The development of taste is like learning to read — and we live in a world where we deny most of those around us access to its alphabet.

A footman opens the door as we approach, and I usher Ben into my house and realise Manon has left the door to the small drawing room open so she can hear us return. She smiles at him, shoots me a glance that says *Where have you been?*, and tells him she'll show him to his chamber herself. It is late, he's travelled long distances and I have still to discover why he is in my house. I am delighted, however, to play host to a man widely described as 'the First American'. The Americas claim to have no aristocrats. But this man is, despite his birth, among nature's natural nobility.

The next morning Celeste knocks at my study door and announces that Mr Franklin has said I might want to hear about the food of her childhood and asks if she can come in. She sits on the very edge of a chair and looks surprisingly nervous for someone willing to describe herself as bored with life at Versailles. Maybe it's Tigris, curled around the corner of my desk in her usual position, her head heavy on her great front paws, who makes her nervous. She receives my suggestion that we swap chairs with gratitude, and she takes my seat and I take hers, leaning against the unfamiliar side of the desk as I begin to make my notes. Her French is heavily accented and mixed with African words. She's not black, she tells me, she's mulatto. Her mother was black, her father is an Arcadian octaroon — one part Iroquois — who moved south with the other French-speakers when the Treaty of Paris gave the Atlantic coast of Canada to the English-speakers.

'You know more about your family than I know about mine.'

She looks to see if she's being mocked, but I'm already making notes about her heritage below the four or five recipes she's given me, and she decides I mean what I say.

'How does alligator stew taste?'

'Like leathery chicken.'

I can't help but sigh.

To cook Celeste's alligator stew

Fillet three pounds of alligator tail and put to one side. Make a basic oil-and-flour sauce, using enough brown flour to stiffen a small wine glass of oil. Add three sliced onions, two red capsicum and two celery stalks and cook until the onion is clear. To this mixture add eight diced tomatoes and cook for another fifteen minutes. Once cooked, add enough fresh water to leave a thick sauce. Now add two crushed cloves of garlic, the juice of one lime, a teaspoon of salt, a tablespoon of dried and well-ground chillies, a glass of dry white wine, and another eight tomatoes that have been boiled to pulp with black pepper, strong treacle and half a glass of brandy. Cut alligator meat into inch squares and put into pan, ensuring the sauce covers the meat completely. Return to the boil and cook for at least three hours, adding water if necessary. *Tastes like leathery chicken.*

Further questioning reveals alligator to be a white meat with a red-meat consistency, somewhat like chicken but with the texture of beef, and, if anything, a little denser and so needing a longer marinate or a slower stewing. Apparently it sits well with dried chillies and should always be served *piquante*. I tell Celeste crocodile tastes more like turkey, in that the meat is dry and slightly musty. But that if one draws a cross — and I drew a cross — and divides the sections into chicken, beef, mutton and pork then it definitely falls within chicken but close to the line signifying the border with pork. I show her the pages of my latest journal, where recipes are categorised into four food groups — fish, fowl, meat and plant — and arranged alphabetically within each.

'This has a purpose beyond taxonomy?' she asks, before adding, 'Which has a value, obviously', and looking to see if she has offended me. I tell her those who come after me will put a value on what I've done with my life. Either that or they'll judge it worthless. Celeste smiles and takes my arm as we make our way downstairs to find the others.

We walk in the gardens, all of us together. Occasionally, one or two of us will sit and the others will keep walking until those sitting are out of sight. Manon likes Mr Franklin's company and I find myself impressed by Celeste's fierce intelligence. I imagine Versailles must do more than bore her. She must find it stifling. In the overgrown maze I had planted for Virginie I kiss Celeste, who seems neither surprised nor offended and kisses me back. She grips my wrist when I begin to raise her petticoats until I explain that I want only her taste and she relents. Mr Franklin smiles when he sees me later.

The week passes pleasantly and makes more of an impression on my memory than most of my recent weeks, which my mind discards as repetitions of weeks that have gone before and so in need of no memory. Celeste holds my arm as

341

she walks, Mr Franklin leans on Manon and she steadies him a little as we make our way down the red brick steps at the back of the terrace. We're about to see an animal killed, among other things.

Celeste shrugs when I say this and tells me she watched her father slaughter hogs back home when she was a child, and Mr Franklin tells me he'd been taught to wring a chicken's neck, pluck it and gut it by the time he was seven. I say those are the skills we should be teaching our children and he laughs. 'Tell me more about this experiment of yours.'

'You can see it for yourself . . . ' We walk round the side towards the stables and the outhouses beyond. Tigris walks at my side, her head under my hand.

'Who's guiding whom?' Franklin asked.

'We guide each other.'

He smiles at my answer but stops in the door of the slaughter yard, suddenly uncertain. The gazelle stands in the middle of the yard, back legs already tied. Her sweep of horns curves back more elegantly than any sketch can capture; but her trembling is more than nervousness, her horns too heavy for all they're beautiful. She's grown too old and too tired to hold up her head.

'Jean-Marie . . . '

'It's her time,' I tell Manon. In one corner a huge range heats a copper cauldron big enough for me to bathe. Steam already rises from the water inside. The third part of today's experiment is hidden in the shed. Usually it would be ready but I don't want to ruin Mr Franklin's surprise. He is looking carefully at a tripod crane I will use later. He looks with the keen gaze of someone who has carried out his own share of experiments.

'My lord . . . ' A slaughter-man brings a bowl of entrails from something killed earlier and stops a safe distance from Tigris, who raises her head and sniffs the air, milky eyes restless. I decide it would be better if she remains outside the yard and lead her back the way we came.

'She'll be safe?' Mr Franklin asks me.

'No one will disturb her.'

His bark of laughter says that was not his worry.

'She'll sleep,' I say. 'After eating she always sleeps.' Taking his arm, I turn him back to the door into the yard and we go in together. The men are waiting. It is a blue-skied day, the kind you remember for ever as a child, and welcome for the ease it brings when old, for all it lacks the significance it once had. Celeste asks what I'm thinking.

'You're not old,' she says, when I tell her. 'Now show Ben your experiment. He likes things like this.' She's right, he's watching closely.

They kill the gazelle cleanly. Now is the real moment. The doors to the brick shed open and two men drag out a hand cart.

'A jar?' Mr Franklin asks.

'Bound tight with strips of canvas.'

He walks to the edge of the cart and feels the thickness of the glass jar and looks carefully at its canvas swaddling. He's already worked out what the canvas does and I let him tell me. He's right, like rope wound round an old cannon, it helps to stop the glass from shattering under the pressure and heat. Mostly it does. Not every glass survives boiling. I tell Celeste we could buy a farm with what that jar cost and Manon's glance is sharp. 'It will become cheaper,' I say hastily, 'as more jars are made and the glass foundry perfects the art. Knowledge always comes at a price.'

Mr Franklin is looking thoughtful. His face is heavy and the flesh beneath his chin rests on the starched linen of his stock. I suspect he looks better as an old man than he did when young, as if the ruined grandeur of his face was something he had to prove the right to inherit. An experimenter himself, he can see the work that has gone into this. My butchers work fast, and the newly skinned, gutted and beheaded animal is manhandled into the jar. A block and tackle then lifts the jar high enough to be lowered into the cauldron. Men scramble up ladders to tip in buckets of brine until the jar is almost full and then a huge cork seal is wrestled into place and hammered down. Now it must simmer, although I'm not sure for how long. Half a week perhaps. If that's not enough I'll try a week for something this size next time.

'I understand the theory,' Mr Franklin says. 'But what's your aim?'

'To make good food widely available the whole year round and abolish famine. Let me show you . . . ' We head back to the chateau, Tigris rising sleepily to her feet and falling into step as I pass. There is still blood in her bowl and on the gravel behind us but she has licked her face

344

clean. In the larder the air is chill and the flagstones cold under our feet, the shelves around us laden with glass jars and resting cheeses. Wind-dried hams hang from the ceiling, mixed with strings of onion and garlic. Sacks of potatoes rest by a wall.

'Remind me to talk to you about those,' I say.

Mr Franklin nods, eyes fixed on our prize. A young warthog is upended in a jar, bristly-skinned and madly grinning through murky brine, its head twisted grotesquely. Evidence of the accident that killed it. Until today this was my biggest experiment. I would have liked to bottle the gazelle whole too, but her beautiful horns prevented it.

'Would you like to . . . ?'

Celeste looks at the hammer and chisel I take from a shelf and shakes her head. Mr Franklin tells me I should have the honour. So I chip away the sealing wax with which the cork is fixed and prise the lid free. The brine smells sweet enough and no foulness rises from the warthog as I dunk my arm into the liquid to my elbow, jab the chisel into the warthog's shoulder and rip flesh away. Celeste, Mr Franklin and Manon shake their heads when I hold it out, their movements synchronised and unconscious. We say we want new experiences, but the opposite is true, and ever more so as we grow older. Tigris wrinkles her nose at the saltiness of the morsel so I eat it myself. The pork is as bland and near-tasteless as only pig can be when boiled without herbs or spices. 'A year,' I say. 'That's how long it's been in here. Just think . . . With this method we can

345

keep meat indefinitely. Store it in times of plenty against the famines to come.'

'Like Joseph,' Celeste says. 'With his dream of seven rich years and seven lean.'

'Exactly like that,' Mr Franklin says. He claps me on the shoulder. 'A noble idea,' he tells me. 'A worthy experiment.'

I've been worried this week has been about more than my company or sight of my experiments, and now I'm certain. When he suggests we take a walk round the garden as there's something he wants to ask me, I'm not even surprised.

★   ★   ★

'What is it?'

I stare at our bedroom ceiling, seeing the light of the candle flame lap at the darkness with every flicker of the wick. Cobwebs in one corner show where a maid has been lax in her duties.

'Jean-Marie . . . ' Manon speaks sharply. Something she only does when we're alone. 'What is troubling you?'

I could say what troubles me is the way she touches the back of Mr Franklin's hand, and the way he leans in to listen to her speak, but then she could charge me with the attentions I've been paying to Celeste, who has a mind as sharp as a freshly-stropped razor, flesh like velvet and a taste like sour honey. And yet, what rankles hurts more than anything that might have passed between Mr Franklin and my wife. He is here because of Charlot, now one of the great

346

ministers of the realm. Ben has been told, and he tells me he believes what he has been told, that I have influence with Charlot in a way few others have. I say Charlot is my friend, quite possibly my only real friend and, complex as that friendship sometimes is, I will do nothing that could harm him. Mr Franklin assures me that what he wants from Charlot can only add to his greatness. He wants me to write a letter asking Charlot to reconsider.

'Reconsider what?' I ask.

It seems Charlot is opposing additional aid to the Americas. He says the kingdom cannot afford it, and Jerome agrees; but the marquis de Caussard quibbles at the cost of everything and it is to Charlot that the new king will listen. Mr Franklin wants me — as a good man, as a modern man — to write to Charlot and say supporting America is something we should do. We should offer aid. More than this, we should enter a military alliance, and sign an accord that neither side will make peace with England without the other. In addition, American independence must be a non-negotiable condition of that peace.

Charlot can persuade the king and Mr Franklin believes I can persuade Charlot. He has travelled all this way to plead his cause with me. He has been summoning his courage all week to ask me to do this. He hopes that I will understand and agree.

'Why did you think he was here?' Manon asks.

'You knew he wanted this?' I sit up with the shock of that thought, swing my bare legs out into the cold air and stop on the edge of the bed, uncertain where my feet should take me.

'I knew he wanted something. It was obvious. Why else would he come?'

'To see my experiments.'

Manon tucks herself behind me, rests her chin on my shoulders and wraps her arms around me as she always did when she was young. 'My poor boy,' she says. 'There is a war on. The American colonies are fighting for their lives. They have more important things to think about than how to grow potatoes or bottle a gazelle . . . ' We sit like that for some minutes, and then she reaches down to find me. I crawl back into bed and fall asleep between her thighs and wake in her arms. As always when I wake like that the world seems kinder.

1784
The Loris

The Treaty of Alliance with the Americas was signed the following spring at the Hôtel de Crillon, with the approval of King Louis XVI and in the presence of Charles, duc de Saulx. Nine weeks after that, on 17th March 1778, my daughter's husband informed the English government in London that France recognised the United States of America as an independent nation and ally forever. I wrote asking her to congratulate him on his part in history. She didn't bother to reply. It occurred to me then that both my children had deserted France. Hélène had her life in London. Laurant lived on his ship, wherever that took him, which seemed to be everywhere but here. I didn't blame them. The sourness I'd first tasted in the air at Versailles years earlier had spread across France like malign marsh fog. Where there had been misery there was now misery and anger. I began to believe that only a truly fierce wind could strip away its sourness.

A few years later I said that to a neighbour at a Christmas party and he looked at the people around us and said he didn't understand what I meant. Shortly afterwards, just before the party ended, he found me alone and told me he agreed. Charlot wrote in the spring to say I was being watched by the police and should guard my words. I asked by reply how he knew, and he told me by return that their masters reported to him and I'd do well to concentrate on my animals. I wrote back suggesting he concentrate on his — since the inhabitants of my zoo were better-housed, better-treated and better-tempered. His reply was typically Charlot: to take my mind off sedition he was sending me an oddity a distant sultan had sent to the king.

'My lord . . . '

I looked up from my desk and made myself smile. The servants would have preferred that I left my study door shut and made them knock, so I could growl at them to go away or hurry up and come in. Sometimes I think half the ritual in our houses is for their benefit. I might need girls to carry water from the kitchen for my bath. But a woman to oversee them, overseen by my housekeeper, overseen by my master-of-house? The man who warms the towels, the man who brings my tea, and my valet . . . Never mind the under-footmen waiting outside my bathroom door. And they wonder why I hide in my study.

My study is at the back of the chateau on the floor below the attics. The room's shape is awkward since it is part of a tower, but windows let out on three sides giving a sweep of the river. I swam there once with Virginie in the very early days. The peasant girls swim there still in the heat of high summer, tiny specks believing their nakedness hidden by bushes. I listen to them, their excited voices and loud laughter, until someone from the castle goes to quieten them in case I might hear, and they scramble for their clothes and hide. They are tiny at this distance. It is like watching flies.

'My lord . . . '

The woman was still waiting.

'This came with the letter.' As succinct and informative as any other information given in this house. Since the door was half shut and she hid herself behind it all I could see was her anxious face and a greying bun of hair. I had no hope of seeing what *this* was.

'Bring it in then.'

She edged her way through the door clutching something the size of a cat and the colour of a fox but with huge eyes made larger by patches like a mask either side of a long, slightly shrew-like nose. The eyes were screwed tight against the light. Instinctively I rose to shut the blinds, casting the study into gloom. 'It must sleep in the day,' I said.

The woman looked at it doubtfully and held it a little further from her body. Perhaps she twisted it, perhaps it was simply distraught at being sent halfway round the world: whatever the reason, it turned and bit her. The obvious happened. She yelped and dropped the creature and it hit the floor and yelped in its turn. It was as well Tigris was asleep in the sun on the terrace or she'd probably have eaten the thing.

'Get that cut treated.'

She looked from the bite on her wrist to the creature on the floor, dropped a low curtsy and hurried from the room. Maybe she washed the wound. Maybe she didn't bother. Maybe she simply didn't wash it thoroughly enough. Within an hour she had a fever and by nightfall servants were clustered in corners whispering to each other and I sent a man for the village priest. An old man at the end of his tenure. The choice of candidate had been mine. She died before morning, her body rigid and bathed in sweat.

I should have sent for a doctor, the village said.

I've seen death and I've seen fever; living near marshes, who hasn't? And I knew the moment I saw her she was beyond a physician's help and only a priest was needed. All the same, perhaps they were right. She was buried two days later and I ordered every servant in the chateau to take that morning off and attend her wake that afternoon. And with the kitchens deserted, I cooked the loris in peace, having killed it as cleanly as I could.

Fifteen inches in length.

I noted the details in my book.

Twenty ounces in weight. More, I imagined, in the wild. The creature was half starved and I wondered what the man who brought it to my chateau had been feeding it. The stomach sac contained apple pulp, also the rotted remains of a spider. The only thing of real interest was a strange gland in the elbow that opened onto the surface like an unhealed wound. It had been licking its elbow before it bit the woman. Skinned, it looked human enough to have me filleting it swiftly and sweeping the guts, skeleton and skin into a sack.

I fried it with unsalted butter and seasoned it

with black pepper and a little paprika. It tasted a little like cat, but the meat was stringy from starvation and I ate only enough to determine the taste, being worried the poison might spread to the rest of its flesh. Some mammals are poisonous to eat, very few admittedly, but there are some and I was not sure if this was one of them.

The early sun of the next day told me I'd survived.

The gardeners found bits of its corpse half-burnt in the ashes of a bonfire. I'd been so furious it had killed my servant that I had tortured the creature to death and chopped it into pieces myself. So they said anyway. They looked at me a little more kindly for a while . . .

★ ★ ★

Laurant is in the Indies, an easy-going naval officer with warm brown eyes and a string of conquests behind him. He writes briefly but often, enclosing leaves and pebbles and shells and dried-out insects of the strangest shape. Whatever he thinks will interest me. He sees me as a scientist, a naturalist, a philosopher. A man who writes to Voltaire and has his letters answered. I'm always amazed how little children know their parents, and suspect we know our children no better. I like his letters, his casual disregard for what others would write. Occasionally he remembers to tell me where he is. Now and then he mentions promotions, awards or prize money from privateers taken. I had to find out from the son of a neighbour that Laurant had been made captain. I'd still thought him a commander.

Most of all, I'm glad my children are where they are. Safe in London, or safe on the way to whichever wild island my son is due to visit next.

In the period between Hélène's marriage and now, Georges Duras has re-made his life and re-written his history. He studied Voltaire for himself, became able to talk easily about politics, reform and the law. Always he combined reform with law, so the authorities would know he was law-abiding. He gave up control of his father's firm to a manager who increased its profits and began to open branches in other cities. Georges himself stepped away from the people he'd been trying to impress, people like me, and began to make very different friends. His election to the provincial assembly as a member of the Third Estate, representing the bourgeoisie and the peasants, made him a man of local importance. His essays and pamphlets and speeches have spread his influence far wider.

Ten years of famine have made France hungry for change, and the Treaty of Paris in 1783, in which the English recognised America's right to independence, convinced the Georges of this world that the future is theirs. They want freedom, not from the English as the Americans did, but from us. We are their English, they are their own Americans.

The irony is that if the king had not supported the Americans their conspiracy would have failed and London would have its colonies still. We defeated Pasquale Paoli's army in Corsica, but the constitution he wrote influenced the Americans when the time came for them to write theirs. The soldiers we sent to fight beside the Americans brought back a revolutionary fervour borrowed from their allies. They have seen first-hand that change can happen. If we had not supported America, France would not be bankrupt and the king would have had no need to call an Assembly of Notables. It was the failure of that assembly in 1787 that led to the calling of the Estates General two years later. Georges was a representative of the Third Estate. He was one of those who, on 17th of June last year, declared the Estates General a National Assembly and voted themselves ruling powers. A month later the prison at Bastille was stormed by the mob and the massacres in Paris began. 1789 changed everything. We are their English and they are the revolutionaries.

Their war for independence has begun.

1790
Revolution

The rest is history or will be for those who come to write it after us. I doubt they will be kind, and why would they? They will see our sins and forget our graces. It is a year since the Estates General became the National Assembly and the Third Estate, led by men like Georges, decided they could do without the First and Second Estates; the Church and nobility having been outgrown. Last summer's riots saw the burning of dozens of chateaux and the massacre of thousands like me. Many of my friends have become *émigrés*, fleeing to London or Vienna or Berlin. Others have adopted the tricolour and sworn their allegiance to the new regime. I doubt it will be enough to keep them alive.

The news when it comes is always old, and something else is always happening as we learn about what has gone before. The provinces are now *départements*. Monasteries have been shut, as have nunneries. I have no idea if the tales of raped nuns are true. Georges' club in Paris, the Jacobins, contains nobles and bourgeoisie and even peasants. They call each other friend and embrace the rights of man. I am no longer the marquis d'Aumout. Last year we gave up our feudal rights, this year we give up our titles. The decree nailed to my door a month ago made that clear.

1. *This day 19th June 1790 the National Assembly declares that nobility by descent is forever abolished. Consequently, the titles of Prince, Duke, Count, Marquis, Viscount, Vidame, Baron, Knight, Lord, Squire, Noble & all other similar titles shall neither be accepted by, nor bestowed upon, anyone.*
2. *A citizen may use only the real name of his family. No one may wear livery or have it worn, nor may anyone use a coat of arms. Incense shall be burned in churches only to honour God and shall not be offered to any person.*
3. *The titles of Your Royal Highness and Your Royal Highnesses shall not be bestowed upon any group or individual, nor shall the titles of Excellency, Highness, Eminence, Grace, Lord, etc . . .*

In my forties and fifties I was out of fashion, lacking the embroidered cuffs and flamboyant coats then becoming fashionable. Now I am à la mode again, my simple dress reflecting the concerns of the age. Peacock is out, owlish seriousness is in. So it goes. My clothes were always simple unless where I found myself absolutely demanded something more ornate. The world changes around me, sometimes in my favour, sometimes against. They say Jerome is murdered, and his sister and Charlot émigrés, self-exiled in London, a place they detest. It occurs to me that my daughter, Charlot's goddaughter, is in London also. I wonder if it influences his choice. They were close, I gather, in those few years following her elopement. In someone less influential than Charlot it might have attracted muttering.

Ben Franklin once told me something said to him by the Swedish ambassador: *The afternoon knows what the morning never suspected*. As I approach the final foothills of old age I wonder if anyone has had time to write what the last few seconds of the evening know. Maybe that duty falls to me. I have sent Manon to London with the best of Virginie's jewellery for Hélène. She took also a box of valuables — miniatures, enamel snuffboxes, loose diamonds, and as many gold coins as she could carry. The box was drab and she wore servant's clothes, leaving quietly without saying her goodbyes. Shortly afterwards, I sent her a letter with an émigré I knew was leaving, told him Hélène's London address and begged him to put my letter into Manon's hands himself. It told her not to come back. I loved her, I wrote. She had given me a peace and a happiness that no other woman had managed and I had certainly never managed to give myself. I apologised for my unkindnesses, of which I was sure there were many, and begged her to take my order seriously. If she returned she would die. Hélène was to have her mother's jewellery but everything else in the box was for her. I would remain at Chateau d'Aumout with my kitchens and my notebooks. Tigris would be here to protect me, as I would be here to protect her. I had no doubt an end would come, and I would try to face it as bravely as I could, but I was too old, too tired and too much of a coward to change countries and begin my life again. She would forgive me, I hoped, and remember me fondly. Laurant would mourn me and — if he had any sense — get on with his life. I doubted Royalist officers would be welcome back in France but some of our colonies must have remained true and there was always America. They liked French aristocrats in America, we'd helped them defeat the English. And if she could persuade my daughter to forgive me, then that was more than I deserved . . .

★   ★   ★

The servants have gone, sent home or left of their own accord. The chateau is empty and echoing, and strangely peaceful for the first time in years, although I suspect that is about to change. Last night a young man arrived at my door and pounded hard on the wood until I abandoned my study and went to see why he bothered me. The guttering wicks of my candelabra lit the face of a village boy I vaguely recognised. He looked at me and held out a sealed paper, letting it drop the moment I reached for it. The letter hit the cobbles and ruffled at the edges in the night wind.

'You will pick that up,' I told him.

He glared at me like the child he mostly was and shook his head. He wore a floppy cap with a

359

three-coloured cockade, and a grubby sash made from a strip of red ribbon. A brace of pistols were pushed into his wide leather belt.

'Your father would be ashamed of you.'

He spat on the cobbles.

'And your mother, if you behave like that.'

'Read that,' he said. 'Obey it.'

I looked at him, then glanced at the dropped paper and began to shut the door. I saw no reason why he couldn't return his letter the way it had come, tucked in his grubby pocket, to whomever sent it in the first place. I doubted it was anything I wanted to read.

'You have to take it.' He dipped to the cobbles, grabbed the letter and pushed it at me, his face suddenly anxious. 'Go on. Take it.'

I shook my head and kept shutting the door. That was when he grabbed for my sleeve to stop me disappearing. There was a snarl as Tigris materialised out of the darkness of the hallway behind me. The door pushed open as she bundled through so fast the boy stepped back, tripped over his own feet and tumbled down the stone steps behind him, the back of his head connecting hard with the edge of the bottom stair.

She went to sniff at the boy.

'Good cat,' I said. 'Old cat.' What else was there to say? She glanced back, although what she really did was turn to listen, her eyes as milky white as the day I first saw her in the zoo at Versailles. She purred as I told her the gardens were hers. The night was hot, the weather close enough to sour milk, so I dragged the boy up the

360

steps, along a corridor, through the kitchens and into a larder, which, with its thick walls and cold stone floors was the coolest place in the chateau. I left him under a shelf on which sat a Parmareggio that Charlot's eldest boy had sent me a few years earlier.

Did I make a mistake, or was Georges Duras always the man who wrote the letter now open on my desk? Worse still, did I make Georges that man? I can see his face that day he whipped his hunter, his eyes fierce with the fury of being shamed. I have not heard he has mistreated a woman or an animal since. His reputation is for ruthlessness and probity. He does not drink, he does not whore, he wears simple clothes and lives with his half-sister, a homely woman who does his cooking and darns his clothes and scolds him if he works too late into the night. He is dedicated to change, they say. A staunch Jacobin of the most incorruptible kind. I would go to see him myself but what is the point? Georges has not bothered to come to see me. He simply sent a sullen messenger to sneer and drop his message at my feet when I reached to take it. Georges would never be that crude. But the messenger was young and needed a man like Georges to tell him what to think. Just as I once needed Charlot to teach me where my loyalties lay.

Last night's letter was addressed to Citizen Aumout. No title, no particule to link my name to the land, no politeness. It simply says my chateau is confiscated in lieu of unpaid taxes judged by the local assembly to come to the chateau's worth. I have a day to make alternative arrangements and hand over the building. There is no mention of my cat. And now Georges' men are at my door. I doubt he's with them. He's probably in Bordeaux, Limoges or Paris doing something important and has delegated my ruin to his subordinates. Georges would regard overseeing my fall as vulgar, an indulgence. What is being done is done in the people's name, his message tells me. This is not a matter of old enmities or even older friendships. It is a matter of justice and historical necessity.

I have no doubt he believes it.

My chateau is old and looks new. This makes it different from most other chateaux in this part of France, many of which are new and designed to look old. Four turrets guard the corners and a curtain wall wraps the chateau and the inner garden. The roofs are slate and the windows glass, the lead flashing is new and the mortar sound. A moat around the chateau itself is filled with carp and has bloomed green with summer algae.

Its official name is le Chateau d'Aumout.

Everyone within a hundred miles calls it *Where the Tiger Lives*.

Soon it will have another name. It has stood against the French army when this part of France was English, and against the English when the lands returned to us. It has stood against heretics and neighbours and the jacqueries that swept through this area five hundred years ago. But tonight it will not stand, because what comes against it is not armies of the rich or the starving; what comes against it is history itself. And what can stand against the waves of history?

I read my words and wonder at their truth. If the *sans-culottes* beyond the walls merely represent a modern jacquerie then my words will be regarded as grandiose and my fears absurd, which would not be the first time. If I am right then the wave of history will roll right over me and I will be forgotten. The thought bears its own comfort.

We seek the immortality of fame around the same time our bodies begin to seek the sweet peace of oblivion. Such is the contradiction of being human.

I look at those words and like them even less.

Men hope to leave some record behind them. A country conquered, a culture changed, some great work that even the simplest can see has been built on a lifetime's striving, perhaps even a lifetime's pain. At best, I leave my recipe book and this journal. The heart and the soul can change. Manon showed me that. The angels of death scratch at my door. Walking through the corridors, with my hollow eyes staring back from every tarnished glass, I can no longer believe the mirrors lie. These are the last days of my life. Schoolmasters say to children start at the beginning. When writing stories people say begin where it begins. François-Marie Arouet, who wrote as Voltaire, began his *Essay on the Customs and the Spirit of the Nations* by tracing human development from its earliest days. But how does anyone know where anything really begins? Did this story begin the day I met Virginie, the day I arrived at the military academy to be greeted by Jerome and Charlot, that day, years before, I first met Emile, or did it begin with the dung heap, when I sat in the sun eating beetles? Looking back on the days of my life, I can't think of any time I was happier.

So let me say it began there, as good a place as any.

Barbarians at the Gate

I say my prayers before a second-rate painting of a messiah with the face of a tortured Spaniard against a backdrop that looks as if the artist simply looked from my study window and painted what he saw. Perhaps he did: the landscape is dark, the lighting on the Messiah's face bad enough to have been done by a local or a jobbing artist passing through this area when times were simpler.

I say the creed and the pater noster, the prayers we say without thinking about the words. *For thine is the kingdom, the power and the glory, for ever and ever. Amen.* I wonder what chance there is of that being true. Realising now is not a good time for doubts. Tigris obviously feels the same because she nudges me from my knees.

'Time to go?'

Her milky eyes say yes and she does that big cat smile which bares her teeth and always sends a shiver down my spine. We leave the altar candles burning for whoever comes to find them. A moth flies into one and falls, singed and wounded. It tastes of burnt hair, bitterness and a sharp need for light. Tigris's nose wrinkles at the smell.

'Our turn soon, big cat . . . '

The beast flicks her ears at the sound of my voice as we head for the stairs. She is old now, almost ancient. I have found no authority to tell me how long tigers live but her age shows in the grey of her muzzle and the yellowing of her teeth. She stinks of cat and being caged inside the chateau for the last few days. I've thrown sand across the floor of a room behind the kitchens and she uses that for her duties. She stinks of urine and discontent and I hate to see her so unhappy. Dropping to a crouch, I stroke her head until it arches back under my touch and a low purr begins deep in her throat.

'What now?' I ask her.

She looks at me with those blind eyes as if I should have the answer. A man should die on the battlefield or in his study. Somewhere unknown or utterly familiar. That my chateau should be turned into a battlefield I find distasteful, hoping that the mob will spare the paintings and the furniture but knowing they probably won't. Why should they? The paintings mean nothing to them and the furniture — in many cases — is too refined to do more than support someone who sits quietly. They will smash the windows and steal the curtains and probably end up giving the building to someone who becomes me in all but name. Old age has its advantages and one of those is resignation. My boyhood self would be scared by what is about to happen, my self as a young man outraged and ready to fight, my self when Tigris and I first met concerned with finding a way out of this trap.

I feel none of those things. I feel the weight of history inevitable as a wave that will roll up the beach whether I stand in its way or not. Now here, at the end of my life, I finally understand what I have not allowed myself to understand before this. History will happen. It cannot be denied. Nor would I deny it if I could. There was both beauty and cruelty in the world now dying. There will be beauty and cruelty in the world now being born. If my death is a part of the price, then that is all it is. A small part only.

There are shouts from the courtyard that say the gates have failed and the sans-culottes are inside the walls. The doors into the chateau are locked and barred, the windows locked and shuttered, all of them strong enough to hold a little while longer. I am glad that Virginie is dead, that Manon is gone and my son safe in the Indies. I think of Hélène in London and hope she'll regret my passing a little. It is too late to say I'm sorry if I was wrong about Georges, or tell her what really happened with her mother; and there are some things parents should not tell their children. It would only be self-justification on my part. *It was more complicated than you knew. There are two sides to every story. I did the best I could* . . . With luck she'll mourn me in time. And, if not, I doubt my spirit will be there to mind.

Just before we die is too late to start calling on God and hoping for Heaven. But if he does exist, and I somehow find myself in Heaven, then I hope Virginie is there also — for all she shouldn't have been buried in hallowed ground — and has been reunited with her elder son. I hope she is happy and that she will be glad to see me as an old friend, because we were that once, along with other things. I know I will be glad to see her. I hope in time Manon will join me there too. I do not expect it, though, believing in my heart that we are what we seem, dung for beetles. But I hope. A man may be allowed that.

Taking a bowl from a table I fill it with water from a jug and put it on the floor in front of Tigris, within easy reach. She looks at me with opal eyes and I sigh, lifting the bowl to hold it for her while she drinks, her huge tongue messily splashing liquid across my cuffs. 'Good girl,' I tell her. 'Good girl.'

I'm sure animals learn words, unless they simply recognise the tone of voice or we signal our intentions to them in some other way. She puts her head heavily on her paws and sinks into silence. She is hungry as I am. Anything truly edible in the kitchens is long gone and I do not dare try to reach one of the storehouses. It is a day since either of us has eaten. I would have liked one last meal. Sitting alone in my dining room, eating from porcelain decorated with my coat of arms and some Chinaman's idea of a tiger or rhinoceros. The finest wines to go with the finest tastes. Something I'd never eaten before, cooked with complexity or absolute simplicity, depending on my whim and what the ingredients demanded. I will say it, what I've said or written before. And I can only say it because I suspect the dream of God and Heaven is a fantasy. I've always wanted to eat human flesh. That strange monkey Charlot sent me is the closest I ever got. We're said to taste like pork, but then everything that doesn't taste like chicken or beef or mutton tastes like pork to those with no palate.

A few years ago I tracked a ship's bosun down to a squalid inn in Marseilles. The man hadn't sailed in five years and no captain would employ him. Men muttered that he brought bad luck but the truth was he served on the *Angélique* and was one of the few who survived her sinking and the subsequent sea voyage in the scuttle boat. Fifteen men set off across the Bay of Bengal and seven landed on the beach at Trincomalee in the Dutch colony of Ceylon. The others died, the survivors said, of hunger and fever and were fed to the sharks; but the Dutch doctor who examined them wrote that those remaining were not so ravaged by hunger as they should be. In the monsoon season fresh water is not a problem. It falls from the sky until all you can do is pray that it stops. So Laurant said in a letter I have in a drawer somewhere. Maybe the remaining crew spoke half the truth, and the sharks were fed the scraps. They were ordered to confess by the Dutch governor, a Protestant of foul temper and little vision. They refused and were imprisoned and tortured. All kept to their story, understanding that to admit to eating the flesh meant death.

When I found the man he was drunk and unshaven and smelt as bad as if he slept every night in a midden. For all I know he did. He regarded me suspiciously and stepped back when I called him by his real name. It had taken money and time and the acquaintance of unsavoury individuals to find him. I laid out what I would offer before I told him what I wanted. Enough gold would be his to re-make his life. He would be given new clothes and a berth to Canada or Louisiana, both places where French was spoken and he could start again. A wine merchant from Bordeaux, a ship's captain from Nice, a fisherman from Brittany . . . He could be any of those things or anything else he chose. Men were less fussy in the colonies about lineage. So long as he didn't claim to be noble, or pretend he came from one of the richer merchant families, he would be safe.

This drunken man stared at me. In his eyes I saw the horror of his last five years and wondered if he was too deep into degradation to save himself by telling me the truth. He asked, because who wouldn't, what I wanted in return. I imagine he knew it had to do with the *Angélique*, for there was little else remarkable about him. I explained I wanted to know the truth about his crossing the Bay of Bengal in a tiny boat on raging seas. That I would tell no one else and would bind myself by oath to this. I left my real reason for hunting him down until later and I doubt he ever knew what it was. He simply thought I wanted to know if he'd eaten human flesh.

I wanted to know if it tasted closer to beef, pork or mutton.

The man had eaten human flesh. On the third day, ravaged by hunger, when a ship's boy died, the remaining men looked at each other and the decision went unspoken. One of them simply pulled out his pocket knife and began filleting.

The sharks got the guts and bones but the men ate everything else. That was the only time and the only victim, and since the boy was dead, the man asked, what harm had really been done? He looked so desperate that I shrugged and said that was a question for the priests but I would have done the same. And he looked at me to see if I was mocking him and then wrung my hand.

He sailed that night, still drunk but now dressed and shaved and with a passport signed by Jerome that made the captain of the ship he took think he was a radical with connections being allowed to go into exile. Before he left he told me his answer. The meat was tender and easily digestible but bland. It could have done with cooking. And it could have done with seasoning. At the very least it needed black pepper. His understanding of food was too crude to tell me if one cut had tasted better than another.

'Ignore the noise,' I tell Tigris, who keeps freezing her position every time there is a thud or a crash outside. From the sound of it men are battering at the main door and a couple of the side doors. They'll find the doors inside locked as well, which will no doubt upset them. 'Go back to sleep.' But she is too restless and I have to leave her there twitching her great tail while I go downstairs.

I always knew it would come to this. Well, perhaps I suspected in the darkest part of myself, that part we keep hidden from our lovers and our children, and often from ourselves because who wants to admit to himself that he is a monster? Everything I can eat, I have eaten. Every taste I can find, I have found. My notebooks, like my experiences, are extensive but they are incomplete. The dead boy lies where I left him, under the shelf with the Parmareggio. His body has cooled in the previous twenty-four hours and the stone of the larder floor has kept him fresh. 'Meat,' I tell myself, 'is simply meat.'

The words fill my head but fail to convince. It is with an elemental sense of sacrament that I cut the clothes from the boy's body and slice strips of flesh from his buttocks and back. The meat from the shoulder is pale like pork, the meat from the buttocks a little darker but not so dark it could be mistaken for venison or beef. I think carefully about how the meat should be cooked, and in the end I opt for simplicity. This is partly out of respect for my ingredients, and partly because, while I can ignore the mob beyond my doors, I'm aware enough of them to know that marinating meat for hours is not open to me.

Hacking free a chunk of Parmareggio, I smash it into fragments with a meat hammer and use the same hammer to flatten the strip of buttock, then crumble stale *pain campagne* and mix the breadcrumbs with the crumbled cheese, adding black pepper, because I tend to add black pepper to everything, and some shredded sage. I dip the flattened meat into a saucer of beaten egg, shake off the excess and dredge it through the Parmareggio mix. As I heat butter in two pans, I shred an apple. The back, sliced fine, I fry simply, without any seasoning at all. It tastes like pork. The buttock cooks quickly, no more than four or five minutes each side, and tastes as I would expect — of sage and black pepper and a good Italian cheese. The shredded apple cuts through its richness nicely.

The tastes of France are changing and we are the last of the banquet. After us, the table will be swept clear as surely as the Chinese plates I use will be smashed by the men and women at my door. A new meal will be laid for them, and the first course will taste pure and clean after what has gone before. I write up my final notes, close the book and smile. My work is done. All that remains now is to end this story as it should be ended; and to do that I need to go upstairs again, to my chamber and then to my study. In my chamber I wash as well I can in the cold water of a jug on the side. Stripping off my clothes, I stand naked on a Persian carpet and scrub every part of me. My body is old and wizened, my arms thinner than I remember and my belly small but low. Fearing that I haven't scrubbed myself thoroughly enough, I find a second jug in another room and wash myself again, removing my wig to wipe sweat from my scalp. I shave my head quickly and rinse it as if readying for a fresh wig, but leave my head bare. This will have to do. Finding the silk banyan Manon bought me with her own money, I drape it over my frame and look round my room. I took Virginie on that bed, Manon too. I have waited out fevers and written letters there to my son and reluctant daughter. It has, in its way, been the centre of my little world.

Tigris looks up as I enter my study, her head

to one side as she waits for my voice but I give her only silence. The noise of the sans-culottes is louder now. They are inside the chateau, outraged at finding all the doors from the hall locked. I hope that I have left enough time and decide I have. It would have been good to be able to say a proper goodbye to Tigris but then what would be the point of washing so thoroughly? And I should have done it earlier if I wanted to do it at all.

★ ★ ★

Now, I think, *do it now*. But first there is this to say.

This is where I have to stop writing and let you imagine the rest.

Putting down the pen I pick up the razor I used to shave my head and check the edge, already knowing it is sharp. Then I check that my study door is locked and slip the robe from my shoulders and return to my chair, pulling it a little further into the middle of the room. I'm sitting naked in my chair with the razor in my hand, and Tigris is restless and growing upset. Her tail twitches and her eyes flick in irritation at the noise outside and the silence in here. Opening the razor, I watch it gleam in the candlelight, because it's getting dark now and I've lit a candle. Virginie liked candles, Manon also. Women do. I smile, but not sadly. I've lived too long and been too lucky to die sad.

Tigris and I have shared what came to me from Versailles, and the offal from the bullocks killed to feed guests at my chateau. It occurs to me, what should have occurred to me before this: she is my closest companion. They say every man — and, for all I know, every woman — has one great love. I have always thought Virginie was mine, and Manon the peace that came after. Now I wonder if Tigris is not the greatest of my loves. The only one that's really lasted. Men are killed for tasting human flesh and so are tigers. I have tasted this flesh, and Tigris has not. It will not matter to her if this is a meal she has eaten before in the way it matters to me. But she is hungry and I am ready.

There is courage in resignation but what I do now takes little courage. If I had free choice of how to end my life, this is how I would have chosen that it ends. Years ago I made a *ragoût* from meat cut from Tigris's mother's flank. The meat needed slow cooking for several hours to make it tender, and strong seasoning to make its sourness palatable, but I fried it first with onions and that seems to work for everything from tiger to rat.

Now it is Tigris's turn. The poor animal is hungry and I can see no reason why she should not have one last meal. Drawing the razor diagonally across my wrist so that blood wells but I don't bleed out too fast, I let blood drip to the carpet and watch Tigris's nose twitch. She freezes for a second the way she always does when she smells food. She's puzzled. She thinks it's me in here with her, but she's no longer entirely sure. Most of my smell is gone and I'm not talking to her as I would usually do, and now there's the smell of blood, and she's hungry. I at least have been hungry my entire life. I cut again a second time and a third, wincing at the pain, which is sharper than I had imagined. The fur along her back has risen now. Her head has turned to face me directly and she sinks low to the ground. I know what she looks like resting. This is not Tigris resting.

We are here, where we were always destined to be.

Some of this book is written on paper, some of it is simply the wash of my memories, much of it you have filled in for yourself. I thank you for listening to the ghost of a life now gone from a world that is dying. And though it pains me to believe it, deserves to die. The mob will ransack my chateau, rebuild it in time and as I've already said, one of them will become me. I wish it were different but suspect this is the truth of it. I want, more than anything, to say goodbye to Tigris. I want this more than I want to say goodbye to Manon or Hélène or my son. It cannot be. Gripping the razor one final time, I dig deep into my flesh in a vertical cut that opens an artery in the second before Tigris pounces. I fed on her mother, she feeds on me. Justice is served and the circle closed. I would live it all again.

Endnotes

Note 1

This work, reputedly the journal of Jean-Marie, *soi-disant* marquis d'Aumout, was found among the possessions of Citizen Duras, mayor of Limoges, following the execution of the Citizen Mayor for treason.

Note 2

Returned to Admiral Laurant d'Aumout, marquis d'Aumout, trusted confidant of l'empereur, on the orders of the president of the General Council of the Gironde.

Acknowledgements

I'd like to thank my agent Jonny Gellar at Curtis Brown, who stayed up one night to read the first draft of a novel then called *Taste*; Francis Bickmore, Editorial Director of Canongate, who telephoned part way through reading the newly renamed *Master of the Menagerie*, to say he loved the characters and would probably bid but wasn't mad about the title; Lorraine McCann, for a stunningly good copy edit of what had become *The Last Banquet*; and finally, Sam Baker, for whom this book was written.

I jotted down the novel's outline in a café over fifteen years ago, on a strip of paper torn from a napkin. (By which time Sam and I'd known each other for ten years and been married five.) I folded the strip into the back of a notebook, knowing I wasn't grown up enough or good enough to write it. Over the following fifteen years I took it out twice, deciding both times I still wasn't ready. At the start of this year I went hunting for the notebook, and with Sam's encouragement started writing. This is the result.

Jonathan Grimwood
December 2012

We do hope that you have enjoyed reading this large print book.

Did you know that all of our titles are available for purchase?

We publish a wide range of high quality large print books including:
Romances, Mysteries, Classics
General Fiction
Non Fiction and Westerns

Special interest titles available in large print are:
The Little Oxford Dictionary
Music Book
Song Book
Hymn Book
Service Book

Also available from us courtesy of Oxford University Press:
Young Readers' Dictionary
(large print edition)
Young Readers' Thesaurus
(large print edition)

For further information or a free brochure, please contact us at:
Ulverscroft Large Print Books Ltd.,
The Green, Bradgate Road, Anstey,
Leicester, LE7 7FU, England.
Tel: (00 44) 0116 236 4325
Fax: (00 44) 0116 234 0205

REGENERATION

Pat Barker

Craiglockhart War Hospital, 1917, where army psychiatrist William Rivers is treating shell-shocked soldiers. Under his care are the poets Siegfried Sassoon and Wilfred Owen, as well as mute Billy Prior, who is only able to communicate by means of pencil and paper. Rivers' job is to make the men in his charge healthy enough to fight. Yet the closer he gets to mending his patients' minds, the harder becomes every decision to send them back to the horrors of the front . . . *Regeneration* is the classic exploration of how the traumas of war brutalized a generation of young men.

HARVEST

Jim Crace

As late summer steals in and the final pearls of barley are gleaned, a village comes under threat. A trio of outsiders — two men and a dangerously magnetic woman — arrive on the woodland borders and put up a makeshift camp. That same night, the local manor house is set on fire. Over the course of seven days, Walter Thirsk sees his hamlet unmade: the harvest blackened by smoke and fear, the new arrivals cruelly punished, and his neighbours held captive on suspicion of witchcraft. But something even darker is at the heart of his story, and he will be the only man left to tell it . . . Timeless yet singular, mythical yet deeply personal, this beautiful novel of one man and his unnamed village speaks for a way of life lost for ever.

THE SHOCK OF THE FALL

Nathan Filer

'I'll tell you what happened because it will be a good way to introduce my brother. His name's Simon. I think you're going to like him. I really do. But in a couple of pages he'll be dead. And he was never the same after that.' There are books you can't stop reading, which keep you up all night. There are books which let us into the hidden parts of life and make them vividly real. There are books which, because of the sheer skill with which every word is chosen, linger in your mind for days. *The Shock Of The Fall* is all of these books. An extraordinary portrait of one man's descent into mental illness; a brave and groundbreaking novel from one of the most exciting new voices in fiction.